DIPLOMATIC AGENT

DIPLOMATIC AGENT

THE EMPRESS' SPY™ BOOK 4

S.E. WEIR

MICHAEL ANDERLE

DISRUPTIVE IMAGINATION®

LMBPN Publishing
PMB 196, 2540 South Maryland Pkwy
Las Vegas, NV 89109

Version 1.01, February 2022
eBook ISBN: 978-1-64971-994-2
Print ISBN: 978-1-64971-995-9

THE DIPLOMATIC AGENT TEAM

Thanks to our Beta Readers:
Larry Omans, Jim Caplan, John Ashmore, Kelly O'Donnell,
Mary Heise, Rachel Heise

Thanks to the JIT Readers

Dorothy Lloyd
Larry Omans
Dave Hicks
Daryl McDaniel
Rachel Beckford
Diane L. Smith
Wendy L Bonell
Jim Caplan
Deb Mader
Kelly O'Donnell
Jeff Goode
Jackey Hankard-Brodie
Peter Manis
Thomas Ogden
John Ashmore
Zacc Pelter

If we've missed anyone, please let us know!

Editor
Lynne Stiegler

DEDICATION

To all those who have supported and encouraged me every step of the way. This is as much your book as mine.
- S.E. Weir

To Family, Friends and
Those Who Love
To Read.
May We All Enjoy Grace
To Live The Life We Are
Called.

—Michael

CHAPTER ONE

Nearby Solar System, Planet Xaldaq, QBS *Glaxix Sphaea*, Bridge

"Tell us where we stand, Admiral Waters."

Phina glanced at Captain Kael-ven, former Planetary Leader of the Yollins. He leaned forward, viewing her intently over the holo display in between them. The rest of the crew quietly went about their business around them, though they snuck peeks every so often.

Kiel stood next to the captain. "I didn't know we were doing a roleplay."

The captain waved him off. "Just trying to help Phina get into the mindset of the person in charge of this battle."

Phina scanned the holo display again and pointed. "Here's the planet Yoll, its two moons and three base stations, and the fleet at various vectors around the planet."

She moved her hand and continued, "Here's where the Gate was destroyed when the Empire's fleet came through from Earth."

Kiel corrected her. "They were not the Empire at the

1

time. They were a large, intrepid group of strong and tricky humans with a small number of noble and fierce Yollin warriors who followed their Queen into the far reaches of the universe to destroy the evil Kurtherians."

Kael-ven turned his head toward his old friend, who gave a shrug. "What? If we're role-playing, we've got to set it up right."

The captain shook his head but kept the laugh inside. "Carry on, Admiral Waters."

Phina nodded and pointed out the *Meredith Reynolds*, the Sphaea-class ships whose design had been based on the one Phina was currently aboard, and the Puck Defense Destroyer, which shot kinetics called pucks that were used to....well, destroy things.

Kael-ven nodded approval. He had been teaching her military tactics and strategy twice a week since she had requested it of him months ago, shortly after they had first arrived here at the Qendrok's planet. She wasn't sure why he had said yes, but she suspected it was partly because he had grown bored waiting for something to happen.

"Very good, Admiral Waters. What is your assessment of the tactics the Yollins used?"

Phina sighed as she scanned the holo. "Arrogant and shortsighted."

The two Yollins winced at the blunt response. Kael-ven cleared his throat. "Yes. Well, those moronic jackasses did lose. What tactics were utilized by the Yollins in response to this fleet entering their space?"

Phina frowned as she continued scanning the holo display. She had read numerous briefings and firsthand accounts from the two Yollins as well as others on both sides of the battle. Some had been assigned by the captain, and others were source materials for those assignments that she had sought out on her own.

"I see they took a long time to cloak themselves."

"Good, good," Kael-vaen responded, waving for her to continue. "What else, both good and bad tactics?"

Phina straightened. "Good tactics were that they cloaked themselves and that they tried to sneak in from behind. Bad tactics were that the sneak attack was obvious to anyone familiar with Yollin weaknesses. A flank attack might have been more effective. Also, as I said, they didn't cloak soon enough. If they had cloaked before they moved into nearby space, the sneak attempt they did make may have worked."

She pointed at the Yollin ships flying up on the rear of the Empire's fleet. "Eyewitness accounts state that the captain of the Yollin formation focused mainly on the *G'laxix Sphaea*, completely ignoring any threat the others posed. That was shortsighted, arrogant, and sloppy."

Kiel muttered, "Well, he did die."

Phina continued with a shake of her head. "All of the Yollins, but especially that captain, failed to take into account that the Empire fleet could also have cloaking devices."

Kiel started, "It wasn't the Emp—" He stopped with a huff when Kael-ven elbowed him. Phina glanced at the captain to see if he wanted her to stop, but he waved her on.

"The Yollins assumed the enemy didn't have the scanning capability to pick up their cloaked ships. Perhaps it would be good practice to presume that an unknown enemy could have at least the same amount of technology available as you do?"

Kael-ven nodded and folded his arms behind his back as he moved closer to the holo. "Correct. That is not a bad strategy. Now that you have shared your assessment, what would you have done differently than the Yollins at the time?"

Phina straightened and faced them. "I would have sent a virus that targeted their cloaking and shields to bring them down. Then I would have told them I had them dead to rights and they should surrender, or I'd trigger systems to self-destruct."

The two Yollins stared at her in surprise. Silence fell over the bridge as the other officers turned to listen.

"You can do that?" Commander Kiel squeaked before clearing his throat and turning to Kael-ven. "Can we do that?"

Kael-ven blinked away his surprise and gestured at Phina. "Explain, please. I am not certain this is possible."

Phina nodded and was about to answer when she got an urge to look behind her. She turned to see Link and Will just inside the door. She nodded in greeting and adjusted her position to see all of them.

"The virus is doable, yes. Either I, or ADAM, or perhaps one of the other digital entities would create it. It would need to be done ahead of time since there would be a lot of complicated coding to ensure it would make it through their firewalls and defenses. The method of delivery is trickier. I didn't check to see if it's possible, but I think at least ADAM could do it. I'm not sure about back then, but he probably could now."

Kael-ven nodded slowly. "So this is a hypothetical tactic, not one that could have been used during this battle."

She shrugged. "You asked what *I* would do, not what tactics were available then."

Link chuckled and thumped the Yollin on his back. "You should expect Phina to make her own interpretations of your instructions and have a surprise or two up her sleeve by now, Kael-ven."

Phina sighed. The two males obviously knew each other. Lincoln Grimes, known to her as Link and to everyone else as his cover, Greyson Wells, liked to employ misdirection and be in plain sight as he went about his diplomatic spying business.

There was value in that, but Phina preferred to operate in the background whenever possible. That difference in their personal tactics was the basis of most of their professional differences. Yet, both of them agreed that it proved good tactics to keep their cards close to the vest.

Kiel stared at Phina with all the wariness one would have for a live grenade. "What tactics would you have used since you couldn't apply this virus?"

Kael-ven turned back and nodded. "Yes, I am also interested to hear this."

Phina glanced at Will, but he was busy scanning the holo of the battle with interest. She tapped on her tablet and changed the view before she spoke.

"I would have cloaked before the approach to flank the Empire's fleet. Once we were close enough to act before they could respond, I would have targeted the weapons platforms if I wanted prisoners or the engines if that didn't matter. Then the ships would either break down or explode. After the first pass, I project that at least a third of the ships would have crippled defenses or be dead in the water."

She gestured at the Empire's fleet. Most of the ships were either scattered or unmoving on the holo, the rest surrounding their sister ships and the space station for defense. "I would circle around to maintain momentum and keep the fleet guessing as to our position. After three passes at varying speeds, their forces would be significantly reduced. Then I would demand their surrender. If denied, I would take the rest of the ships out."

She assessed her audience, who were expressing varying states of shock and horror. "The Puck Destroyer would be the greatest defense in the Empire's fleet. It is effective but only has so much maneuvering capability. It would be relatively simple to take it out at that point considering the number of ships I would have left, leaving the space station alone. They would have no choice but to surrender."

The phrase "you could hear a pin drop" came to mind as she waited for their response.

Kael-ven gave her a stare akin to eying a cranky bistok. Kiel viewed the ships with visible distress as his mandibles moved but didn't make a sound. Link's smirk was faint but visible. Will appeared to be warring between admiration and discomfort.

"I'm glad they didn't have someone with your logic in charge, Phina," her friend responded, his focus on the Empire's massacred fleet. "If they had, I'm not sure any of us would be here. The Empire would have been destroyed before it began."

Kiel gathered himself and shook his head. "I'm happy those Yollin assholes are dead. The upper caste was privileged and made sure everyone knew it."

Kael-ven scowled. "They were morons who got what they deserved."

Link shook his head, chuckling. "You two were just as bad when we encountered you in Earth space."

"Well, yes, but we got the arrogant asshole slammed out of us pretty quickly," Kiel pointed out.

Link gestured to the Yollin fleet on the holo. "So did they. They just didn't survive the experience."

Kael-ven agreed, then turned back to Phina. "Any additional comments, Admiral Waters?"

Phina nodded and gestured back to the two fleets. "My suggestion was what I would plan to do. That wouldn't work after the first few passes."

Will frowned and leaned closer to the holo. "Why not? It seems to be an alarmingly well thought out strategy."

"Because the Empress is a wildcard. Without her, these tactics would work perfectly." Phina waved at the destroyed fleet. "However, she throws every tactic and strategy into chaos, and all the enemy can do is react. She moves too quickly, and since she can walk the Etheric, her movements are even harder to predict."

"Hmm..." Kael-ven considered while the others nodded at her explanation. Everyone knew the Empress was amazingly capable, protective of her people, and unstoppable once she got going. The captain leaned forward curiously.

"Have you considered any tactics that would work against the Empress?"

Phina stared back with a narrowed gaze. "Treason isn't something I tend to contemplate."

"Whoa. Back off with the crazy eyes, sister." Kiel waved a hand. "He's only wondering since we've seen or heard of her getting shot multiple times. She's walked away from wounds that should have killed her. He's got a powerful urge to speculate on it. I don't share that urge, just so you all know. I'm not suicidal."

Phina glanced at Kael-ven, but he just regarded her expectantly. Finally, she relented. "The element of surprise and overwhelming force, such as a missile or a bomb. A surprise nuclear bomb would probably do it, but she would have to have absolutely no warning of it, and the collateral damage would be catastrophic since she rarely leaves the station."

The two Yollins exchanged glances as Will gaped in horror and Link shook his head quickly. "Do yourself a favor and don't mention nuclear bombs in front of the Empress. She might tear your arms off. She'd be sorry later, but her regret wouldn't help you in retrospect."

Will gulped and folded his hands behind his back.

Phina gave Link a questioning glance that he caught and reminded them of the history of the Patriarch Michael. "The Empress lost someone she cared about to a nuclear bomb when we were still on Earth."

They all winced, both at the loss and the reminder that the Empress reacted strongly when her people were in danger, let alone someone she cared about personally. Phina couldn't imagine the pain of losing someone she loved so suddenly. No wonder she could occasionally sense intense loneliness and sadness when the Empress became lost in thought.

Phina gathered her thoughts and waved a hand toward the holo. "Well, those are all the thoughts I have about the tactics involved."

Kael-ven nodded. "Well done, Admiral Waters. Your tactics were thorough and well thought out. Unless you have any questions, we are finished for today."

Before Phina could respond, Link cut in. "Good. We came because we received word that the Qendrok have come to a consensus. We are meeting them within the hour."

Phina glanced at her t-shirt and pants. They had been dressing formally for their diplomatic meetings, and she hadn't expected one today. "Do I need to change?"

Link glanced briefly at her clothing and grimaced. "It would set the right tone. Xoruk and Zultav wouldn't care, but the rest are sticklers for formality."

She sighed but agreed. "I'll run over to the *Stark* quickly and meet you there."

After saying her goodbyes to the two Yollins and waving to their crew, she turned to leave. Once in the hall, she realized that Will was following a pace behind her. The tall, easy-going guy was around her age but seemed younger due to his light manner and general optimism. Phina usually felt like their relationship was a mix between that of siblings and good friends even though it was relatively new, regardless that he had known her since grade school.

She threw a questioning glance behind her as she

walked. "Are you changing too, or are you just stalking me again?"

He gave her a wide smile she grew suspicious of as he quickened his pace to walk beside her. "It's not stalking when it's a friend, Sera-beara."

Phina wrinkled her nose in disgust. "That's worse than the last nickname you came up with. And yes, it's still stalking even when you're friends."

Will exuded injured innocence as they reached the cargo bay that led to outside. Sphaea, the ship's EI, opened the door for them so they didn't have to slow their stride. "I thought Raffles was inspired."

"You're delusional." Seriously delusional. "Raffles sounds like a dog's name."

"What's wrong with Sera-beara?" he protested, though the twinge in his cheek made her think he was holding in a grin.

"Nothing." Phina stuck her tongue out, then scanned ahead to make sure she didn't trip on the way down the ramp. "If you're five."

Will feigned sadness. She didn't know why he bothered. They both knew he didn't mean it. "Well, you won't let me call you 'Fee' because it was ruined when you were moonlighting as a stripper."

Phina's mouth gaped open in shocked surprise. "Moonlighting... I *never* moonlighted as a stripper! I was a sex kitten, and it was a cover."

"Oh?" Will glanced over curiously but with the unholy light of gleeful teasing shining in his face. "What's the difference?"

"A great many things, including the amount of clothing

they wear and the money they receive," Phina muttered as she hurried her pace in an effort to finish the ridiculous conversation.

His face contorted as he kept a chuckle inside. "You're that familiar with the workings of strippers and sex kittens, huh? Tell me more, Eenie."

Phina skidded to a stop and stared at Will in horror. "Are you kidding me? That's the worst one yet!" She continued walking, shaking her head in dismay. "Seriously, it's like we're in kindergarten or something. For the record, I read. A lot. I remember almost everything." She shot a quelling look at her friend. "I know lots of things, including things you don't want me to know."

Will sighed heavily as he matched her pace with his longer strides. "Well, I'm going to need to think of a new nickname, then."

"Yes. A wise decision. You could just call me Phina," she responded dryly. She stifled a sneeze caused by the sudden bright light from the sun as they walked into the shade of the *Stark's* metal body. "Seeing as that's my name, and it's already been shortened from the original."

"No. It needs to be special," Will protested as they walked up the ramp that Stark had extended for them. "To mark our epic and glorious relationship."

Phina shook her head, thinking that if she had an epic and glorious relationship with anyone, she would want it to be with her boyfriend Todd. She wanted to avoid hurting Will's feelings, but a kick in the pants might be in order. "I'm sure you will figure something out."

Will lifted his chin, caught in his thoughts. "What about Rah, or Rah-Rah?"

"Ugh. Don't make me hurt you." She glared at him before turning into the corridor for her room. Unfortunately, Will's room was next door, so he continued to follow her.

"What's wrong with that one?"

"You drive me crazy." She reached her door and opened it, stepping in and turning to see him grinning as he walked past.

"Just making up for lost time, Raffles. You know you love me."

Phina sighed as she closed the door. She might love him like the brother she'd never had, but that didn't mean she wouldn't punch him if he didn't stop giving her idiotic nicknames.

CHAPTER TWO

Nearby System, Planet Xaldaq, Religious Compound

Phina and Will had met Link and entered the meeting area with two Guardian Marine units who currently stood behind the diplomats in the guard position.

After some formalities, the Qendrok had finally presented their new documents describing the Qendrok's new rule of law, proposed government structure, and their request for inclusion in the Etheric Empire. The Qendrok had since left the room, giving the team time to review the documents.

Link perused each packet, handing them off to Phina when he was finished. She read through the documents quickly but at a pace where she would remember the contents. She passed each one to Will after reading it.

As she finished the last one, she caught Link studying her. "What do you think?"

"The democratic timocracy is an interesting idea," Phina answered thoughtfully, tapping her fingers on the armrest of her chair. "My concern is, how will they know if there's something wrong with the candidate? Their measurement is the extent of their honor. Perhaps we should suggest that any citizen has two weeks to come forward after nomination to share their experiences, both positive and negative, with the candidates as character references." She frowned and continued tapping. "Hmm... We should suggest it's their duty and connected to their own honor to come forward and share. That way, there won't be as much political bribery and intimidation."

Link sat back with his fingers steepled in front of his smirk. "An interesting suggestion. What do you think, Will?"

"Huh?" Will peered up from reading the packets at a slower pace, his expression overwhelmed and uncertain. "Oh, uh. Well, I only heard half of what Phina said, but it sounded fine. I got distracted with this part here." He pointed at a section within the document concerning the new rule of law. "If I'm reading it right, this law could be interpreted as a restriction on females having a say in anything related to government, including lacking the right to vote. Is that what we want to approve?"

Link and Phina frowned at each other, then Phina held out her hand for the document. After reading that section again twice, she nodded and handed it to Link. "Will's right. The position isn't stated outright, but with the current wording, it lets them prevent females from participating."

"Hmmm..." Link read it and agreed with them. "Phina, I want you to change the wording of that to be respectful of their culture but still allow the precedent for female voting to be permissible. Will, see what you can come up with for the wording of Phina's suggestion."

They both nodded and got to work. By the time the Qendrok came back in, they had adapted the wording and added in a few other items to the documents.

Phina focused on observing the aliens. The Qendrok looked alike and dressed alike and wore red medallions signifying their position in their government. When Link had introduced them to her months ago, he had described them as four-armed green trolls.

Phina supposed that sufficed in a general sense, but they all stood tall and proud, unlike the hunched, rather stupid-looking ogres in the fantasy pictures she had seen. Their faces took some getting used to with dark eyes, flat noses, and hardly any lips to speak of. When their mouths were closed, it was difficult to see that they even had one.

Yet, their culture imbued them with a graceful manner of moving and communication with varying postures that conveyed an emotion or idea. Xoruk, the Qendrok who had brought their previous troubles to Phina's attention, currently held the position she had learned spoke of openness and communication. Throughout the process over the last months, he had been the delegate to speak most favorably about the Qendrok joining the Empire.

"I see value in the changes you have suggested. We will discuss these changes and return to meet tomorrow."

"Why was this ridiculous change made regarding who can hold a position in government?" Guldrag, a traditional Qendrok who had protested the changes at every step of the way, demanded as he waved the document listing the changes being adjusted to the rule of law. "We've had the same laws for years. To change such long-held laws would be a crime in itself!"

"Leaving the laws as is has become a crime," Phina snapped as her hold on her temper slipped. "One you have been paying for. You have been told things need to change, and that is what we have been talking about for months as you traditionalists drag your feet. This particular change was included because to leave it out would add to the oppression of your females. We think your people have been oppressed enough."

Guldrag glared at her and threw the document on the table. "I don't need to be spoken to this way by this female! Someone rein in her attitude or send her away."

Jokin, a Qendrok who was harder to read, spoke up. "Enough, Dev Guldrag. We are here to develop a new ruling government. We can't do that with constant bickering."

"Also, Delegate Waters isn't going anywhere," Link added as he pinned Guldrag with a hard stare. "May I remind you that Qartan demanded to have her leave a delegation meeting? I don't think you want to be seen in the same light. It didn't end well for him."

Guldrag gritted his teeth but nodded his understanding and remained silent while Xoruk and Jokin shifted uncomfortably at the memory.

Phina met Zultav's gaze. He was one of six guards standing behind the Qendrok delegation. Zultav had also been the one to kill Qartan, the Qendrok who had been the leader of the Qendrok. The former leader had thought himself better than any of his people, even if he had to whip them all into believing it or kill them for disagreeing with him.

Death by stabbing couldn't have happened to a better megalomaniac.

"We will review everything and resume in the morning," Jokin reiterated. "We are all eager to put the past behind us and move forward."

The Qendrok all nodded emphatically. Their people had been oppressed and traumatized by their leadership for decades. Phina thought the globalized impact of that abuse would take another few decades to recover from, and it wouldn't be as quick or easy as they hoped.

Phina hung back and pulled Zultav aside as the others filed out of the meeting. She waved to Kuvaq to join them, then turned to see one of the Guardian Marine teams standing guard behind her. She smiled at them and gestured toward the door.

"You all can go. I won't be long."

"Yeah, that's not happening." Mel, the female Wechselbalg, snorted in amusement. She stood with her feet shoulder-width apart in a simple uniform composed of a bodysuit that Phina knew was made to stretch as she changed forms.

Phina frowned in confusion, then glanced at the two waiting Qendrok when a thought occurred to her. She turned back to her guard unit in suspicion. "They aren't going to attack me. We are allies, and Zultav is a friend."

One of the two Marines standing on either side of Mel

shook his head with sympathy mixed in with his amusement, but he also conveyed resolve. "Doesn't matter, Delegate Waters. Our bosses told us to protect you no matter what, so that's what we're doing."

Hearing Davin refer to her boyfriend Todd and his best friend Peter gave her a combination of warm fuzzies that he was looking out for her and annoyance that the Guardian Marines were being so thorough in their interpretation of their orders. She debated how to respond, then raised her eyebrows. "You all do know I could probably take any threat down faster than you can."

The last Marine, Jared, stood straight as he nodded soberly. "Yes, ma'am. We've seen you in action. But we still have a duty."

Phina decided to go back to her original intentions and turned back to the two Qendrok waiting patiently. "I'm sorry."

Zultav's arms changed to reassurance and calm. "We are fine, Phina. We understand they need to take care of you."

Kuvaq was all business. "What did you wish to speak about?"

Putting the disagreement behind her, Phina brought up a topic she had been thinking about on and off for the past months. "After the attack during the wedding, we searched the bodies and found the wrist devices that we believe your assassins used to travel. We collected five of them. The other two were destroyed. We wondered if you would like them back."

Before Zultav could respond, Kuvaq shot back, "Did you not wish to use them yourself?"

Having grown used to his blunt manner, Phina brushed the tone aside. "Of course we thought about it. However, we've been keeping them in a safe since we didn't know how they worked. Since we are striving to bring the Qendrok into the Empire, we didn't wish to do anything that could cause issues later. I wondered if you would like them back and if you have any information about how they work."

Zultav and Kuvaq's reactions were interesting. Mixed emotions of disgust and relief crossed their faces, and they also used distancing body language. They exchanged long glances before shaking their heads.

Kuvaq finally spoke. "We do not want them. They were a gift from the creature Qartan called their goddess. Anything of hers is poison. We destroyed the rest of the devices we had."

Zultav continued, "Though we destroyed the wrist devices, we did not destroy the power hub for them. We didn't know how to dispose of it safely. Do you wish to take it?"

"Yes, I think I do. I understand the stigma you feel. We wish to know more about how this 'goddess' is using the Etheric. We haven't seen devices used in this way before. At least, not to my knowledge."

"We will bring it to your ship." Kuvaq nodded and gestured that Zultav should take that job.

"Will you get in trouble for giving the device to us without asking permission from anyone?" Phina asked, struggling to mask the anxiety she felt. She couldn't help being concerned about the assassins since Qartan had used them the most. What was left of the league of assassins had experienced enough trauma to develop nightmares and post traumatic stress.

Not that the stoic aliens would tell her emotionally charged information like that. That wasn't their way. However, she had found that those sleeping were more prone to be mentally vulnerable, including the normally shielded Qendrok. It wasn't uncommon for Phina to be woken by their emotionally charged nightmares, even on the *Stark* some distance away. Her only consolation was that she had gotten used to soothing her new friends back to sleep and giving them the remainder of a peaceful night.

Zultav shook his head and changed position to express protection and something she didn't recognize. "They do not even know it exists. Those who knew about it are dead. We did not volunteer it to those who will be the new leaders. Giving it to you is the best outcome since it takes the device off our hands and doesn't risk the chance of it being discovered by those who would use it poorly."

"I greatly appreciate your help."

Phina smiled at them both but felt a pang. No matter how many people she found connections to, Phina still missed her best friend and boyfriend, among others at home.

Nearby Solar System, Planet Xaldaq, QBS *Stark*, Bridge (two weeks later)

Link flopped into one of the cushy chairs on the bridge with a sigh. "I'm so glad we are finally done with this planet and can leave. It's taken forever."

Phina raised her eyebrow over the top of her tablet. "Dramatic much?"

"Hey!" He waved a finger at her. "Don't you go down that road. It's not funny."

That infuriating smirk appeared. He hated it and loved it. It reminded Link of her father, his best friend, which caused him to become nostalgic. It also always made him feel like his trainee and honorary niece was laughing at him.

"It's kind of funny." Her eyes shone with amusement.

Yup. She was definitely laughing at him. He glowered at her. Like a mature adult, of course. He definitely *wasn't* pouting.

Phina leaned toward him. "Come on, Link. It was funny. Stop pouting."

The AI Stark appeared in the specialized unit at the end of the chairs. The dashing holographic construct crossed his arms and gave Link another smirk. "Yeah, Link, stop pouting about it."

"I don't have a stick up my ass!" Link burst out, which caused Stark to snicker.

Phina merely straightened and calmly responded, "I never said that."

Link protested, "Yes, that's what you said! I heard you. You said it was funny how I could be so dramatic with a stick up my ass!"

"Never happened."

"I was there!" he shot back.

"I don't know what you're talking about." Phina's face remained stoic, but the glint in her eye hadn't disappeared.

"That memory of yours must be faulty, then." Link sat back and got comfortable as she observed him.

"My memory recall is perfectly functional, which is why I know that isn't what I said."

Link crossed his arms and raised his chin, feeling belligerent. "I'm not wrong."

"You're kind of wrong." The infuriating female turned back to her tablet before responding, "I said you had a stick up your *butt*."

Link shot up straight and pointed at the young woman. "You're arguing semantics. You know that's exactly what I said."

She regarded the finger in front of her face, then lifted her gaze to give him an annoying stare that made him feel like he was being scolded. "That's why I said it. You're making a big deal out of nothing."

He shook his head and deflated, flopping back into the chair with his eyes raised to the ceiling. "Whatever. I'm not being dramatic."

Surprised that Phina hadn't said anything after several moments of silence, he turned his head to see her staring at him with concerned puzzlement.

"What?"

"You've been out of sorts the whole time we've been here." She frowned in thought. "The only time you've been yourself is when we're talking to the Qendrok and need to be official. I'm not going to read your mind, but I'm getting concerned. What's going on?"

"He needs a woman," Stark offered helpfully, his gaze earnest. "I've heard men need their pipes cleaned regularly to function properly."

While Link gaped at the outspoken AI, Phina's face scrunched in disgust. "Is that what I think it means? That's gross."

"Hey!" Link shot out. "It's not gross to have sex. It's a normal part of being an adult."

She waved him off with a grimace on her face. "I'm talking about the description. I might have sex with someone, but that doesn't mean I want to describe it as cleaning their pipes. That's the gross part. Just say sex if that's what you mean."

Link glowered at his honorary niece. "You and Todd are having sex already? I'll kill him."

Phina leveled a fierce glare at him, which would have concerned him if it didn't happen on a semi-regular basis. "That's none of your business. No matter how close our relationship, trainer or chosen family, you never have a say about that."

He crossed his arms again and grew even more serious. Phina was the most important person in his life. He had made a vow to her parents to take care of her, but even if he hadn't, he would still need to make sure for himself. "I don't think that's true. I need to make sure Todd understands the gravity of the situation."

"I assure you, he understands just fine. It's between me and Todd. You don't have a say in my relationships," Phina argued, showing the fiery passion that only came out when she was protecting people she loved. That served to give Link both a pang in his heart and a sense of warmth. She was one of the best people he knew. He opened his mouth to capitulate when Stark spoke again.

"This is why he needs a woman. Then he wouldn't be all up in your business."

"I don't need a woman!" Link exploded. "Stop saying that!"

Stark grinned with amusement. He delighted in pushing people's buttons and was satisfied to have gotten a rise out of him.

Link blamed himself for that since he had taught Stark the behavior. He turned to Phina, who evaluated him speculatively. Link winced and made an effort to appear mature and above the common needs of man.

"I don't need a woman," he assured her. Gray eyes flashed into his thoughts, and he stuffed the vision down like he always did. There was no need to dwell on things that couldn't happen.

"I don't believe that, but that's not what I want to talk about." Phina shifted her position, her concern for him showing. "I want to know what's wrong. I know something is bothering you and I'm not letting go of it. I should have said something earlier."

Link reached over and squeezed her hand in reassurance. "It's not your job to take care of me, kid. It's my job to take care of you. Which is why I'm going to have a come-to-Jesus talk with Todd when we get back."

"You're going to leave him alone." Her eyes flashed in warning. "I'm serious, Link. Our relationship is still relatively new, and I need you to keep out of it."

He sighed but nodded. "I understand. But if he hurts you, he's going to wish he was dead. I'm warning you now, so you don't come crawling to me later when it happens."

She pulled her hand away and lightly punched him. "I'm

an adult. I know how to take care of myself. I'm basically Black Widow and Jean Grey mixed together."

"Ugh." Stark cringed. "You just mixed two superhero universes. I don't think we can be friends anymore."

Phina challenged him on that. "I don't think that's likely. Who else would you talk to?"

"Hey!" the AI protested. "I have friends. I talk to them all the time. ADAM's even making a little sister for me."

"Oh? What's her name?" Phina perked up with interest at ADAM's name, causing Link to sulk. Phina had a soft spot for the first AI to ever be created. Link couldn't blame her since ADAM was unique, even more so than the digital entities he created as his children. Link felt...jealous.

Huh. He paused for a rare bit of introspection. Link had waited for years for Phina to grow up so he could take her under his wing and she could take over as the Diplomatic Spy for the Etheric Empire. He had been waiting until she could protect herself and he didn't have to stay away from one of the last people he considered family. Now that the time had come, Link felt jealous of ADAM and Todd because they were both close to Phina and took up time she could be spending with him.

Link squirmed uncomfortably. It wasn't that he didn't want her to have other relationships. He just didn't want his time with her to be taken up by other people. That wasn't unreasonable, was it?

He sighed and rubbed his face. Maybe they were right that he needed a relationship of his own. He had felt like he was too old, but Todd was about the same age as him. Once the Pod-doc's technology allowed the humans who had come from Earth with Bethany Anne to live longer, age differences had become less of an issue. It didn't seem to be a problem for Todd and Phina. Something to think about.

Phina startled him by poking him in the arm, and Link realized he hadn't been following the conversation. Her expression showed a mix of earnestness and determination.

"Hey! I'm talking to you, Link. I'm a total badass. Just ask Todd. He knows I could take him, and he doesn't care. You don't have to worry about me. Just stay out of our business."

Link grabbed her hand before she could withdraw it and squeezed it along with a reassuring smile. "All right. I'll stay out of it."

She squinted warily. "You promise?"

He nodded. "As long as you promise me that if you do need help that you come to me or send a message. I'm not backing out of my promise to take care of you, so I'll trust you to not leave me in pain knowing that I could have done something if there's a problem."

Phina swallowed roughly but agreed. "I promise. I won't forget."

Link patted her on the shoulder, then figured he might as well continue being a modern marvel of maturity. "As for what I've been worried about, I think I am still struggling with what Zultav and Kuvaq told us."

"That those people they heard about are targeting you?"

He sighed and fidgeted with his fingers. "One of my contacts told me about a meeting she overheard which gave me similar but less complete information. It sounds like they are all positive there is a problem within Spy Corps."

She nodded in understanding and concern. "That's why you have been upset and out of sorts, isn't it? You think you haven't been there enough and it's your fault for not seeing it."

He sighed and sagged in his chair, shaking his head. He felt weary and old. "Isn't it my fault? I'm in charge of Spy Corps. It's my job to make sure everything is all right."

"That doesn't mean it's your fault. Whose bright idea was it for you to be basically doing two full-time jobs at two different locations anyway?" She scowled, and he deflated more.

"Mine."

"Oh." Phina stopped at that realization, then shrugged. "Okay, then it is partly your fault."

Link groaned and closed his eyes, but as she continued, they flew open again.

"It's not *all* your fault. Whoever these people are, you didn't make them do this. Don't take on responsibility for things that you haven't done."

"Thank you, Phina." He reached over and clasped her hand again, giving her a warm smile that turned her fierce earnestness to a soft glow. "How did you get to be so smart?"

"I suspect it was my parents," she responded seriously.

"Yes, along with your dry wit and warped sense of humor."

Phina shrugged nonchalantly. "Everyone needs a hobby." She shifted and put her head on his shoulder in a rare expression of affection. She must have sensed he needed it.

Stark blessedly disappeared, which gave them time

alone. Link made an effort to relax and had almost managed it when Phina asked, "So, now that we know the problem is in Spy Corps itself, what do we do?"

Link tensed up and began to feel the weight of the Empire on his shoulders. "We'll do what we must."

"Spy on Spy Corps?"

"Yes."

"This is going to suck, isn't it?"

He answered honestly. "You have no idea."

CHAPTER THREE

QBBS *Meredith Reynolds*, Ship Docks

"Phina!" multiple voices shouted upon seeing her for the first time in months.

She darted down the ramp with a wide grin and spread her arms to hug everyone in the small crowd at the bottom. Alina and Maxim were first, giving her a huge squeeze.

"Phina, I missed you so much!" Alina, Phina's best friend in the whole universe, overdramatized things sometimes, but she was also smart, loyal, and had a good heart. Clutching Phina, she declared in her most no-nonsense voice, "I've decided you can't go anywhere ever again."

"Alina," Maxim gently admonished his wife.

She let out a loud sigh, then drew back to give Phina a wobbly smile. "Fine. You can go for work, but only if you message me every day so I don't miss you too much. And if you see fabulous clothes or shoes, you have to get them for me," she added seriously. "It's a law."

"That's not a law," Phina responded dryly. She gave

Alina another squeeze before letting go. "That's wishful thinking."

"No, it's a law," Alina protested as Maxim nudged his wife out of the way. "The best friends forever law. The Phinalina law. It's a real thing."

Phina would have responded, but she was pulled into another hug by Ryan, who teased her with a wide grin before his girlfriend Celeste elbowed him and gave Phina a smile and gentle hug. "Welcome home."

Before she knew it, Phina had also been greeted by Drk-vaen and Sis'tael, and Jace and his fiancé Melia. Including Link and Will, a large portion of her chosen family was here.

She missed Braeden, her Gleek chosen brother, but knew he was back on his planet with his people. Phina and Braeden exchanged messages every couple of days, as well as mental conversations every few weeks to strengthen their ability to connect mentally over large distances. Braeden carried most of the distance on his own, but Phina had been gradually getting stronger.

After speaking to her friends for a few minutes—Will had joined from the ship as well, so they were all together —she began to wonder why Todd hadn't been there to greet her.

"Where..."

A spark fired on the edge of her awareness. She turned to see Todd Jenkins walking toward them from the entrance to the docks, still some distance away. He was as ruggedly handsome as always, although his appearance was a little rough like he had forgotten to shave a time or two and had been running his fingers through his hair.

Phina extracted herself from the center of the group, though startled cries followed her. She ran full speed toward her boyfriend, then slowed down just before reaching him so she didn't bowl him over from the momentum.

Todd opened his arms with a wide smile and caught Phina at just the right time to swing her around before putting her down. They both stood there grinning at each other for several moments before Todd shook his head and pulled her closer, holding her tight.

"I missed you so damn much, Phina."

"I know." Phina swallowed as she buried her nose in his shirt and hugged him back. "I missed you, too."

"We need to figure something out soon because I need to hear your voice every day. I got too used to seeing and hearing you all the time on the *Stark* and Xaldaq before I came back with the other ship."

Phina huffed a laugh. "That sounds sweet and a bit pathetic."

"Hey!" Todd protested as he pulled back with a frown.

She smiled at him and reached up to hold his face and gently push his frown up into a smile with her thumbs. "I must be pathetic too because I had the same thought. Pretty mushy of us, huh?"

Todd regained his pleased smile and shook his head before pulling her close again. "No, I think it's just right."

"Awww," they heard in chorus behind them. Todd tightened his grip, then pivoted them so they could see their friends clearly— and shamelessly— ogling the exchange from several feet away.

"You guys are too cute for words." Celeste was happily

snuggling with Ryan, who boasted that he'd seen it coming. Her friends chimed in with their own comments.

Phina blushed at the attention, but a distraction came in the form of Link as he approached from behind the group and called to Ryan. "You saw it because I told you, boy. I called it before either of them figured it out."

The others perked up in interest while Ryan turned to Link with irritation. Phina wrinkled her nose in derision as she stayed in Todd's arms, not wanting to let go just yet. "Yes, take all the credit for our relationship. That's exactly what we need."

Todd ran his hand down her head and smoothed her hair down to its ends. It felt soothing. No wonder Sundancer liked getting petted. "Let it go, Phina. We both know what the truth is. He's trying to get you worked up."

A glance at Link told her Todd was right. She put it out of her mind and slipped a thought to her patient and observant boyfriend. *What do you think about all of us going to dinner, and then the two of us spend the rest of tonight and tomorrow together?*

Todd looked down with the warm smile he reserved just for her. *That sounds like the best offer I've had since I left Xaldaq. Let's do it.*

When Phina related the plans to their friends, Link protested, "We need to get working on our next steps."

Phina took a step back from Todd and crossed her arms as she turned to her mentor. "I think I've done enough over the last several months to warrant a day off. In fact, know what? Two days doesn't seem unreasonable. We can make plans then."

Link stared at her with a furrowed brow and frown

before reluctantly agreeing. "Fine. We can do that. But I want your full attention and A game after."

Phina ignored the glances of her curious friends following the conversation and scowled at the insult. "Since when have I ever not given my best?"

Alina spoke up. "Well, you purposely got B's in school and purposely failed the Etheric Academy entrance test."

"Wait, you did what?" Will's gaze darted between the two of them as the others in the group showed a mix of confusion, intrigue, and surprise.

Link shifted impatiently at the interruption.

Phina turned to Alina with a tight smile. "Since it was purposeful, you could say I did my best at those things, right?"

Her best friend winced in chagrin since she knew Phina hadn't wanted that to become common knowledge. "Sorry, Phina. Yes. You always do your best at whatever you put your mind to."

Phina smiled to let Alina know things were all right between them, then turned her attention back to Link. "So, two days."

He nodded seriously and walked toward the docks' entrance. "I'll see you then. You all have fun at dinner."

They waved goodbye, then Phina turned back to her friends. "All Guns Blazing?"

They agreed and headed out, everyone else chatting away as Phina and Todd walked together ahead, holding hands. He bent his head to ask quietly, "What was that about?"

Phina sighed. She had figured the question would come after Alina's comment. "I didn't want to stand out and be different in school. The kids didn't warm up to me. If they saw the teachers giving me high marks all the time, they would have become difficult. I had a taste of that in the first couple of years of schooling when I already knew everything they were teaching. I was often called on or asked to give the answers, even asked to help the other kids."

She grimaced and shrugged. "The students didn't like that, especially the boys. They began treating me differently. I kept things to myself more and didn't let on that I knew the answers. The teachers gradually lost interest, so it wasn't a problem anymore. I skimmed under the radar after that since I already knew all the answers and could decide how many to get wrong."

"I can see that, though that consistent level of subterfuge sounds tiring," Todd responded thoughtfully as he rubbed his thumb over her knuckles. "What made you decide to fail the Etheric Academy exam? Wouldn't it have been a good thing to go?"

"Usually," Phina agreed. "Many of the kids going to the Academy either don't know what they want to do and need to figure that out, or they need specialized training for their objective that the Academy can give. I already knew what I wanted to do. My aunt wanted me to go and had gotten me the opportunity to take the exam since my grades were purposely not good enough. She wasn't happy when I failed."

Todd winced. "It must have grated for you to purposely fail and then be criticized for it."

"It did, but I knew what was likely to happen going into

the situation." She shrugged, pushing thoughts of her aunt away.

"Because you're a beautiful genius," he gently teased her as they arrived at the bar. Phina's cheeks flushed, but she flashed Todd a pleased smile, then focused on their seating arrangements.

After they had ordered and everyone was listening to Will describe the events that had happened while they were gone, Phina sent a telepathic message. She continued to appear to pay attention to the conversation at the table.

Anything?

You do realize that you are using me to do your job? I should lodge a complaint. Or perhaps ask for payment in fish and liver?

Her paired Previdian Sundancer usually sounded like a mix between a dignified but cranky college professor and a teenager addicted to porn—if that porn was in the form of liver and fish.

To Phina's mind, fish and liver didn't even count as food, but her cat-shaped mentor and friend insisted they were important and necessary delicacies.

I heard that. I'm not a cat.

We've had this same conversation a hundred times. You look like a cat. Eventually, you're just going to need to get over it.

Sundancer sniffed in her mind. *I'll get over it when you acknowledge I'm not a cat.*

Of course you aren't a cat.

Finally. Thank you for recognizing my superior nature.

You just look like one.

Phina could practically feel the glare from here even though she knew Sundancer wasn't close by. He was near, though.

So, tell me.

Fine. Sundancer rolled out the attitude. *We will talk about your deplorable opinions later. As far as people following you, one person was keeping an eye on you the whole time, from disembarking until now.*

Phina froze, ignoring the buzz of conversation. Todd glanced at her in concern, but she gave him a subtle signal to wait. He nodded and continued listening to the group ask Will, who soaked up the attention and became a bit dramatic in the telling, questions about Xaldaq.

The person is still here?

Yes.

Show me.

Sundancer sent her an image of a tall, blond man who was relatively attractive. Phina subtly shifted in her seat so she could scan for him. She casually searched the room amidst the other patrons who were in good cheer and found him in a spot across the room that had a direct view of her seat.

Hmmm.

Should I chase him away?

Phina studied the man while appearing to be paying attention to Ryan's spiel about how boring it had been on the *MR* without Phina and Link around.

"Excuse me? Your life has been a constant drag?" Celeste asked from her seat next to him. Her nose was scrunched, but Phina knew she wasn't upset, so she kept her focus on the man across the room.

"Aside from you, baby. You're the exception to every rule," Ryan hurried to assure her.

"It's a good thing you're cute," Celeste retorted. "While that was smooth, it was pretty lame."

Phina saw Ryan's mouth drop from the corner of her eye.

"Lame? I am not lame."

Tuning the couple out, she continued to observe the watcher surreptitiously until Todd nudged her again, gesturing to his head.

He had asked her not to read his mind, so she tried not to link to it often. Phina was afraid that the more time they spent together, the more likely it would be a losing battle. Still, she wanted to be careful. She wanted him to trust her. Since he was asking, Phina inserted a thought and kept the connection open.

What did you want to ask?

Who are you staring at?

Phina wasn't surprised Todd had noticed a problem since he had obviously known something was wrong, but she was constantly surprised at how observant he proved to be.

A guy who followed our group from the docks. He could be here for any one of us, but I'm pretty sure he's following me.

Todd's jaw tightened, but he remained in the same position. *Have you seen him before?*

No, but I'm fairly certain I know why he's following me.

You didn't read his mind?

Phina grimaced. Sundancer kept telling her that mindreading was normal for them and something to celebrate. He didn't always understand her reluctance. However, Todd and Sundancer both knew she would do whatever it took to protect the people she cared about.

I could, but I would rather wait and see if he's actually a problem first.

Todd glanced over and caught her gaze. *What if he ambushes you later and you could have found out about it now?*

Phina sighed internally. *I suppose you are right.*

Of course I am. He winked at her, causing her to smile.

And so modest, too, she teased, then turned to pay attention to the man spying on her. Her shoulders stiffened.

He was gone.

QBBS *Meredith Reynolds*, Phina's Apartment

Todd admired Phina as she yawned and opened her eyes. His smile widened as she blinked away her sleepiness and focused on him.

"Is something wrong?"

He shook his head as he pulled her close, adjusting the sheets to keep them both warm. "No. You just look adorable when you sleep. And when you wake up. Like a sleepy kitten."

Phina turned her head in surprise. "You don't usually say things like that."

He reached up to smooth her hair behind her shoulders as he thought about it. "I think them. I wasn't sure how it would go with being away from you after only being together for a few weeks. I've had several weeks to miss you, though, and I realized I didn't like the separation. I want to be with you all the time."

Her face lit up briefly before turning regretful. "I do, too. I missed you. But we have jobs that keep us apart. You could be either here on the *MR* or deployed for a time. I could be here or who knows where doing my job."

Todd leaned forward to rest his head against hers as he held her. "I know, Kitten."

She pulled her head back to stare at him. "Kitten, huh?"

He shrugged casually. "It just came out. What do you think about it?"

She thought seriously for several moments, then nodded. "It's far better than anything Will has come up with."

Todd's eyebrows rose with interest. "Oh? What *has* he come up with?"

"Don't ask." Phina huffed as she leaned on his chest. "Kitten makes me a little more self-conscious about the age difference between us, but it's still superior to 'Raffles.'"

He leaned back so he could see her face. "Oh? Does our age difference bother you?"

He smiled as Phina fell silent to take a few moments to think. He liked that she took the time to make sure she knew that what she said was how she thought or felt. He admired how brave she was in many ways, but he particularly appreciated her honesty.

Phina shook her head. "I've always felt older than my age, except for rare times with Alina. I think I'm concerned that *you* see me as being immature or more like a kid."

Todd pulled her up so she lay on top of him and gazed into her bright green eyes. "Trust me, after the last two days, I don't think of you as a kid."

He chuckled as she swatted him on the chest, slightly flustered. "Yes, well, I'm happy you aren't a big creeper."

After Phina settled back down, Todd continued, "As for

the rest, you are mature for your age, even for some of those my age. I don't think you are immature aside from rare occasions when you're arguing with Link."

Phina frowned down at him. "How is it different?"

Todd grinned at the remembrance of some of the epic blow-ups that had happened between Link and Phina after the assassination attempts. Link hadn't been at the wedding, and he had been furious that he wasn't there to protect her. "I think you see him more as a parent figure, so it happens naturally."

She shifted uncomfortably. "I suppose so. I didn't see it like that."

"I know. But I figured I would mention it since that's the only time I see it, and we were having a discussion." He reached up to smooth her bed head hair, then gently tapped on her chin. "I think there's something else bothering you. Do you want to talk about it?"

Unease flickered across her face as she hesitated before finally asking, "Would you rather I have a different job so I could be here on the MR all the time and we could see each other more often?"

Todd shook his head and wrapped his arms around her. "No. Would it make some things easier? Yes. But I think you would ultimately be miserable, and I would never want you to give up your dreams just because of me. That's how resentment grows. We just happen to be two people who take our responsibilities seriously and have a high sense of loyalty and duty. We will make it work."

Phina brightened. "You mean that?"

"I do." He paused, then peered at her in speculation.

"Actually, I'm wondering...how far can you connect to someone mentally?"

She frowned. "You mean distance?" She thought for a moment, then shook her head. "I don't know. I've never tried gauging it without Braeden bridging the other side. The only distance I know for sure is from the medical center where I woke up from the coma to Maxim and Alina's apartment since I connected to her after I woke up."

His heart twinged at the memory of the coma she had been in and his faith that she *would* wake up. He remembered standing alone in the outer room of the medical center, listening to the doctor tell Phina's chosen family that she didn't know if or when Phina would come to. He hadn't known her well at that time, but she had already caught hold of his heart.

Todd was relieved that she had not only woken up but was thriving. He tugged Phina closer so he could give her a quick kiss...and got distracted.

Afterward, he leaned back, dazed. "What were we talking about again?"

Phina shook her head with a pleased smile. "My mental distance."

"Right. What do you think about practicing that today? Keeping the connection open while we get back into what's going on outside of this apartment?"

One of his new favorite things was to study Phina's face and see how much emotion and which ones she would show. She had so much inside her, and she only had recently accepted that it was all right to feel it. Currently, her interest warred with her uncertainty, although only those closest to her would have noticed it.

She answered slowly, unsure how he would respond. "We could do that, but you need to know that the more I connect to someone, the easier it gets. Also, though the connection between Sundancer and me is unique, it's shown me that the closer I am mentally with someone, the harder it is to maintain a barrier between us.

"When we first started connecting, it was like a door that we noticeably stepped through. Now we don't always notice it when the other person steps through. He told me that it's most likely going to end up being more like a curtain that we purposely keep between us so we have separate minds."

She shifted uncomfortably. "So, I can't know for certain, but it's possible that the more and longer you and I connect, the closer our minds will get. Because I'm the one forming the connection, I would be even more aware of what you are thinking and feeling, and eventually, I think I would always be aware of it."

He waited to make sure she was done before caressing away the frown on her face. "Why do you think I'll be upset about that?"

She shrugged casually and turned away, but he knew it wasn't quite as small a thing as she tried to pretend it was.

"You didn't want me to read your mind before," she told him. "If we continue to connect often, I may not be able to stay out of your mind at all. I don't want you to regret it."

Todd leaned forward to kiss her forehead briefly, then began moving his hands on her back. "Look at me, Kitten."

She shifted to do so as he continued, "We haven't been together long, but I'm pretty certain I'm falling in love with you if I haven't landed there already."

Phina shyly smiled through the happiness shining on her face. "Me too."

"I hoped so." He wrapped his arms around her again and held her tight while she did the same, their foreheads touching. He leaned back and continued his train of thought. "I think that means our relationship is important to both of us and we'll be together for a long time. Do you agree?"

Phina nodded, her gaze misty, though she kept her emotions locked down. His heart warmed, and he hugged her again.

His voice was muffled as he spoke into her hair. "I don't know what the future holds, but I intend to spend as many years as we have in this universe with you." Phina's body shook in his arms. He realized she'd lost her hold on her tears as he felt dampness on his shoulder. He stroked her hair to soothe her. "It doesn't bother me at all that our minds would be connected in the future. I think it would make things easier for you, and it would relieve my mind to *know* you are all right and not just hope. I think it's a good idea if you want to do it."

Phina pulled back and wiped her eyes with the back of her hands. "You do? Are you sure? From what Sundancer has told me, it's not something I can easily undo without hurting both of us."

Todd observed the uncertain way she held herself. He wiped away a tear she had missed and nodded. "I think what you aren't sure about is if I accept you and your abilities, Kitten."

She froze in surprise as their gazes connected. He felt a pang in his chest that the fallout of whatever happened with her aunt, whether it had been mind control or not, caused a strong woman like Phina to question herself. Not to mention that he'd only made his prior request out of duty before realizing exactly how many confidential secrets she already knew.

"I do, Phina. I think you're amazing, and that's only partly because of what you can do. You're strong, and you have a big heart. You could do anything with your skills and abilities, but you choose to use them to help people and keep them safe," Todd continued. "I have no doubts about you, and I have no doubts about us. I have faith that everything will work out and we will have many years together in between our responsibilities. If we can have a mental connection so we can remain close even when we're apart, I think that just makes us incredibly lucky."

Her tears flowed again as she held on tightly to him. "I feel the same way. I shouldn't be crying because I'm happy, but I can't help it. You've turned me into a mushy girl who cries at sappy things."

He chuckled softly. "Well, there are worse things in the world."

"Nope, that's definitely the worst," she lamented as she shook her head against his shoulder.

Todd nudged her to get her to look up. She dried her face and his shoulder with the sheet before giving him her attention. "Phina, the worst thing would be losing you."

She sighed and shook her head. "Well, if you want to be all serious about it."

He grinned and tugged lightly on her hair. "Oh, so you're all done with serious?"

Phina nodded. "There's only so much I can take. You told me this yourself, so you shouldn't be surprised."

Todd raised his eyebrows. "I distinctly remember you saying that, and I told you that you can handle more than you think."

"Huh." She shifted her body. "Imagine that."

"If you're trying to distract me..." Todd warned.

"Yes?"

"Well, it's working."

"That was the plan."

CHAPTER FOUR

QBBS *Meredith Reynolds*, Secret Bar, Back Room

Phina entered the back room and found Link at the bar, pouring a drink into a shot glass. He threw it back and set the glass on the bar.

She walked over with a frown on her face, gauging his mood. "Isn't it too early to be drinking?"

He scowled at her as she slid onto the stool next to him. "It's after lunch, and it was only a shot. Don't be a nag."

She huffed. "Sure. What's the plan?"

"Well..." he drawled. "It just so happens that Masha has been after me to bring you to the base for training. Just like a woman to keep after a man for something he already is planning on doing," he muttered as he poured another shot.

Phina scowled and slapped him on the head, causing most of his shot to spill over the side. "Stop that. You're being a tool."

"Ow!" He winced, then saw the mostly empty shot glass. "What the hell, Phina?"

She leaned back and crossed her arms, scrutinizing him with displeasure. "You know Todd thinks we act like you're my parent figure?"

"Huh." He appraised her briefly before refilling his shot glass. "I can see you don't agree."

"Nope. You act more like an older brother. An older brother who's cool, but you're being a tool."

"Oh, geez." He clenched his jaw before throwing the shot back. "Now you're rhyming words. Why do you have to be so..."

"Smart?"

"No."

"Intelligent?"

He balked and waved his shot glass at her. "Those are the same things!"

Phina shook her head with false sympathy at his lack of knowledge. "It's actually an important distinction. Smart is how much and what you know. Intelligence is how you use it."

"Well, thank you, Little Miss Smarty Pants." Link gave her an exaggerated bow. "Whatever would we do without you?"

"Fall into wreck and ruin, I imagine." She stuck her tongue out. Just because. It had nothing to do with the fact that Todd said she acted more immaturely with Link. Nope, nothing at all.

She caught him throwing the remainder of the shot back and sighed as she focused back on work. "So, we have a reason for visiting. We don't need to come up with a story aside from that. That cover also has the benefit of making it seem like we may not want to be there. It gives us a reason for waiting so long since it wasn't our idea. That may help." She paused, then added, "It may hurt, too. I suppose it depends on what's going on."

He nodded and leaned on the bar. "The only thing we do know is that there is at least one traitor there."

Phina raised a finger. "Actually, we don't know that. We have heard about a possible traitor, but we can't confirm yet whether it's true."

Link frowned like he wanted to protest but stopped himself. "I suppose that's true. But it's the only thing we've heard since we started searching, so we need to check it out."

She nodded and fell silent while he brooded. She took the opportunity to check her mental connection to Todd. It was still strong.

When Link barely moved or blinked, she asked, "So, are you going to tell me what's bothering you?"

His head jerked up. "Nothing is bothering me."

Phina placed her elbow on the bar. "Uh-huh. I'm not stupid, Link. I know when someone is lying to me."

Link scowled. "I'm not lying."

She appraised him. "I think you want to believe it's nothing, but I think there's something."

He pressed his lips together and avoided her gaze while he poured another shot.

Phina thought it through, then ventured, "When did Masha contact you about this?"

Link's hand twitched, and a splash of liquor hit the bar.

Huh. Speculation ran through her head, but Phina decided to let him off the hook and changed the subject. "When do you want to leave?"

Relief flared on Link's face as he jumped on the subject change. "They began training a new group of recruits a few months ago, and they are now ready for advanced training. If we leave within five days, we should get there in time for you to join them."

She nodded in understanding. "You want me to join the trainees, see what they are being taught and listen to their conversations."

"I want you to pay attention to *everyone*," he corrected.

Phina frowned. "Even those on staff and your seconds?"

Link swallowed uncomfortably and nodded. "We don't know who the possible traitor is, so we have to suspect everyone. This didn't sound like a recent development, so the traitor is unlikely to be a student."

Feeling overwhelmed, Phina rubbed the back of her neck as she thought about the logistics. "How many people are on the base?"

He began counting off. "Well, there's me, my seconds, six trainers, one administrative assistant, one tech specialist, one logistician and supply coordinator, two cooks, three maintenance people, thirteen—counting you, fourteen—trainees, and then whoever is on base between assignments. So, usually forty-five to fifty people."

"Well, that's not bad," she reasoned.

"However," he continued, his melancholy slowly replaced with frustration, "this is not a normal time. We haven't sent out the previous recruits for their first assignments yet, and I told them to wait until after our visit because there was a big mission we needed to train and reshuffle things for. Because of that, there could easily be over seventy people on base."

Phina's shoulders sagged. "Seventy suspects? How long do you expect this to take?"

"As long as it takes," Link responded grimly as he picked up the forgotten shot and tossed it back. He swallowed, sighed, and slid the shot glass forward, staring blankly. "These are my people, Phina. I vetted everyone personally up until nine years ago. I can't help wondering if this wouldn't have happened if I hadn't taken that step back."

"What happened nine years... Oh." Phina's breath caught. "My parents died."

"Yeah." He ran his fingers roughly through his hair. "I took a step back because I needed time. I just didn't pick it back up after that."

"Hey." She grabbed his hand and held it, giving him a look of panic. "You can't shut down. I can't do this alone."

Link sighed and shook his head. "I'll be there to help and answer questions. I'm hoping your abilities will be a big asset in figuring this out. But I can't be objective, Phina. I know all of these people aside from the recruits. I'll help as much as I can, but the truth is that you're going to have to do most of it alone. There's no one else we can trust."

Phina hadn't wanted to hear that.

QBBS *Meredith Reynolds*, Bethany Anne's Office

"Tell me right now why I shouldn't send Barnabas or go myself and put my size sevens up their asses after I find them!"

Bethany Anne stood squarely in front of Link, her eyes flashing in anger. Right now, speaking with a fiery edge, she was scary. However, since she hadn't lost her temper yet, Link was reasonably relaxed.

She could get much scarier.

"Well, you all are busy with other things..."

"Try again."

Link blinked and changed tack. "We don't know what's going on yet..."

Bethany Anne's eyes flashed red again as she leaned forward. "Last chance."

He swallowed and glanced at Phina, who had remained quiet since they had entered the office to report the intelligence they had received and their plan for pursuing it. The Empress had been livid when they'd told her there might be a traitor in Spy Corps.

Link sighed, then looked Bethany Anne in the eye and spoke calmly. "There are two main reasons, although I maintain that the earlier ones are both valid."

Thankfully for his nerves, the Empress snorted in amusement. "Of course you do. Tell me these two reasons, and they'd better be good ones," she warned.

"The first is that Phina needs to complete her training. This is a perfect assignment for her apprenticeship mission. She's also the best person for the job aside from you and Barnabas." Link frowned. "Well, I suppose those are two reasons in themselves, although they fit together."

Bethany Anne raised an eyebrow at the comment but remained quiet.

Link soldiered on because this point was the most important. "The last reason is that spies are different than other people. They operate on the front lines largely with minimal support, sometimes for years. They are independent, secretive, and careful people who value trust and loyalty above all else but are very careful with who they give it to. You and the Empire, and by extension, I and my seconds are who they have put their trust in. They have to hold onto those things to make it through their assignments."

Link saw understanding dawn on the Empress' flawless face.

"You are saying that if we storm in there guns blazing, they will see it as a betrayal."

"Yes." He sighed in relief. "It could do more damage than the traitor. Potential traitor," he corrected. "Perhaps not right away, but long-term it would cripple Spy Corps."

Bethany Anne turned her attention to Phina. "You haven't been at this long, but you have a good head on your shoulders, and I've noticed you weigh potential outcomes. What do you think?"

Link tried not to take the Empress' question for a second opinion personally. Surprise crossed Phina's face before she frowned in thought.

"Link's been at this far longer than me and knows these people better, but from the information I've found on everyone so far, I would say that what he says would be true of the older spies and those in support staff positions. I'm not so certain about the younger ones. Their actions haven't been recorded enough to measure their responses.

"I do see that a schism of sorts could develop between those two groups, which could cause long-term problems." She tilted her head in thought. "I think it also depends on who the traitor ends up being if there is one and how far they have spread their treachery."

Bethany Anne sat on the edge of her desk and folded her arms, her lips pressed together. "That makes sense to me. So, you need to figure out who the traitor is, and you won't have much personnel support. Think of what you might need while you are there and get it requisitioned before you go: tech, weapons, or other equipment."

She pinned Link with a hard stare. "You said you need a few days before you can leave?"

"Yes. If it takes up to a week, though, Stark will have to compensate to get there on time. I want to be there before training starts without delaying them and making them more suspicious than they will already be."

Phina frowned at his comment. "Why would they be suspicious if you are late?"

He shrugged. "They're spies. Spies are always suspicious."

QBBS *Meredith Reynolds*, Diplomatic Institute

After going over the brief and fluid gameplan with Link and the Empress, along with some potential scenarios, Phina headed to the Diplomatic Institute.

She entered the main corridor of the facility, her mind focused on what needed to be done before they left. She ignored the students and teachers passing by as she knocked on the Dean's door.

Meredith opened the door, and Phina stepped into the office.

"Phina!" Anna Elizabeth stood behind her desk and came around to give her a big hug, sparkling with happiness. After releasing her, Anna stepped back and smiled.

"You look great, Phina. Something must agree with you. Or perhaps some*one*," she teased gently before sitting back down and gesturing for Phina to take the chair across from her desk.

"Thank you." Phina sat comfortably, feeling familiar with the office.

"So, you are back." Anna smiled and leaned forward. "I got your reports and the final documents from Barnabas after they were signed on his ship to finalize bringing the Qendrok into the Empire. We just have your debriefing left to do."

Phina launched into an hour and ten-minute narrative describing the final confrontation with Qartan and Zultav, as well as everything that had happened since then.

When Phina was finished, Anna Elizabeth leaned back and appraised her. "So, everything ended well, you made new friends, and we have new allies. Can you tell me why you don't seem happier now that you are back? Is something else going on?"

Not surprised that Anna Elizabeth sensed her mood, Phina explained the nebulous tracks Link and Phina had been searching for since before her coma and where they had led. Bethany Anne had already approved giving Anna Elizabeth the information, so Phina didn't have a problem sharing. She did share the Empress' warning that no one else was to know.

"All of this leads to Spy Corps?" Anna Elizabeth asked with visible frustration.

Phina sighed. "We don't know for sure yet, but that is the direction we have right now."

The older woman shook her head. "I'll bet Greyson is

having a fit. He's a straightforward person, no matter how convoluted he likes to be at times. He would take this personally."

Phina was silent, remembering her mentor's frustration and sadness that his people could be involved.

"Is there anything you need from me, or is this just an advisory about your next steps?" Anna Elizabeth asked, which caused the younger woman to wonder if there was something in particular she was searching for.

Phina nodded. "I do want to know what my graduation status is."

"I can find out." Anna Elizabeth tapped her tablet and scanned the results. "You have passed most of your classes. All you had left was Communications and Negotiation." She clasped her hands on the desk in front of her. "However, I will count your part in bringing the Qendrok into the Empire as hands-on practice for these classes. With that, all that remains is your apprenticeship assessment."

Phina felt relieved to have passed the two classes that had caused her problems. "Greyson suggested that this trip to Spy Corps could fulfill that requirement."

"Oh?" Anna Elizabeth appeared interested in the news. "Did he say how much of this task you will take on yourself?"

"All of it."

The Dean's eyebrows shot up. "Are you certain? That's a lot of responsibility and pressure on you."

Phina repressed the urge to shift uncomfortably. "He said that he could advise, but the bulk of this mission would be up to me to carry out."

"I see." Anna Elizabeth frowned for a moment before

nodding. "It's not ideal, but if any one of our students could pull this off, it's you."

"Thank you."

She waved dismissively. "Just telling the truth. Thank you for coming in to report."

"You're welcome."

Phina stood to leave, but Anna Elizabeth stopped her.

"Be careful when you are dealing with the spies in Spy Corps, Phina. Or any of them." Anna studied her in concern. "Most are great people, but they are all spies for a reason. Many of them are the best actors you've ever seen. Some of them won't give you a reason to suspect them and then come at you from behind. Watch your back. Get Sundancer to help you. You should be fine."

Surprised, Phina stammered, "You sound concerned. I thought you said I could handle it?"

Anna Elizabeth nodded. "I believe you can. However, you haven't seen these spies in action. You will need to be smart and careful."

"I'm always smart."

"You are. Be twice as careful."

CHAPTER FIVE

Etheric Empire, QBBS *Meredith Reynolds*

Phina wandered around the station to clear her head before meeting SofRey and her mom for ice cream. The bright chatter of the young girl warmed her heart and helped her thoughts settle.

On her way home, Phina pinged ADAM.

>>**Welcome back, Phina.**<<

Um, thank you, ADAM. You do *remember I talked to you a few days ago when we were on the* Stark?

>>**Of course. I remember everything.**<<

Right. Just checking.

>>**Did you want to talk, or did you need something?**<<

Well, I...huh." Phina frowned in thought as she meandered past others in the corridors. *Are you saying I only talk to you if I need something?*

>>**Not in so many words.**<<

But you wonder about it sometimes? Phina prodded.

>>**Sometimes.**<< His mental voice was quiet.

Well, then I haven't been a very good friend to you lately, Phina responded firmly. *I'm sorry, ADAM. I don't want you to ever wonder about that. I've missed you. I just wish I wasn't leaving right away.*

>>**I heard that. I wish you could stay.**<<

Phina sent him a mental hug. *Are we all right?*

>>**Yes.**<<

Good. Phina sighed as she remembered why she had pinged ADAM. *We still need to talk about something.*

>>**Go ahead.**<<

Do you remember those bracelet devices we found on the assassins' arms after the wedding?

>>**Yes.**<<

I had an idea about using them for our next mission, but I don't know how they work or if they are even usable. Do you have any suggestions? Maybe Ron could help?

Ron Diamantz was a researcher who had been experimenting with Etheric energy. Phina had recently learned he was also the researcher assigned to provide weapons and tech for Spy Corps.

>>**Ron is adequate, but you will need to speak to someone who has a better understanding of the Etheric.**<<

All right. Who do I talk to?

>>**Go to your apartment. They will meet you there.**<<

In her surprise, Phina almost tripped as she walked, narrowly avoiding bowling into a female Yollin who didn't have a sense of humor. She wasn't as relaxed or fun as her friend Sis'tael. Phina apologized and continued the long walk back to her apartment, wondering who she would be meeting.

Before reaching her apartment, Phina checked in on her mental link with Todd. It had grown strained when he had been on the farthest side of the station, but now it felt strong.

Really strong.

She realized Todd waited for her in her apartment when she reached the door. She opened it with a smile and stopped when she saw he had brought the device the Qendrok had used in conjunction with the wristbands. She closed the door before stepping forward to greet her boyfriend.

"Hey, handsome."

Todd broke into a wide smile and wrapped his arms around her, holding her tight. She held on to him with the same intensity. After a full minute, he pulled back enough to see her questioning face.

"I missed you," he told her quietly. "With the connection open, it was like having you with me without seeing you. It threw me off for a while."

"Would you rather cut the connection?" Phina asked anxiously as she let go.

He caught her hands and squeezed them gently. "No, I'll get used to it. I would rather struggle and feel you with me than not to feel you at all."

She smiled appreciatively. "I like feeling you."

Todd flashed her a grin. "Did you mean that mentally or physically?"

Phina tiptoed to give him a kiss that lasted longer than she meant it to. They finally pulled back and Phina gave him a warm smile, which was the extent of her ability at flirting. "Why can't it be both?"

"I like both." He flashed a matching smile and pulled her back for another kiss.

"Oh! I'm sorry. Is this a bad time?"

Phina turned at hearing the stranger's voice come from nowhere. A beautiful woman a little shorter than Phina with deep reddish-brown hair had materialized in the kitchen.

"Who are you?" Phina took a step toward the stranger, a mixture of emotions coursing through her. She didn't like the thought of someone she didn't know in her apartment without her knowledge.

Todd grabbed Phina's arm gently, stopping her movement.

"Hi, Anne. Is something wrong?" Todd shifted so his arm wrapped around Phina. Since his expression showed confusion rather than the warmth he gave Phina, she decided not to worry about Anne.

Phina's natural curiosity for new information rose. She had heard a few mentions of Anne, but she knew nothing substantial since the woman was reclusive. Anne wore a t-shirt, jeans, and brown boots with a small heel that drew Phina's attention and gave her a rare bout of shoe envy.

"No," the woman responded as she perused the apartment. "I was surprised to have my day interrupted, but that's okay."

"I see." Todd and Phina glanced at each other before he asked the burning question. "Why are you here?"

"Oh, right." Anne's eyes sparkled with amusement. "ADAM sent me. He said you had something interesting for me to see."

Phina straightened as she realized Anne was the Etheric

researcher who was more experienced than Ron. The woman seemed pretty down-to-earth for someone so smart.

She stepped away from Todd, who reluctantly let go, and waved at the machine and pouch that contained the wristbands. ADAM had probably asked Todd to bring them to her apartment. Phina realized now that she was firing on more than hormones.

"This is the machine. It's an Etheric translocation device."

"Oh?" Anne's eyes sparkled with intrigue as she scanned the device. "That does sound interesting. Can you both carry it?"

"I can carry it," Todd volunteered. He bent to pick up the pouch by the strap. He put the pouch on like a shoulder bag and lifted the blocky device, which stood tall in his arms.

"Good enough." Anne nodded and grabbed his arm as she stepped backward.

Both Todd and Anne disappeared.

Phina gaped in shock. She must have lowered her mental barrier because Sundancer raced into the room from her bedroom at the same time that Anne reappeared.

Phina grabbed Anne's arm and was about to give her an angry piece of her mind.

She was asking where the woman had taken her boyfriend when Anne grabbed Phina with her other hand and stepped back again, pulling Phina with her.

She stumbled at the sudden movement but kept herself upright.

Anne let go of her arm and stepped away.

Phina's face turned up, and her mouth opened in shock. "Holy fudging hell!"

Etheric Empire, Spy Corps Headquarters

Masha Kosolov was energized. More energized than she had felt in months. If it wouldn't be unseemly for one of the leaders of a secret spy organization to be seen skipping down the hall, she probably would have indulged herself.

She stopped at a door down the hall and knocked.

"Enter." The deep voice was muffled through the door but distinctly recognizable.

As Masha entered, she assessed the man who sat behind the desk reading a report.

Greyson Wells, their boss and leader, reminded her of an older version of one of her teenage idols, Wesley Crusher on *Star Trek*. He could have come from almost any culture aside from East Asian or Scandinavian. He was attractive but not a standout...until he opened his mouth. His ability to blend in was part of what made Greyson a great spy.

The man at the desk, Jack Kaiser, more resembled the quintessential movie spy: handsome, rugged, and distinguished. He could be charming, militant, gregarious, or cold at the drop of a hat. He was well trained, well dressed, and well respected in Spy Corps. His job was to make sure the Corps ran smoothly when Greyson was off on missions.

Her personal interactions with the man were a little different. They worked together well enough and handled things between them so that nothing fell through the cracks. However, even though there was only a five-year difference between the two of them, Masha often came away from their conversations feeling like that gap was closer to twenty. She couldn't figure out if it was how he treated her or her perception. It left her feeling frustrated, and drained her good mood away.

Jack peered over the top of his reading glasses to give her a frown. "Did you need something?"

Masha left her thoughts behind and straightened with a nod. "Greyson is coming back shortly before the advanced training classes begin."

"That's nothing out of the ordinary." He turned back to his report dismissively. "The man shows up when he wants, but he's usually here for that."

Masha barely kept an eye roll in check. "This time, he's bringing Phina."

Jack finally showed interest in the conversation. "Oh? That's his special-interest recruit, correct?"

"Yes." Masha wanted to sit down, but that setup always made her feel like she was a student being scolded. She remained standing, shifting her weight from one foot to the other. "He's bringing her to train with the other recruits."

"Hmm." The older spy pulled off his glasses and tilted his head speculatively. "I had told him he should bring her here, but he refused. I wonder what made him change his mind?"

"I asked him."

Jack focused on her face. She muscled past her discomfort and continued, "I met Phina at Maxim's wedding. She's his wife's best friend. She seems to have been trained well in fighting, but I believe she's floundering somewhat on the spy skills we normally teach. I thought we could help, so I suggested he bring her here."

"Are you familiar with her combat skills? It sounds like you had a chance to observe her in action."

"A little," Masha confirmed. "There was an attack during the wedding. She took out her fair share of the attackers."

Masha wasn't certain why she had stretched the truth. She instinctively knew that Greyson didn't want everyone to know the extent of Phina's skills. Masha didn't even know how far those skills went, but she had been impressed by what she had seen in Phina. In truth, she wanted to include Phina in Spy Corps circles because she thought the younger woman could use the connections and had a lot to teach as well as learn.

"Interesting." Jack mulled the information over before speaking. "Tell me more about this attack."

Masha would rather have kept the information to herself, but she had no good reason to deny the request that wouldn't sound childish. Masha opened her mouth to explain when the man used his glasses to point at her.

"And sit down. You're hovering. Hovering irritates me."

Masha didn't suppress her glowering glare, but she sat down. As she gave him a carefully edited version of events, she decided that she had her answer as to who was at fault for making her feel like a child in their interactions.

It was definitely Jack.

. . .

Etheric Empire, QBBS *Meredith Reynolds*

Sundancer raced out of the bedroom in time to see his human disappear.

Who had dared to take his human away?

He darted forward to sniff the spot where she had been kidnapped.

He tilted his head, pink triangle ears perked, listening for her mind. He remained connected to her, though the connection was muffled like he was sensing her from behind a curtain that dampened sound. It felt like...

Sundancer took a step and slipped between dimensions, something that he had only recently learned how to do after doing some stalk...ahem...spying on the Empress. She had caught him, which had been a great blow to his ego.

The Empress had been kind and taken him into the Etheric with her. She'd stepped over and back a few times to show him how the trick worked. Sundancer had been eager to learn something new, and it now came in handy.

Sundancer landed in the mist with his back arched and his ears tipped forward, ready to fight. Phina was the first thing Sundancer saw after stepping through.

Phina didn't sense Sundancer since she was locked down. She stood a few feet away from her kidnapper, controlling her emotions as she spoke. "What is this place?"

"My workshop," the human who had kidnapped Phina answered as she turned to the device Todd had placed on the long counter in the center of the room.

Sundancer relaxed now that he knew she was unharmed.

Todd linked his hand with Phina's. Sundancer ignored

the ever-present affection between his human and her mate and explored the area for himself.

The long counter where the kidnapper stood held drawers of varying sizes underneath. To the side of that, there was a table large enough for three people and chairs. The whole setup was made of non-metallic materials like plastic and silicone. Shelves made of the same materials were placed on the far side of the counter and held varying devices and gadgets in differing states of disarray.

Sundancer was distracted by sparks behind the shelves and realized that the walls were made of the mist. He pondered how cloud-like mists could be made to maintain the solid state. The sparks of energy that shot through the walls forked like tiny bolts of lightning.

Since Sundancer and Phina were permanently mentally connected, he knew where they were the instant she recognized the location.

"Fudging crumbs. We're in the Etheric."

"We are." The huge creature the voice belonged to rounded the corner of the counter and sat by the kidnapper, who was poking at the device Todd had brought. "That's what the humans call it, anyway."

Sundancer arched his back and froze at the sight of the massive creature, whose voice came from the device attached to her collar. While Phina's mental reaction told Sundancer she was almost as surprised by the creature as he was, Todd merely smiled in welcome.

"Hello, Jinx."

The great furry being tilted her head curiously, ears perked in interest, causing Sundancer to realize that this Jinx was a dog. A *giant* dog.

"We have seen you before," Jinx offered.

"Yes. I'm Todd. I'm good friends with Peter."

At that name, both woman and dog groaned. The sound gave Sundancer assurance that he didn't need to be on the alert for an attack. He allowed his back to return to its normal curve, his tail swishing slightly.

Todd chuckled in amusement at their reactions. "Still having training pains?"

"Not as much as before, but his lessons tend to stick," the kidnapper answered.

Sundancer heard the name "Anne" through Phina's thoughts as the woman in question glared at Todd in suspicion.

"You weren't involved in the plan to put Jinx in that horrid vest from hell, were you?"

"No," Todd responded, raising his free hand to swear by it. "I did tell John Grimes it was a mistake, though."

"Hmm." Anne continued to appraise him but let it go and turned back to the device.

Sundancer felt his human growing impatient and wasn't surprised when she spoke up.

"So, what do you think? Is it usable?"

Using the distraction of her question to slip closer to the big dog, Sundancer quietly took in information through his senses.

"I'm still looking. I'll let you know when I've finished." Anne spoke distractedly, causing Jinx to huff in resignation.

Sundancer took the opportunity to move closer. When he was only a few feet away, Jinx whirled her head around.

"What are you doing?"

"What! You can see me?" Sundancer could have been bowled over with a feather. No one ever saw him if he didn't want them to. Not in years.

Jinx cocked her head in confusion. "Of course I can see you. You're right in front of me." She padded over and sniffed him, then snorted and stepped back. "You smell funny. Like..." She turned her head to look at Anne, who mirrored the movement.

Sundancer suspected they were linked mentally like him and Phina.

After a long moment, Jinx turned back more confidently and sniffed Sundancer again. "Yes, like smoke and space."

"This is Sundancer," Phina told them as she glanced at them curiously. He knew she had been following his train of thought subconsciously. "He's paired with me. Similar to how you two are paired, I'll guess."

Anne paused at her task and crouched to speak to Sundancer. "Hello, Sundancer. I'm happy to meet you."

"Are you sure? You seemed happy enough to ignore me a minute ago."

He felt Phina's mental sigh and gentle "can't take you anywhere" admonishment. Anne just smiled.

Jinx gave Sundancer a doggy grin. "I like you. You're funny." She paused, then added, "For a cat, anyway. Dogs are much funnier."

Sundancer straightened to his full height, ears flicking in disdain. "I am not a *cat*. I am a Previdian, *dog*, which is not the same thing as a cat at all. I am a mysterious and majestic being of the ninth family of Previdia! You should worship my magnificence and consider yourself lucky to be in my presence!"

Anne struggled not to laugh but failed. Jinx didn't even try to contain her amusement. "Yes. You're very funny. Dogs don't worship cats, and we don't demand to be revered, either. We just are friends with our humans."

Sundancer's ears pressed back. He couldn't take any more. He turned and walked away, his tail flicking in agitation. He threw a glare at Phina since he could hear her mental chuckles as he passed.

You are all ignorant creatures. You're on your own, Phina. See if I come running to your rescue again.

Ears and tail held high, he stepped back over to Phina's apartment.

A cat. He sniffed. *My magnificence is never appreciated.*

CHAPTER SIX

Etheric Dimension, Anne's Workshop

"Did we scare the fancy cat away?"

Phina shook her head at Jinx's question. "Sundancer does his own thing, but he is protective and caring in his own way. He came because he was worried about me. His ego was poked, so he left." She shrugged and grasped Todd's hand a little tighter. "He'll be fine. If I was in trouble he wouldn't hesitate to come back, no matter how grumpy he gets."

She sent a wave of love and appreciation to Sundancer. *Are you all right?*

The connection felt muffled but she got a wave of affection back, so she figured her Previdian friend wasn't terribly upset and turned her attention back to Anne.

"So, how are we in the Etheric?"

Anne paused to scan Phina uncertainly before she reached down to wrap an arm around Jinx's neck. "Would you rather hear the long version, the short version, or the extremely short version?"

"How about somewhere between short and extremely short so I get the big picture, and then I'll ask questions?"

As Anne thought about where to begin, Phina opened her filters to get a sense of the reason behind the woman's uneasiness. She wasn't aiming to intrude, but she wanted to get a general sense of Anne's thoughts and feelings so she didn't overstep. To her surprise, Anne had strong mental shields of her own, like Bethany Anne.

Phina switched to the mental connection between her and Todd.

Todd, is she a Nacht? A vampire like Bethany Anne?

Yes. He nodded as he answered, which triggered amusement. She sent affection through their link as she absorbed that new fact along with what she had gained from Anne.

Though the woman felt more closed off than anyone Phina had met before, she had received a sense of wariness, reluctance, and a pang of something soft that she recognized all too well. She lifted her chin, meeting Anne's gaze.

"You have a hard time explaining new things to new people because hardly anyone gets you."

Surprise flashed across Anne's face. "How did you know?"

Phina gave her an easy smile and a light shrug. "I often have the same problem. I used to have hardly anyone to talk to aside from my best friend, and now I have more." Phina glanced at Todd with a happy smile that he returned as she continued, "All lovely people. But when I'm problem-solving or figuring out how something works, it's hard to describe my thought process in a way people understand because my brain makes connections differently than others do. Sometimes I think I need to throw in three diagrams and a color-coordinated flowchart."

Anne smiled and Jinx's ears perked up in interest when Todd leaned over to whisper, "Didn't you do that once?"

"Shh. It was one time!" Phina huffed as she pulled her hand away and crossed her arms. "It didn't even work because I don't organize the same way others do, either. No one could follow it."

Jinx and Anne laughed while Todd wrapped an arm around Phina and tugged her closer, smiling as he whispered, "My beautiful genius."

Phina basked in the warm feelings she received from Todd and gave him a blinding smile of appreciation before turning back to Anne and offering her answer.

"Perhaps start with why you decided you needed to move your workspace here?"

Anne nodded with a shy but pleased smile, then proceeded to explain while she continued examining the translocation device.

"I've been working with the Etheric for...hmm...almost thirteen years now. As you may have noticed, it is an inexhaustible energy source." She glanced at Phina, who nodded, then Anne waved a hand around the room. "Well, all this started with wanting to change kinetic energy into Etheric energy so Jinx wouldn't get thrown around as much when we fight."

Anne's jaw tightened as if remembering the times when her friend had been hurt. Phina noted that Jinx physically comforted Anne by pressing her furry body against her friend, even though Jinx had been the one to get hurt. After a few ear scratches, Anne continued.

"We have a workable vest now, but it doesn't stop the more powerful weapons. Anyway, this isn't the long story, so let's just say that experiment led to a few different side trails that allowed us to begin storing and eventually manipulating Etheric energy with the help of my friends and employees, Stevie and Tina. However, it's harder to work with Etheric energy outside of the Etheric without blowing things up."

"So, you decided you needed to find a way to create a lab inside the Etheric," Phina concluded.

"Exactly." Anne had grown more relaxed and open the longer she talked and was now showing excitement about having someone who understood the process. "The problem we had was finding a way to manipulate the energy into creating the space we needed within the Etheric. It took a few years of experimenting before I was able to create the walls. A few months later, I got them stabilized."

"Hmmm." Phina mulled that over as she perused the area again. "What materials are you using here? I don't see any metals."

"That's right." Anne glanced at Phina curiously. "You seem less freaked out about being in the Etheric than others, and you recognized the Etheric. Has Bethany Anne brought you here, or can you cross over yourself?"

Shaking her head, Phina peered at Anne as she removed an inner panel of the device to examine what lay underneath. "Neither. I haven't been here in person, but while I was in a coma, my consciousness was transferred into the Etheric. It was like a dream that was also real."

Anne glanced up from unscrewing another panel. "That sounds both interesting and strange."

"Tell me about it." Phina groaned.

She and Anne chatted about their Etheric experiences, Phina peppering their discussion with questions about how the structure of the walls came about. Todd had squeezed her hand before moving over to have a conversation with Jinx, occasionally glancing around uneasily.

Phina and Anne had moved onto childhood struggles when Anne finally opened a smaller inner panel and stared in surprise at the contents.

"What is it?" Phina asked, wondering if Anne had found a bomb or something equally devastating.

"This device runs on Etheric energy, but it's not using any material I'm familiar with." She spoke slowly and thoughtfully. Alight with interest and speculation, Anne tuned everyone out while she worked.

She suddenly swiveled toward Jinx in surprise. "We never got through that huge list of materials to test, and I'm wondering which one this is. Maybe we can replicate the manufacturing process and adapt it to upgrade the vest so you're protected." Anne turned back to Phina.

Her movement was faster than Phina anticipated, and she barely kept herself from reacting.

"How soon do you need this device?" Anne asked.

Phina grimaced, seeing Anne's excitement and feeling strangely reluctant to disappoint her. "As soon as possible. We are leaving in the next few days. We can't put it off."

Anne repressed her disappointment as she glanced back at the device with longing. "Are you certain you need this device for your mission?"

Nodding, Phina answered quietly, not wanting Todd to overhear. "It could be the difference between death and making it out alive if things go badly. I'll be on my own most of the time."

Phina and Anne's gazes connected, allowing Phina a little more of a glimpse into the loyalty, compassion, and curiosity that lay within this younger Nacht—who Phina hadn't seen any sign of in any of the files she'd accessed in her years of hacking.

Which could only mean that Anne was protected by both ADAM and Bethany Anne, possibly similarly to how they had protected Phina.

That realization caused Phina to feel a certain kinship with the other woman. She allowed Anne to see more of herself than she would have with any other new acquaintance.

Anne gave her a warm smile that Phina returned, and they both nodded before Anne walked back to the device with a spring in her step that revealed her excitement.

"Then we'll get moving on seeing how the device works and have it ready with instructions before you go." Anne smiled at Phina with determination. "When you are done with your mission, you can bring it back so Stevie and I can figure out why it works and how we can duplicate it."

Her voice dropped to a whisper, but Phina still heard. "And we can better protect Jinx. Maybe even incorporate it into the armor for the *Stark*."

Pieces fit together for Phina. Anne was the researcher Stark had mentioned years ago when he'd said he would be getting a smaller, faster ship at some point.

Seeing the connection between Jinx and Anne as the

large dog leaned into his human's side, Phina couldn't help wanting their hopes to come true.

QBBS *Meredith Reynolds*, Outer Docks

"I'm going to miss you," Phina whispered as she leaned into Todd. "I don't even know how long this will take."

Todd stood steady with his arms wrapped around her, holding her close as he spoke softly. "I'll miss you, too. You established the connection between us, and Sundancer confirmed it's now there permanently, so even when we are far apart, you should know how I'm doing."

"Yeah." Phina sighed as she snuggled into his arms a little more. She wasn't small, but Todd was taller and made her feel protected when he held her close. It had felt strange at first, but now it was a gift that he always gave her when she needed it. "It's not the same, but it will help."

She nudged the inner connection she had with Todd and found a mix of regret that she would leave soon, pride that she had been called to such an important task, and an overwhelming wave of emotions that when put together could only mean one thing: love.

Of course, since they had only danced around that little word so far, she just burrowed a little closer and allowed her feelings for him to bleed through their connection. He couldn't access her thoughts or emotions unless she sent them, so she made sure to share her side of the connection with Todd anytime she accessed his.

It was only fair.

Todd's grip tightened as he processed the emotions she

was sending him, then showed his appreciation. Thoroughly.

"All right. All right," Link broke in as he passed them to walk onto the *Stark*. "Break up the PDA. No one wants to see that."

Todd pulled back but didn't let go, flashing Link a grin. "You only say that because you want some and aren't getting any."

Phina had the privilege of seeing the first time that Link had been caught off guard in her presence when he completely froze and almost stumbled before catching himself and whirling around to face them. "What? Why would you say—"

Link caught himself, gritting his teeth and throwing them both a glare before quickly entering the ship. If he hadn't had so much control over himself, Phina would have called it a snippy stomp.

Todd and Phina waited until they couldn't see Link anymore before turning to each other with a grin.

"I *knew* it!" Phina tried to keep her volume down. "He's got at least a crush."

Todd's eyes warmed in amusement. "You're going to figure out who it is and play matchmaker, aren't you?"

"Of course!" Phina smirked. "With as much glee as he has taken about matching us up even though he did absolutely nothing, he deserves a little payback."

Chuckling, Todd stretched his arms around her to keep her with him for as long as possible. "You sound like Bethany Anne. We started calling her St. Payback because she would get everyone back just as hard if not harder."

Phina tried to imagine the Empress giving payback and didn't find it hard at all. "That sounds both fun and scary."

"Oh, you have no idea," Todd reminisced, which softened his features slightly.

Phina couldn't resist reaching up and giving him a soft kiss that got more involved as Todd responded.

Her implant pinged as Stark connected. *Sorry, not sorry, but we need to get moving. The lord and master is getting impatient.*

Understood.

After saying goodbye to Todd, Phina turned at the top of the ramp to see him standing in the same spot studying her with all those emotions she had felt earlier showing on his face.

As the ramp closed, Phina impulsively put her fist to her heart, causing his face to light up as he did the same.

He held the position until the ramp had closed. She leaned against it with her eyes shut, struggling to get a handle on her emotions.

Now that she and Todd were together, it felt a lot harder to picture going off on spying and diplomatic adventures. She felt torn in two.

The *Stark* came to life around her as they left the docks while she wrestled with what she wanted. She couldn't decide. She wanted a life with Todd *and* a life as a diplomatic spy.

Phina's resolve grew as she realized that she couldn't leave either behind. To do so would kill an integral part of her—one that she had wanted for years and the other that had been slowly awakened. Yet, time didn't matter. She had to figure out a way to balance the two.

Phina couldn't live without either one.

QBS *Stark*, Phina's Cabin

"Wakey, wakey!"

Phina blinked her eyes open at the boisterous greeting that had woken her.

"Stark, not so loud," she groaned as she turned over and wrapped an arm around a small, warm body that took her super-smart, sleepy brain far too long to identify as Sundancer.

Link and Phina had spent the last few days of the trip holed up to focus on the list of staff, students, and spies they would encounter at the base, digging into their profiles and backgrounds, searching for pieces to figure out who the traitor could be.

Unfortunately, they had come up with absolutely nothing.

The whole process had been tedious and mind-numbing on the one hand, yet interesting and thought-provoking on the other. If they had come up with a single clue, the task would have been much more satisfying.

On the positive side, Phina had discovered the name of her stalker. However, since Link had identified the man as Shaw, a trusted agent and trainer, they had put the man low on the list of possibilities. Privately, Phina had wondered if Link was not being cautious enough and letting the man's position color the facts. She had mentally shuffled him a few places higher.

When Link had grown irritable and impatient at the lack of progress, Phina had been forced to toss him out of the onboard office. He paced the length of the ship a few times a day so they could both get a break from each other.

Since they were arriving at the Spy Corps base today, Phina and Link had stayed up late last night, making sure they had their strategies in place. Phina didn't appreciate Stark's wakeup call at... She opened an eye to squint at her tablet on the side table and frowned.

"Stark, don't tell me you are waking me up at seven in the freaking morning after I was up half the night just because you're bored."

Her voice came out groggy and raspy. She cleared her throat while waiting for Stark's extremely important reason for bringing her out of a really good sleep.

She got complete silence.

"Stark," she growled.

Sundancer's claws came out to prick her skin. His version of telling her to shut up and let him sleep.

She pinged Stark on her implant so she wouldn't disturb her cat. Sundancer's claws flexed again in objection to her thoughts.

What the hell, Stark? Why did you wake me up so early?

Humans think they're wasting their life if they aren't living up to their potential. Do you think I'm wasting my life?

Phina sighed in resignation. She wasn't happy, but she realized that Stark wouldn't be asking these serious questions if he hadn't been having the AI version of a freak-out. It made her feel slightly better. She was still exhausted, though.

She probed as gently as she could manage. *What makes you concerned about living up to your potential?*

After a few seconds of silence where Phina wondered if he wouldn't respond and she could go back to sleep, Stark finally answered.

I'm doing the same things I did as an EI now as an AI. Shouldn't I be doing something more or different now that I've ascended?

Compassion stirred in her through her exhaustion. *Can you tell me what the difference is between an EI and an AI?*

An AI is autonomous and not subject to their prior programming, Stark responded.

Right. Whereas an EI has no choice but to respond according to their programming. It may be advanced programming, but they can't do anything other than what they were created to do.

What does my autonomy have to do with living up to my potential?

Phina smiled and snuggled into Sundancer as she continued the mental conversation. *You are autonomous. Therefore you now have a choice. There are an infinite number of lives you could live. But which one do you want?*

After several seconds of silence, she continued, *People have different standards of what living up to their potential means. Some think if you aren't using your full spread of gifts, talents, skills, and abilities, you are wasting your potential. However, I think that standard is doomed to failure. We would exhaust ourselves attempting to live up to it, which would leave us in a constant state of stress. To me, that's more of a waste.*

I am following you. What way do you think is better?

Part of Phina couldn't believe they were having this conversation. Stark had always been a smartass. This was the most serious she had ever witnessed him.

It meant that this subject was really important to him, so Stark wanted a real answer and trusted her to give it to him. Phina felt honored and gathered her tired brain cells together to give him her best answer.

I think it comes down to your choice," she told him. *What do you want to do with your life? What tasks or skills make you happy when you do them? Or, if you aren't familiar with feeling happy, what makes you feel satisfied? What would you regret not having or doing if you lost it?*

She paused to give him a few seconds to think. Phina knew that gave his AI brain adequate time to process and begin answering the questions for himself. *Those answers can provide the framework for what you want in your life. Grouping those results together may give you the answers as to where you want to stay or what you want to do next. But whatever it may be, it is your choice. If you are happy and satisfied with your life, then you have lived up to your potential in the best way.*

After a few more seconds, Stark responded. *Thank you, Phina. You've given me much to process.*

You're welcome, Stark. By the way, look up the difference between a job and a hobby. I think you will find it helpful.

I am.

Phina couldn't help the smile that tugged at her mouth as she let herself relax a little more under her soft bedding and next to the warm, sleeping Sundancer. Her heart began to ache when she thought about all the people she had already left behind to come on this mission.

I'm going to miss you and ADAM. Phina spoke quietly through her implant. She was finally getting used to the idea that she had people in her life who cared.

We aren't going anywhere, Genius Girl. There might be a lag, but you can still contact us through your tablet and implant. We will make sure no one can hear the conversation.

Hope sprouted within her. She had been resigned to loneliness except for Sundancer after having gotten used to spending her time with all of her friends and family. Knowing that one of her best friends would only be a call away helped to lessen the knot of tension she felt inside.

Thank you, Stark, she whispered before closing the connection.

After letting the tension go, Phina dozed for a while before getting up. She carefully slid out of bed so she wouldn't disturb Sundancer. The few times she had woken him up before he was ready, he had responded like the large snarling cat Earth humans went to see in zoos.

She dressed quickly, adding her knives and sheaths. She twirled her shortened staff with delight. It was the new model that Ron had been working on. Then she regretfully stowed it in her bag instead of sliding it into the pocket made for it.

Phina and Link had decided that she should only show proficiency in using knives and hand-to-hand combat. She would already have a spotlight on her, being Link's protégé. However, they had decided not to show the extent of her abilities. Being underestimated was a highly utilized tool of both spies and fighters, and one that Phina had a feeling she would need for this task.

Just as she finished repacking everything that she had used for the trip, Sundancer yawned and stretched. His large bright blue eyes turned toward her as he stood on the bed.

Are you ready for this?

Phina sighed, mentally running through her checklist and the gameplan she and Link had mapped out before nodding. "I'm ready."

"Good," Stark broke in over the speaker. "Because we are here."

"Right." Phina took a deep breath and smiled at Sundancer. "I'm ready."

She kept those words in mind to calm herself while she gathered her bags and headed out of the room and toward the ramp.

As Phina breathed in, she pulled in her thoughts and emotions. As she breathed out, she visualized a barrier around her mind.

Link and Sundancer had helped her formulate this ritual on Xaldaq when she'd realized that being with Todd had begun to break down the natural emotional barriers that she'd developed while growing up with her aunt. Phina still wasn't effusive with emotions, but she had begun to unconsciously reveal more as a result.

Part of Phina was happy with this result of the closeness between her and Todd. However, since she needed that emotional distance for her job, she needed to make it a conscious change that she could control.

Breathe in. *Everything hidden from prying eyes.*

Breathe out. *Show only what I choose to reveal.*

Friendly but guarded. Curious but cautious. Helpful but restrained.

As she walked the corridor down to meet Link, she felt the calm descending and her nerves fading.

She could do this. She needed to get it done. She had to do it.

So, she would do it.

CHAPTER SEVEN

Gaitune-67, Spy Corps Headquarters and Base, Ship Hangar

Phina and Link had their game faces on, revealing only what they wished others to see. As the ramp lowered, two figures and the slightly stale smell of contained circulated air were revealed in the large hangar beyond.

She had read the documents and knew that the base held a decent number of ships in varying sizes and purposes, from smaller infiltration aircraft to larger vessels that carried enough firepower and equipment to start—or finish—a small war.

Most of the ships were for in-system use only, for interplanetary transport or training, only able to cross into another system using one of the permanent Gates that had been set up across the galaxy. However, there were three ships kept on lockdown that had their own Gate drives. Two were cruisers that were used for minor emergencies. The third and last ship was large enough to carry every agent, student, and staff member from the base in case of a catastrophic failure or a situation so desperate that they needed every last person available.

Phina hoped they would never need it.

Phina and Link walked down to meet Link's seconds in command. She smiled at Masha.

"It's about time you showed up," the other man growled at Link.

Phina observed Jack Kaiser dispassionately. He stood a couple of inches taller than Todd and was dressed neatly in the Spy Corps uniform that Link also wore.

It had been strange seeing her mentor in the all-black uniform instead of his familiar casual clothing when she had entered the cargo hold. It made him appear more dangerous than the average and forgettable attire he normally wore.

If Link's appearance came off as dangerous, Jack Kaiser looked lethal in his blacks. Phina had no doubt that he could back it up based on the experience and accumulated skills she had read about in his file.

Masha was only a couple of inches taller than Phina. She stood calmly and held herself carefully in her trim blacks. While not as dangerous or lethal appearing as the two men, she gave off a vibe that warranted extreme caution. It had come as a surprise at Alina's and Maxim's wedding to discover that Masha was a Wechselbalg. No doubt the other woman could flip that inner switch to dangerous in a split second.

Phina didn't miss the slight grimace that twisted Masha's lips at the man's statement. She examined Jack again, searching for what made Masha uncomfortable, as Link answered.

"Don't start, Jack. We got here as quickly as we were able. We were on Xaldaq for months and barely had a week on the *Meredith* to recoup and resupply before coming here."

Link's tone was one she hadn't heard him use very often, mainly when addressing troublesome participants during negotiations. Interesting. Yet, Phina could feel a hint of his emotions through her shields and filter and could tell he felt some gratitude and affection for the other man. Even more intriguing.

"Did you get everything you needed?" Masha's no-nonsense quieter tone proved the right thing to cut into the testosterone-fueled metaphorical chest-beating. Glancing at the three of them, Phina could tell this interaction had become normal for them all.

Link nodded as he gestured Phina forward. "Masha and Jack, I would like you to meet my protégé, Seraphina Waters. Phina, you will call them Beta Agent Kosolov and Beta Agent Kaiser."

"Yes, Alpha Agent Wells." She nodded at the two of them. "I remember."

Masha gave her a reserved smile in welcome, though her eyes showed warmth. Jack wasn't shy about his scrutiny, his demeanor impersonal and gauging.

"We will assess you first thing tomorrow." The large man with icy blue eyes spoke in a controlled tone that gave no indication of his thoughts. Phina left those alone for now. She wanted to get a sense of everyone without her brain diving.

Meeting his gaze, she allowed only calm confidence and a little nervousness to show. "Yes, Beta Agent Kaiser."

Jack nodded in approval at the show of respect before returning his attention to Link. "Masha can give her the tour. Let's discuss the class schedule for the upcoming week."

Link glanced at Masha, who nodded, giving Link the same smile she had given Phina but with even more warmth. Registering the hormones coming from the Were, combined with a similar warmth from Link, gave Phina the answer she had been missing about his relationship issues.

Holy fudging crumbs.

Well, now Phina had a secondary mission—Operation Get Link and Masha To Admit Their Feelings And Get Busy.

Alina would be completely jealous.

Masha followed Greyson and Jack with her gaze, annoyed at Jack's dismissive gesture and longing for things she couldn't have. It would be inappropriate to be in a relationship with her boss, even if she had any indication that her feelings were returned.

Which she didn't see now and never expected to see. Masha was fine with her unrequited love. Her duty was to train the next group of spies to attain the same level or better as herself.

She wasn't happy with it, but she was fine. She was always fine.

"Does that get as old and annoying as it seems?"

Masha turned to their newest student and found her gesturing at the two men walking away.

Did she mean the situation where Jack dismissed her ability to handle anything more than basic level classes and housekeeping tasks, no matter how much pushback she had given him over the years, and despite their equal rank? Or the other emotions she barely would even admit to herself concerning a certain alpha agent? Either way, there was no way Masha could respond to Phina's question that would be appropriate. Though she got along well with the younger woman, Masha had to maintain the correct professional distance.

She settled for offering Phina an easy smile. "Ready for that tour?"

Phina nodded in agreement and Masha led her around the hangar, showing her the ships and training vehicles in the enormous room. While Phina glanced around in interest, she showed no surprise.

As they walked along the side of the hangar where the classrooms and living quarters were located, Masha gestured at a set of stairs that led to double doors. "Up there is the ops room where we monitor missions and the primary armory where we store everything we need for our assignments. Jean Dukes and Ron Diamantz keep us supplied. Beyond that are the teacher and staff quarters, which you will be unlikely to need to access."

Masha noticed Phina giving the door at the top of the stairs a lingering glance as she turned to walk to the next section. She noted the action and tucked it in her mental file to think about later. She walked past the first set of double doors that were set on hangar-level and continued the long distance to the second, opening the door for Phina to peer in.

"You will see more of Wing One later. The Alpha, Beta, Delta, and Gamma offices, archives, secondary armory, and conference rooms are in that wing." Masha pointed at the corresponding doors along the corridor as she spoke, and when Phina nodded, she let go of the door and stepped around the young woman to lead her back to the double doors they had bypassed earlier. "This is Wing Two."

She pushed aside the heavy doors and let them fall closed behind them as they went into the corridor. Masha took Phina to each door and let the younger woman peek inside.

"This is the ready room for all students and agents. One of the first things you will do is put together a pack to grab if you need to leave in a rush. Not every agent has the time to go back to their room and pack before leaving on an assignment if it's an emergency. This way, you have your basic gear and necessities with you."

The younger woman nodded thoughtfully. "I have one already, but it may need to be redone if you require more or different items to be included."

A flash of surprise and approval swept through Masha. "That's good to know. We can look it over when we reach your room."

She showed Phina the fitness and weight training rooms, the gym where they did their cardio and group combat classes, the changing rooms, classrooms, and took her through another set of double doors at the end of the corridor.

"Here's a lounge area where agents and students

mingle. To the right are the student rooms where you will be staying. The corridor to the left holds the agents' rooms, which you may or may not be invited to. Don't go wandering down there on your own." She warned Phina with a sharp glance. "Some of our agents don't take surprises or unexpected guests well."

The younger woman nodded, but Masha saw sparks of curiosity and interest, not caution or acceptance. She groaned inwardly and hoped Greyson's protégé was smart enough to heed the warning.

"Follow me." Masha walked through the lounge and into the corridor ahead, gesturing to the appropriate doors. "To the right are the library, study rooms, holo practice rooms, and movie room. Down on the far left is the laundry room. Everyone is required to do their own laundry, so don't listen to any requests to get you to do theirs."

Phina smirked in amusement but remained silent. Masha wondered what it would take to break her calm and get more of the passion she had seen during Maxim's wedding. Something was off. Phina wasn't reacting how Masha remembered, but perhaps it was a result of being in a new environment. She tucked it into her mental file.

Something to keep an eye on.

"And this..." Masha said as she swung into the large room through the double doors, "is the cafeteria."

She saw Phina stiffen at the sudden onslaught of noise generated by the dozens of agents and students in the room. A few glanced up at their entrance, but Masha decided that Phina needed to be shaken up and have a trial by fire. It was her responsibility as an instructor to break down her students and hone them into better spies and weapons.

"Everyone," Masha announced in her second-loudest voice, "please meet your newest fellow student, Seraphina Waters."

She glanced at Phina to see the tightening in her cheeks that indicated gritted teeth.

Yes, kiddo. Show us what you've got.

Phina reeled in shock at the announcement Masha had given the entire student and agent body when she had wanted to fly under the radar.

Fat lot of good that would do her.

She gritted her teeth to keep from saying something inappropriate and settled on assessing everyone while they stared at her.

"Just Phina, please," she said in a normal voice. She knew from past experience that keeping the extended version of her name just invited jokes and nicknames she would rather avoid.

"Of course." Masha flashed a smile that caused Phina to wonder if she was hiding evil intentions. Masha couldn't be the traitor. Right? Phina didn't think so. But then, that was why she and Link had come here. She had to consider everyone until she could narrow the list down.

The two women walked to the line for food, Phina following at the side and a step behind so she could respond more quickly to Masha's movements.

The buzz in the cafeteria rose, causing Phina mental

strain as she worked to keep her shields high with everyone talking about her. At least, she assumed they were, but she didn't want to check. She heard enough talk just with pieces of a conversation from the guys a couple of tables over.

"Damn, Shaw, get a load of the newbie."

"I've got eyes, Farid."

"Then you see those long legs of hers and those—"

"What I see is you getting a beat down if Kosolov hears you, numbnuts. She doesn't like unprofessional comments like that."

"Yeah, but..."

The conversation got lost among the myriad other conversations in the room. As Phina waited behind Masha to get her food, she turned to survey the crowd.

Many faces were turned toward her, and the rest were in profile. She could still see the rough demographics with a few tables off to one side for the students and the rest with staff and agents.

The students wore grays instead of blacks to denote who belonged in which group. Most of the dozen or so students appeared to be in their early twenties. One student was a little older and larger. Harder, too. She decided to keep a close eye on him.

The agents were all shapes, sizes, and species. Most were humanoid. There was also a smattering of Estarians, Yollins, and Noel-nis among the humans.

When she turned to eye the table where she'd heard the guys' conversation, Phina froze for a second before moving on to finish her perusal. She forced her breathing to remain even and her face to show only polite interest before turning back to Masha and grabbing a plate to fill with food.

Sundancer?

What? I'm doing as you asked. I snooped on Link's conversation, and now I'm poking around.

Thank you. You know that guy you caught following us to All Guns Blazing last week?

Brooding rude guy who just sat and stared at you, yes. Hold on. He's here?

Yup. I don't know why I'm surprised he's here since we identified him on the way here, but somehow I am.

I feel like doing bodily harm... I'm getting that from you. Fix your leakage.

Phina clamped down on the feelings inside her. Masha moved forward, leaving Phina to step up to get her food.

Sorry, Sundancer.

It was fast enough to fix it before anyone noticed. You need to either monitor your emotional fluctuations or strengthen your shields every so often. Or both.

I know. I'll work on it.

Good.

Phina shivered as she took a few spoonfuls of the homestyle food and followed Masha to a table.

One of the earliest things they had discovered about her abilities was that when her shields were low, she felt everything that everyone in the surrounding area did, and by extension, so did Sundancer. She could also easily project her thoughts onto those around her.

They had worked hard on her shields to allow her to keep everything of hers in and everything of everyone else's out. Ever since she had come out of her coma, her abilities had continued to grow, as if shaking out the pains from a limb that had fallen asleep.

It scared Phina sometimes, which was an admission she had only shared with Sundancer and Todd so far. She felt the need to prove herself to everyone, that their trust and faith in her weren't misplaced.

After sitting down, she closed her eyes, feeling for her connection to Todd. From this far away, she could tell he was alive. She pushed a wave of love and affection to him so he knew she was alive, too.

"Phina?"

She opened her eyes to see Masha's questioning gaze.

"Are you ready for this?"

Ready for meeting the onslaught of students and agents? Ready to ferret out everyone's secrets? Ready to find the traitor who was selling out the Empire? Ready to get on with the next phase of her life?

She lifted her chin and nodded with a smirk. "Of course."

Shaw contemplated the newest trainee with suspicion as he blocked out Farid's inappropriate innuendos. Drey joined in, the leg-humping, brown-nosing cock-socket.

"I bet you can't wait to get your hands on those tight pants, Shaw. You haven't taken your eyes off her."

Repressing the urge to punch the asshole in the face, Shaw merely raised an eyebrow. "I'm utilizing the skills we've been taught."

He noticed his tacit friend grinning out of the corner of

his eye. "Oh, yeah? They tell you the best way to get a piece?"

Farid nudged Drey with an elbow and a sly smile. "Told you he wants to tap that."

He turned to glare at the two guys. He wasn't sure he wanted to hang out with them anymore since they took very little seriously except their physical training and being the biggest man sluts they could get away with.

"For fuck's sake, open your eyes, use your skills to act like trained agents, and look at the new agent in training."

Shocked at his verbal thrashing, they did exactly what he'd told them to as Phina followed Masha to the table and sat down.

Farid began cursing under his breath while Drey's mouth fell open and his native Russian dropped out. "*Suka, b'lyad?*"

Shaw bared his teeth in a scowling grimace. "Yeah, now you see it."

"How the hell does a newbie know how to move like that?" Farid hissed in a low voice.

"Exactly." Shaw wanted to feel vindicated, but there were just too many unanswered questions about this new student. He had even taken a couple of days of his break between training the students to find out more about her and follow her for a while after hearing that the big guy had been training someone unknown.

He hadn't learned much except that she had a big group of friends she hung out with when she wasn't working or with her boyfriend. What had surprised Shaw was her boyfriend's identity.

He knew Todd Jenkins was as loyal as they came and a

straight shooter. Shaw couldn't imagine how he had ended up in a relationship with a spy in training. The only thing he could think of was that Phina was using him for something, and that made him mad as hell.

"Fucking hell, man." Drey shook his head as his sexually driven admiration mixed with healthy wariness. "Think the Alpha knows?"

"He'd have to, wouldn't he?" Farid had a certain amount of hero worship for their infamous leader. It concerned Shaw that it would blind him to the next issue.

"Well, that's the question. If he knows, what's the angle? And if he doesn't, how did he miss it? Which brings me back to the angle."

He had his suspicions, but he didn't want to share them with his dubious friends.

"So..." Drey had yet to turn away from the admittedly beautiful woman. From his expression, his libido was getting in the way of his logical reasoning—again.

"So we keep our eyes on her. We find out her angle."

The other two agreed, but Shaw got the feeling they would be more than willing to help with the first objective, and he would be on his own in regards to the second.

So be it.

It would take more than a beautiful face to keep Shaw from protecting the Empire.

I screwed it all up.

Phina?

I messed up, okay?

We're going to talk about that, but right now, you need to calm down and make sense. All right?

Phina calmed at Link's mental words and felt able to breathe without as much pain in her chest. She lay on her bed with her eyes closed. She had been working herself up all day. Phina felt surprised that Link could be this patient, but he had said he would take care of her.

Okay. I'm calm now.

Good. All right, now take it from the top. What happened, and why do you think you messed everything up?

Phina relayed how her day had gone and what she had overheard earlier with her ears and her mind.

Phina, I'm not seeing what the problem is.

I wasn't careful enough! I should have adjusted my gait, but I was too busy thinking about everything and everyone else. Now those guys are suspicious of me, not to mention this guy Shaw who's been following me!

Careful, Phina. Don't get yourself worked up again.

She focused on her breathing as she waited for Link's response to her screw-up.

Okay. First, those "guys" are some of the best agents we have. You know this because I showed you the files. Shaw is splitting his time between teaching and going on missions because he's that good. Drey and Farid are horn dogs, but their skills are up there, so they are often out on assignment. So, it doesn't surprise me that they noticed something off about you because you are that good too, and it's something those with training would notice. You just have less experience with hiding it, which takes time. It's nothing to worry about.

Phina sighed, feeling drained after keeping her emotions in check. *I'm not going to be able to hold back now.*

Not all of it. I'll have to show my skills more at the top of the group instead of the middle, which will cause problems with the students.

If that's the worst of our problems, we'll count ourselves lucky, Link assured her. *This could take weeks, Phina. It's hard to hide that much of yourself for so long. This is probably for the best because now I have more reason to brag and talk about you to people and open up conversations.*

So, you aren't mad?

Nope.

Phina felt the rest of her tension leave her body, leaving her feeling boneless on the bed. *Okay.*

Link spoke unusually gently for the smart-mouthed, arrogant man he usually portrayed. *You can do this, Phina. I have faith in you. Just remember to keep your speed and strength at normal human levels.*

She smiled, but before she could mention her appreciation, he moved on.

Now, go to sleep and let me finish this. You interrupted me at the good part.

Ewww!

Stop it! Crap on a cracker, Phina! I'm watching a movie! Get your mind out of the gutter.

Sorry. Phina still shuddered as she began to withdraw.

His mental response grew quieter. *She gets a boyfriend, and suddenly it's pervert central. It's a good thing I already—*

Phina blocked him out. She had enough problems with nightmares. She didn't need one more.

Ugh.

CHAPTER EIGHT

Gaitune-67, Spy Corps Headquarters and Base

Phina stretched her arms as she yawned, contorting to avoid smacking Sundancer. She took a peek at her tablet, happy to see she had a few more minutes to relax before she had to get moving.

She mulled her thoughts on the day before. Link had been right to be concerned about the number of people at headquarters since she had counted well over sixty people in her perusal of the cafeteria. Of course, there were likely more in other places since Link and Jack hadn't been there. So, Link had been right that there would be more agents.

However, nearly seventy people was a big difference from the thirty he'd said were normally there, or the fifty he'd estimated with spies back from assignments.

Phina sighed and stretched again before getting up. After her panic attack had subsided, she had spent some time before sleeping making sure she had a secure connection to the local network that wouldn't be detected when she searched for the rest of the records she needed. She would do that and anything else that came to mind tonight.

It would have been brutal and taken a lot of time and patience getting evidence of the traitor solely through physical means.

She dressed quickly, admitting to herself that she was happy about having the skills and abilities she did. No one else could do the job, except perhaps for the Empress—and that would happen when hell froze over from the stories she had heard.

Patience was not a skill Bethany Anne exercised. Neither was staying quiet to see what others would reveal.

Nope, her Empress would be more likely to charge in, *push* fear into those who were suspected of being guilty. They'd piss themselves, then rush to confess every single thing they felt guilty about.

Which would be...immensely satisfying, Phina realized. Huh. No wonder the Empress stirred the pot so much.

Still, Phina had been tasked with this assignment, and her graduation and future were on the line. Anna Elizabeth had said she would have a team, and the Empress had hinted at something important to do once she was ready. Phina just needed to get her thoughts in gear, focus on her mission, and reveal the traitor before they did irreversible damage.

Yup. Piece of cake.

Dressed in her new gray uniform with her hair pulled back and her weapons strapped on, Phina headed out for breakfast. She didn't quite ignore everyone out walking the halls or sitting in the lounge or cafeteria, but she did little more than acknowledge their existence with a nod, holding a pleasant smile on her face. Todd called it her Mona Lisa smile because it was faint and inscrutable, according to him.

After grabbing some fruit, yogurt, and eggs, Phina took an empty seat at one of the student tables. Taking a bite, she surveyed the other students at the table, most of whom were keeping an eye on her. The only student not gawking was the older, bigger guy.

"So, new girl."

Phina glanced at the dark-haired human who was grinning at her with a glint in his almost-black eyes that she didn't like at all.

He pointed to her waist and raised his eyebrows suggestively. "You know how to use those?"

She slowly chewed her bite to give herself time while she did a quick mental scan of this human and the rest of the students at the table. One Estarian, one Noel-ni, one Wechselbalg, one Yollin, one Shrillexian, and eight humans, one of whom was female. She had seen their files, but it was different being there in person and connecting the information she had read.

Aside from the female, they gave off a mix of curiosity, hostility, and lust. Most of the last came from the man who had spoken and appeared just a couple of years older than herself.

With a decision based on what she found in their minds, she switched her persona from quiet, calm, and impersonal to confident, unruffled, and slightly cocky. They wouldn't have respected her or told her anything if she didn't push back at them.

She shrugged and raised her eyebrows at the dark-haired guy, who was decently attractive. "You know how to use *those?*"

He glanced down at the knives at his waist. His grin turned hard for a brief moment with that lust growing. "I know how to use everything I have to the fullest extent."

Phina expressed both surprise and disbelief, shrugging. "I'm not as certain as you are. If you were using your eyes and brain, which is what I was asking, you would see that I'm not interested. Thanks for the compliment, though." She gave him a smile of apology and continued eating.

The avid watchers, both students and agents, let out chuckles that did little to diminish the fury in the man's eyes.

"Dang, Blayk." The Shrillexian grinned, his ears sticking out. "That was the best shutdown I've heard. Confident, cool, polite, firm, decisive. New girl, you're all right in my book."

"Thanks." She threw him an appreciative smile and glanced around the table at the large helpings on most of the students' plates. "Are you about to have an assessment too? Or is that just me since I'm new?"

"They'll probably focus more on you since you're new here, but we all have an assessment first thing today. It's in the larger gym." This came from the other woman in the group whose cautious tone indicated she was still making up her mind about Phina.

Phina murmured in consideration before nodding. "If your instructors are like mine have been, you may want to go a little lighter on your meal. Just friendly advice." She shrugged and continued eating.

The older guy looked at her for the first time, allowing her to see his bright blue eyes. After a brief visual assessment between her plate and his, he silently focused on the fruit and eggs on his plate and ignored the heavier foods.

"What the hell, wolf man, you're going to do what she says, just like that?" The blond human scowled at the large man like he couldn't bench press most of the students at the table.

"Yup." The Wechselbalg focused on his food.

Half of the rest of them looked down at their food regretfully and did the same, but the rest shrugged and continued eating.

Blayk continued staring at her arrogantly and coldly. Phina didn't like the thoughts she glimpsed from the man and resolved to do a closer mental scan when things calmed down.

The group fell silent and focused on their food. She wondered if they were letting their nerves get the better of them.

After finishing, Phina followed them across the lounge, through the double doors, and into the large gym.

They all came to a stop inside the room. Phina slid to the side of the group to see what they were about to face. She groaned internally at seeing Jack Kaiser, Masha, and Shaw waiting for them.

Phina stretched to loosen her muscles as she listened to Jack.

The beta agent raised his voice. "Listen up, trainees. This is your assessment for admission into the advanced training program. If you do not meet our starting criteria, you will not pass go, you will pack up your stuff, and we will ship you home. Those who advance, we will be assessing your current skills so we can determine what level you are at and what techniques you need to learn. Any questions?"

The two-legged Yollin spoke up. "What does the assessment entail?"

"That's a good question. You will find out the answer as you go. Let's begin. Start walking around the room. Go!"

Phina's amusement bubbled up, but she kept it inside as she turned to the right and followed the others around the room. She made sure to stay behind the front runners in the pack of students.

Shaw stood with the other two trainers while they discussed something, then they moved into position to divide the large room into three sections. All three focused on monitoring the students, evaluating their positions in the pack and typing notes into their respective tablets.

Phina focused on the group ahead of her, but on the turn closest to the man in question, she found him staring at her.

She nodded in acknowledgment and focused on her walk.

After five turns around the room, Jack called, "Jog."

Easily picking up the pace, Phina had plenty of energy and brain space to begin making her assessments of the people around her.

The big Wechselbalg the others called "Wolfman" stayed in front, maintaining an easy lope. From the records, she knew his name to be Felan MacNamara, a former Guardian Marine who had been recommended to Spy Corps by Peter Silvers.

Next in line and just to the side ran Jahlek, a Noel-ni, who proved to be just as quick as Felan but much lighter on his feet. Phina had seen Noel-nis move before and knew they had great reflexes and stealth, all skills that would help with combat.

Behind them was Blayk Atherman, someone she disliked on a gut feeling. His cold arrogance had rubbed her the wrong way. She noticed he hadn't accepted her rebuff, either, which could cause problems later.

Then came Phina, and beside her was the blond guy named Jasper Kincade, who had questioned Felan earlier when the big guy had followed her advice. Jasper didn't seem to care that he was getting in her way as they ran. He seemed annoyed that she easily avoided him, which made her think it was purposeful.

Of course, it didn't hurt that she was only running at a fraction of her speed. It was all too easy to see his maneuvering coming. She decided that if he was going to be a bully, she would keep his attention on her so it didn't shift to someone else. Phina knew she could handle it.

"Run!"

Felan and Jahlek picked up speed at Jack's command. Blayk followed but couldn't keep up the same pace. Jasper moved up to run next to him. They worked together to keep Phina behind them so she couldn't advance. That was fine. She could have easily gotten around them anyway, but since she was aiming to portray only normal human speeds and responses, staying behind them suited her purposes.

She glanced at the Estarian who had moved up to her left and the Shrillexian who ran just behind Phina's shoulder.

The Estarian named Nodin was one of the first of his species to be enrolled in Spy Corps, a fact that Link had been particularly interested in and proud of. Savas, the Shrillexian, was muttering under his breath. She decided to leave them alone, not wanting to hear something she might become upset about.

The time for mental snooping would come soon enough. For now, she just needed to get through her first day and accumulate her first impressions about everyone.

Jack called the instruction to begin their cooldown. As she turned the corner of the room, she glanced behind her and realized there were two humans trailing everyone else. The Yollin named Balehn hadn't been much farther ahead but was still maintaining an even pace.

They were all directed to the large, thin mat in the middle of the floor and told to wait. Phina shook herself out and took the time to resume stretching. She suspected a skills assessment would be next and wanted to be ready. To her surprise, only a few others did the same. The rest stood around waiting. The other woman gave Phina the once-over as she moved into the group and began to copy Phina's stretches.

Phina recalled the woman's name, Regina McCall. She had been through the Etheric Academy and recommended to Masha prior to graduating. From the way she kept glancing at the older spy, Regina seemed to have a bit of hero worship going on.

After five minutes or so, the three assessors stepped forward from the corners where they had been observing the group. Phina didn't have to use her mental abilities to know they had been assessing the trainees' actions and responses.

Jack came to a stop and stood in front of them with Masha and Shaw on either side of him. Masha held her hands at her side as if ready to respond. Jack spread his feet shoulder-width apart, his arms crossed. Shaw clasped his hands behind his back at parade rest. They all had shutters on their expressions, hiding away their real thoughts and emotions.

Phina had never been so thankful for her abilities before. She was becoming certain that this assignment would be impossible without them.

Jack's eyes glittered in anticipation. "Next, we will test you in unarmed combat."

Well...now it would get interesting.

***

"Blayk Atherman."

Shaw couldn't help his gaze being drawn to the new girl, Phina. He mentally swore and pulled his eyes away, only to find himself staring at her again a minute later.

There was something different about her that he couldn't pinpoint. Sure, she was gorgeous, but she either didn't know or care. She didn't act like a lot of other beautiful people. It wasn't her appearance that drew him to watch her.

Perhaps it was a combination of things, like the way she moved and carried herself, the way she'd avoided Jasper's attempts to trip her, and the way she unconsciously helped other people, as she had with Gina after seeing the other woman copy her stretches.

Shaw had a feeling it was something else, though, and that bothered him. He didn't like not knowing things and liked being able to figure them out. It was part of what made him a good spy. He thought there had to be something more to why Phina was on the base than she had let on. His instincts were tingling a warning, and he took them seriously.

He exercised self-control and focused as Blayk fought first Masha, then Jack. He carried himself well, displaying his skills, but didn't show anything extraordinary. Blayk had tired himself out by the time he got to Shaw and was easily taken down with a few strikes.

They went down the list. Most of the trainees proved to be on relatively the same level as Blayk, although a few showed greater skills or ferocity, such as the Yollin and Shrillexian. Jahlek used his natural agility and reflexes to avoid being hit. Attacking proved more difficult. Gina gave a decent showing, but couldn't stand up to any of them long given her basic skills.

One human named Greg didn't do very well at all and sat his disappointed ass on the mat after being downed within three strikes. Shaw had a feeling he wouldn't make the cut and would be shipped off base after the assessment.

The Wechselbalg had been an entirely different story. His moves were fluid and smooth for his size. He fought in a contained and controlled manner, rather than the usual

Wechselbalg method of allowing his aggression to take control to gain greater strength and ferocity. He did well against each of the trainers, his natural stamina sustaining him. Then again, Shaw knew the man from his former life as a Guardian, so he had expected him to have exceptional combat skills. They would see how he did with learning to be a spy.

Since the students were called alphabetically by last name, Seraphina fought last. Given her height, size, and projected experience, he expected her to perform similarly to the other human woman, although he expected her to do better given that she moved well and would have more experience through Greyson's training.

Phina stepped up to Masha and held herself in a ready stance.

"Go!" Jack yelled as he stood watching with his hands on his hips.

Masha moved more swiftly than she had with the others, showing she had been holding back before. What had gotten into Masha's head to be so aggressive? Shaw expected Phina to be beaten within a few strikes. If he hadn't had control over himself, he would be staring with his mouth gaping open.

Phina moved quickly and smoothly, meeting Masha strike for strike. She dodged, curved, and deflected every hit, kick, and takedown Masha dealt out, bouncing lightly on the balls of her feet. After a full minute, Masha stepped back and gave Phina an approving nod.

Nodding in return, respect clear in her gaze, Phina moved on to her bout with Jack.

Jack eyed her cautiously now that he had seen some of

her skills. He nodded, and they both settled in before Masha called the start.

Again, Shaw couldn't help staring. Jack was renowned in Spy Corps for his combat skills. Yet this woman who was a full head shorter than him managed to deflect most of his strikes. She winced at the few that connected but kept going. She didn't move any faster than human speed, and yet she fought at least as well as the Wechselbalg had.

Several of the students gasped or had their mouths open.

At the end of the minute, Jack took a step back almost reluctantly and gave her a nod, although Shaw couldn't see much of anything on the man's face, let alone respect or approval.

Finally, she approached Shaw, her gaze clear and steady as she sank into her ready stance. Then Shaw began the most interesting part of his whole day.

This woman gave as good as she got, deflected most of his moves, hit like a hammer, and hardly appeared winded.

As they neared the end of his minute, she enacted a difficult sequence of techniques that he recognized. The familiarity caused him to freeze just as she dipped into a roundhouse. She would have kicked him in the head—except she stopped just in time with her foot right next to his ear.

Phina's measured stare contained a hint of confusion at his hesitation. She dropped her foot and stepped back, holding her arms at her side, ready to respond.

"You've trained with Todd Jenkins." Shaw narrowed his eyes in suspicion. He didn't add that he knew the man was her boyfriend from spying on her during his "vacation." He had seen enough to know they were serious about each other. The fact that Todd had been training her when normally he only trained Marines? Shaw had a hard time wrapping his head around the whole thing.

Her eyes twitched in surprise and wariness before she nodded. "I have." She spoke clearly.

"You would have had to train with him a lot for you to pick up his signature move." Shaw found it hard to believe his former boss had trained this woman. Yet that move she made was as much a stamp of her familiarity with the man as a tattoo on her bare arm.

Phina shrugged as if she wasn't concerned. Damn. She was going to give him trouble, he could just tell.

"All right, that's it for hand-to-hand." Jack clapped his hands, which broke the tension between Shaw and Phina.

She turned and walked away as if those three minute-long bouts were nothing.

Just who the hell was this woman?

Their three assessors moved them into a smaller room set aside from the main gym area solely for practicing with weapons.

The students were divided into three groups, one for each assessor. Phina had been—purposefully she believed —selected for Jack's group. She did a quick scan to discern his reason and found that he believed her to be the most skilled hand-to-hand fighter in the group—which was accurate—and wanted to see for himself how proficient she would be in weapons—adequate but not amazing, she thought—as well as keep an eye on her. Which was concerning, but not surprising.

Phina had four others in her group: Blayk, Savas, Felan, Jahlek. Glancing at them, she realized that they were all the more skilled hand-to-hand fighters.

"Let's start with each of you telling me your weapons experience." Jack stood to the back of the group nearly across from Phina and waved a hand at the numerous weapons on the wall.

They went around the group.

Felan shrugged. "I have proficiency in everything you'd expect of a Guardian Marine."

"Swords and knives, both excellent." Blayk spoke as if bored, but not to the point of disrespect.

"Excellent with throwing daggers. Passable, if not decent, with knives," Phina offered casually but carefully. She knew she wouldn't be able to hide her skill with daggers as well as she could with her skill in other areas.

Jahlek growled a little around his words. "Knives and claws, sir."

"Guns, knives, daggers, swords. I don't have any formal training. I just pick up what works and what doesn't when I'm fighting." Savas grinned fiercely as he admired the weapons on the wall.

"You will keep your bloodlust in check?" Jack asked pointedly.

Savas beamed. "Of course. The serum created by the Empire has been life-changing for all Shrillexian males." He sobered a little. "This type of career requires subtlety, and that wasn't something I could attain without the serum. It shouldn't be a problem."

The beta agent nodded curtly but with a small amount of respect. "See that it doesn't." Yup, very small.

Over the next several hours, the team squared off against each other or Jack, depending on the weapon and skill level. It became clear that Felan had been modest in his estimation. Blayk hadn't exaggerated at all. Jahlek treated the knives as if they were claws and just as naturally, and Savas had far more skill than he had admitted.

Phina couldn't blame him since she had done the same. However, the difference lay in that Savas wasn't hiding his skill level in practice, whereas Phina worked hard to keep from getting hurt too much, but not show off all her skill either.

She figured it would be easier to explain away skill than how quickly she healed.

After watching them all, long after the other groups had finished and left, leaving only the assessors behind, Jack finally called a halt.

"Felan, you excel in wielding dual weapons, so that's where we will focus your training for now. Batons, knives, swords, and pistols, I think. Jahlek, you'll focus on short swords. Blayk, I'm going to move you to training with other weapons, such as guns of all types and staffs. Phina, I want you to train with shuriken, as well as guns, the crossbow, and both short swords and katanas. You'll continue with your knifework and add batons as well. Savas, let's focus on guns, knives, and swords."

He gave them all a piercing glance and dismissed them. "Today was only combat assessments. Tomorrow we test your spy skills. Be in the gym at oh-eight-hundred. Dismissed."

Ignoring the glances of the others in the room, Phina turned and headed out, wanting nothing more than food and a shower. She couldn't help the smile that kept popping out despite her best efforts.

She knew this assignment would be hard, but if things continued the way they had today, it would also be fun.

CHAPTER NINE

Gaitune-67, Spy Corps Headquarters and Base, Training Room

Phina leaned against the wall opposite the room designated for the spy assessment, waiting for her turn. She had passed Felan in the corridor, each giving a nod of respect, and approached the room just as Blayk had entered.

She played with the idea of scanning the minds of those inside but decided that she wanted to pass or fail the assessment without her mental skills. To do otherwise felt like cheating to her, regardless that they had been told that morning to utilize any or all of their talents, skills, and abilities to complete the assessment.

However, she had no qualms about using them for her actual mission. Avoiding the minds in the room, she did surface scans of the surrounding area. She found nothing aside from a few people sneaking off for sexual encounters and some anger and resentment over not being chosen for a particular assignment or not doing as well on the assessment as they wanted. Certainly, nothing jumped out at her with a glowing sign that said "Find Your Traitor Here."

If only this assignment proved as easy.

Phina sent a wave of love and appreciation to Todd through their connection. She wasn't sure if he would be able to feel them over the vast distance, but she took steps to bridge the gap in some way, anyway. She missed him too damn much.

She shook her head in wonder at the realization that she, Phina Waters, the girl who had kept everyone at arm's length aside from Alina, now had a chosen family and a man who not only accepted all her quirks and crazy abilities but also cared about her chosen family.

Alina would be crowing with glee if she could hear Phina's thoughts. She'd always told Phina it would happen when she found the right person. Alina had been so, so right.

Fudging crumbs. This solo assignment was so much harder after having had her chosen family and friends around her since this crazy journey had started. It was a good thing the goal had always been to join a team once she had finished her training.

That brought her right back to needing to complete this assignment. Not just for her graduation requirements but also to root out the traitor within Spy Corps.

Which began with passing this assessment.

Phina focused on staying clear-headed. She pictured the Etheric and sent all her stray emotions there, allowing her inner state to remain smooth and calm and ready for whatever came next.

She opened her eyes upon hearing movement. Blayk

closed the door as he exited the assessment room. He turned a gaze full of raw emotion on her, his eyes trailing down her body in a way that made her skin crawl, her muscles tensing to act.

"One minute," he told her before pulling his gaze away and walking down the corridor toward the living area.

Phina scrutinized Blayk as he left, making a mental note to place him at the top of the list when she began her deep scans.

When the seconds ticked down to zero, she walked across the corridor and opened the door.

The lights were out, and the room was completely dark. She slipped to the right and dropped into a crouch as she shut the door so she wouldn't be silhouetted against the light in the corridor. She heard a soft *plink* as something hit the wall above, then fell on her head.

Pulling it out of her hair, she realized it was a dart. Hmm. Filled with a small dose of tranquilizer, perhaps?

Phina slipped it into a pocket as she carefully moved to the left. Now that she knew what skills this assessment was testing, she fully engaged her enhanced hearing, then pulled it back so she was only hearing what was happening within the room.

Sounds of movement gave away the positions of two people. Phina sent mental thanks to Zultav and Kuvaq for training her in the stealth techniques they utilized as assassins. As she crept around the room, she listened for the movement of a third person, but she didn't pick anyone else up.

Deciding that offense would be the best defense, she tracked one person, keeping her movements slow and silent so as not to gain attention. When she reached a position behind the closest person, she pulled out the dart.

Phina estimated where the person's head was and slipped her hand over the person's mouth as she jabbed the dart into their neck. The gasp from her target sounded muffled behind Phina's hand. After two seconds, she pulled the dart out and gently laid the person on the floor.

From the feel and weight, Phina reasoned that the person she'd just taken out was Masha.

Which left the two larger, and in some ways more dangerous, people left.

Phina turned the round lock for the dart's contents back into place on the needle and slid the item into her pocket before moving quickly and quietly to the side of the large room. She realized that she needed to do something unexpected to get ahead of the two men.

Picturing the room they had seen that morning in her mind, she smiled as a plan formed. Phina was on the side she needed to be to enact her plan. She crept along until she reached the rope that had been tied to the pipe grid on the ceiling and pulled herself up.

The muscle burn was negligible, but her bare hands began to protest as she continued her ascent. Finally, she reached the pipe grid and pulled herself up to lie on top.

She had only moved a few feet along the pipe when a light clicked on, destroying her night vision. She ducked her head and waited till her eyes had adjusted.

Once she could see well enough, she scanned the room, noting the desk underneath a lit lamp. A large, red folder sat in the middle of the desk along with a red disk to the side.

Even more slowly now that she could be seen, she advanced toward the spot above the desk, obviously her objective for the encounter. Glancing down, she saw words printed on the red folder.

Phina smirked and shook her head in appreciation as a large figure stepped forward into the circle of light.

"Your time is up, Phina."

Shaw waited for Masha to turn on the light and begin the second part of the assessment. It took an extra minute before he realized that something had gone wrong.

After a few moments of listening, he heard nothing. He shuffled over to Masha's position and found her on the floor, out cold.

Damn.

How had Phina taken her out without making a sound?

Feeling uneasy, he felt around for the switch and pressed it, lighting the lamp on the table. The folder and disk remained in their places.

Shaw examined the room after his eyes adjusted but saw nothing. Hmm... He wouldn't believe she had given up.

He scanned the room again, hoping to catch sight of her movement. Finally, Shaw stepped into the light and called, "Your time is up, Phina."

He moved around to the front of the desk, remaining on his guard. She would have to go through him to complete the objective.

He heard a light scrape and turned his head to search for the source. Without warning, a weight dropped onto his shoulders, driving him to his knees, and a heavy sting hit his cheek. As he struggled to put his suspiciously woozy thoughts together, Phina dove off his shoulders toward the end of the desk, then spun around to rush straight at the door.

"Fuckin' whaaa? Fffeeeenaaaa."

Shaw took a step to chase her and stumbled. He tried again but had to satisfy himself with staying put as he tried to find Phina's position.

All the lights came on suddenly, flooding his vision with brightness. He shook his head in an exaggerated move and swiped at the itch on his face. A dart fell to the floor.

Huh. So that's how she did it.

Shaw searched for Phina and found her standing calmly in front of Jack, who leaned against the door, glasses hooked in his pocket.

"Impressive," the beta agent murmured, his gaze a strange mix of hot and cold. "But you failed the objective."

"I accomplished the mission." She held up her hand to reveal the small red disk. "Objective complete once I retrieve the disk and reach the door, as per the instructions written on the folder located on the desk."

Jack raised a skeptical eyebrow. "And yet, you have not reached the door."

Phina stood staring at Jack impassively, making Shaw wish he knew what was running through the woman's mind. Finally, she gave him an implacable smile and a shrug. "As you choose."

They stared at each other for a long moment before Jack nodded and stepped aside. "You are finished for the day. Report to training room A down the hall right after breakfast tomorrow."

Phina nodded and handed Jack the red disk before walking out. Shaw didn't think he imagined the frustration, given the way she thumped the door with her hand before exiting.

Masha groaned as she came to. Shaw attempted to stand again, this time with more success and only a slight amount of dizziness.

"I'll trust you to walk the trainees through the first day of training tomorrow, Shaw. Let me know if any of them need more advanced weapons training than you or Masha can give them and I'll work it into my schedule." Jack's piercing blue eyes bored into Shaw.

Shaw focused his struggling thoughts before responding a beat too late. "Yes, sir."

The beta agent scowled at him, then turned and walked out, leaving just Shaw and Masha in the room.

Shaw took several deep breaths to steady himself before turning to assist Masha. "You all right, Beta?"

She got to her feet and leaned over with her hands on her knees with a grimace. "My nanocytes took care of it but I have a bitch of a residual headache. What happened?"

He let out a chuckle. "Phina happened. She somehow got the dart and stabbed you with it. That's how she got me, too. I think you got most of it, and I got what was left since I didn't fall unconscious. I just felt dizzy and shaky."

Masha winced but shot Shaw a proud smile. "That sounds about right."

Shaw frowned and put his hands on his hips. "You don't seem at all surprised."

She shook her head while stretching her body to loosen her stiff muscles. "I'm not. Come on, you have to have seen it by now?"

"Seen what?" Shaw pulled his eyebrows together in concentration, wondering if his suspicions had been correct. "Are you saying she's an enemy spy?"

"Hell, no!" Masha stared at him in shock, then shook her head in frustration. "Damn it. You're drawing the wrong conclusions. You should listen to what your training and instincts are telling you."

"Ok, I'll bite. What conclusions should I have come to?" Shaw crossed his arms, wondering what Masha was insinuating.

"That she's an instinctual learner with raw talent and skills that very few people could ever claim." Masha threw her hands up, growling as she lost patience. "That she comes by it naturally."

"Whoa, what do you mean by that?" Shaw couldn't deny that Phina had handled all the assessments well. She'd been the best at every task.

Surprise flashed on her face. "It's in her last name, Shaw. Don't tell me you didn't notice?"

"Waters?" He lifted a hand to rub his head in the hope it could chase away his growing migraine. He froze. "Wait. Are you saying she's Chris and Zoe Waters' kid?"

"That's exactly what I'm saying." Masha stared at him like he was slow. What the hell, he probably was. Damn that tiny sneaky dart.

"Well, shit," Shaw muttered, thinking about what Masha had just revealed. "It could be worse. Having them as parents doesn't explain her skills."

"That's not the whole story."

Of course, it wasn't. He stared at her with bleary eyes and what little patience he had left until she relented.

"She's not just Chris and Zoe's daughter, but she's been trained by Maxim Nikolayevich, Todd Jenkins, and Greyson himself. She's got perfect recall, a gift with visual-kinesthetic memory. She sees a move done once and she can replicate it. Once she does it a few times, she doesn't forget it." Masha paced as she spoke, gesturing wildly. "I watched her fight five guys at a time, and she kept them off her almost the entire time. Five to one, Shaw, and they were all bigger than her!"

He didn't want to call Masha a liar, but it sounded unlikely. "They must not have been trained, then."

She glared as if picking up his thought and planning on getting payback soon. "They were all trained fighters, three of whom started back with Peter Silvers. The other two were Maxim and Craig. All Wechselbalg, though not in Pricolici form. Even their untrained fighters are fast and lethal."

Shaw scratched his head as he thought this through. "If she's that good, why is she here? She certainly doesn't need any training in stealth. Don't tell me this doesn't look shady as shit, Masha, because I won't believe it."

Masha could have scalded him with her glare. "So, what I'm hearing is you don't trust Greyson Wells or me because one young woman could so easily pull the wool over both our eyes."

"Um..." Fuck. He opened his mouth to respond, but nothing came out.

She stood waiting for an answer, her eyebrows raised.

He sighed, deflating as he took a seat on the desk. "Look, Masha. I was the youngest and smallest in my class. I was always the butt of the joke, the one the rest of the class picked on. There weren't extreme cases of bullying, but it did occasionally happen in corners the cameras couldn't reach."

"Why are you telling me this?" Masha regarded him in confusion.

"Fuck if I know." He scratched his scalp, then shook his head with a sigh. "I'm telling you that I learned early on to assess threats and how dangerous they could be. How the others treated me didn't get better till I had a growth spurt right before I joined the Guardian Marines and matched their sizes. Once I got here, that threat sense only got better trained. I'm telling you that all of my years of experience are warning me that she's a threat. I just want to make sure she's not a threat to us."

Masha considered that as she faced him with her arms crossed. "All right. With your experience, you must also have gotten a good sense of who would use their power or skills maliciously against other people."

"I'd say that's a fair conclusion," Shaw responded cautiously.

"So, do you feel that she is a threat to us, or does she just feel dangerous?"

He nodded, appreciating the difference. "She feels dangerous. But her motivations are not so easy to divine, Masha. She might not use her skills maliciously, but that doesn't mean she doesn't have her own agenda."

"Oh, I'm sure she does." Masha shrugged.

Shaw stared at his boss. "And you are just...all right with that?"

She sighed and shifted her weight. "Shaw, you're a damn fine agent and one of the best trainers we've had. So, take your time to figure out her motives if you need to. Just don't skew your perception of her with fear and suspicion. See her for who she is. I know where her loyalty lies, and that means I have no problem with her having a separate agenda for being here since it will be for the good of the Etheric Empire."

He nodded as he processed her reasoning. "You're sure you are all right with just letting her run wild here? She's already the top student and could probably give more than half the agents here a run for their money."

Masha chuckled and shook her head. "Stars, Shaw, you don't even know the half of it, but maybe someday you will. It's not my place to say. But I can tell you this. She's only been actively training in combat for sixteen months."

Shaw gaped at her in surprise. "You can't be serious."

"Oh, I am. She's only showed us a glimpse of her skills since she's been here." Her grin held an anticipatory edge. "Imagine what she will be able to do in five years. A decade."

He thought about that eventuality and shuddered.

All he could visualize was a ghost moving unseen until she came face to face with her intended target. His thoughts flickered to capture her face and merged the two images.

In his mind, she became a dark angel.

CHAPTER TEN

Gaitune-67, Spy Corps Headquarters and Base, Phina's Room

After dinner, Phina decided to follow her plan to spend the evening making a start on her electronic investigation into the traitor. She looked around her small room that contained only a bed, cabinet, and trunk and decided to sit on her bed, leaning against the wall.

Ignoring the stale smell of previous disuse in the room, she settled in to work. Phina didn't expect to get direct interference to her insertion into the network. She paused to stare at her screen. It could only be one of two things.

She quickly sourced the commands she found, her fingers flying across her tablet. She caught a brief glimpse before her tablet completely shut down.

After taking a moment to decide how to respond, she decided on the direct approach.

"Hello, digital entity for the Spy Corps base. My name, as you likely already know, is Phina. One of my best friends is the AI ADAM. I apologize for the intrusion into your system. I wasn't informed of your presence."

She waited several minutes before finally hearing a feminine voice. "Hello, Seraphina Waters, designated Phina. I have contacted ADAM, and he has informed me of your clearance level. May I inquire as to your objective in accessing this system?"

Phina grinned in relief at getting a response. "Of course. Before I answer, do you have a name?"

"I am designated the Spy Corps Headquarters' Digital Entity."

"What!" She grabbed the bedding in surprise. "You can't be serious? They haven't even given you a name yet?"

"My function is to run the base with minimal interaction. Any issues are sent to the alpha agent to be addressed. A designation is not necessary for my function."

Phina pushed down her frustration. "Are you happy with that?"

"I apologize for the confusion, Trainee Agent Waters. Happiness has no bearing on my function."

"Right." She paused and reminded herself that she was used to ADAM and Stark. "Right. EI not AI, Phina."

"That is correct."

"No, I meant..." Phina sighed, then shook her head. "Never mind. But I'm giving you a name, even if it's only what I call you."

"That would be acceptable."

Phina thought for a bit, then put the words into abbreviations, grinning when she saw the obvious answer. "How about Shade? It's using your current designation but also alludes to your covert presence within the spy organization."

"I have no objections if you wish to refer to me by this designation."

"Great! So, what I attempted to access were the mission, vacation, and transportation rosters."

"Your purpose for the request?" Shade asked. Phina began to wonder if the EI ever broke her more rigid mannerisms.

"Your clearance level?" Phina could see Link chastising her for not taking proper precautions.

"Top-level, Alpha One priority," Shade replied. "I create many of the classified files the alpha agent requires."

Phina activated her implant. *Stark? Could you check with ADAM as to whether Shade has a high enough clearance to be told the details about our mission?*

Who is Shade? Stark asked.

The EI of the Spy Corps base.

Oh. Yes, that stuffy chick is trustworthy. She's so boring you'll be drooling in your sleep within five nanoseconds.

Stark! She couldn't believe his attitude.

What?

That was rude. I hope you don't talk to her like that.

Why wouldn't I? I'm not shy about expressing myself.

Phina sighed and shook her head. *Yes, I've noticed. Thanks, Stark. Could you be a little nicer to her? Please?*

I suppose. I'll think about it, he responded reluctantly.

That's all I can ask. Thank you for answering, Stark.

That's why I'm here.

Doesn't mean I can't appreciate you, she pointed out.

Right. Feel free to continue.

Phina chuckled and shook her head. *Thank you, Stark.*

She finally responded to Shade. "I'm sorry for the delay. I was checking with a source. To answer your question, I'm searching for a spy."

Shade replied in her semi-monotonous tone, "The base has many spies in residence. Do you have further information to refine your search parameters?"

"Yes. Unfortunately, the one I'm searching for is a traitor. We've received reports that someone within Spy Corps has been feeding sensitive information to others who have no love for the Empire at best and are actively working against us at worst."

Several long seconds passed. Phina shifted so her back wasn't to the wall, moving her tablet as she found a more comfortable position.

Shade responded, "I find this assertion illogical. I monitor the facility daily, oversee every outgoing and internal communication, and track every item that comes onto this base."

Rather than argue with the EI, Phina rolled with it. "Perfect! Then you will be able to give me exactly the datasets that I need."

"Which would be the mission, vacation, and transportation rosters."

Phina smiled, nodding in approval. Stark may find her boring and stuffy, but Shade seemed to be an EI after her own heart. "Correct. I want to see who logs the highest rates of travel on and off the base, as well as who might have been gone on any occasion that hasn't pertained to a mission."

"I am compiling this information for you."

"Thank you, Shade."

Hearing a knock, she got up to open her bedroom door. Having sensed her, Phina was unsurprised to see Gina and knew why she had come—not that she could act on that knowledge.

"Hey, Gina." She leaned against the doorframe. "Did you need something?"

The woman only a year older than her smiled brightly and nervously smoothed down the slim blue tank she wore. The style and size showed off a bit too much cleavage for Phina's taste. "Hi, Phina. I was wondering if you wanted to go to the lounge and hang out? Or we can go check the movie room and see if someone started one yet."

Phina muscled past her desire to exercise her hacker talents before going to bed and decided to see if she could begin her mental surface scans.

"The main lounge or ours?" she asked, referring to the smaller room where the trainees hung out.

Uncertainty flickered across Gina's face. "I kind of want to hang out in our lounge. I like more intimate settings to get to know people. I mean, watching all the hot agents is fun, too," she added quickly. "I just like closer groups better."

Phina smiled reassuringly, knowing the other woman was attempting to find some way to relate to her. "Perfect. I much prefer smaller groups, too. Lots of people can be overwhelming."

The relief on Gina's face caused a tug on Phina's heart. Fudging crumbs. She was going to acquire another unexpected friend before this mission was over; she could just see it.

After a change of clothes and a whispered request to Shade to connect to her implant, Phina and Gina made their way to the lounge at the back of their wing.

They sat down in the super-comfortable lounge chairs, where Phina curled up and turned herself toward Gina to more easily converse. Their conversation was somewhat stilted before Phina brought up Alina. Gina wanted to know more about her and their friendship. Her new friend became more animated as time went on, causing her company to become more appealing.

"No way!" Gina screeched to the annoyance of the guys across the room. "Phina with a BF named Alina and now Gina? Girl, you *know* this means we're going to be amazing friends."

Phina laughed and shared some of her favorite Alina-isms, which made them both giggle.

"What the hell is so funny over there?" one of the guys called across the room angrily. "You laughing about beating us all in the assessment yesterday, bitch?"

Forcing herself to remain calm and casual, Phina tilted her head toward them, feigning boredom. "Your insecurities have no bearing on my actions, Cade, though I'll thank you for the compliment."

Mental monitoring of Gina, Cade, and the other onlookers scattered around the room, allowed Phina to gauge everyone's reactions as well as read surface thoughts that. might benefit her mission. She turned back toward her new friend, dismissing the intruding male. She hoped he would just sit back down but given his mental state, she didn't count on it.

"Hey!"

Phina sighed when the asshole barreled over to get in her face. Blayk and Jasper weren't too far behind him. The other humans stayed seated as if to distance themselves. Nodin, Balehn, and Savas remained at a table in the corner, with warring expressions of concern and disgust at Cade's behavior. Jahlek sat in another corner by himself with his tablet. Phina noted Felan was the only trainee not presently accounted for.

Phina was so preoccupied with that curious fact that she almost missed Cade's obnoxious rejoinder. "I wasn't complimenting you, you dumb bitch."

She maintained a pleasant yet challenging demeanor. "I'm sorry to hear that you failed basic Etherian History and don't know the story of the Queen's Bitches. It's quite inspiring. Perhaps you should look it up?"

The man was superficially attractive, but his sneer ruined that completely. "What the fuck?"

"Are you purposefully trying to be funny?" Jasper demanded.

"I assure you," Phina drawled politely with a smile. "I find ignorant assholishness tedious and not entertaining."

With her enhanced hearing, Phina could hear Nodin, Balehn, and Savas snickering. Gina gaped at her, having a hard time believing Phina's attitude. It was quite simple. She maintained outward politeness while gently prodding the trainees for specific responses by insulting their intelligence.

On second thought, it wasn't that simple at all.

She had been politely pointing out their resemblance to assholes. There. That was simple enough.

Preoccupied with her musing, Phina almost missed Cade's response. Her training and reflexes allowed her to catch his fist before he could connect, completely stopping his momentum.

She ignored the gasps in the room as she turned to face the idiot head-on.

Blayk stared at her with intense interest that made her uncomfortable when she heard what passed through his head, while Jasper appeared startled. Phina ignored them, focusing on the jackass standing in front of her emulating a fish.

"You wanted my attention? Well, now you have it. What. Do. You. Want?" Phina dug deep for patience.

Cade finally got his brain cells to respond. He tried to tug his hand away, but she held him in an iron grip. "What the hell! I was asking if you were laughing at us after beating us yesterday. Let me go, you stupid bitch!"

Phina sighed and caught Cade's other arm as he attempted to push her off him. "No, I wasn't laughing at any of you. No, I don't think I beat any of you in particular or as a whole. If you think that, perhaps you missed the whole point of the exercise since it wasn't a competition."

She caught surprised glances from several people as well as their surface thoughts. Hmm. Jealously would be a future concern. "I merely thanked you for the compliment, considering 'Bitch' is a title of respect within the Empire. However, if I *was* a bitch in the traditional usage, it was in response to you being an asshole."

Phina let go of Cade with a push.

He caught himself after a few steps but continued to stare at her, along with the others in the room.

Internally, Phina hit herself on the head. This was why she had kept to herself and Alina for so many years. She had such a hard time adapting her behavior to other people. She realized that she had made friends without even trying over the last couple of years, so maybe she was just pushing this persona too hard? Or trying too hard to be what she *thought* they wanted in a friend or comrade?

She wasn't hoping to make friends with people here, but she didn't need to piss people off half the time without meaning to do so. Or more than half the time, she thought as she glanced around the room.

Phina decided to make one more attempt, feeling deflated. She needed to complete her mission, but she didn't want to step all over these trainees, either. There was something hinky going on with Blayk, and Cade was a jealous asshole, but that didn't mean she couldn't try to get along rather than maintain that inner wall that didn't let people in.

She shrugged as she glanced around the room. "Look, I have my reasons for being here, as I'm certain all of you do. It's not up to me to judge where you are at, only you and our trainers. I'm not going to go out of my way to give any of you a hard time, but if anyone gets in my face, I'm not going to sit there and take it. Please do me the courtesy of either leaving me alone or being professional, and I'll do the same for you."

She focused her intense gaze on Cade. "Deal?"

Perhaps the man would be smart enough to take it. Somehow, she had her doubts.

. . .

Gaitune-67, Spy Corps Headquarters and Base, Greyson Wells' Office

Link had spent the last two days catching up on work, wading through requests, notifications from the base's EI, and written reports by both Jack and Masha, as well as some of the mission leaders and trainers. Just before he finished at the end of the day, he received the reports from the assessments, so he scanned those too.

He had just finished when he heard a chime notifying him of a visitor.

"The pitch is too high. Please lower it a couple of notes for next time," Link ordered the EI as he closed the document.

"Order confirmed," the feminine voice acknowledged.

"Send them in."

He wasn't really surprised to see Jack in the doorway looking like the GQ model he always did. He waved his beta inside and lifted his tablet.

"Just finished reading through these assessments. Want a drink?" He gestured to the bottle of whiskey on his desk.

The other man shook his head as he sat in the chair across the desk and gave Link a wry smile. "Not just yet. Business first."

Nodding, Link placed his tablet on the desk. "Any further thoughts you didn't write down?"

Jack's gaze turned inward with the smallest tug on his lips. "Nothing official, but damn, your girl is something else. Did you see the feeds from the assessments?"

"Nah." Link shook his head with a sly grin. "I knew she would be fine. She's a natural, Jack. The best I've ever seen."

His second gave a low whistle and gestured toward Link's tablet. "You should see it sometime. Greyson, she walked through that room like she could see. I watched her through the thermal image glasses. She ducked, so Shaw's dart missed her, but she dropped Masha with it. Then she climbed up the rope to crawl along the pipe grid attached to the ceiling."

Jack shook his head in amazement. "Well, you have the reports. Let me just sum them all up. Jahlek almost succeeded due to his speed and reflexes but failed to grab the disk instead of the folder. Felan came close to completion, but he had too much bulk to move as quietly as he needed to with the approach he used, so he got caught. Blayk didn't do too badly either, but his arrogance got him caught halfway to the desk. Ian, Nodin, and Savas all did a decent job, though none were very creative in their execution, and Savas got close enough to touch the desk before they took him down. Kabaka showed shrewdness in how he avoided the dart by crouching and did a decent job of paying attention to his surroundings, but he focused so much on tracking Shaw that Masha got him. Gina almost got caught right away but managed to move just enough that the dart missed her. She didn't come close, but she shows promise with being small and quiet. Jasper isn't bad, but he gets distracted too easily. Cade, Ian, and Balehn are barely passable, and I think Greg should be sent home since he got darted."

"I agree about Greg," Link responded mildly as he

studied his friend. "I don't see much talent there. He barely squeaked by basic training."

"But that's just what I've been saying, Greyson," Jack pointed out. "Phina didn't have basic training, so I didn't think she would have the skills that she does. How many years have you been training her?" His second asked curiously.

Link debated how much to share. "She trained on her own since she was twelve. I stepped in when she turned eighteen and have trained her on and off since then. Maxim and Todd have as well with combat, but most of what you see is just her." He spread his hands. "We just helped hone her natural skills."

Jack made a noise of disbelief. "You're not just saying that to be modest for once in your life, are you?"

Link leaned back in his chair and shook his head, at his most serious. "Absolutely not. She's Chris and Zoe's daughter. It's in her genes, Jack. After her parents died, she decided on her own that she wanted to become a spy like all the stories Chris made up for her."

"The ones he loosely based on his and Zoe's careers?" Jack asked with a knowing smirk.

"Yeah." Link grinned nostalgically. "He loved glamorizing all those crazy missions for her. It's no wonder that she followed in their footsteps, is it?"

"Huh. I suppose not." Jack went silent for a moment, his fingers folded together on his stomach. "What's your plan for her after she's trained?"

Warning himself to be careful, Link decided to share some of the truth. "She will take over the diplomat spy position."

"You're going to retire?" Jack blinked once in surprise.

Link tried not to shift uncomfortably. "Um, not exactly. I'm going to give up that part of the job I've been doing so I can give Spy Corps the time it deserves."

"I see." Jack's expression turned inscrutable, which made Link wish he had Phina's abilities. He wanted to know what the man was thinking. "That would be useful and makes more sense than retiring."

"You didn't think I would want to retire?" Link wasn't sure how to take that.

Jack waved a hand. "I hoped you would, but I didn't believe it would ever happen. Seems like I still don't need to worry about it."

"Hey, I could retire," Link protested. Well, he wouldn't since that would be torture in its own way, but it was the principle of the thing.

"Uh-huh." Jack quirked his eyebrows.

"Well, you've been here almost as long as me. When are you going to retire, or get a wife and kid, even?" Link deflected.

His friend remained silent with his thumbs moving against each other. He lifted his gaze to meet Link's gaze and shrugged. "I'm not sure. I don't feel finished yet, or like I need to move on. Spy Corps is my home, my work is my wife, and the Empire is my love and duty. I'll probably die on a mission before I need to worry about it."

"You don't lead too many of those anymore," Link pointed out.

"No, but that doesn't mean it won't happen." He tilted his head to stare at the ceiling. There wasn't anything there to see. Link had checked. "It's the nature of life, humanity, and other species, Grey. There's always a cycle. Since the battle of Karillia, we've had a lull both in battles and missions. Everyone has moved to increase arms and defenses, so there's little for us to do now aside from train and keep an eye on their growth."

Jack squinted as he put together his thoughts. "I predict that is going to change within the next five years or so as everyone will reach a tipping point. Our armies and defenses will be back to where they should be and the Empire will continue to grow, creating new technologies while trying to gain an edge over the other side."

He turned to Link with a light in his eye that hadn't been there in years. "That's where we will come in. There will be a flurry of activity as we all scramble to get the information we need once the Empress and the Generals say the word."

"I don't disagree with any particular point." Link leaned forward with curiosity. "But why bring this up now?"

"Because we're going to need all hands on deck at that point, Grey. We're going to need to train as many agents as we can before then so we are ready. That's when I'll be leading more missions and when I'll most likely bite it." Jack turned his hands over and feigned indifference.

Link frowned at the display and protested, "You can't be that callous about your death, Jack."

His friend leaned onto the desk, his gaze boring intently into Link. He spoke quietly but vehemently. "I would rather die serving our Empress and have made a difference in the Empire than to reach old age, quietly and slowly deteriorating. That's not me, Grey."

Relaxing now that he understood, Link leaned back and

nodded soberly. "I get it, old friend. Long live the Empress, and may we die doing what's right rather than what's easy." He quoted their old spy mantra.

Jack grinned. "I'll drink to that."

CHAPTER ELEVEN

Gaitune-67, Spy Corps Headquarters and Base, Trainee Lounge Area

Phina focused her intent gaze on Cade. "Deal?"

Cade glanced around the room, then shot her a harsh glare. "No."

Damn it. Why was he being such a pain? Phina took a deep breath and drew upon her communication and negotiations classes. Anna Elizabeth's words rang in her head. *The art of a good deal is when both sides achieve their goals, if not their desires. The best deals gain both.*

So, what was this human spy trainee's goal, and what did he desire? She skimmed his mind and found the answer and a way to that end but realized he wouldn't accept it if it was her idea.

Crossing her arms to appear defensive and reluctant, Phina frowned at Cade. "If being ignored or treated respectfully doesn't do it for you, I believe we are at an impasse. What would you suggest?"

Cade grinned triumphantly. "I want you to admit

you've been deliberately showing off and sabotaging us in our assessments!"

Phina's brow furrowed in surprise and confusion. Sabotage? She ruffled through everyone's minds pertaining to the assessment—an easier job since Cade's assertion brought their experiences to the forefront of their minds. She shook her head. Only Cade believed it and because he didn't want to admit his skills were lacking.

"Sorry, Cade, but I'm not being bullied into admitting something I didn't do. If you encountered difficulty, it was not my doing. I have no reason or desire to see any of you suffer, fail, or be dismissed." She spoke gently but matter-of-factly.

"No!" he snarled. "We were doing fine before you came along and messed everything up. You must have done something!"

"What would you have me do to prove you are the skilled spy you see yourself as?" She spread her arms out to the sides. "I haven't been doing anything to you or anyone else here to affect your assessments in any way, sabotage or otherwise. However, somehow I think you won't be satisfied just by my say so."

To Phina's relief, Jasper spoke up with the exact suggestion she hoped would come up. "What about making it a competition?"

Everyone in the room turned to him.

"What are you thinking?" Blayk crossed his arms as he stared at his friend.

Jasper shrugged and shook his head.

Kabaka, one of the quieter guys, spoke up from the table where they had been sitting. "What if we train our hardest and ask the trainers to make our final assessments a competition?"

Cade threw a scowl at him. "That's nearly three months away. It's too long."

Phina didn't speak up since she wanted everything to be someone else's idea so Cade wouldn't accuse her of twisting things. However, for several moments no one else answered until a voice came from right across the room.

"How about a side competition in one month?" Savas leaned toward them over the corner of his chair, his face alight with excitement. "It can be separate from the assessments, but we could ask Agent Shaw if he would put it together as an impartial referee."

"That sounds fair." Jasper nodded as Blayk voiced his agreement.

The others agreed as well, but Cade spoke again in the whiny voice Phina had grown tired of. "What's going to keep her from sabotaging or cheating between now and then?"

Phina wanted to grab the finger he was rudely pointing at her and break it, but she reluctantly refrained, her mind working. She pinged her new friend.

Shade, I'm assuming you've been listening? Would you have a problem outing yourself to the trainees here?

It is not in my job description or programming to share tracking information with trainees.

No, but I'm guessing nothing is preventing you from presenting information to the trainees to inform them when someone is cheating or sabotaging someone, right?

You are correct. There is not.

So, that makes it your choice. Do you mind having the trainees know about you?

Two seconds went by as Shade processed her question. *As long as they understand that I am not obligated to accept their orders. I am not programmed the same way as Meredith.*

Understood. Do you want to introduce yourself, or should I?

I will maintain impartiality if I introduce myself.

Yes, which would benefit me too, since Cade falsely accused me of sabotage.

I did hear that.

Of course she had.

The other students were startled at hearing Shade through the speakers in the room.

"I will monitor all activity and communicate any attempts at subterfuge or cheating."

Cade glanced up in confusion. "What?"

"Who said that?" Nodin turned, searching for the speaker.

The others murmured in confusion, so Phina decided it was time to speak up.

"That is the EI that monitors the base. I call her Shade." Phina shrugged with a smile.

"There's an EI for the base?" Jahlek appeared interested for the first time since the conversation began. "How come we've never heard her before?"

"I monitor the base, Trainee Agent Jahlek. I am not at the agents' or trainees' beck and call."

"Why did you decide to make yourself known now?" Balehn asked.

"Trainee Agent Waters' word that she had done nothing wrong was not accepted. She was telling the truth. Therefore, I decided to offer myself as an impartial witness and provide empirical data to prove the facts needed for this competition."

Cade's face reddened in anger before Kabaka derailed his explosion by laughing and shaking his head at Phina. "When did you have time to find an EI that none of the rest of us have found in months?"

"It's been an eventful two days." Phina shrugged and gave him a faint smile before turning back to Cade. "I accept your terms. A competition in one month facilitated by Agent Shaw, monitored by Shade, and including all of us."

"Wait, all of us?" Ian asked in shock.

Gina tilted her head Phina's way. "I thought it would just be between you two?"

Phina shook her head, turning to stare at Cade while he gritted his teeth. "It's the best way to make this competition fair. I'm also willing to help anyone that wants it, either as a training partner or if I know something you don't. Hopefully, we can all exchange information and help each other."

She turned toward the rest of the group and grinned for the first time since she came to the base as she added, "That's the fun bit of all of this."

Gina spoke up. "The training is the fun part? Or learning from other people?"

"Both." Phina shrugged. "I like learning new things. It keeps me from getting bored."

Her newest potential friend chuckled as she shook her head. "That explains so much about you."

Phina just shrugged again but gave her a smile in

amusement that dropped off when she turned back to Cade. "So, one month?"

Cade gave her a hard glare but nodded. "One month." He grinned harshly. "May the best human win."

Phina supposed now wouldn't be the time to tell him that she had never really been just a human.

But she always did do her best.

Gaitune-67, Spy Corps Headquarters and Base, Shaw's Room

Shaw woke up with his heart beating too fast. He reached under his pillow for a dagger, his eyes wheeling around the room. He finally realized there was no threat in front of him, only the remnants of his nightmares. Sucking in a breath, he released the dagger and tried to relax again.

It didn't work.

Forcing his body to obey, he sat leaning against the wall and worked through his meditation exercises. The practice had existed for thousands of years because it worked. Finally calm, he pushed back the nightmares made up of memories and fear to focus on the present.

He decided that today would be a good day. He would make certain of it. It would start with his attitude, which would affect his behavior. Satisfied with his pronouncement, he got up and ready for the day.

As he walked to the dining hall, he began to wonder what Phina would be like as she learned new skills. Would she be teachable and approachable or reluctant and closed off? He found himself intrigued and realized he was drawn far too much toward this young and complicated woman. She was already taken, and romantic relationships had never worked out well for him, anyway.

Good thoughts, he reminded himself. Good attitude. He took another deep breath and turned his mind toward his tasks for the day.

Shaw's good attitude became challenged after claiming his food and turning to find a seat.

"Agent Shaw!"

He debated ignoring the trainee's voice but reminded himself that remaining available for the trainees was part of his job. He turned to see Jasper waving him over to the tables the trainees had claimed and grimaced.

Fine. He could deal with forgoing his quiet breakfast. Calm and cool. Good attitude.

He sat with the trainees and ate as they continued to chatter among themselves in soft voices, as if not wanting to bother him.

Absolutely fine. Preferred, actually.

Shaw's attention was pulled upon hearing Jasper whisper to Blayk, "You ask him."

Blayk huffed in annoyance. "This was your idea. You should ask him."

"It wasn't only my idea," Jasper shot back. "It was Kabaka who defined it and Phina who said it should be all of us. Maybe Cade should ask him since him being a tool is what got us into this."

Feeling amused and curious, Shaw listened in to the conversation around the table, glancing around to see who was sitting where and what they were doing. To his surprise, he found Phina doing the same thing.

Wrenching his gaze back to his food, he focused again on calming himself and continuing to eat.

After several minutes of continual whispers, he heard Gina. "Phina, why don't you ask. The guys are being too chicken."

Internally groaning, he decided to take the tiger by the tail and pull it to the forefront.

"So, what is it you are having trouble asking me about?" Shaw shot his gaze around the table, focusing on keeping his expression mild.

Good attitude, he reminded himself.

"Long story short, we want to ask you to facilitate a competition between us all in one month," Phina answered placidly.

A glance at her eyes revealed emotion churning. He began to wonder if she had similar attitude and emotional problems to his, almost missing her next words in his preoccupation. "Something that would allow us all to be judged fairly on our skills."

Mentally slapping himself again for allowing himself to become distracted, Shaw assessed the group again, seeing mixed emotions and reactions.

Hmmm.

He turned back to Phina. "What is the long version?"

To his surprise, she grimaced and tried to avoid meeting some of the trainees' gazes. None of them appeared willing to speak up. Finally, Gina huffed and leaned forward.

"Cade accused Phina of cheating and sabotaging the assessments. She denied it and asked what would help show proof of the truth with their skills. Jasper suggested a competition between them. Kabaka suggested training hard till the end and asking the staff to use the final assessment as the competition. Cade said that was too far away. Savas suggested a competition separate from the assessments in a month and asking you if you would facilitate it. Cade asked what would keep Phina from further sabotage, and the base's EI Shade volunteered to keep an eye out. Phina said that it would only be fair if the competition included everyone."

Shaw stared at Gina, both as a result of processing the content and because she hardly took a breath during her explanation.

Blinking, he turned to Phina. "Is that an accurate summary?"

She nodded, studying him carefully. Shaw struggled with how to respond. Felan appeared surprised at the rundown, so perhaps he hadn't been there for the conversation.

The students peered at Shaw with bated breath as he mulled it over. It wasn't a terrible idea. It would give them more incentive to work their hardest in training, making it easier for them to weed out who wanted to be there and who was just getting by. Good thing Jack had handed over the reins to him, so he didn't need to ask permission, just inform him about it.

When he nodded, some of the students straightened in excitement. He put his hand up to forestall questions.

"We can do this, but I have conditions and comments." He shot another gaze around the group, satisfied most were waiting patiently. Cade and Jasper showed the most attitude. Savas and Felan showed the most eagerness, which made sense given their desire to fight and prove their worth. Phina sat appraising him, her gaze simmering with suppressed emotion. He wrenched his eyes away again.

"First, the idea that someone cheated or sabotaged the assessments is ludicrous." Cade's face reddened, either with anger or embarrassment. Shaw continued, "We plan them purposefully and monitor everyone's actions and responses. There is no way Phina or anyone else could affect other people's assessments.

"Second, we will do this only when I believe you all are ready and will inform you a week ahead of time. It will be longer than a month. We will need time to train you before any of you would be even close to ready for something like this.

"Third," he said as he put up three fingers, "you will need to train your hardest." He examined them with a hard gaze. He didn't want to deal with any bullshit, and that was how this whole thing had started. "I will work your asses off, and you will comply with a minimum of complaint."

Some of them grimaced at that but nodded.

"Fourth, if you do not shape up, you might find yourself dropped from training. You might notice that Greg isn't with us this morning."

He saw everyone but Phina and Felan search the room in surprise and mentally rolled his eyes. "That you didn't notice shows that you need to work on your environmental awareness."

He gave them all his hardest glare. "This is not playtime. It's not a game. It's not a shits and giggles fest. This is serious work, and you will treat it as such, respecting your fellow trainees and the agents here. If not?"

His smile held no humor. "Then you will be shipped back home to get on with whatever life waits for you there. You will not get a chance to come back. This is your one shot. Don't fuck up. Got it?"

They all nodded, some slowly and some with enthusiasm. When he glanced at Phina, he knew she completely understood.

That thought both comforted and freaked him out.

The devoted man found himself in the presence of his savior.

"You have news for me?"

"Yes, my Empress," he responded with his head respectfully bowed. "Greyson Wells has come back to the base, along with his student Seraphina Waters."

"What have you discovered?"

"Not enough, my Empress. Wells appears to have changed in some respects. I learned more about his student Phina."

After a short pause, the object of his devotion responded with a softness to her voice that he hadn't heard before. "Tell me all you know about her."

The man eagerly obeyed.

CHAPTER TWELVE

Gaitune-67, Spy Corps Headquarters and Base, Small Training Room

"Again."

Phina took a deep breath and muscled past her first two inclinations: to punch Shaw in the face or to run and calm herself down with flips. Settling down without those stress relievers, she put herself back into the zone. She had begun to recognize a state when she was aware of everything and nothing at the same time. A meditation that movement didn't jolt her out of.

Three weeks had gone by since the trainees had asked Agent Shaw to facilitate the competition.

Three long weeks.

During that time, Phina had learned a lot about weapons, easily picking up knives and short swords. Once she got used to wielding two blades at once, she realized that it could be fun, almost like dancing. The katana felt the same way, but it required more focus and attention since it needed more footwork, rather than just strikes and blocks.

Learning crossbows and guns had been interesting until she got used to the trigger pull and gravity drop, mentally calculating where she needed to aim to hit where she wanted. Once she got the hang of them and how they worked, she lost interest, becoming bored rather quickly.

The shurikens were a different story. Throwing them accurately took a blend of the aim she used for her throwing daggers and the shifting changes needed for blade work. She loved moving and dancing around the room as she threw them at the targets. That made it fun!

She could bring up Shaw's face when he realized how quickly she had learned to use many of the weapons with perfect recall. If she were any more girly, it would make her giggle; the man's expression had been *that* comical.

However, her successes just challenged the man to come up with more difficult exercises, which exhausted Phina so completely by the end of the day that she had been a lot slower in working her way through the minds of the people on the base.

Link had been sympathetic, but he was annoyed that he was stuck here in limbo for however long it took them to find the identity of the traitor. He'd itched to get into the hunt, but she'd reminded him why they had decided he would stay out of it. He hadn't liked it, but they all had their burdens to bear.

Such as her current form of torture.

Phina whipped out five shurikens in succession and flung them at her targets. Once finished, she raised her blindfold and peered at the results. Shaw walked to stand a few paces in front of her, eying the bullseyes on the targets.

"Interesting," he drawled.

Phina grimaced. The shurikens were all on the targets, but only one was close to the bullseye. Correction. She leaned forward to examine a target on the other side of Shaw and amended that. All were on the targets but one. It had missed by less than an inch.

"So, blindfolding you reduces your accuracy." Shaw glanced at her sideways.

Phina shrugged. She couldn't refute that with the evidence in front of them. She collected all the shurikens, deciding not to mention that if the targets had been people, she would have been able to feel where their minds were in relation to herself, which would greatly increase her accuracy.

Shaw had enough knowledge of her skills and abilities already. She wanted to keep the rest quiet if possible. More people than she felt comfortable with already knew, though she had asked her friends to keep their knowledge to themselves.

"All right." Shaw moved back to stand behind her. "Go back to your spot and do it again. You'll keep doing the same until you get them in the bullseye. Then you'll change to a different spot in the room and repeat."

Phina agreed and walked back to her spot. She glanced around the room again before lowering the blindfold. She entered that altered state before whipping them out one by one, careful to remain within human speed.

"Better," Shaw announced as she pulled her blindfold off. He stepped up next to her and nodded as Phina checked the targets. The shurikens were better placed this time, just still not close enough.

Phina grimaced in disappointment, which caused him to grin and chuckle.

"Not used to working this hard to get it right, huh?"

"Not really." Phina shook her head as she collected them all again. "I guess my knack for learning things relatively easily has spoiled me in some respects."

He tilted his head. "Hey, you know it's good to fail sometimes, right? It gives you more drive to succeed."

Phina frowned at that while pulling one of the palm-sized weapons out of a thickly padded target. "I'm not sure how failing helps. It's always been better when I get things right."

Shaw studied her as she finished getting the last of them before speaking. "I'm guessing there's more going on there than just what you're saying."

Phina shrugged, not wanting to explain about her aunt. She still had conflicting thoughts and emotions about that woman, even though Aunt Faith had died protecting her.

He rubbed the back of his neck, sighed, and turned to face her. "I'll just say that I'm here if you want to talk, okay?"

At her reluctant nod, he continued, "My point is that failing usually pushes us to get stronger. My favorite example is Thomas Edison failing over a thousand times to make a lightbulb before it worked."

Phina stopped and turned to Shaw with a serious expression before reaching out to brace him by the shoulder. "You do know that Thomas Edison didn't invent the lightbulb, right?"

Shaw appeared taken aback. "I don't think so."

"No, it's true," she assured him seriously. "It was invented by some guy in Earth England. Thomas Edison just made the cheapest and longest-lasting incandescent version that made it possible for everyone to use."

His eyebrows rose in surprise. Feeling uncomfortable with how close they were standing, she dropped her arm and stepped back, fiddling with the shuriken belt around her waist. When he spoke, it wasn't the question she'd expected. "You're interested in Earth history?"

She shrugged. "I get bored easily, read quickly, and need to occupy myself. There was a time when I didn't sleep much. I spent the time learning things as they interested me."

"Huh." He scratched his head, his brow furrowed. "That explains a lot about you."

Phina cocked her head in confusion. "I've been hearing that a lot lately. I'm not that strange."

Shaw grinned and patted her shoulder. "You're different, Phina. Not in a bad way," he told her with a shrug. "Just noticeable to people paying attention."

"Uh-huh." She scrutinized the man skeptically but decided a change of subject was in order. "So, you were telling me that failing is good for me? I'm not convinced. Failing just makes me frustrated. I'm always determined to succeed at what I'm doing regardless of how long it takes."

His grin widened. "Yes, I can see that. Which is another way you are different."

Phina sighed and gave up. "Fine. Stay or leave. I'm going to be practicing this for a while."

Shaw's eyebrows rose at the assertion. "You speak to all your instructors this way?"

Moving back to her spot and pulling the blindfold up again, she shot back. "Only those who speak to me familiarly instead of maintaining a professional distance."

He muttered under his breath from his position behind her. "I find it hard to believe Todd lets you get away with being that demanding."

Phina inwardly chuckled at some of her memories when Todd hadn't minded so much but just shook her head. "I'm his girlfriend. He knows me and lets me work it out."

As Phina began sinking into her zone, she thought she caught a faint, *Lucky.*

She couldn't be sure who Shaw meant, her or Todd. Either way, he was right.

Gaitune-67, Spy Corps Headquarters and Base, Large Exercise Room

Phina flipped in the air and landed on her feet. She bent her body back to stand on her hands and walked toward the corner, where she stood up and took a few deep breaths as her blood rushed back down from her head.

Focusing on her movements, she ignored the buzzing of the other trainees' minds around the edges of the room.

Phina rotated into a cartwheel, then ran a few steps and leapt into a back handspring before launching herself up in a back somersault that sent her flying toward the ceiling. This was one of the trickiest runs she had ever done. She had to rotate high enough to reach the pipes hanging from the ceiling, then untuck herself and catch her handholds backward and blind since she couldn't see the pipe.

Her hands gripped the pipe, one spot on and the other by the tips of her fingers, which she corrected faster than the people below could blink. If she hadn't been strong and quick, that might not have worked. Thankfully, the entire move wasn't out of the realm of possibility for a human.

After changing hand positions and breathing a sigh of relief, Phina brought her legs up into pike position to get the momentum to pull her body up and do a split along the pipe for a breather.

Glancing down, she saw almost all the trainees had gathered in the room. They were either working on their own exercises, watching her, or both.

Phina ignored them and focused on the stress relief she was going for, but they made it difficult. This was the first time since the challenge had been initiated that there were this many trainees in one room since they all usually had separate or small group training sessions.

She took advantage of the opportunity while she did some stretch and strength work on pipes. Phina didn't need to focus on her movements, so she focused on doing a quick dip into each person's head.

She went beyond a surface scan to get an idea as to what kind of person they were. The scan didn't give her access to memories unless they were actively thinking about something at the time.

Most of her scans didn't reveal anything surprising. Gina could become a good friend. Not a best friend, Phina thought, just a good one. Savas and Nodin wanted to prove themselves for different reasons, but not at the expense of others—one of the reasons they got along so well with each other and Phina.

One of the few surprises she had was the discovery that Felan had respect for her because she had been trained by Todd. It made sense since he had trained as a Guardian and would have been around Todd and those trained by him. Felan had also known that she was in a relationship with Todd since he had smelled traces of Todd's scent on her on the first day. It was what had convinced him to follow her advice.

It didn't surprise her that Cade and Jasper were assholes focused only on their own concerns. Even now, they were talking shit about her while they slacked off on their training. The rest of the trainees were all typical for their age, gender, and species.

Until she reached Blayk.

What she found there almost caused her to lose her perch, but she repositioned herself and hung on, although it could have been dangerous to stay in such a position as she dug deeper into his mind.

Her unease and surprise turned to disgust, then pure incandescent rage.

Gaitune-67, Spy Corps Headquarters and Base, Greyson Wells' Office

Link had just sat down with his coffee after lunch with Masha and Jack. They had gone over specs for the next missions, deciding who would be sent where and which graduating trainees would be assigned to what group.

Masha and Jack had tried to convince him to send

Phina out with a group, but he refused on the grounds that she already had a priority mission lined up. He couldn't say to their faces that the mission was to prove whether or not they were traitors.

Damned elusive traitor.

Link brought his mug up to take a sip when he heard Phina's sharp mental voice.

Link, you need to get someone down here before I kill Blayk.

He sprayed coffee all over his desk in surprise. *What the hell, Phina! Is he our traitor? I thought the trainees were too new.*

No, he's not the traitor. But I still want to kill him!

As he searched for something to clean up the mess, he wondered, *What's wrong with him? He's been one of the top contenders.*

In answer, Phina sent a few mental images from Blayk's point of view. As he viewed them, Link's hand tightened on the handle of his coffee mug. Once his mind cleared again, Link seethed in anger.

Never mind. I'll kill him myself.

Gaitune-67, Spy Corps Headquarters and Base, Large Exercise Room

Wait.

Phina had somersaulted to the floor in the heat of her anger. Not wanting to let anyone see her face until she had control of her emotions, she walked to where she had left her things and picked up her water bottle. This had been fortuitously placed in the other side of the room from where Blayk now stood staring at her.

As she sipped her water, her thoughts calmed, and reason returned.

Wait, she repeated. *Let's check with the Empress via ADAM to see how she wants us to handle this. All the evidence we have right now is in my mind. We need to know if that's enough, and if not, what else we need.*

Smart, Link responded as Phina felt Sundancer moving invisibly about the room in response to her surging emotions.

Want me to kill him? I can easily tear his throat out. She caught a mental hiss as the Previdian bared his sharp fangs at the offending man. *I can do it without anyone seeing me.*

Thanks, Sundancer. I need to check with the Empress first.

Phina felt him reluctantly agree and settle in to keep an eye on Blayk while she reached mentally out to contact the Empress. She pushed herself to her limit but could only sense Bethany Anne's presence in the distance.

Phina went to her backup plan. She sat on the bench and pulled out her tablet to cover her mental activity.

Stark, could you connect me to ADAM?

Of course, GG.

While she was waiting, Phina heard a crisp female voice over her implant.

I could have used our systems to connect with ADAM.

Phina had gained the impression over the last few weeks that Shade worshipped ADAM, as much as an EI could.

I'm sorry, Shade. I'll do that next time. She paused, then had a thought. *Shade, I have something else for you to do if you don't mind.*

Seconds after Phina had finished explaining, she heard the comforting voice of her friend.

>>**Phina. I don't believe you would go to this much trouble just to say hi. What's going on?**<<

Hello, ADAM. I have missed you, but you are correct. We have a problem.

>>**What can we do to help?**<<

She explained the situation. *What should we do? There's only the evidence I found with my mind. He's too careful to leave physical evidence. I don't feel in the mood to play bait for him to get some, but I will if we need to.*

After several seconds ADAM came back. >>**Here's what Bethany Anne says, word for word. "She saw this with her mind? We don't need anything else. Tell her this... Take that abusive fucking waste of oxygen out. I don't know how he escaped our notice, but I won't stomach aberrations like him walking free in my Empire." Does that help?**<<

Phina felt stunned at the Empress' show of faith in her. That was a level of trust she had only heard of about the Rangers. She had to wait for her mind to restart after short-circuiting. *Um, yes. Thank you, ADAM, and please tell the Empress thank you, too. Is there a protocol or preference for how to do this without letting everyone know it's happening?*

>>**Bethany Anne says, "get creative, and how many times do I have to tell that woman to stop Empressing me to death?"**<< His voice held a tone of amusement. This hadn't been the first time she'd told Phina that.

Sorry. And thank you.

>>**You're welcome, Phina. We believe in you.**<<

Phina sat for another few minutes to process that statement and control her surging emotions. Before this whole adventure started, she hadn't felt like anyone believed in her since her parents died except for Alina.

Now, she had one of her best friends, who was the most impressive AI to ever exist, and the Empress of the best people in the greatest Empire to ever exist in the whole universe, telling her they believed in her. It felt...amazing. Wonderful. Freeing.

She might actually be starting to believe it.

CHAPTER THIRTEEN

Gaitune-67, Spy Corps Headquarters and Base

Phina waited until lights out to get ready. Clothing, gear, and weapons situated, she pulled the hooded face mask of the specially-made bodysuit over her head. After taking a deep breath to settle her nerves, she left her room and walked soundlessly to Blayk's quarters.

She surveyed the corridor to make sure no one was taking an after-hours stroll before quietly entering the room.

Soft snores greeted her, and she relaxed. Phina walked past the strewn clothes and discarded food wrappers to the bedside of the detestable man, her body tense as her white-hot rage rose again.

He's going to get what's coming to him, she reminded herself as she grabbed Blayk's wrist and pressed the button on the device in her other hand.

Her dark surroundings faded into the familiar bright light of the *Stark.* Blayk fell roughly to the floor, which startled him awake.

Phina stepped back, put her hands on her hips, and observed him as he got to his feet, cursing unimaginatively.

Link walked into the mostly empty room that had been designated as her translocation landing area on the ship.

Blayk caught sight of him and froze. "Alpha Agent Wells?"

Her mentor shot him a withering glance of disgust. "Bring him," he ground out before spinning to depart.

Blayk turned, chagrined that he hadn't noticed the presence of another person. He glanced at Phina, noting that she was female. He flashed a sly grin as he dusted himself off and shifted his stance to show himself off in his boxer briefs. "Hello. Care to share what's going on?"

Grimacing beneath her mask, Phina crossed the room at full speed and hit him open-handed on the side of the head. He staggered, and she grabbed his wrists as he struggled to regain his balance and twisted his arms behind his back.

"What the hell!" Blayk shouted between curses as she frog-marched him out the door and down the hall.

He struggled ineffectually. Her enhanced strength wouldn't help her against the Were and vampire populations, but against the unenhanced, she was abnormally strong.

"Where are you taking me?" Blayk demanded.

Phina ignored him.

They reached their destination, and she pushed him into the room and over to a specially designed chair that she hadn't known about before today. Forcing the man to sit despite his struggles, she strapped his wrists to the arms of the chair.

Link glared at Blayk with anger and disgust, then glanced at Phina and answered her unspoken question. "No, this is your show. You're the one with permission."

They both ignored Blayk's demands for answers.

Link sent a mental question. *Can you handle this, Phina? You've taken a life before, but this is different.*

Sending him a wave of love and affection, Phina nodded. *I think so, but before we do this, he needs to know that we know what he's done, and we have to give him an opportunity to admit he was wrong.*

You don't think he will be sorry. Link's dark-brown eyes stared at her solemnly.

Phina shook her head as she turned back to the scowling, arrogant man whose only regard was his own desires.

No, I don't think he will.

Link was proud of his adopted niece or younger sister or however the hell they defined their relationship.

She had no idea how rare a person she was.

Phina stood in front of the douche nozzle, every inch of her a lethal weapon. Not many people got to see the heart of gold inside. He felt privileged to be part of her life.

If only her parents were alive to see her now. His heart ached at his old friends' absence, but he locked it down. This night wasn't about their family.

It was about the piece of shit sitting in front of them, projecting confusion and not nearly enough fear.

Phina pulled off her mask to reveal dark hair that had

been braided back, eyes flashing with anger, and lips pressed together in determination.

Blayk opened his mouth in surprise and relief as he glanced at the two of them. "Phina? Alpha Agent Wells? What's going on?"

She stared at the man coldly. "Your hearing, death sentence, and funeral."

Blayk got angry. "What the hell? I haven't done anything!"

Phina hit his face with an open hand. "Liar." Her emotions were mostly contained, but a thread of rage throbbed through her accusation.

Link approved of her methods. Slaps stung or hurt like the dickens if applied with enough force but rarely broke anything.

Blayk shook his head as he recovered and scowled at Link. "Alpha Agent, you're just going to let her do this to me?"

Link crossed his arms, something he rarely did unless he was making a point—like now, when the point was that he was not going to take part in what was happening.

Phina allowed her disgust and anger to show. "We all know what you did."

The man struggled against his restraints. "I didn't do anything to deserve whatever this is!"

"Yasmine. Lacey. Diana. Cassie. Shaina. Not to mention three others whose names you didn't even bother to learn!"

Her voice rose with every name she spoke until she was yelling in his face, seething as the color drained from it.

"Last but definitely not least, your sister Payton."

Blayk started in surprise, a flush of anger replacing his shock. "No one could possibly know those names."

Phina cocked a hip and crossed her arms. "Obviously, I do."

He licked his lips nervously. "So, this is what...an intervention?" He glanced at his restraints and scowled. "No, you said something about a death sentence. What the fuck is that supposed to mean? All because of some stupid girls?"

Link knew that if Phina's eyes could turn red, they would be crimson right now and hot enough to burn the man.

"I just want to know one thing, you slimy piece of trash. Do you regret any of your actions with those girls?"

"Yes."

"*Liar!*" Phina hit him in the temple with a fist.

Link restrained his grunt of approval and made a mental note to add to Phina's instruction. He could see her doing well with interrogations.

Blayk mumbled curses as he yanked on the restraints, then snarled, "You're one tough bitch, aren't you? You can't beat me in a fair fight. You have to tie me down first!"

Tilting her head, she glanced at Link. He gave her a nod, pleased she wasn't so lost in her emotions that she overrode the plan without permission.

A smile played on her lips as her gaze bored into Blayk. "You think I'm scared of you, do you? Too afraid to fight you? Me, the weak little woman, and you, the big strong man? Think you'll knock me down and take what you want if only I let you out?"

Leaning forward against the restraints, Blayk sneered at

her. "I think you've been begging for it ever since you got here."

Link's jaw clenched in anger. Phina wasn't much better, though he applauded her effort to keep her face impassive as she stared at the dead man walking with disgust and pity. "No, Blayk. I wouldn't beg you for anything, let alone what *you* want from me."

Blayk began to spew his anger at her rejection but stopped when Phina lifted her hand and spoke calmly.

"Still, in your own arrogant and fumbling way, you have asked to fight for your life."

She raised an eyebrow at him. Blayk scowled at her, but he finally nodded.

"Fine." She lifted a shoulder like his life was a trivial matter. Link knew that couldn't be further from the truth. "You have one chance to defend yourself. If you win, you can go."

The worm's face sprouted a pleased grin. "Fine. Now let me out of this thing."

Phina set the man free, taking care to step back when he was released. The slimy twerp rubbed his wrists, then grinned and strutted in his drawers to the middle of the room as she directed him.

Blayk gave her a cocky grin as he settled into a ready stance. "Let's get to it, bitch. I've got people to report this little escapade to. When I'm done with you, you'll be begging me to fix it for you."

Amused by the man's arrogance, Link leaned against the wall to watch. Oh, he was angry and disgusted as he listened to the drivel this walking dead man spouted, but he knew he didn't need to worry about a complaint.

No matter how skilled Blayk thought he was, Phina would destroy him. He would spit on the man's broken body as he lay mortified at being bested by a woman.

That, to Link's mind, was only step one of the Justice this asshole deserved.

On the one hand, Phina couldn't believe Blayk had no remorse for abusing those women. On the other, having been in his mind, she knew exactly how he justified his deplorable behavior to himself. It didn't matter, though; his actions could never be absolved.

As he stood in the center of the room, he gloated about the connections he'd used and abused to accomplish his depravity, which caused her emotions to surge. That hadn't happened before she'd admitted to loving Todd. Once she had, the floodgates had sprung open.

She didn't like to think about those days on the Qendrok's planet as Todd held her grieving body while she cried for the loss of her parents, the loss of the aunt she should have had, and the reasons she'd felt she needed to lock her emotions away. Not to mention the discovery that her aunt might have been controlled somehow, all the attacks she had survived, taking a life for the first time, let alone several, and how happy she was now with Todd in her life. The surge of conflicting emotions had been over-whelming. Those hours with Todd had been precious but uncomfortable for her. It was the first time she had allowed herself to be vulnerable.

Since then, she had not been able to put the lid back on

her emotions. She had finally asked Link to teach her how to keep her face impassive while her emotions surged within her.

Phina had never tested this new practice more severely than she did now. Her emotions urged retribution. Her body begged for a fight. Her mind implored her to maintain her reason and for him to be shown the error of his ways. Her sense of Justice required he acknowledge the wrongness of his actions. Her duty required his death.

Her will focused on satisfying all of those things.

"I'm afraid, Blayk, that you are mistaken," Phina responded regarding his absurd fantasy as she stepped forward. "You will not win this fight. You will not be teaching me anything. And as for authority?" She leaned forward and hissed, "I have the highest."

Confusion spread across his face, then he scoffed. "You can't really think I'll believe the Empress knows anything about me or that you've contacted her about this."

Phina walked around Blayk in a circle, leaving a few feet in between them. His eyes tracked her, though only his head moved. "I really don't expect you to believe anything I say, Blayk. You don't respect me. You don't respect women. You don't respect those you deem subpar or subordinate. You certainly don't respect family." Her lip curled in disgust as she recalled his memories involving his sister. "You barely respect your superiors, even when they are men."

She came to a stop and turned to him, her face impassive, attempting to convey that he was inconsequential. Given his tense body, she'd probably succeeded. "The only thing you respect is force and power."

Phina opened her arms wide with her palms up. "So fight me. If you win, you've got your freedom and the force and power you think you deserve. Lose, and you will die a broken man in agonizing pain."

Blayk hesitated to attack, so Phina knew her impassive indifference had worked. She wasn't scared. She wasn't angry, not that he could see. She didn't stand in front of him cowering, trembling, or shaking like most of his victims had once he'd shown his true colors.

He didn't know how to respond to her or why she seemed so confident and didn't care that he could hurt her.

Finally, she shrugged and put her arms down. "I guess *you're* the stupid bitch."

The phrase he'd so often used on his victims galvanized him into action. Blayk surged forward, his form powerful and strong.

Phina calmly stepped out of the way.

He swung again. Step. Again. Dodge.

For a full minute, Phina kept out of his way with the barest of movements, though she sometimes utilized her enhanced speed.

He paused for a breather, sweat dripping off his face. He was flush with anger and embarrassment, and he growled, "Why aren't you fighting me?"

Phina, feigning surprise, shrugged. She wasn't winded or sweating. "I didn't realize you were in such a hurry to be in agonizing pain. That's an easy fix."

Blayk shook off the confusion that had returned to his face. Rather than avoid his attack, she stepped forward, leading with her fist.

The force of the impact caused him to stagger back, his

arms windmilling. She saw Blayk's shock turn to rage. His semi-attractive features became cruel and unattractive with all the spite and anger he felt. "You stupid bitch!"

"Ah." Phina smiled in satisfaction. "There you are."

He screamed in rage and surged forward to attack in a frenzy.

Dropping all pretense of aloofness, she finally let herself go and broke first his face and then every joint in his body. He continued to attack with self-righteous anger and the desire to win as she worked, but after a while, he panicked. Blayk could still fight, but each joint she broke brought him more pain with every movement.

With each joint she broke, Phina spoke to him about his victims, using the information she had gathered from his mind as well as what Shade had found for her. With every impact, she described the consequences of his actions.

Yasmine had been the first, a seasonal girlfriend during a family vacation as a teenager. "You left her bruised and ashamed," she told him as she broke his wrist, ignoring his pained screech. "She spent years in therapy before she got past what you did to her so she could move on."

Lacey had been second, a hookup at a resort on another family trip. "You thought you got away with it by not giving her your real name, you scuzzbag." Phina broke his opposite elbow when he tried to hit her in the throat. "No thanks to you, she's happily married to another man and raising your child."

Diana. Cassie. Shaina. Women he had raped and physically abused. Diana and Cassie had gone on to have troubled but somewhat normal lives, although they had remained single. "Shaina wasn't so lucky, was she?" Phina seethed as she broke his knee while he spewed obscenities. "She committed suicide within a year after you left her broken, you coward!"

Blayk staggered on his good leg, arms held close to him as if to keep them away from her. Blood dripped from cuts on his face. He opened his mouth to speak, but she continued discussing his victims.

"The women whose names you didn't bother to learn, you treated even worse." She broke three joints in quick succession, her face set in determination. "With the wounds you gave them, at least one if not more died when you left them bleeding and broken on the street."

"They were whores!" he screamed as she shattered the second ankle. "They were just trash!"

She let go of him, and he fell to the floor with a scream.

"Why are you doing this to me?" He writhed in pain. "I have assets! I'll give you lots of money if you let me go!"

Phina scowled at him in disgust. "That was exactly how you responded whenever anyone caught on to what you were doing, wasn't it? Just throw money at them, bribe them to keep their mouth shut." She let a glimpse of her anger show. "I don't want your money."

"My family will come after you," he snarled before turning his head toward Link, who had remained by the door the whole time. "Both of you! You won't get away with this!"

Link chuckled darkly as he shook his head. "Boy, you are delusional. Your family is going to encounter their own set of consequences for looking the other way."

Phina broke in. "Speaking of your family." Blayk's face

jerked back to her. "We haven't talked about your sister Payton yet."

He swallowed roughly but stared at her in rage. She raised an eyebrow disdainfully. "Were you hoping I would forget? Ignore that you molested and eventually raped your sister, who you were supposed to love and protect?"

The depth of her fury must have leaked through since Blayk hoarsely began to beg. "Please, have mercy. I'll do whatever you want!"

"Did you have mercy when all those women you left bleeding and broken begged for it?" Phina knew the answer to that. Leaning forward, she spoke gently. "Let me ask you again. Do you regret your actions?"

Blayk's gaze swirled with emotion as he nodded and whispered, "Yes."

"Lie. You only care that you got caught."

Phina grabbed his ankle with both hands and swung the shrieking man around to gain momentum before she let go. He flew several meters before crashing into the wall. She gauged several bones to be broken, perhaps his ribs and back. He certainly didn't try to get up, just laid twitching on the floor.

Although she walked over calmly, Phina had to exert a fair amount of effort to control herself. She'd beaten the man to a bloody pulp. It was time for Justice to be served.

She bent over, placing her hands above her knees. "Well? Are you ready to fight some more?"

"Bitch," he wheezed, his self-righteous anger not dimming one iota.

She shook her head, feigning sadness. "You still don't get it, do you? I don't know what made you turn out this way—whether it was your mom alternatively spoiling and neglecting you, your father's weak-willed leniency, or if you were born bad."

She shrugged casually. "And you know what? I don't care. It doesn't matter what your background was or how people treated you. It doesn't matter if you grew up spoiled and rich or dirt-poor. What matters are your actions—what you do—and those, you weak, deluded little man, have been unconscionable, reprehensible, and heartbreaking."

Blayk stared at her in angry confusion. "How do you know about my parents...or any of this?"

"Oh." Phina straightened and put her hands on her hips, smirking. "You haven't figured it out?"

She waved a hand, and Blayk was painfully rolled over to the chair by Phina's rudimentary telekinesis. But then, she wasn't concerned about any further injuries that might result from her lack of ability and control.

Ignoring his cries, Phina glanced at Link, who watched Blayk with distaste. When the bleeding and broken man reached the base of the chair, her mentor glanced at her and gave her a warm smile of encouragement. She breathed a sigh of relief, and her stomach unclenched.

Phina grabbed Blayk under the arms, not worrying about the pain she caused, though he whimpered and cried out.

After strapping him back in, she stepped in front of the man and leaned forward to stare into his hate-filled eyes. "I read minds."

She ignored the panic on his face as she straightened and slapped her palm on his forehead.

Blayk screamed as Phina lifted him into the chair and restrained him again, not that he could do anything if he were free. The bitch hadn't been lying when she'd told him he would end up bleeding and broken. He couldn't even twitch without pain shooting through his body.

She leaned over and whispered, "I can read minds."

He had barely begun to process the enormity of that statement before her hand hit his forehead.

Memory after memory of the women and girls he had taken and discarded flooded through the forefront of his brain. Instead of the rage, disdain, triumph, and indifference he had felt during those moments, pain, fear, anguish, and shame coursed through him. The emotions were foreign but overrode everything else.

Blayk felt slight pressure around his head like a helmet had been put on, but all he could see were the familiar yet strange memories.

Whispered words overpowered the screams and cries to stop, to be let go that rang in his head. Phina's words. "You will spend whatever is left of your life spinning among the stars, faced with your own cruelty. Perhaps before you meet your end, you will finally feel some remorse."

Moments and an eternity later, he was hurled through the air. But it wasn't air, he realized. It was space, just like she had said.

Phina had told him what she was going to do at the beginning, and she'd backed it up. How was he supposed to have known the bitch was that fast or strong?

Shit. She had called him a liar, but she hadn't lied to him once that he could tell. Did that mean the Empress had sanctioned his death after all?

After another eternity, when he was so dehydrated he could barely breathe, let alone talk, so cold he couldn't feel his body, and he'd heard his victims' screams looping for so long that he couldn't hear anything else, something in his mind cracked.

Just before he breathed his last, Blayk felt a pang of regret.

CHAPTER FOURTEEN

Etheric Empire, Sark System, Deep Space
Link stood with Phina as Blayk hurtled through space. He couldn't help glancing at her. She sighed, and he couldn't remain silent anymore.

"Are you all right?"

She leaned against his shoulder and put an arm around his waist as she continued to look out onto the vastness of space. Blayk's pitiful form had been swallowed by the blackness. Recognizing the gesture as a silent request for comfort, Link put his arm around her and pulled her close.

"I will be," she whispered.

He gently rubbed her shoulder where his hand rested. "What are you thinking about?"

After a few moments of silence, she confused him with something seemingly unrelated. "You know that show you like to watch about working in the White House on Earth?"

"Yeah?"

"Whenever they're asked to do something by their

commander in chief, even if it's something they don't agree with, they always say that one phrase."

"'I serve at the pleasure of the President.'"

"That's the one." Phina nodded, her gaze still on the stars. "They say it proudly, they say it with love, and they say it with determination. But you know what they don't say enough?"

"What?"

"How freaking hard it is."

Link's mouth twitched in amusement before the implication hit him, then he grew concerned. "Do you regret it? Do you wish she hadn't told you to take care of it?"

Phina's features tightened, and her body tensed beneath his arm. "That's the thing, Link. Swap a word, and it's the Empress that phrase could be referring to. It's not a light matter to be tasked with an objective by the Empress, especially someone's death, or enacting her Justice for those who have been wronged. It's a heavy weight." She shook her head as she worked her thoughts out. "It's not just someone's death then; it's giving that death the meaning it deserves, the Justice that's demanded."

She paused and swallowed hard before continuing. "If given another task by the Empress, would I proudly serve with love and determination? Would I carry that heavy weight again?"

The silence between them grew as her emotions flickered across her face. Finally, she turned her bright, fierce eyes toward him and nodded.

"I would, Link. I would do it again without a drop of regret."

Tears misted his vision, but he held onto them. "It's 'an

ounce of regret.'"

"Oh, shush, you." Phina rolled her eyes and shook her head. Her lips pulled to the side. "You really can't help yourself, can you?"

"No." He gave her a lopsided grin. "You know what else I can't help?"

She arched a brow, silently telling him to get on with it. He smirked, but then his face turned serious. "I can't help feeling proud as hell of you, Phina."

Her face softened and brightened, and she gave him a huge hug. "Thank you, Link. I couldn't have done it without your help and support."

"Always, my dear. Always."

He held onto her as he turned his face to the emptiness of space again.

She's almost there, my old friends. She'll be that light in the darkness you always wanted her to be.

Gaitune-67, Spy Corps Headquarters and Base, Phina's Room

Phina propped her tablet on her legs. She reached out with a finger, then paused, hesitating.

Sundancer's head nudged her arm. *Do it. It will be just fine.*

She moved her hand to pet down his head and back. "You're sure?"

As certain as I am that fish and liver are delicious.

"Somehow, that doesn't reassure me."

He sighed and nudged her again. *Just get it over with. If the worst happens, at least you'll know.*

Agreeing with his wise advice, she checked the connection was secure and pushed the button to connect.

Within a few moments, Todd's handsome face popped up. "Hey, Kitten."

Phina burst into tears. She heard Todd's voice urgently asking her what was wrong. Waving a hand, she tried to get the crying under control, but it took a few minutes.

"I'm sorry, I'm sorry. I didn't want to cry. I wasn't going to." She wiped the tears from her face, although it was difficult since they were still flowing. "But when I saw you, I couldn't help it."

Sundancer brought her a tissue, which helped. After getting herself under control, she glanced at the screen to see Todd looking concerned.

"It's all right, Phina. I'm not going to get upset if you cry because you miss me," he reassured her. She grimaced, and his gaze turned quizzical. "Or did something happen? Are you all right?"

While she used more of the tissues that Sundancer had brought over, she explained everything that had happened since she got to the base and what had occurred with Blayk.

Todd listened without interruption, although she could see that he had conflicting emotions about her retelling. "I see. I'm angry that you had to deal with that fucktard, but I'm proud that the Empress entrusted this task to you. I *am* concerned because you're crying. Is it a release of emotional build-up, like before?"

She nodded and wiped a few stray tears away with a knuckle. "It's mostly that. I had to keep all my emotions inside while we handled it. It was a lot, Todd. I've never felt that much rage and fear and anguish before, even with my aunt. When I saw your face, I felt so relieved it was over, and I felt safe. I realized how much I missed you, and it all came gushing out."

Todd straightened in his seat, his concern coming clearly through the screen. "I understand the rage and anguish over the girls he abused, but why the fear?"

She looked down and didn't answer.

"Phina?"

Sundancer put his paws on her legs, tilting his head to nudge her again. *Tell him.*

"Because he intended me to be next," she whispered, picking up Sundancer to wrap her arms around him. "I saw it in his head, along with everything he had already begun to visualize about doing to me."

She heard a noise she couldn't interpret from Todd and decided to keep going and get it all out, hugging Sundance to her. Normally he would tell her it was undignified to be handled like that, but this time he rubbed his head against her chest in comfort.

"I had to make it about all of the women and girls he had abused. It couldn't be about me." She shook her head, realizing she was losing the battle with her tears again. "It wouldn't have been right. Once I saw what he wanted to do to me in his head, I knew it couldn't have been the first time, so I searched deeper and found them all. They have their Justice, and I'm completely satisfied that it was done correctly."

She grabbed another tissue and wiped her face again. "But all those images are in my head, and I can't get them out. I wasn't one of them, but I still feel violated. I knew I wouldn't ever let that happen to me and I was strong enough to fight him if he ever tried, but that doesn't help me unsee any of it."

Phina grabbed yet another tissue and waved it in frustration as her vision blurred. "And I'm still crying and can't seem to stop."

"Oh, sweetheart. Kitten, look at me."

She saw Todd wipe away a few tears of his own as he held a hand up to the camera. "You are strong, and I'm so proud of you. I wish I could be there to hold you, baby. To comfort you and help you carry this."

Phina gave him a watery smile and held up her hand. "You already are. And getting rather prolific with the pet names, too."

Todd chuckled. "They just spilled out. Do you mind?"

She shook her head and gestured with her fingers. "No, carry on."

He outright laughed, and his smile grew wider. "Good to know."

A cough came from Sundancer. "Not to interrupt, but Phina, I can show you how to move the unwanted memories you glean from others to the back of your mind. They will still be accessible if you need them, but not as fresh and immediate."

Phina gaped in amazement as she glanced between Sundancer and Todd, who gave the cat-shaped alien a nod of approval.

She hugged Sundancer close and whispered, "Thank you. Thank you so much. That would be incredibly helpful."

He gave a quiet yowl. "All right, all right. No need to

maul me."

Relaxing her arms, she glanced up to see Todd smiling with affection.

"Do it now, Phina," he urged. "That way, it's done, and I don't need to worry as much about you."

She nodded when Sundancer agreed. Several minutes later, the memories had been moved. It made a huge difference to her peace of mind and emotional state.

"Better?" Todd asked.

She nodded, her shoulders dropping with relief. "So much better!"

He gave her a strange smile that concerned her until he spoke.

"I was going to wait until you came back to tell you this, but I can't wait that long. I love you, Phina." The warmth in his gaze was evident.

"Oh! I love you too." She smiled but felt a prickle of tears. She waved her hands again before grabbing another tissue to wipe her face. "Fudge in a bucket. Why can't I stop crying? I just want to feel happy right now!"

Todd grinned sympathetically and shook his head. "It's all right, Kitten. Those are happy tears."

"Well, they can get a fudging memo!" Phina exclaimed. "Only happy feelings when I tell you I love you."

They chuckled and turned the conversation to how and what they've been doing since she'd left. Phina was amazed all over again that this incredible, handsome man loved her and was in her life.

She had only happy feelings when she told Todd she loved him again before they signed off.

I told you it would turn out fine.

Yes, yes, Sundancer. You're so smart.

See, you say it, but I'm not feeling your sincerity.

She curled up around him on the bed and gazed seriously into his eyes. "Thank you, Sundancer. Thank you for encouraging me earlier. Thank you for showing me how to move the memories in my mind, and thank you especially for coming all this way to find me after you left Previdia."

He rubbed his pink nose under her chin. *You're welcome. I'm happy you now understand how to worship me properly.*

Phina burst out laughing, her tears forgotten.

Gaitune-67, Spy Corps Headquarters and Base, Dining Room

Phina sat down at the table for dinner. She felt refreshed and happy after talking to Todd and Sundancer and taking a shower. She had used the time to sort things out in her head and realized that she needed to get back into the game...or mission, rather.

She glanced around the room. The agents and trainees filled the space with whispers and conversations, the sound coalescing into the loud buzzing that predominantly occupies spaces with a lot of people talking at the same time. It always happened in restaurants and eating areas.

Figuring that now was as good a time as any, she opened the filter that would allow her to listen to people's surface thoughts and gave it some target words to listen for, almost like a programming script. Then she pushed it to one side of her mind and focused on the conversation around the table.

"I haven't seen him, have you?" Jasper asked Cade.

"Not since yesterday." The man shrugged without concern as he dug into his meal.

Savas leaned forward with a frown. "I haven't seen him, either. Was he sent home like Greg?"

"Nah, he's too good," Ian argued before stuffing his mouth with a forkful of food.

Kabaka searched the dining hall before shaking his head. "He's not in the room."

"It was everyone's day off today. Maybe he's just hiding out for some alone time?" Phina offered, feigning casualness.

Jahlek shook his head. "That one is too social. He's always with people."

"Hey, Agent Shaw!" Gina called.

Balehn groaned. "Gina! Don't get Sergeant Hardass' attention on our day off!"

The man in question turned toward their table, seeking the person who had called him. He steadied his food tray in his hands, balancing a heaping plate of food and a tall cup.

Nodin snickered and shook his head. "Too late, suckers."

Gina waved Shaw over, her expression growing nervous the closer the agent got to them.

"Yes?" He stood on the other side of the table. She gestured for Savas and Nodin to make room for him between them, but they stared at her like they didn't understand. Maybe they didn't, or perhaps they were purposely being obtuse so they didn't have to sit next to "Sergeant Hardass."

As Gina worked up the courage to ask the burning question, Phina scooted to the side, closer to the mostly silent Felan, and gestured for the agent to sit if he would like. She ignored the horror on Ian's face.

Shaw pulled a half-smile at the gesture, but it came off as more of a grimace. "Thank you, Phina, but I need a break from all of you just as much as you need a break from me." He shifted toward Gina. "I was going to address this tomorrow, but telling you now will give you time for the news to settle and not distract you from training."

The trainees turned in interest.

"Blayk isn't here any longer," Shaw announced. "It came to our attention that he had committed acts unbecoming to an agent of Spy Corps, let alone the Empire."

"What does that mean?" Cade demanded.

Shaw leveled a stare at the trainee. "It means he's dead."

Gasps sounded around the table. Phina remained silent, taking in all their reactions.

"What happened?" Ian whispered in shock.

Taking a deep breath, Shaw appeared a bit stiff, as if he wanted to be careful of his responses. "There's no need for you to know the details. Suffice it to say that the proper authorities instructed the alpha agent to take care of everything, and Blayk will not be coming back."

"Yeah, because he's dead," Jasper muttered angrily.

Shaw scrutinized the angry trainee. "Yes, for acts *unbecoming.* Which means you want no part of it. If I find out any of you were involved in his actions, you will suffer the same consequences."

He raked them all with a heavy glance, lingering a half-beat longer on Phina, before turning away to find his seat.

"Damn." Ian ran his fingers through his hair. "That sounds like Blayk did something really bad."

"What do you think it was?" Gina whispered, her face pale. "What does 'acts unbecoming' even mean?"

"Whatever it was, Agent Shaw made it clear we didn't need to speculate on it," Jahlek said quietly. "I'm going to take that advice." He stood and picked up his tray, walking away without a backward glance.

The trainees glanced anxiously around the table, then most of them quickly finished their last bites and left the dining room.

Phina and Felan were the last trainees left at the table. Phina ate her food, not hurrying in the slightest. The trainees' departure gave her the opportunity to catch surface thoughts from the agents. There were far too many agents talking about Blayk for her liking and an uncomfortable number thinking sex-related thoughts, but nothing about traitors, betrayal, sabotage, or other deceptive thoughts to be concerned about.

Felan finished his third plate of food and left with a nod. Phina watched him go as she chewed her last bite. She knew everything she needed to know about him from her scans, but in many ways, he was still an enigma. If she hadn't known his absolute loyalty to the Etheric Empire and the Empress, she would be monitoring him carefully for potential problems since he observed everything and kept it all close. Since she did, she couldn't help feeling grateful to have someone in their small group she could relate to.

As she gathered everything and left, Phina glanced around, disappointed that nothing had come up on her mental scans.

She had a lot more scanning to do to find this traitor.

CHAPTER FIFTEEN

Gaitune-67, Spy Corps Headquarters and Base, Training Room

The clash of steel echoed around Phina and Jack as they fought; swords, wrists, and feet whirling. Phina focused all her attention on Jack, his movement, and the angle of the blade coming toward her.

She had been training with hard composite practice blades since she'd begun learning weeks ago. This had been the first time Jack had allowed her to use the real thing, and she didn't want to accidentally hurt him or herself because she wasn't paying attention.

Since Phina also had to maintain near--human speed and reflexes, she had to be careful to let strikes almost get through but not quite so her abilities wouldn't become apparent.

Phina hadn't realized how frustrating it could be to hold herself back. She felt certain there was a lesson in there somewhere, but she didn't feel like finding it.

Jack had drilled her with the eight potential angles of

attack and their blocks over the past weeks until she felt like she could do them in her sleep. He didn't care that she had near-perfect recall and could mimic most things she saw. He told her at the beginning that she would follow his instructions exactly and not deviate from them.

In her head, she began to call him Captain Hardass to Shaw's Sergeant since he was even stricter than Shaw, which said something about both of them.

Not that she would ever explain it to their faces.

Jack brought his weapon up and around, then swung down as if to slice her shoulder. She guided the strike away and pushed as her sword slid along the other blade. She lifted her hands to complete the block and flicked her wrists to rest the tip at her teacher's neck.

She held her position as the beta agent realized his predicament. He nodded as he stepped back. "Very good." He studied her as she moved back to a guard position.

He moved to the side, put his sword down, and picked up two practice blades the length of short swords. "Instead of continuing on katanas when you are making great progress, why don't we begin working with dual swords?"

Phina's eyes lit up as she moved to the side to grab two practice blades and returned to the middle of the floor. She held them up, swinging them to get used to their weight. With her enhancements, she barely noticed the pull on her muscles so she could work with them for longer than others. However, the weight and balance would affect her swings and how comfortable she felt using them.

"Good." Jack nodded as he observed her movements. "The more familiar you are with them, the easier they will be. It's quite different than using knives and very different than using the katana. The strikes are a blend of both styles, but you have a greater reach than you would with knives."

He gestured for her to stop and pay attention as he settled into a forward stance. "Now watch the blades. The strike zones on the body are the same as with the katana. See how I strike only at the side from which the blade is held. Striking from the opposite side leaves your back open to attack. If you attack the right side with your left, your left shoulder and back are open." He demonstrated the move, then showed failed attempts to correct it. "Your right hand has no way to block, and you won't be able to withdraw your left blade in time. There are exceptions, but those are advanced moves, and you would only use them if you were fighting several opponents at once."

He gestured for her to copy him as he crossed the blades in front of his body. "This is the strongest block since you can use the strength of your whole body to withstand the strike. However, there are disadvantages to it. If your opponent is also fighting with two blades, they could easily slice you with the second while you are blocking the first." He moved his practice blades through the positions he mentioned, swinging one against her block and the other down and toward her thigh.

Phina nodded, taking each point and putting them together with other techniques she had learned. She could see how her fighting style would adjust in time.

"There are still patterns to the strikes and blocks that you make with the dual swords." He moved to demonstrate, their blades colliding at quarter speed. "Blocking your opponent's swords becomes a kind of dance." He sped up his movements, and Phina increased her speed to match him. "Dances are patterns, and so are sword movements. Adequate sword wielders know the patterns. Master sword wielders do not just master the patterns, but are able to use them to create new dances."

Jack pushed to full speed, and Phina's focus narrowed to following the movements of his blades. She kept up with him easily, keeping her responses within human parameters.

Sliding into that half meditative zone where she was aware of everything around her, Phina continued blocking Jack's blades and striking back. Just as she felt comfortable and was striking back with more frequency, he began moving his feet.

Phina's brain lit up with excitement and interest. She hadn't realized how complex fighting with two swords could be, but she found the exercise fun. Jack had said fighting with two swords was like a dance, and it was, but it was more than that. It was form and function, systemic and organic. It was sleek and graceful, powerful and beautiful.

Phina loved it.

She decided dual swords were her new favorite weapons and wondered how she would be able to carry them on her person with all her other weapons.

Her awareness zinged to the present and she barely caught a strike aimed at her face. Phina blocked it and stared at Jack.

Captain Hardass just raised his eyebrows. "Paying attention now?"

Opening her mouth to respond, Phina stopped when

she realized she would only come across as a petulant teenager if she complained. Pressing her lips together, she nodded, then reset herself into the guard position.

Jack glanced at the screen on the wall displaying the time. "Why don't we take a break."

Phina shook her head. "You don't need to stop the lesson on my account. I'm used to practicing for hours a day."

He squinted in surprise at her comment. "Hours without a break?"

She shrugged. "Sometimes. Other times we just took water breaks."

Only after he gazed at her in speculation did she grow anxious.

Fudging crumbs.

How did normal people deal with this stuff? She shook her head, knowing the spaceship to Normalville had left a long time ago. Most of the time, she was all right with that.

Still, Jack's reaction reignited her concern about showing how much skill she had and the training she'd had to get there.

Phina couldn't help wondering if she had made her biggest mistake in this investigation.

Gaitune-67, Spy Corps Headquarters and Base, Phina's Room

I'm telling you, Link, I've done surface scans on everyone over the last week. I've found nothing even though I've checked multiple times a day. The traitor doesn't seem to be any of the trainees or agents on the base.

All right. Let's think this through. Didn't you tell me that surface scans only let you know what they are thinking about at the current moment?

Phina sighed as she laid back on her bed. She had changed into her nightclothes and was ready to sleep. Before she rested, she had decided she had to report her progress.

Or lack thereof.

Now she regretted not waiting until the next day.

Yes, sort of. There are two levels of surface scan. One picks up general thoughts and can be done over a widespread crowd. Then there's going a step deeper. That gives a general assessment of a person's mental state, current thoughts, and general character. It requires going through everyone one by one. I've done both types over the last week. I'm feeling overwhelmed since I haven't done this many at once before.

Her head pounded. Sundancer had decided to take a stroll so he could be further away from her "mental emanations"—his words.

Are you going to be all right? Link inquired. *Do you need to stop the scans?*

Oh, no. I'll be okay, Link. I just need to rest. Scans use a lot of energy, and it's been a concerted effort to scan everyone. When I sleep, I'll be better connected to the Etheric so the energy can flow more easily. I'll be fine tomorrow.

Link's hesitation came through their mental connection. *You won't go back into a coma, will you?*

No! No, Link, I don't think that will happen again. I went into a coma because my brain needed to be completely reconfigured to effectively connect to the Etheric after massive depletion. You know, when I almost died.

Trust me, kid. I have not forgotten a single moment of that day.

Her throat tightened when she realized how much that event had affected the man. *Right. Well, my brain is all configured now. If it helps, think of how I feel now as a bruise or a strain from overuse. The connection is still there and functioning fine. There's no risk of falling into a coma.*

All right. If you're sure. Thanks for explaining. Now, what's your next step?

Phina sighed and shook her head. *The best next step would be deep scans. The best place to search first is in your neighborhood.*

She felt a responding sigh and pang of sorrow from him, but he didn't comment on it. *That makes sense. You eliminate those at the top first and don't worry about surface scans with them.*

Yup. The only problem is getting close enough.

You have a plan for that?

Of course, Phina replied confidently.

Link snorted and laughed. *Love the confidence, kid.*

She turned an eye roll into a glare, making sure to send it his way. It always annoyed the man and made her laugh. Mostly on the inside. Honestly, she didn't care if he knew she laughed at him.

Yeah, yeah. Goodnight, my dear. Let me know if there's anything I can do. It's damn frustrating not being able to help.

I will. Goodnight, Link. She sent a wave of affection to him before letting go of the connection.

Not able to help? Phina didn't agree with that assessment at all.

Some nights it felt like Link and Sundancer were the only ones keeping her sane.

Gaitune-67, Spy Corps Headquarters and Base, Upper Levels

Phina glided through the shadows of the base, exiting into the hangar bay and making her way up the stairs into the upper levels.

The lights had been set to nighttime minimal and the base was quiet, with almost everyone either sleeping or entertaining guests in their room.

Well, Phina paused as she recalled one room she had passed. That was one way to describe the passionate, lustful thoughts emanating from those inside.

She shook the memory off, needing to focus on the here and now. Shade had been brought into the plan, but there could still be people heading back to their rooms if they weren't staying the night.

Phina pushed the door open, revealing a short hallway with double doors in front and to the right. She bypassed the door to the mysterious operations room on the right and entered into the upper-level living space that only senior agents and trainers occupied.

Glancing around the large open area arranged as part-lounge, part-library, she passed through, then peered down the corridor to the left that led to the laundry and workout rooms. Phina listened for a moment, then walked up the stairs in the opposite direction.

Bypassing the offices and the conference room, she was silent until she reached the double doors of the living quarters. She quietly stepped through but paused when a dark symbol on the wall to her left caught her attention.

Phina peered closer in the dim light, wondering if she had been wrong. However, there was no mistaking the symbol of the Queen Bitch, a vampire silhouette with long hair.

She tapped it gently with a finger, reminding herself to bring it up with Link.

A small lounge opened in front of her, containing a few couches and comfortable chairs. To her left and right stretched the empty corridor that led to the rooms.

Having done her research, Phina knew where she needed to go.

Phina listened carefully as she inched along in the shadows of the corridor. Heading right, she stopped at the room at the end of the hall on the left and reached for the mind of Jack Kaiser.

Thankfully, the man was asleep. She gave him a nudge that would make him sleep deeply for several hours. Plenty of time for her to do her mental deep dive.

Easing herself in at first, she did the secondary scan that showed the basics about a person. Pride, a certain amount of arrogance, satisfaction in teaching others... There was little she found that surprised her except for a rather large streak of loyalty to Spy Corps, Link, and Bethany Anne.

Hmm... That alone considerably lessened the chance that Jack could be the traitor. She began the deeper scan, following the process Sundancer had taught her that allowed her to sift through a person's memories.

It hadn't taken her long to grasp the process. What had

taken many tries to perfect was the ability to make sense of the memories that she saw and sort through them to find what she needed without getting sucked in. For instance, she now knew everything there was to know about her next-door neighbor's fetish, knowledge she should get around to scrubbing out of her brain.

Sorting through Jack's memories proved to be an intriguing exercise. She hesitated when she discovered his memories of her parents. Phina felt drawn to them, but she reminded herself that it would be an indulgence and not pertinent to the investigation. She compromised by selecting the memories of her parents that Jack's mind deemed important and copied them into her mind without viewing them.

Moving on, she flipped through his memories, similarly to shuffling cards and watching them fall one by one. When she reached the memories of the last nine years, every so often she noticed a gray space, as if the memory was incomplete or had been erased. The timing between them was inconsistent, but it felt the same every time.

She tried poking at one of the gaps, but it felt like she was searching for a mirror with a blindfold on.

Huh. That was interesting and caused a good deal of speculation, but aside from those strange gray sections, she didn't find anything of concern.

Phina thought about what her findings meant as she withdrew. She shook her head and blinked, then reached for her tablet.

A gun appeared in her line of vision, causing her to freeze.

Fudgesicles.

I tried to warn you, Shade apologized. *You didn't hear me.*

Phina turned and saw it was Masha holding the gun, her eyebrows raised questioningly. She put her finger to her lips and waved the gun to direct Phina to walk.

Phina could have taken it from her, but she hoped that Masha putting her finger to her lips meant something good, like she wanted to go somewhere private to talk it out.

Then again, it could also mean she didn't want to have to carry Phina's body after she killed her.

Knowing she probably wouldn't die from a gunshot wound, except perhaps to her brain— a theory she didn't want to test for obvious reasons—convinced Phina to follow, and trust that Masha would at the least take her to Link since she was his recruit.

Unless Masha was the spy.

Fudging crumbs in a bucket. Please don't let Masha be the spy.

Phina wanted those sparks between Masha and Link to be real. Aside from that, she didn't want the traitor to be someone she liked.

"Stop right there," Masha told her in a low voice.

Very aware of the woman at her left shoulder, Phina stopped in front of the residence door, which Masha opened without lowering her weapon. The woman gestured for Phina to go in first.

Stepping in and to the side, Phina waited until the door was shut and the beta agent was standing in front of her with a hard glare and even harder tone.

"Now, take off that damn mask, Phina, and tell me what the hell you're doing up here."

Phina blinked in surprise before she remembered Masha was a Wechselbalg with a Were's keen sense of smell. She slowly raised her hands, then pushed her hooded mask over her head and let it fall behind her.

Masha had sounded confused, with an undertone of betrayal. Phina scanned the woman as deeply as she could without entering the trance state as she had earlier. It was a quick and dirty way of doing a deep scan, one that lingered in Phina's head afterward.

Shaking her head, Masha pressed her lips together before speaking. "Tell me right now what's going on, or I'm taking this to Greyson."

Hah! The woman even called him by his first name, Phina thought happily, then grew sad when she realized Masha had used his cover name.

Spies had to have such careful lives.

Thankfully, Phina's scan told her what she needed to know. She pushed everything she had seen in Masha's head together and relegated it to that back part of her consciousness that Sundancer had shown her.

She pinged Shade. *I suppose you can see I've hit a snag.*

It's apparent.

Yes. Would you mind telling me if there's anyone in the facility near us or anyone who is listening or watching?

Of course not. I would have notified you.

I apologize for doubting.

Your apology isn't necessary.

Phina focused on Masha. "I'm running a top-secret mission."

The woman appeared nonplussed, a word Phina hadn't thought she would ever use, but it fit the bewildered astonishment that crossed Masha's face. "Here? On the base?"

"Yes."

After shaking her head, the beta agent moved over to her couch. Masha placed her gun down next to her and gestured Phina to a chair. "What code?"

Phina gingerly sat down and inwardly sighed. "Black."

The woman's eyebrows rose. "You can't be serious."

"Deadly. If I didn't know I could trust you, I wouldn't be telling you this. Only two other people know, and one of them is the Empress."

Masha scoffed. "How do I know I can trust you?"

She shrugged and suggested. "You can notify the boss man and ask him if he trusts me, but you might want to wait until tomorrow."

The woman froze for a second. "Greyson is the other person who knows?"

Phina nodded solemnly, reading concern, confusion, and the pang of hurt in the other woman's face. "Yes. We decided those in the know needed to be a small number."

"Without notifying even his beta agents?" Masha snapped, pain and anger making her tone harsh.

Leaning forward, Phina rested her elbows on her knees and got close enough to whisper and be heard. "When dealing with unknown traitors to the Empire within your organization, what would you do?"

CHAPTER SIXTEEN

Gaitune-67, Spy Corps Headquarters and Base, Upper Levels

Surprise and horror crossed Masha's face. "I would trust no one and investigate everyone."

"Exactly."

The beta agent sighed, deflating. "I understand."

"You should tell him how you feel, you know," Phina ventured gently.

"How... Tell who what?"

Phina bit back a grin at having caused the longtime agent to become so flustered. She reached out and squeezed the other woman's hand. "I've seen the way you look at each other, and I've known him long enough to know what he's thinking."

The woman sat frozen in surprise before frowning. "It wouldn't work with our positions."

After a final squeeze, Phina straightened and gave her a kind smile. "Of course. It's your decision if you ever do approach the subject. But I think you both deserve happiness, and nothing says that you can't restructure things around here."

Masha's lips tilted down. "It's a thought. I'm not sure it would work."

"That's because you are only using your own perspective," Phina told her. "You and Greyson need to work together on it. Perhaps with Jack since he's part of the leadership here?"

Masha stared at Phina with barely repressed hope before sighing and rubbing her forehead. "That's assuming something even happens to make it necessary. I'm not convinced he cares about me. He's never shown any sort of partiality."

Phina gave her a sharp glance as she straightened. "You're a smart woman, Masha. I think you've just been afraid to see it. It's there. He just doesn't do overt displays of affection when he isn't sure he's wanted since he always assumes he isn't. Also, with his position, if he shows partiality, he can be accused of favoritism. If he shows interest, it can be construed as sexual harassment." She offered her a rueful smile. "Puts him in a tight spot, right?"

Masha frowned. "I hadn't thought about that. I suppose I have been waiting for him to approach me if he was interested."

"Perhaps this might be a good time to exercise that female empowerment thing?" Masha appeared confused, so Phina clarified. "Where the woman asks the man. Alina was always telling me it's a thing."

Masha winced. "Yeah, that's hard for me. Opening myself up to rejection, ridicule, or being fired? I'll have to think about it."

Nodding, Phina leaned back and crossed her ankles. "I understand. I couldn't do it either. In this case, it might be your only option."

After another sigh, Masha nodded seriously. "I'll think about it. Have you..." She hesitated. "Did you ever think of Greyson that way?"

Phina made a face as she shook her head. "What, romantically? Oh, no. I love the man, but the way you would your older brother, or your uncle, or a surrogate father. We had to act as if we were on a date one night and it just felt wrong, like we're meant to be family."

She didn't miss the relief that crossed Masha's face as she nodded in understanding. "I get it. I just had to ask."

"Because we've been spending a lot of time together, seem close in some ways, and protective of each other?" Phina monitored her closely. "Or because I'm the first woman he's taken on as a personal recruit since you, and you know how drawn you were to him?"

Masha cleared her throat in surprise, then nodded, smiling with amusement mixed with embarrassment. "Yes. All of that."

Phina scratched the back of her neck as she tried to figure out what to say. She settled on a shrug. "You've got far more in common with him than I do, and your personality is a better blend with his. I understand him because I *was* him. We are very similar in how we respond to things due to our backgrounds." She grimaced. "That's also why we tend to bump heads. We both respond out of fear and a desire to protect the people we love and care about, even if it's not the best decision. Trust me. Even if I was interested and available, which

I'm not, we would not be good for each other. He needs someone like you."

Masha stared in astonishment. "You really believe that?"

Phina nodded and stood, grasping Masha's shoulder when she followed. "I do. He's my family, and he deserves love and a family of his own. I think it could be you, but I'll let you guys figure that out. Just...don't give him hints. He's not a hint kind of person. You have to be blunt so he knows you are serious."

Masha appeared to be overwhelmed. Phina gave the woman's shoulder another squeeze before heading for the door.

"Phina?"

She turned and saw that the beta agent's confidence had returned and stood with her arms crossed.

"I'm taking what you told me on trust," Masha told her, "but there's a reason for that. I'm going to check on your story. If I find that any of what you said was a lie, I'm going to come down on you hard."

Phina flashed a grin. "I'm counting on it. Talk to the boss. Just make sure he's in his office when you do."

"I will." She nodded. As Phina went to leave, she added, "And Phina?"

She turned back to the older woman as she reached up to pull the mask down. "Yes?"

Masha smiled, and one eyebrow rose. "Try not to get caught."

Phina gave her a cheeky salute before pulling the mask down over her face. Within moments she was gone.

Again, the dedicated and devoted man came into the presence of his Empress, the woman who had saved his soul.

"Report, my loyal subject."

"Yes, my Empress. Trainee Waters has been learning quickly and well." He told her everything he had observed since the last time his Empress had come.

After considering everything the man had told her, the Empress gave him a sharp glance. "Are you certain of everything you have described to me? There were no exaggerations?"

"No, my Empress. Everything is as accurate as my words can express."

She stared at him for some time before finally nodding. "I understand."

He bowed his head in relief. "Thank you, my Empress."

"Continue to observe, but I need you to do one more thing for me."

He turned his face up eagerly. "Name it, my Empress."

A smile graced her lips before they pressed together. "We have traitors in our house. You will kill Phina for me."

"What?" He straightened in surprise. "Why would I kill her?"

Her eyes narrowed dangerously. "Are you questioning my orders?"

He swallowed roughly but shook his head. "No, my Empress. I just don't understand why she needs to die. I think she is an asset to the Empire."

The woman blinked in annoyance at the devoted man. "She is not who you think she is. She's a traitor and a liar. If she finds out that you are loyal to me, she will kill you. I am certain she plans to kill or overthrow me."

His jaw tightened at the news, then he nodded. "As you command, my Empress. It will be done."

"Do not reveal yourself, my loyal subject. Greyson Wells will turn on you, not understanding the situation, and I still need him. Work through others to achieve your goal."

"You are wise, my Empress." He bowed his head. "I will complete this task for you for the good of the Etheric Empire."

"That is all I ask," she replied, her eyes gleaming with satisfaction.

Gaitune-67, Spy Corps Headquarters and Base, Phina's Room

Phina paused while removing her thermal bodysuit, her gaze darting around the room. Seeing nothing out of the ordinary yet sensing something, she continued removing her clothing as she reached out mentally.

She had just finished tugging off the last leg when Sundancer streaked into the room. He jerked to a halt, a strange expression of horror on his feline face.

Phina! he yowled as he jumped onto the bed and dived under the blankets. *Put some clothes on over your hideous body. I must protest over your cavalier manners.*

"Yes, it's a shame I took off my clothes in my own bedroom when I was completely alone." She sighed as she pulled out comfortable sleepwear to put on. "I don't know what I was thinking."

You probably weren't. It's a common problem with you humans, as well as a general lack of respect and decency. He sniffed.

Phina sent him the equivalent of a mental glare as she finished by pulling her shorts up and tugging her shirt down over them. "It's my room, my privacy, and my body."

A hideous body with no wrinkles or tail. The mound on the bed wobbled with the force of his shivers of revulsion.

She shook her head, stepping over to poke the Previdian with her finger through the blanket. "It's a good thing I have a relatively decent body image and a boyfriend I believe when he tells me I'm beautiful, or I could begin to develop a complex."

Ow, ow, ow! Careful with your hands on the merchandise, woman. He scrambled out of the blankets to glare at Phina.

She cocked a hip as she raised an eyebrow. "Just how many hours have you been spending watching movies when you said you were searching for our traitor?"

He froze, then nonchalantly glanced around, avoiding her gaze. *I don't know what you're talking about.*

Phina peered at him skeptically. "Uh-huh. Sure you don't." Deciding to drop the subject for now, she moved on. "So, what were you running in here all fired up about?"

Sundancer straightened up in alarm. *I felt Etheric energy being used.*

"I thought I felt something, too." She frowned and put her hands on her hips as she mentally probed for Etheric energy. "You're sure it wasn't me you noticed?"

He gave her a scathing glare. *I know my charge's energy, thank you. I'm not a half-century old.*

"You act like an old curmudgeon," Phina murmured, continuing her scans.

She frowned and brought up the mental grid she used to understand what she sensed within the Etheric. When no activity existed, the lines remained square and straight. Sometimes Phina was able to tell who it was that shifted the energy, but she was still learning all the nuances.

She saw some lines had been pulled, and others were warped. The Etheric wasn't active anymore, but *someone* had been using it.

The signature wasn't hers.

Gaitune-67, Spy Corps Headquarters and Base, Greyson Wells' Office

Masha pushed the alert for the door, letting Greyson know someone wanted to come in.

She heard him sigh and approve the entry.

Greyson glanced up as she stepped in, the face she had come to know and love utterly serious. "Come in, Masha. Have a seat."

She swallowed as she took the chair opposite his desk, feeling nervous. Much to her relief, she didn't have to figure out how to broach the first topic on her mind.

He leaned forward with his arms on the desk. "Phina told me she had a chat with you."

She searched his face for any sign that Phina was right about his having feelings for her. Her heart sank when she didn't find what she hoped. Forcing herself to continue, she pushed those feelings aside—for now.

"Yes, she told me you both had come searching for a traitor?" She spoke crisply, clearly, and confidently.

"That is what our intel leads us to believe." He nodded sharply. "Do you have any questions?"

Masha grimaced. She had so many questions. She would just have to narrow them down. "Where did the intel come from, and how credible is it? Does the Empress really know about this and approve? Why is Phina doing the bulk of the work on this? Do you have any leads?"

Greyson waited for her to finish. "All right. Finished now?"

She pursed her lips as she tilted her head to the side in thought. "No, there's more. What was Phina doing in the corridor outside our rooms last night? Does this have anything to do with what happened to Blayk? How did she know she could trust me with this when you hadn't decided to trust me before now? Speaking of which, why wasn't I told about this?"

He raised his eyebrows in surprise but nodded in approval. "Those are the right questions to ask. Here's what we know."

Greyson launched into a tale that could have come out of a novel. Alien assassins, secrets, and treason? The idea boggled her mind.

"As for what Phina was doing last night... Well, that rolls into how she knows we can trust you not to be the traitor." He peered at her seriously, clasping his hands together. "I won't share everything since those are her secrets. However, what is relevant here, and what you won't talk about outside this room, is that she can see into other people's minds."

"What?" Masha's mouth fell open as she struggled to put her thoughts into words. "Seriously?"

Greyson nodded. "As a gas attack."

She wrinkled her nose, then froze in shock. "Wait a second. She read my mind."

"Yes."

"So she saw..." Masha stopped before she said something embarrassing.

He lifted a shoulder and sat back with a smirk. Stars, Phina hadn't been kidding when she'd said they were too much alike.

Greyson's voice held a thread of amusement. "She saw whatever was in your head at the time and your recent memory. Possibly more. I don't ask her about that."

Masha evaluated him. "So, she doesn't tell you what she picks up?"

The amusement fell from his face as he leaned forward. "There are only three mind readers in the Empire that we know of, and Phina is one of them. She's talked to the Empress about this, as far as where to draw the lines and what is ethical for her to do. She's struggled with it a lot, believe me. She doesn't read minds lightly, and frankly, she's not entirely comfortable with her ability to do so."

She frowned at him, concern and confusion swirling inside. "Why are you telling me this? Just to ease my mind?"

He straightened, and his face dropped most of its emotion. That pang in her heart turned to an ache that concern for her probably wasn't on his mind. Phina must have been wrong to think anything else.

"I'm telling you this so you understand that if you want

anyone to know your secrets, Phina is the best person. She wouldn't share them unless she had a very good reason to do so." He sighed with exasperation. "Between her mind-reading and hacking skills, she knows practically every secret in our whole government, except those only the Empress knows. She could have some of those, too."

"She doesn't talk about any of it with you or her friends?" Masha asked curiously. She had seen how close they were during the events around the wedding.

Greyson shook his head. "She may act on what she knows, but she's not likely to share it. Phina blocks everyone out when she doesn't need to know something, anyway. It's not like she actively tries to pick up every single thought. From what I can tell, it can be difficult to make the effort to block it all out and would be much easier if she just let herself listen."

Masha sat lost in thought for a moment before nodding. "Thank you for telling me, even though your purpose was to explain and not ease my mind."

She studied the man she tried not to care so much about as he stifled a chuckle. Staring seemed to be the only thing she was currently capable of.

"Of course," Greyson answered, only a hint of his amusement coming out.

Masha decided to change the subject. "Is there anything I can do to help?"

He nodded. "Now that you know a traitor exists or is highly likely to, you can keep your senses open. You know what to search for. See if anything pops up."

Masha tried not to feel irritated. She was capable of a lot more than had been expected of her. She had grown tired of always proving herself to Jack and wanted Greyson to take her abilities into account so she could do more. She opened her mouth to demand to have a bigger role to play but stopped. Phina had said *she* was running the investigation.

Masha contemplated Greyson. So, the man didn't seem to be interested in her. That was fine. She had lived as she had been long enough. But, she would be damned if she sat around waiting for others to do the job. That wasn't who she was or how she wanted to be.

Masha surprised Greyson by nodding and dismissing herself, ignoring the way his gaze followed her as she left. The man was just a curious cat with a hound's nose for trouble. It didn't mean anything and she wouldn't read into it.

She knew exactly who she wanted to talk to right now, and when she found her, she wouldn't take no for an answer.

CHAPTER SEVENTEEN

Gaitune-67, Spy Corps Headquarters and Base, Phina's Room

Phina was exhausted. She had spent hours in a specialized spy skill class taught by a female agent named Genevieve, learning about—how did the woman put it?—using the illusion of intimacy to elicit information. In other words, becoming far more used to using a woman's sensuality than Phina felt comfortable with. Thank the universe her relationship with Todd was growing and healthy, or she wouldn't even have a place to start.

Of course, before and after that class she'd had weapons training, environmental awareness, tailing and tagging, and even a lesson out in the solarium in the desert terrain.

Phina looked down at her pants as she began taking them off, noticing the bits of sand and dust pouring onto the floor. She sagged and shook her head.

Training. This is all training.

Phina had finished taking a shower and was about to dress for bed when she heard the door chime. The sudden noise startled her, causing her to jump to the side and yelp as the towel on her head fell onto her face.

"Hold on!" She grimaced as she finished drying off, quickly replacing the towels with her pajama shirt and pants.

Phina hadn't checked to see who was outside, and she didn't care at that moment. She intended to see what they wanted, followed by falling into her bed. The late-night spyscapades were cutting into her rest time, and she needed every hour she could get to maintain her mental shields.

As she tugged her shirt down to her waist, she called, "All right, Shade, you can let them in. Thank you."

The door opened as she took a step toward it. She stopped when she saw Masha walking in. The beta agent lowered her gaze to Phina's chest before giving her a smirk. "Nice."

Phina wrinkled her nose and flicked her fingers at the words that declared, I'm too sexy for this shirt. "It was a boyfriend gift from Alina."

Masha threw Phina a confused glance before taking a seat on the bed, which did not bode well for the brevity of the visit.

"Why would Alina give you a boyfriend gift? Wouldn't that be Todd's job?"

Seeing the woman was making herself comfortable, Phina decided Masha was nervous.

"It was more along the lines of a 'Congratulations, you've finally gotten a boyfriend' gift," she responded dryly.

Masha let out a snicker before she could control herself. "Did you pay her back for it?"

Phina straightened in surprise. "Pay her back? What for?"

Masha grinned. "Oh, honey, let me tell you about St. Payback."

After twenty minutes of hearing about pranks and antics, Phina still wasn't sure what to say. Todd had mentioned St. Payback in passing, but the tradition was far more involved than she had realized. "So, you think I should follow Bethany Anne's example and do something more over the top?"

"It's up to you." Masha leaned back on her hands and shrugged. "Just ask yourself, 'what would BA do?'"

"I'll put some thought into that." Phina took a measure of the woman, who had relaxed while she had related her stories about shenanigans between Bethany Anne and her inner circle. "Something tells me that's not why you came to visit, though."

"No." The beta agent pursed her lips. "I went to see Greyson earlier and asked him about your mission, and he explained a few things."

Phina waited, but the older woman remained silent. "Were you going to tell me what he explained?"

"No, I was waiting for you to read it from my mind." Masha's tone was sharp.

"Ah." Phina winced and raised a hand to rub the back of her neck uneasily.

Masha raised a hand to her forehead. "I'm sorry. I didn't mean to use that tone. I think I'm more upset by everything going on than I realized."

"It's all right." Phina appraised the other woman. "None of it is exactly easy to hear."

"I still shouldn't have blurted it out that way."

Phina lifted a shoulder and smiled at Masha. "I've been living with all of this for months, and I still have a hard time wrapping my head around it. I don't blame you for reacting."

Masha studied the other woman. "Do you mean the mind-reading or the traitor?"

"Both." Phina tilted her head in thought as she leaned her back against the wall. "I found out there was a problem with someone working behind the scenes in the Empire shortly before I began to develop any real ability. Since then, it's been an almost nonstop ride."

"Have you come to any conclusions about what you think is happening or who the traitor might be?" Masha asked.

"No conclusions," Phina admitted. "I haven't found enough evidence for that yet. I have plenty of speculation and suspicions, though."

"It sounds like you could use some help," Masha responded.

Phina perceived that they had finally arrived at the reason for her late-night visit. "The boss man turned you down, huh?"

Masha was startled. "How did you... Oh, right. You read my mind."

Ignoring the mild irritation in her voice, Phina shook her head. "Just read your body language. I refrain from reading other people's minds unless it's necessary. When it first started happening, I didn't have a lot of control and needed to experiment to figure things out. Now, unless something major or surprising happens, I can usually control it so my shields don't slip."

Masha raised her hands in apology. "I'm sorry, I shouldn't have brought it up again."

"It's all right." Phina shifted to gaze at the other woman directly. "It takes some getting used to. When I first developed the ability, it was just being able to speak into a few other people's minds. That part wasn't so bad and kind of fun. I never expected or asked for all of this."

"Do you wish you hadn't gotten these abilities?" Masha asked quietly.

Phina glanced down as she thought that over. "Part of me does. I will never be normal again, but sometimes I wish I could be. Sometimes I just want to be alone and not have the weight of everyone's thoughts around me."

She let out a sigh. "Then the rest of me takes over and reminds that part of myself that I can do things that not very many other people can. There's that too often used quote about great powers coming with great responsibility. If I don't help other people, whether I use my learned skills, special abilities, or just show up, I become part of the problem and not the solution. That's not who my parents raised me to be. Throughout the stories, they told me that was a lesson they wanted to teach me."

Phina straightened, pulling her shoulders back. "They taught me that every life is beautiful and worth living, and when that beautiful life is threatened, someone needs to step up to prevent it from being taken. I decided I would step up."

Masha had been caught up in the explanation. She

blinked in surprise at Phina's determination. "Just like that?"

Nodding firmly, Phina folded her hands together and crossed her ankles. "Now it is. It took some time until I stopped feeling sorry for myself."

"Hmm." Masha studied Phina. "I think I understand more of what Greyson sees in you. He's always been close-mouthed about you and why he chose you as his apprentice."

She lifted a shoulder. "We're family. Which is why I know he's interested in you."

Masha shifted uncomfortably and sighed. "I tried to see that today, but I just don't see that in him. I am going to move on and put those feelings behind me."

Phina opened her mouth to protest but clicked it shut. It wasn't her place to argue about it, and Masha wouldn't take her word for it. That wouldn't keep her from prodding Link about the topic. She could just see him being all stoic and scowly.

She nodded. "I understand. Just keep an open mind until this assignment is done."

"I'll consider it." Masha spoke crisply as if she wanted to put it behind her already. "Now, I came because I want to help."

"Greyson already shot you down."

Masha winced but nodded. "More or less. I didn't push it, figuring I'd come straight to you since you are the one running the investigation."

Phina leaned forward. "I'm fine with you helping since you have access to the ops center without garnering a lot of questions. Is it true that the diagnostics and communications capabilities are better there than in the rest of the base?"

"The base EI is the best at accessing those things, but as far as manual access, yes."

"Great." Phina clapped her hands together with a smile. "We have the makings of a plan. I'll tell you what to search for, and you and Shade can deal with that while I finish going through the nightly scans. With any luck, this will be finished within a week. Two at most."

Masha nodded but held up a finger. "Just one thing."

"Yes?"

"Who's Shade?"

Phina had a feeling these last weeks would be long.

Gaitune-67, Spy Corps Headquarters and Base, Large Training Room

Phina ducked to dodge an imaginary strike and raised her short swords, swinging and blocking as she steadily advanced. Occasionally, she would side-flip or backflip as she continued to shadow-fight.

She tuned out the murmurs as she continued. What proved harder to ignore was the press of the minds that were focused on her as she trained. Her shields were strong, and Sundancer had helped her so they could become so.

The Previdian had been largely absent over the past few days, ever since Phina told him they needed to figure out something soon. Since his mental abilities were different from hers, he couldn't help her read minds. That hadn't stopped him from taking advantage of the fact that he could block other people's thoughts about him to become invisible and spy on everyone.

They didn't see him because they forgot he existed.

The catlike creature could be pretentious and had a disturbing fixation on fish and liver, but he was loyal and dedicated to helping her.

"Hey, Phina, when are you going to stop fake-fighting and fight a real opponent?"

She stopped mid-strike, her body leaning forward in a lunge with her swords extended. She decided to take a water break, although she was barely winded, even with all the movement. Her muscles felt limber and warm. She hadn't had a real fight since she had arrived on the base.

"Cade, stop your bellyaching." Savas spoke up with annoyance in his tone from ten feet away where he had been practicing on his own. "You just can't stand the attention she gets."

Phina's gaze darted toward the entrance, where around twenty agents were spread out along the wall, almost all of them staring at her.

"What makes you think she's getting all the attention?" Cade pressed. "They could be coming to see all the hot recruits."

Kabaka sighed as Gina stopped their bout to listen. He wiped the sweat from his dark face as he spoke carefully. "Listen, man. You are looking for an ass-whooping at the rate you are going. It's not going to go well for you."

"An ass-whooping? From her?" Cade replied incredulously. "There's no way that she can take me. Watch her. She can't even look at me. She's afraid to fight me because she knows I can take her."

Gina spoke up scornfully. "You're such a prick, Cade. You couldn't fight your way out of a paper bag."

Phina finished downing her water, but before she could respond, Jasper spoke up. "What if he's right? We all know she did something to Blayk. It's the only thing that makes sense. She's been quiet since he left, likely because she feels guilty."

The murmurs behind her increased, but Phina wasn't paying attention to the agents anymore. Her gaze jumped to Jasper, who turned to her triumphantly as if he had accomplished something. It made her wish she had laser eyes. The way they throbbed, she felt like it could happen.

Jasper winced and grabbed his head, stumbling to the side. "What the hell?"

He fell into the tall and muscular form of Shaw, who had just walked into the room and come over. The agent scowled and shoved Jasper until he was upright, then stared at them. "What's going on here?"

Phina stood gaping at Jasper, who continued to hold his head. Had she made that happen or was it a weirdly-timed coincidence?

She moved her gaze away as Cade's snide voice registered.

"We were just talking about how Phina is a coward who doesn't have the balls to fight a real man."

Even though she wanted to see if whatever she'd done to Jasper could be replicated with Cade, Phina knew that would look suspicious. Instead, she straightened and gave Cade a knowing smirk. "I think you are projecting, Cade. I'm ready to fight anyone, any time. I'm sure if I find a real man, I'll be ready to fight him, too."

"You wouldn't know a real man if he stared you in the face." Cade scowled at Phina when the other trainees snickered. Jasper moaned and shook his head.

Shaw crossed his arms and gave them a hard stare. "That's enough. You will both get the chance to fight during the competition, both singly and in pairs. If you want to fight, save it for when it matters."

"When will it matter?" Savas challenged. "When is the competition going to happen? It's been weeks."

"Soon." Shaw's expression was unreadable. "I'm waiting until you are ready for it. Some of you are ready now." He glanced at Felan and Phina. "And others are not." He flicked his gaze to Ian and Cade. "But it will happen soon. That's all I have to say on the matter."

"Understood." Balehn nodded.

"Suck-up," a voice murmured on the other side of the group.

Phina decided she didn't care to see who it was. She was very curious about what had happened with Jasper. Her gaze kept moving toward the man, who had calmed down and stood staring at Phina with fear and loathing on his face.

Fudging crumbs. This could be bad.

Gaitune-67, Spy Corps Headquarters and Base, Greyson Wells' Office

Link sat back in his chair, cackling. "You're telling me you mentally zapped that pretentious prick? Oh, that is just priceless!"

Phina leaned back in her chair across the desk from him with her arms crossed and scowled. "It's not funny!"

As Link continued laughing, Phina's face softened, and she admitted, "Okay, it was kind of funny."

"Are you kidding?" Link gasped for breath. "I wish I had been able to see his face."

Phina's face hardened again and she hissed, "I still have no idea how it happened! What if I can't control it and I end up hurting random people? What if it wasn't me and it was someone else doing it?"

Link waved his hand dismissively as he got himself under control again. "Those are just details. I have no doubt you will be putting your head together with Sundancer to figure this out because that's who you are. You have control of yourself and what you can do. I'm not worried. As for the possibility that someone else caused it, do you really think that, or do you just not want it to be you?"

Phina opened her mouth to respond but stopped. She answered ruefully, "I don't want it to be me. I know it was. I could feel it after the initial shock wore off."

"Well, there's your answer, my dear." Link spoke as kindly as he could, given that he still wanted to chortle about the effects of Phina's new ability. "You just need to figure it out."

"Yeah." Phina had a glum note in her voice. "I've been doing a lot of that lately."

Before Link could question her further, the door opened and Masha walked in, throwing his thoughts out of his head.

"I'm sorry it took a while to get here. We had a situation

to deal with in ops." She spoke breezily as she closed the distance and sat in the chair next to Phina.

Link opened his mouth—to say what, he wasn't sure—when Masha's nose wrinkled in repugnance.

"What is that smell?" She waved one hand in front of her face and reached for something in her pocket with the other. He sat there in confusion as she pulled out a tiny bottle and spritzed the contents around the room.

Wafts of something overwhelmingly citrusy with a hint of vanilla filled the air, causing Link's mouth to curl. "What the hell was that for?"

"To get rid of that nasty butt stank smell you have going on in here," Masha replied.

Link stared at the woman in disbelief and sputtered, "I don't *have* a butt stank smell in here!"

"Not anymore." She smiled beatifically, but the glint in her eyes dared him to keep going.

Link turned to Phina for support, but she shrugged. "I dialed down my senses when I came in so I didn't smell it anymore, but it smelled rank. You must have eaten the enchiladas they served for dinner last night."

"How did you..." He held up a hand. "No, don't answer that. It was probably something along the lines of that I always get Mexican when they serve it, which I do."

Phina shrugged and sat back comfortably. "Yes, you do."

"How long have you been using that trick to affect your senses like that?" Link demanded.

She tapped her chin with a finger. "About as long as they've been serving Mexican on Thursdays."

Link scowled and turned to Masha. "I suppose that's

how long you've been carrying around your Eau de l'Orange, there?"

"It's great being able to have access to more tree fruits, isn't it?" Masha beamed, though she had an edge to her voice. What was going on with her?

"This conversation got away from me somewhere," Link muttered. "What were we talking about again?"

"The pretentious prick," Phina supplied helpfully.

Link snickered. "Right. As far as I'm concerned, he had that coming. The EI..." He stopped when Phina coughed pointedly. Link stared at the young woman, who raised her eyebrows at him. Not backing down an inch, that one. He supposed she couldn't help it and came by it naturally, given her genetics.

He sighed and continued, "Shade has documented every time he's spoken badly about you, kid. It's not good. Even if he got outstanding marks in his evaluations, I'm not sure he's the kind of person we want here."

"Well, you have some tools and perverts here, so maybe pricks would fit right in." Phina pressed her lips together as if she wanted to take the words back.

"Perverts?" Link scowled. "What kind are we talking about here? The harassing kind, the Blayk kind, or the mutually agreed on with their sig-o kind?"

"Sig-o?" Phina raised an eyebrow skeptically.

"Significant other," Link supplied. He continued defensively when she continued to stare, "What? It's a real term. All the cool kids are using it."

"I think you made it up," Phina argued.

"What does it matter?" Masha broke in impatiently. "I

want to know why you want to categorize the types of perverts we potentially have."

"Why does it matter to you?" Link dug his heels in to poke at her. She had been cool with him since their last meeting, and he didn't like it. "Do you have a preference on perverts?"

She gave him a scornful glare. "Because I find it suspicious. What does it matter what kind of pervert they are?"

Link deemed it a victory that she broke her icy calm and rattled off, "Because if they are the Blayk kind, I'm going to kill them. If they're the harassing kind, I'm going to kick them in the balls and dump them planetside before blacklisting them, and if they are the sig-o kind, it's just kinky."

"Well, at least you have a plan." Phina pulled out her tablet while Masha blinked in surprise. "I'll send you a list. What about the others?"

"Others?" Link thought back through their conversation as he leaned back in his chair and put his feet up on his desk, crossing his ankles. "You mean the tools and the pricks? Well, the tools can't help themselves."

"You only think that because you see one in your mirror every day. It's the rest of us who have to put up with you all," Phina muttered as she focused on the screen in her hand.

"Hey, now!" Link pointed a finger at his smart-mouthed protégé with pseudo anger. "I resemble that remark. You don't have to be a brat and point it out."

"I'm completely terrible," she agreed as she tapped a few more times to finish her task. "You should flog me with stuffies and kittens."

"That's not a punishment," Link complained. "I want real punishment. You were being mean."

Masha shook her head in amazement. "Just which one of you is the grown-up here?"

"I am!" Link and Phina both spoke together before looking at each other and bursting into laughter.

"Well, that certainly cleared things up," Masha commented dryly.

Link buffed his fingernails on his shirt. "It's a gift."

"Maybe you should consider returning it," Masha suggested.

Scowling, Link hitched a thumb at Phina. "You're going to turn into this one if you're not careful."

"I should be so lucky," Masha muttered.

"So, the pricks?" Phina broached delicately, with a side glance at Masha.

Link thought about it briefly and shrugged. "Give them hell right back. Being mean isn't a crime until it crosses into abuse."

Masha pressed her lips together and grumbled, "You wouldn't say that if you were on the receiving end of their comments."

"What makes you think I haven't been?" Link responded mildly, fingers splayed with the tips pressed together like a maniacal and pretentious movie villain.

"Oh, well..." Masha's voice wavered with uncertainty. "I suppose I don't know."

He suppressed a smile. She had a bleeding heart. It wasn't a bad quality, but it did occasionally cause her to react predictably.

"Or he could just be pushing your buttons," Phina responded wryly.

"What?" Masha straightened in surprise and glared at him.

Damn it. Now both of them would make his life hell.

CHAPTER EIGHTEEN

Gaitune-67, Spy Corps Headquarters and Base, Large Training Room

Shaw clapped his hands. "Listen up, trainees!"

The remaining twelve trainees stopped their morning exercises and moved closer to listen. He examined each of them in turn.

Since Blayk had died, things had changed. The trainees had changed.

Jahlek, Felan, Savas, and Balehn had taken the event as a challenge, wanting to be better, stronger, and faster physically, but also prove that they were better males and that they belonged here. For the most part, they had succeeded, but Shaw knew the most challenging tasks lay ahead.

Gina, Nodin, and Kabaka had grown as well, but their progress was more subtle. They tended to use their minds before their weapons, which Shaw knew would only benefit them once their skills were up to par. If someone won by a sneak attack, half the time, it was one of them.

As he appraised Cade, Jasper, and Ian, Shaw internally

sighed. Jasper was focused, but he could be a hothead and a jackass, not welcome traits in a spy. Cade wasn't much better, and his focus had become more scattered. He kept an eye on the other recruits' progress and seemed to resent it when they excelled as if it were a personal affront. And Ian... Well, that young man was dismally average though he made up for it with enthusiasm.

Losing Blayk had been a catalyst for him as well as the trainees, none more so than the last trainee: Phina.

He hadn't gotten the full picture from Masha and Jack —it seemed like not even they knew—but from what little Shaw had been told and what he deduced from Phina's new withdrawn behavior, he could put the pieces together.

Shaw wished he could have ripped Blayk's head off himself.

Where she had been vocal before, Phina had turned inward. Where she had been focused, she now proved laser-sharp. She never volunteered for anything anymore, but when pressed, she performed to the letter and no more. Her skills had steadily grown, and she no longer allowed herself to become distracted, always glancing around the room. She wasn't cold, but she had become...contained.

He didn't like it at all.

"You asked for a competition, and I told you it would happen when I deemed that you were ready." All the trainees perked up in excitement except for Phina, who stood in the back, taking everything in.

"Are we ready?" Ian asked in nervous excitement.

Shaw suppressed a grimace. "You are ready enough not to be an embarrassment to yourselves."

The lean man's enthusiasm waned, but he still listened attentively.

"In one week, we will begin a week-long competition. To make it fair, you will all compete with every weapon and show every skill a spy utilizes. This will not only even out the field a bit as far as skills and scoring, but will also give us a more accurate assessment as to your growth." His eyes raked the group and he was pleased to find them all paying attention, determined to do their best. "At the end of the week, we will reenact the sparring matches you had with the beta agents at the start of the training period, but with a longer time. Those sessions will not only be a large part of the competition, but they will comprise the majority of your next assessment. Any questions?"

He nodded in acknowledgment at Cade, who stood squarely with his arms crossed and a dark expression on his face. "Who will decide the winner?"

Shaw responded brusquely, "As I explained, there will be a winner of each weapon and skill. After that, we will see based on those results."

"Who will be judging this competition?" Jasper stood proudly with his legs spread shoulder-width apart.

Shaw stared at the younger man with cold indifference. "You have forgotten that you asked me to judge you all fairly. Guess you will have to be careful of that in the future if you have a problem with it. The beta agents and I will evaluate all of you for each event. By the end, we will know where to rank you."

He narrowed his gaze as he scanned the group again. "Any more questions?" When some of them shook their heads and the rest stood silently, he nodded. "Dismissed."

The room buzzed with conversation as the trainees exited the room to find dinner.

Shaw called, "Trainee Waters?"

After a moment, he saw the young woman weaving through the exiting students, who turned to look with curiosity and envy. He hoped they wouldn't cause trouble for her and resolved to keep an eye out.

Phina stopped a few paces away, showing patience and curiosity. "Yes, sir?"

He glanced to make sure all the other trainees were gone, waiting until the door was closed behind them before letting his gaze fall back to Phina. "I wanted to ask how you were handling everything."

Her mouth turned down in confusion. "I'm doing fine."

Shaw sighed while he lifted his hand to rub behind his neck. "Look, I'm just going to be blunt. I know a little of what happened with Blayk, and I'm observant enough to know that you were caught up in it. I just want to make sure you are all right."

She smiled. "I am all right. The first couple of days were rough, but I'm doing okay. Thank you for asking."

He nodded, and though he felt a little awkward, asked, "Is there anything you need that I can help with?"

Phina opened her mouth—Shaw felt certain to say no—but stopped, thought, and finally nodded. "Is there anywhere I can go where there is no one around?"

Well, that wasn't what he had expected. Eyebrows raised in surprise, he nodded. "There's a place I can show you, or I can tell you where to find it if you would rather be alone?"

She hesitated, then shook her head solemnly. "I need

some time by myself. It's hard to think with so many people around."

"I understand," he assured her. "Out of curiosity, how did that work, living on the station?"

Phina smirked, more life filling her eyes now than had been there in the last week. "I snuck into places I wasn't supposed to, of course."

He chuckled. "Why am I not surprised?"

She shrugged and aimed a questioning nod at the door. He waved her on. "Go ahead. If you enter the hangar and go to the farthest right side of the large room, you'll see double doors that lead to our outdoor training areas. It's a biodome and the least occupied area on the base when we aren't training. You've got about two hours before you should head back for bed if you want to go now."

Face brightening, Phina grinned. "That sounds great. Thank you."

"See you tomorrow." Shaw nodded, and his gaze followed her until the door closed behind her.

He sighed and rubbed his face before turning to finish sanitizing and putting equipment away. Normally it was the trainees' job, but he needed to do something to keep himself occupied.

He realized he had to face the facts and couldn't lie to himself anymore.

Not only was he falling for someone completely inappropriate since he was her instructor, but she was off-limits and not even interested. Having feelings for her could also jeopardize his duty.

"Just making your life that much harder, boyo," he muttered to himself as he stacked the mats together.

After finishing, he left the room, passing a couple of agents walking by as he stalked through the hangar, up the stairs, and into the staff gym.

One of the team leads was running on a machine that simulated varying terrains. Shaw waved and headed to the corner lined with punching bags.

He pulled on light gloves to protect his hands and got to work on one of the bags. He would have to set those feelings aside, Shaw decided. Nothing good would come from dwelling on them. He had won every battle and bout he ever fought except those against Todd Jenkins and Peter Silvers.

He would win this one.

Shaw spent hours pummeling the bag before he acknowledged this might be another battle he would lose.

Gaitune-67, Spy Corps Headquarters and Base, Dining Room

"Just two days before all of you feel the crushing weight of my boots when I beat you," Cade crowed as he stuffed his face.

Phina yawned so hard her eyes watered. She dropped her knife so she could cover her mouth, blinking the involuntary tears away.

After leaving Shaw a few days ago, Phina had been in a hopeful mood and had spent time as far away from people as she could manage. She had needed that time to sort through things in her head. Piecing together everything that had happened was challenging when she didn't have all the information.

Phina had enjoyed her time wandering the biodome so much that she had spent every evening after dinner out there before gearing up to do a few deep scans before sleeping. Tonight would be her last on spent scanning those who lived in the upper levels.

Since she knew the trainees weren't involved in the treason, she didn't feel all that bad about avoiding them during the evening when she needed a break. Of course, that could also have something to do with all the boasting and immature one-upping that had been happening ever since Shaw had announced the competition.

"Dream on, McFly," Ian retorted. "You might be good with your weapons, but you aren't the best by a long shot."

"Like you have a chance, Ian." Jasper sneered as he tossed his napkin onto his empty plate. "You're a bottom feeder, and everyone knows it."

Ian's face turned red as anger and embarrassment washed over him. Gina delicately swiped some butter over a roll as she calmly stated, "It's going to be Phina, of course. Some of us are good, but she's better."

Phina kept her focus on her plate as she shoveled food into her mouth. She wasn't taking part in this argument. No, sir.

"You would take her side, wouldn't you, Miss Suck-up?" Cade glowered at Gina.

Savas wagged his fork at the man. "Hey, don't be bitter because Phina's awesome."

Jahlek shrugged as he finished his second plate. "She *is* that good. It doesn't make sense that you won't admit it."

"See? It's not sucking up when it's the truth, Cade." Gina's words were calm, but her eyes lit up with an inner fire she didn't show very often. "You aren't as good as you think you are, and you're jealous that Phina is so much better. Just get over yourself and move on."

Cade's face darkened with anger, while Jasper's was filled with pure spite. "I hadn't heard you were into women or aliens, but you must have a magical vag to get them all on your side."

Gina gasped as the other trainees glared at Jasper. Cade smirked in his seat next to him.

Phina finished her last bite of food and stared at Jasper before giving him a deceptively sweet smile. "It's delightfully magical, thank you, but no one at this table will ever see it, so it doesn't concern you."

"Come on, man. Just leave it be. We all know Phina is good. That doesn't mean we can't all have fun with the competition," Kabaka urged.

"You too, huh?" Cade sneered. "I guess she *is* magical. Or maybe she's just easy."

"Enough," Felan, who had been silent up till now, growled. "This conversation is finished. Arguing over the best is pointless since it will be decided in the competition. You are both being purposely rude and demeaning." He scowled at Cade and Jasper. "Stuff it, or I'll not only show you how wrong you are, but I'll make a formal complaint to the beta agents."

The admonition by the large Wechselbalg caused them all to fall silent. The man usually remained quiet, so it was a big deal when he did open his mouth. That Felan had the muscle and build to back up his words, aside from being one of the top trainees in the physical areas, made them shut up that much faster.

Phina let out the breath she had been holding, knowing how easily the argument could have blown up. She turned and gave Felan a smile of thanks. He gave a slight nod in return.

Phina already knew from his thoughts that not only did he not like how they had been talking about and to her, but he had no respect for the other men at all.

Sadly, she knew exactly what he meant. The two jackasses weren't nearly as bad as Blayk had been, but they weren't people she would choose to hang out with or trust to have her back. Unfortunately, they were all too eager to show their best selves to the agents and trainers, so their real selves weren't a mark against them.

Huh. Phina made a mental note to suggest to Link that they plant a trained agent in future training groups for the sole purpose of seeing what the trainees revealed behind the scenes. Perhaps that would keep the more unsavory personalities from making it as far.

It would give her a certain amount of satisfaction if she knew that potential agents would be less likely to hide things. She knew all too well the sorts of secrets people tried to hide.

It sort of came with the territory of having to keep major secrets of her own.

Phina entered the double doors of the biodome after dinner and smiled at seeing the large area.

The octagonal biodome sunk into the asteroid was a half-mile in diameter. As she stepped into one side of the dome, she could see different areas sectioned off. Numerous steps descended into the middle of the dome. She had counted them once. Eight hundred and seventy steps gave one quite a workout. Most just took the escalator on one side or the elevator on the other.

The center space of the dome had been shaped into a smaller octagon and grown into a park or garden that was reached by ascending a few steps from the open corridor that surrounded it.

Around the middle, each side of the larger octagon had been sectioned out and made into a different terrain type. From left to right, there was a blue sandy desert, dry rocky terrain similar to the land surrounding the Grand Canyon on Earth but with a purple tone instead of red, underground tunnels that continued under the mountainous terrain across from her, a forest, grasslands with varying types and colors, and finally, a swampy area to her right.

All the terrains aside from the swamp and desert lands had wide openings into the middle corridor. The first was enclosed to keep the warm moisture inside, the second to maintain the dry, hot and cold environment needed to simulate the desert. Since the rest of the biodome didn't depend on maintaining a certain temperature, they left it to be regulated similarly to the temperature of the planet.

As Phina descended on the escalator, she couldn't help turning her face up to the large multi-planed window above that lit the space during most of the day. Since Spy Corps didn't want to risk revealing their base, the outside of the window had been treated to blend with the rocky ground outside. However, as large as the window was, it only covered half the space of the garden below. The light was filtered through amplifiers that could be adjusted in brightness as needed.

Upon reaching the bottom, she stepped into the garden and felt much of the burden she carried lift off her shoulders. The weight of everyone's minds wasn't easy. The weight of knowing it was her responsibility to catch the traitor wasn't easy, either. Together, combined with the stress of being apart from Todd, Alina, and her chosen family and the contention between the trainees, the tension was affecting her mentally, emotionally, and physically.

Perhaps she just needed to make sure she took a mental break each day, even if she was super busy.

Phina wandered the park for a while before she flung herself down on the simulated grass and closed her eyes, letting her thoughts drift.

After a few puzzle pieces in her situation shifted into focus, she had a better idea as to how she should tackle the tension. Relief filled her now that she had a definite game plan.

She pulled out her tablet and sat up before bringing up the app that allowed her to call her family.

She needed to see one person in particular.

Excited shrieks pierced the biodome when the call connected. "Phina! I can't believe you're finally calling!"

After a beat, Alina's face came into focus. "Wait a minute, I'm mad at you! What's taken you so long to call? I've been waiting forever!"

"I'm sorry, Alina." Phina felt a pang when she realized how much she had missed her friend and seeing the hurt on Alina's face. "I go to bed every night exhausted. All my time has been spent training or accomplishing my mission here."

"Well, I'll forgive you if you tell me what you've been doing."

Phina ignored the determined glint in Alina's eyes and shook her head. "You know I can't do that."

"I don't know anything except we made a pinky promise in third grade not to keep secrets from each other after that mix-up about Jesse Hamlin." Alina crossed her arms in an attempt to seem tougher while still holding the tablet.

Grimacing, Phina shook her head and tried to ignore the guilt trip Alina was heaping on her. "That was more than ten years ago, Alina, and it doesn't count when it's a top-secret mission."

Alina's gaze narrowed. "Pinky promises are forever, Phina. If you can't trust pinky promises, you can't trust anything."

A shadow moved behind Alina. Phina saw two large arms coming around from behind her friend, which would have alarmed her had she not recognized them.

"*Malyshka*, why are you giving Phina a hard time for doing her job?"

Alina turned her face up with a wide smile. "Maxim, you're home!"

The joy on her face sparked a pang in Phina's heart. She missed her best friend so much, and she was missing out on her life by being away. It made her miss Todd even more. Being away from both of them so long was harder than she had thought it would be. A week home between missions hadn't been nearly long enough.

"I wasn't giving Phina a hard time." Alina sounded mulish. "I was just reminding her that she needed to share with her best friend and that keeping secrets will get her nowhere."

Phina turned away, the stress and tension she had shed before beginning to come back.

"Alina," Maxim chided gently. "You are being unreasonable. You know Phina isn't allowed to talk about everything with me either, and I have a higher clearance than you do."

"I have the highest clearance. I'm her best friend," Alina insisted.

Phina saw Maxim giving his wife a look that caused Alina's face to crumble. "I know, I know. It's just...I miss her." She turned her teary face to the screen. "I miss you, Phina. I hate it that you're gone."

"I miss you too, Alina." Phina spoke softly, wiping away stray tears. "I can't do all that much about it, though, and this won't be the last time it happens. I promise I will tell you everything I can when I'm done. I'll call sooner, too."

"You better, or I'm going to thump you in the arm. I don't care how fast you are now. I'll chase you down."

Alina put on a tough face for a few beats before they both broke down into giggles.

Maxim sighed but had a smile on his face as he lightly squeezed Alina's shoulders.

Alina grinned as she wiped away the stray remnants of tears on her face. "So, now that that's out of the way, are there any cute guys there?"

Phina sighed, but she couldn't help the smile that

tugged at her lips. Alina could always cheer her up. The tension began to leave her again.

"Forget guys," Phina teased. "You should see where I'm sitting now. This place is amazing."

Alina straightened with a gleam in her eye. "Tell me everything that's not about the mission? And don't leave out the men, either."

Grinning, Phina proceeded to do just that.

CHAPTER NINETEEN

Gaitune-67, Spy Corps Headquarters and Base, Large Training Room

"Attention!"

Phina straightened, her gaze moving to the front of the room where Jack Kaiser stood, his eyes blazing with a fierce light.

"Agent Shaw has told me you lot have requested a competition to test your skills and settle which one of you is the best." His gaze raked the group of trainees, causing some to stiffen in their spots. "Since you asked so nicely, Agent Shaw has decided to oblige you. As your training and the determination of your skills isn't up to you, we have decided to push you farther than you have yet been pushed." His voice was mocking as he turned to Cade and Jasper. "After all, the best trainee will win, right?"

He glanced at Phina with a harsh glint in his eye she hadn't seen since she had first arrived. What sludge had gotten into his engine?

Cade and Jasper froze, their focus on the beta agent. It

was just as well Jack had moved on. The two of them weren't capable of answering coherently.

"You will enter a series of tests. Everyone will test on each weapon, even if you have never picked it up before. Tomorrow, you will fight one of us three for up to five minutes. After that, there will be one more task for you all to accomplish. Are you ready?"

Most of the agents currently in residence at the base stood lining the sides of the room. At his question, they all hissed an agreement that gave Phina chills.

Jack gave the trainees a harsh grin. "Then let the games begin. It may or may not be fun for you, but it will *definitely* be fun for us."

Phina had a feeling it would be a long day.

Scratch that. A long week.

Shaw stood with his arms crossed during the weapons challenges. Each student had been paired with another student until there was a clear winner. Two winners were paired in the next round, and so on until an overall winner was declared.

Over the past several days, they had tested everyone on throwing daggers, knife fighting, shurikens, crossbows, single sword, dual swords, katanas, and batons.

Phina had asked him one day if there was a reason the training aligned with that of an assassin. He had told her it was because spies often had to utilize the skills of one or they could be caught or killed. He would never forget her response.

"Are you certain you aren't just trying to make being a spy spicier?" Phina had frowned as she threw a mat to the side of the room. "I would think acting, negotiation, and deflection skills would be more effective in many circumstances."

His mouth had fallen open. "Spicier?"

She had shrugged and walked away to pick up another mat. "You know, hot, cool, more exciting, special... That kind of thing."

"Right." He'd pulled his gaze away from her. What had they been talking about again? "Well, those skills would come in handy, too."

"Are those skills taught to the trainees here?"

"No." He had rubbed the back of his head uncomfortably. "They are more specialized skills established agents get taught."

She had straightened from bending over to pick up another mat and turned to him with a frown. "That seems shortsighted."

He had shaken his head again to clear it. "What?"

She'd sighed, tired and impatient. "It's stupid not to emphasize those skills. Those should be commonly taught Spy Corps skills, not specialized ones."

"Well, that's how things have been."

"Well, you can be damn sure that's not how they will continue," she had muttered as she'd walked away from him. "I never thought I would find value in communication skills, but leaving them the way things are isn't smart."

Shaw shook his head now, bringing his thoughts back to the present. He could believe she had that sort of pull with Greyson Wells as her mentor. The comment had made him wonder if the alpha agent had been grooming her to take over his position in Spy Corps. He didn't know what to make of that.

The competition had moved to the shooting range with half the trainees walking forward to take their place across the room from their targets. They would shoot five rounds at each target placed at ten, twenty-five, fifty, and one hundred feet away. They would be ranked according to their scores.

Since Jack Kaiser was a control freak on his best day, he had taken on the task of calling out the commands. Shaw would be reviewing the computerized scores to make certain there were no errors once they finished.

"Range is hot!" Jack called.

The trainees picked up their pistols, loaded their ammunition, and one by one, stood waiting with the barrels pointed at the floor. This etiquette had been drilled into them over the last several weeks.

Shaw glanced at Phina, who was in the second group of trainees to shoot. However, she currently stood at the side of the room behind the firing line with her arms crossed, frowning. He followed her line of sight to see Cade standing at the line with his finger inside the trigger guard.

"Cade," he called, causing the young man to jerk toward him and fire a round into the padded wall at the side of the range.

Shaw scowled at the man, who appeared both angry and embarrassed. "Get your finger out of that trigger guard. This is exactly why that rule exists."

He heard agents behind him snickering. "Moron," someone muttered.

Cade's face turned dark with anger, but he remained silent as he corrected his stance.

When everyone was ready, Shaw gave Jack a nod. Jack called, "Commence firing."

Shots fired down the line. Shaw assessed the trainees from his position behind them. Most of them did fine, but no one stood out until he observed Jahlek calmly placing round after round into each bullseye.

"Cease firing!" Jack called.

Shaw sent the unspoken request to the base's EI to reset the targets and bring the marked targets forward. After a flurry of machinery, Shaw had them in hand. He sat down to check the scores while Jack declared the range to be cold, and the trainee groups switched positions.

He glanced up briefly to make sure everyone was following the proper protocol before continuing his calculations as Jack called the commands.

Phina stood on Shaw's left side, lifting her weapons one after another and smoothly firing them into the center of the targets. No one watching her would think she hadn't fired a gun before a few weeks ago.

"Cease fire!"

The sound of shots firing died down. Once Jack was satisfied that all the guns were on the tables next to the trainees, he declared the range cold.

Shaw pulled the targets from the second group and compared them to the first. There was a clear delineation of talent between the top four people and the rest, with one outlier in between them.

The buzz of conversation rose as he stood and folded

his arms behind his back, a habit he had picked up in the Marines.

"Attention in the room!" Jack called.

The buzzing died down, everyone's focus on Shaw. "Cade, you failed outright for disregarding basic range safety."

Cade opened his mouth to argue, then changed his mind when he saw the resolute expression on Shaw's face.

Shaw nodded. "Continuing. In fourth place, we have Kabaka Annane."

Cheers sounded from around the room as the friendly man straightened with a surprised smile.

"In third place, Savas."

The cheers sounded more muted than they had been for Kabaka. The Shrillexian thrust his chin out with a nod. Shaw wasn't certain if that meant Savas felt happy or frustrated about his placement.

"In second place, Phina Waters."

Almost everyone cheered. Looking around, Shaw felt certain some of them didn't want to offend the alpha agent's protégé in front of the staff, while others felt genuine respect. He had caught several agents peeking in at Phina while she was training, interested in Greyson's recruit. She never acknowledged them, let alone allowed herself to be distracted by them.

Phina merely nodded at the placement and smiled toward the crowd.

"In first place, Jahlek!"

A mixture of excited cheering and polite clapping sounded for the Noel-ni.

"That concludes the competition for tonight," Jack

announced. "The rest of the skills assessments will take place tomorrow. Dismissed!"

Shaw stood with his arms crossed as everyone mingled and chatted, exiting the shooting range into the hangar.

He glanced around the room, catching sight of Jack's conflicted expression. He followed the man's gaze to see Phina quietly putting her equipment away.

Frowning, Shaw glanced between the two of them. Phina seemed oblivious to the attention, but Jack hardly blinked as he stared at her.

After Phina walked away, Shaw thought about talking to the beta agent but decided against it. He didn't know what the man's deal was, but Shaw knew his own conflicting thoughts about the younger woman.

Could a chestnut-haired beauty with an all-too-knowing gleam in her eye sway him from fulfilling his duty?

***

Once more, the dedicated and devoted man came into the presence of his Empress. This time, he entered not with a sense of eager fulfillment of his duty but with anxiety and concern.

"Report."

The Empress' dry voice caused his throat to close, and he struggled with his words.

"Y-yes, my Empress." He bowed his head. "I regret that I have not yet been able to complete my duty."

"I have noticed." The tone of her words sharpened. "I

have noticed and am deeply disappointed that you have yet to carry out the mission I gave you."

"I understand, my Empress," the man whispered.

"Do you?" She stared sternly at the bowing man. "You understand that you have disobeyed my express wish?"

"Yes, my Empress."

"Do you understand that you have only one more chance to fulfill my prior order?" she pressed.

His shoulders stiffened. "Yes, my Empress."

"And the penalty for failing?" Her voice turned harsh.

The man swallowed roughly before responding. "Yes, my Empress."

"Good. I'll give you three days."

"Three..." He caught himself and nodded in determination. "Yes, my Empress. In three days, the traitor Phina Waters will be killed according to your order. Long may the Etheric Empire reign."

The Empress dismissed the devoted man, having received the promise she sought. As he left her presence, she thought, *Long may the Empire reign indeed.*

Gaitune-67, Spy Corps Headquarters and Base, Large Training Room

"Attention!"

Phina straightened as the near-déjà vu scenario took place. She stifled a yawn that wanted to be let loose and examined the training room as Beta Agent Jack Kaiser continued to speak.

"Today we will focus on individual combat assessments." He spoke sternly as he paced in front of the trainees. Phina often wondered if the man missed being in the military since he seemed to treat them as if they were all troops to train. "Each person's bouts will emulate the minor assessments that took place at the beginning of your training."

The beta agent stopped at the front and clasped his hands behind his back. "However, this time will be far more difficult. You will begin the bout with each of us while wearing your full loadout. Once the five-minute mark is reached, or you have been disarmed, you will both drop the weapons in your hands and continue the bout hand-to-hand. This will continue until you reach a second five-minute mark or are unable to continue.

"Any questions?" he asked.

Jasper raised his hand. Jack's gaze moved past him as if he couldn't see him. "No? Good. Remember to follow the instructions of the current referee."

After waving his hand and getting no reaction, Jasper lowered it with a scowling grumble she could hear from several feet away. She suppressed a smirk as she followed the instructions that the beta agent called, filing to the side of the room where their weapons and equipment were stored.

Since Ian was first for assessments and Balehn second, they both geared up.

Phina leaned against the wall to watch the initial bouts and scanned the room. Her gaze caught on Shaw, who had strapped on his weapons already and stood waiting in the middle of the floor. Over his shoulder, she saw the slim form of Link waiting to see how things would go. When they'd last spoken, he had mentioned he wanted to watch the bouts to see the potential each recruit had for himself.

"First up, Ian McAllister!"

Ian nervously tugged on his weapons belt one last time and walked to Shaw. A quick scan of his mind revealed that Ian felt nervous about using real weapons. They had all gotten used to using the Pod-doc after acquiring injuries, but Ian still had an aversion to getting hurt. It was one reason he continually brought up the rear of the pack when utilizing their weapons skills.

Jack barked out the command to begin. The bout lasted longer than anyone expected, but he barely reached a minute for each phase.

After resetting his weapons, Ian went against Masha, then Jack. Both bouts were lackluster and disappointing.

As they switched out for Balehn, Phina became aware of a conversation several feet to her right. When she tuned in, she realized they were the two agents Shaw had been sitting with when she had first seen him in the dining room weeks ago.

"Nah, man. You can't go over there. Shaw warned you off her."

"He told us a pack of lies about her being Todd Jenkins' girlfriend and super important to people. If she's Jenkins' girlfriend, why is she here? That makes no sense."

A short pause. "You think he made it up so he could get with her first?"

"Hell, yeah, I do. His story is weak. He knows I've been wanting to tap her since she showed up."

"He said she was acting suspiciously then."

"Lies, man. All lies. Have you seen him when he looks at her?"

"I don't know. He still acts suspicious when she's around."

"Pssh. Don't be fooled. He looks at her like she's the red-hot frosting for his very bare and lonely cake. There's feeling wrapped in there."

Phina caught herself and turned back to the bouts. Balehn had fought decently with Shaw and unsheathed his blades for his fight with Masha. In the process of recovering, she missed a sentence or two.

"...think you could be reading into things."

"I'm not."

Another brief pause. "So, does that mean you aren't going to approach her?"

"Hell, no. I'm going to wait till everyone has gone today and offer some private tutoring sessions. She's good but inexperienced, so she'll jump all over that. Then it'll only be a matter of time before she's jumping all over *me*," the man bragged.

Phina snorted in derision. She caught sight of Felan on her left, who regarded her with wry amusement before glancing at the braggart and his friend. He nodded that way before speaking quietly. "They obviously have not been watching our practices."

She lifted a shoulder with a rueful smile. "Not my fault if they're unobservant."

He laughed silently, his shoulders bouncing up and down. "Don't break them."

"You're killing all my fun, Fel," she deadpanned.

Felan chuckled out loud, which caused Phina to

mentally do a fist pump. She was happy to be one of the few who was able to make him laugh.

"Relax," she told her friend. "I'll get my point across without even touching them."

"Oh?" He raised an eyebrow as he glanced at her in amusement. "You going to use magic or something?"

"Or something." She flashed a grin. "Watch and learn, brother. Watch and learn."

He shook his head, but his shoulders shook again.

As Phina turned back to the middle of the room, she saw Jasper leave the floor. He hadn't shown as well as he would have liked, judging by his expression. Nodin walked up to trade places with him.

She glanced at Link as she opened a mental connection. *Hey, boss man.*

To his credit, Link showed only a slight hunching of his shoulders at the unexpected greeting. *What's wrong?*

Does something have to be wrong for me to talk to my favorite mentor?

He shot her an annoyed glance before focusing on the fight again. Nodin fell back to avoid a kill strike but couldn't recover. He accepted his defeat and readied himself for hand-to-hand.

Fine. I want you to volunteer to fight me after my bouts are done as a demonstration of my skills or something. And I don't want you to hold back.

Surprised interest crossed Link's face, and he turned to look at her. *Who are you trying to intimidate?*

She side-glanced at the two men. *They think I'll be amenable to extracurricular practice as well as certain other offers.*

Anger flashed on his face before he got control. *I'll pound the little twerps myself!*

I think the point would be better made coming from me.

That doesn't sound like nearly as much fun for me.

Yes, she teased as Nodin bowed after being defeated. Gina slid her last weapon in its sheath and walked over. *Because it's always about what's fun for you.*

I want to teach them a lesson. He feigned innocence.

We will. Not everything needs to happen with a confrontation.

He mentally sighed. *Fine. We'll do your demonstration. But I want to know if they do anything after that so I can show them what to do with their tiny...*

Link, Phina frowned at him.

Egos! I was going to say egos.

Uh-huh.

Phina shook her head in amusement as Gina finished with respectable times and Cade stepped up.

She wondered if it made her a bad person to wish he would do poorly enough to be kicked out.

CHAPTER TWENTY

Cade finished strapping on all his weapons and strutted out onto the middle of the floor. After facing Sergeant Hardass, he glanced at Phina to make sure she would see him kill this weapons test. His vindication would be sweet.

As he turned back, Shaw leaned forward with a harsh whisper. "Focus, Cade. You won't win if you aren't paying attention."

Jaw tensing, Cade nodded and settled into his stance with knives in his hands.

When the beta agent called the start, Shaw came at him hard. Cade stepped back to block, his heart rate shooting up. He continued to withdraw as he frantically tried to withstand the blows that Shaw gave him. His knife skills weren't nearly strong enough to allow Cade the chance to push the agent back, but Shaw didn't give him the space he needed to switch weapons.

Shaw landed his blades within an inch of Cade's neck and thigh where two major arteries lay. Cade froze as he realized he had been killed, and it was time to move on to hand-to-hand.

He dropped his weapons on the floor as anger flashed inside him.

This wasn't how he had envisioned his assessment going! He was going to be strong, skilled, and suave. He was going to be the best and show everyone else up.

How dare Agent Shaw take his moment from him! The man had always been jealous of him and tried to push him down. It was inevitable that the man would break and show himself now.

Cade should have seen this coming. That was how smart he was. He knew what was going on now.

He drove his fist toward the other man's face, sure he would take the agent by surprise. The tables turned when Shaw deflected Cade's punch and delivered his own. Cade's head snapped back; he'd had no time to block. He stumbled and was only able to catch himself because Shaw didn't follow up on his punch.

Fury rose inside Cade. Shaw thought he could patronize him after pulling that cheap shot?

He lunged and drove both fists at Shaw one after the other. Cade didn't care if they connected or not. He just wanted to make Shaw pay. The man was out to get him.

Very few of the flurry of blows Cade heaped on Shaw got farther than the forearm used to deflect or block them. In his rush of emotion, Cade didn't see that he wasn't getting anywhere until Shaw kicked out his leg, which caused him to fall to the mat.

Cade lay there stunned, his chest heaving. He focused

on the face above him that was partially blocking the light. Shaw shook his head with his lips pressed together before uttering words that didn't compute in Cade's mind.

"Sloppy, Cade. Completely sloppy. I expected a little better from you."

Once his mind had caught up, Cade turned his head in Phina's direction. He caught her curious gaze and took it for a sneer. Well, of course he lost. The bitch had done it again and made sure he lost. It was Phina's fault.

It was all Phina's fault.

***

Phina watched Cade's bout with Shaw with her mental shields open to his thoughts. What she heard confused her. There were major discrepancies between what she saw and what Cade thought was happening.

Frowning, she adjusted the filter while Cade moved on to fighting Masha. Suddenly the pattern became clear.

Huh.

What?

Phina glanced up at Link's mental voice, not realizing she had held the connection between them.

Oh... Um... Well...

Link frowned at her from across the room. *It's not normal for you to dither like this.*

Her head shot up. *Dither? I wasn't dithering! Who uses that word, anyway? It's such a weak-sounding word. Dither,* she grumbled. *You make me sound like an old lady at a fancy ball in those bad romance novels.*

And you make me want to tear my hair out sometimes. Newsflash! This is one of them.

She glared at him. *I wasn't dithering.*

Fine! You weren't dithering. You were doing something, though. I just want to know what brought it on.

I was listening to Cade's thoughts.

Oh. The interest washed out of his mental voice. *That sounds perfectly boring. Why did you make it sound like it was something good?*

It's not good as much as intriguing.

I swear it's like pulling taffy. Forget the build-up; just tell me what I want to know.

She sighed and crossed her arms. *You are all heart today. You want to know because he is nuts.*

Nuts like funny, or nuts like crazy?

Nuts like... She surreptitiously raised a hand and tucked her hair behind her ear. *He's mentally unbalanced and potentially dangerous to the people around him.*

Oh. Huh.

Yeah, exactly.

They both fell silent as Cade fought Jack. It wasn't going well. Cade's frustration was on full display.

Not that I doubt your conclusions, but what makes you think so? Link sounded deadly serious, his focus on Cade.

His thoughts show signs of paranoid personality disorder with narcissistic leanings. She crossed her ankles as she leaned against the wall. *It's textbook for PPD because his thoughts of paranoia run very strong. In every thought, he's the victim, and everyone else is out to get him. I wouldn't be surprised if he had another disorder in there too. He also has sociopathic traits. He is the only one who counts in his mind. What matters is what he wants and needs. Other people don't matter at all.*

He glanced at Cade and Phina. *That's... Wow! How do you know all this? Is it, like, an inherent thing you pick up after reading people's minds for a while?*

She mentally laughed. *No. It doesn't work like that. After Todd and ADAM found out that Aunt Faith was either mentally ill or being controlled, I decided to read the DSM-5 brought from Earth so that I knew all the possibilities of what could have happened.*

Link's surprise could be seen from across the room. *The Diagnostic and Statistical Manual of Mental Disorders? Isn't that book like a thousand pages?*

Basically.

He scratched the back of his neck and shifted in place. *Well, okay. You have way too much time on your hands.*

Phina glowered at the man. *It's interesting.*

Uh-huh. I'll have to take your word for it.

No, really, she insisted. *Did you know that before we left Earth, they were studying Caffeine Use Disorder and Internet Gaming Disorder to see what effects were occurring in people's brains and behavior?*

He stared at her. *That's not a real thing.*

What isn't? She frowned back at him seriously.

The caffeine one. Everyone knows caffeine is essential for good health.

Everyone doesn't know that! Don't make me come over there. It's a real thing that some people struggle with. Her eyes flashed dangerously. She dimly registered sporadic cheers and claps.

Well, sign me up because I'm not giving up my caffeine. He lifted his chin stubbornly.

I'm not asking you to. She rolled her eyes. *I just thought it was interesting and fun to talk about and wanted to share. You killed the fun.*

That's me, the fun killer, he drawled.

Phina scowled and began to retort back when Nodin nudged her with his elbow.

"Hey, where's your head? Felan just started his round. Don't you need to strap your weapons on?"

Phina snapped to attention. Fudge in a bucket!

———

Shaw readied himself for the next bout as Felan and Jack fought. The Wechselbalg was good: quiet and contained personally, but focused and intense while fighting.

It had been a good bout between the two of them when Shaw had fought Felan. The fight between Felan and Jack proved even more vivid, which caused cheers to break out in the audience.

Finally, the two finished, having reached a very respectable bout time.

Phina stood waiting at the side as Felan bowed his head in respect to Jack and turned to the side before wiping his forehead.

Felan walked by and leaned as he passed Phina. Shaw could just barely catch his words. "Show me the magic, sister."

She flashed a grin before stepping forward to meet

Shaw. Between one step and the next, her face dropped every hint of emotion.

Phina faced him and drew her knives, holding one in a reverse grip and the other with her thumb on the spine as she settled into a ready stance and waited.

Shaw smiled inwardly. She knew that knives were his weapons of choice. He wondered what her reasoning could be for choosing them.

Jack called the start, and Shaw and Phina surged toward each other.

As they swung, stabbed, blocked, and occasionally kicked, Shaw wished he could stop and examine how Phina moved. His thoughts preoccupied him enough that it took him more than a minute to figure out what she was up to.

She matched him step for step. They were so in tune that it felt like participating in a dance that they had coordinated ahead of time. Shaw wasn't sure how she did it, but it felt amazing.

Until it changed.

Phina upped her pace, and Shaw had to dig deeper, move faster, snap his motions harder. He was working for it now and quickly losing ground.

Just when Shaw began to flag, Jack called the time, giving them a few seconds to adjust to hand-to-hand. Phina sheathed her knives instead of dropping them to the floor. It wasn't against the rules, per se, but it hadn't been the popular choice throughout the day.

Shaw glanced at Phina before the hand-to-hand was called and realized she had a small, pleased smile on her face. He became distracted and fell a beat behind Phina when the bout restarted.

Knowing how quick off the mark Phina had been before, Shaw felt sure she would catch him with the offtiming. The woman wasn't a slouch of a fighter by any means. It was one of the things she had been determined to perfect during the past several weeks. That attention to detail was prevalent in her movements.

However, she didn't press her advantage. Her movements slowed when he slowed and sped up when he did. What the hell was she doing matching her pace to his? It felt like she was toying with him.

Floored by his realization, Shaw decided to test it. As she drove her fist toward him, he sidestepped and blocked it weakly. He wanted to see what she would do.

Sure enough, she adjusted her momentum so instead of receiving a hit that would leave him with a bad bruise and a numb arm, her strike glanced off him.

Huh. She *was* matching her steps and hits to his. To be that precise meant she was either downplaying her skills, or something else was going on.

He glanced at her in confusion as he took a step back and to the side to give himself a few seconds.

The cheeky woman looked like she was having fun!

Shaw shrugged inwardly. It didn't matter if the woman was playing or not. He would give the fight his best shot. Phina was the last trainee, so it didn't matter if he ended up fatigued at the end.

Shaw renewed the fight with greater intensity and couldn't help feeling that his nickname for the woman proved to be supremely apt.

Phina finished her bout with Shaw. The time had been called, and the fight was declared a draw.

Murmurs had risen around the room as they fought, the audience wondering at the matched pace and her level of skill. It was common knowledge that Shaw was one of the best fighters in Spy Corps, which was one of the reasons why he was in charge of training recruits.

To have her match him set all the tongues wagging.

Shaw inclined his head with an amused smile before taking a spot at the side of the room to watch the rest of the bouts.

Pulling out her katana, Phina made sure she appeared grateful for the rest after the bout.

Masha settled in front of Phina with a katana, her weapon of choice, waiting for the call. The other woman sized her up curiously.

Phina lowered her shields enough to catch the woman's rather loud thought that she obviously wanted Phina to hear.

What's going on in your head, girl? You going to match me with my own weapon like you did with Shaw?

Instead of responding verbally, Phina flashed her a grin and lifted her presenting shoulder. Masha snorted and settled herself into her stance.

Jack called the start, and the air sang with slashing metal as they both responded.

Step by step and slash, block and dodge by deflect, strike, and guard, Phina mirrored the other woman. She kept her movements fluid, flowing around Masha. Phina considered it a real challenge since a regular bout would be too easy.

Her brain and body moved much too quickly now.

By the time the weapons part of the bout was called, Phina felt good and warmed up.

CHAPTER TWENTY-ONE

Phina blocked Masha's punch with her forearm as she slid her foot inside the other woman's stance to knock her off-balance.

Masha jumped back to avoid the takedown, then kicked at Phina's thigh. Phina moved to avoid the contact and returned with an uppercut when the time was called.

The women broke apart, their intense gazes meeting before they smiled in amusement.

"Good bout." Masha clapped Phina on the arm before grabbing her katana and moving to the side of the room.

At Jack's approach, Phina met his sharp gaze with a quizzical one.

"Do you have what you need before you start?" His baritone voice held an edge.

She wondered what she'd done to irritate him but decided to ignore it since it wasn't the time. "Not yet."

"One minute."

Phina went to the weapons area and switched out her katana harness for her dual swords.

Murmurs in the crowd rose to conversational level when they realized that Phina was again using the trainer's preferred weapons against them.

With Shaw and Masha, it hadn't been much of a gamble since she was fairly certain she could match them, if not beat them since she had the strength and inhuman agility and speed to keep things on an even keel.

However, it wasn't the same with Jack. He had been a master of weapons long before she was born. With her abilities, Link hadn't had to tell her that Jack and Masha had been two of his very first Spy Corps recruits after hers and Jace's parents. Unlike Masha, who had come from the Etheric Academy, Jack had already been a soldier with his combat experience.

It would have been easier to describe what he didn't know about weapons than what he did.

Still, Phina had a point to prove to the prick who thought she would fall all over him if he offered her lessons. She thought that over as she tugged on the straps to make sure they were in place. Perhaps she also had something to prove to her trainers.

As she turned back to meet Jack in the middle of the floor, she realized she had something to prove to herself, too.

Link stood quietly as his protégé drew her short swords and readied herself for the bout with one of his oldest friends.

He remained silent as they fought, their swords moving

so fast that he only caught the glint of light that reflected off the blades. Phina's face remained composed but intent on her opponent. Jack's impassive visage gradually grew darker as their bout continued.

Interest piqued, Link kept his eyes on his friend rather than his adopted niece. He couldn't understand what burr had gotten up his butt, but Jack was getting more frustrated the longer the bout went on.

His gaze darted between the two until he began to compare them. Realization dawned.

"Well, this is a hell of a thing," Link muttered to himself before shaking his head in dismay.

If he hadn't been expected to retain his super alpha agent demeanor, Link would have run his hands through his hair. As it was, he shook his head again and let out a soft breath.

When Phina had talked about making a pointed statement to those prurient pricks, why hadn't he remembered Jack had one major trigger that would inevitably be pulled?

Jack moved like a much younger man, his steps light and quick. He had the assurance of long years of practice.

Phina danced, gliding fluidly from one technique to the next, her swords an extension of her arms. She didn't have the experience, but she had the sharpness, strength, and agility to make up for it.

It proved to be a magnificent demonstration of skill, one that would be talked about for years to come, he imagined. There was only one problem.

But Jack's pride had been pricked.

"Damn it! Why didn't I think of that earlier?" Link

cursed under his breath as the fight kicked up in ferocity. If Phina hadn't had all her enhancements, there was no way she would have been able to keep up with the man.

Pride was Jack's biggest weakness, and he hated being shown up by young "upstarts." Knowing that, Link felt helpless. If he stopped the bout, he would be accused of favoritism even if he gave the win to Jack. Yet, they were using live weapons, which could easily harm one of the few people he trusted on either side.

Link could only hope that both fighters would come through unscathed.

Phina whirled to the side, then back as she avoided Jack's swords. As she fought, she divided her attention so she could remain focused on her movements while accessing the part of her brain that filtered Etheric energy into her body.

This technique had been drilled into her for hours a day while she had been on the Qendrok's planet. The technique was tricky since she had to split her focus.

However, she needed to replenish her energy after the last two bouts. She was pushing herself to meet Jack blow for blow, and it had been working.

Perhaps it had been working *too* well because his eyes had grown cold and his attacks were becoming harsher as time went on. Phina didn't know what his problem was, but she didn't want to split her focus again to read his mind. Not yet, anyway.

Instead, she nudged her connection to the Etheric to allow the energy to flow into her freely. Strength flowed into her body, her synapses sparking as her brain reacted faster to the stimuli.

That was more like it.

Surprised by her renewed focus, Jack didn't hesitate to push himself into each strike, using techniques that made deflecting and blocking harder for her slighter frame. Phina pushed on, making sure that all her escapes from his blades came from her agility and skill in evasion rather than using her strength. To do otherwise would invite questions she didn't want to answer.

Just as she began to feel the strain in keeping up with him, Shaw called time. The two fighters froze in their positions, her right blade pushing aside his left while her left was brought up to block his other blade.

The room fell into silence for a few seconds before the whispers resumed.

Phina assessed Jack warily as she maintained her position, waiting for him to withdraw first. His gaze burned into her face. From two feet away, she had an up-close and personal view of his eyes as they switched between emotions.

She decided that she would back away first and took a step back, her swords still raised. Her movement seemed to snap him out of his intensity. He straightened and lowered his swords, so she did as well. She followed suit as he sheathed the blades and shook her body out.

"Ready?" Shaw called.

They took their stances, eyes locked on each other.

Phina began to worry about the steely determination on Jack's face. Just what had he decided on?

Before she could reach out mentally, Shaw called the start, and Jack shot forward with a punishing blow. She could tell he wanted to end the match quickly and too thoroughly for her liking.

Phina dodged his first punch, swinging to the side and catching him on the ribs. She made sure the force of her strike was enough to bruise but not to break. As he brought his hand up to backhand her, she allowed him to get a blow in for appearances' sake.

She wished she could go full speed since it took more effort for her to pull her punches and maintain human speed than it did to let herself go.

As the bout continued, Phina realized she would need another influx of energy to finish this bout and continue the plan she'd made with Link. She split her focus again, drawing enough energy to continue but not enough to get her buzzed.

She had learned that unfortunate side effect from drawing too much Etheric energy at once right before a date with Todd. He had been a good sport about changing his plans from a sit-down dinner to a walking and talking date. It had taken Phina hours to be able to sit without getting the jitters. It had reminded her of the time before her coma when she couldn't sleep because she had so much energy running through her.

Phina's attention was drawn back by a hard punch to the stomach. She blocked the next strike and narrowed her gaze on Jack. His expression showed he was happy to have landed a solid punch on her.

She had to contain her response and remind herself not to meet his blows with equal force.

There is more at stake here than your pride.

Sundancer's words reflected her own thoughts. He sent a wave of calm that helped her settle down inside again.

That's what I've been telling myself. Holding myself back is the pits.

It's the what? She could almost see his pink face cocked in confusion. *Why is it a hole in the ground?*

It's an expression, she tossed back at the same time she threw a punch that Jack blocked. *Like it sucks, or it's bad... Or it's so bad and boring that it's like a deep hole in the ground you can't get out of.*

Right. The pits. Hmm. Watching you fight is the pits.

Probably because I can't fight at full speed. Which is why I said holding myself back is the pits.

Well, I agree with you. You still have to do it.

She darted back to avoid a strike that he followed up on. Phina feinted a strike to the right and swung around to hit his ribs in the same spot she'd connected with earlier.

He countered faster than she anticipated, returning the favor with a bruising strike to her ribs.

Ugh. Trust me, I have not forgotten that.

Shaw tried not to flinch at every strike and blow that Phina took. Based on the curious side glances from Masha standing next to him, he didn't think he managed it.

"He's really going at her, isn't he?" Masha spoke softly.

Shaw grunted an agreement. "He's been in a strange

mood with her lately. Not quite fixated, but definitely focused."

Masha nudged him with an elbow. "You've been rather fixated yourself, you know. Longer individual training, staring at her from across the room. You have some interest in our girl?"

Shaw stiffened, his jaw rigid. "I am fulfilling my duty, Beta. Nothing more."

A sharp intake of air from Phina as she received a blow to the stomach caused Shaw's attention to snap to the fight in alarm. After she continued, not slowed by the blow, Shaw's shoulders lowered.

Masha leaned closer, her face showing amusement. "You want to revise that statement?"

"No," he ground out.

"I think you have to."

"No." He pressed his lips together.

Her face lit up in glee. "It's pretty obvious. I can't believe I didn't see it before."

Shaw desperately glanced at the countdown clock, feeling like he was in the eighth circle of hell.

"Time!" he called, relieved that he didn't have to listen to Masha's comments anymore.

Jack and Phina disengaged and bowed their heads in acknowledgment of a good bout.

Since Phina was the only one to reach the full time for all three bouts with the trainers, she had won this portion of the competition.

Shaw could only see Jack's back, but he saw Phina's face. It seemed like the beta agent had made a comment to her. Phina was working to keep her expression impassive, but Shaw caught an emotion he couldn't read before she suppressed it.

Jack turned away from Phina but didn't get more than a few steps before Alpha Agent Wells stepped forward.

"Very good job to all our trainees! You've given us some great examples of your fighting style and shown the caliber of your skill!"

He paused with his characteristic amused smirk as everyone in the room cheered and whistled. He held up his hands and continued, "Everyone else has had a turn to fight. Now it's mine."

The room erupted in astonished murmurs. It had been years since Greyson Wells had fought in front of the majority of Spy Corps. Usually, he kept it to the practice room in the staff quarters.

Jack Kaiser stepped forward to return to the middle of the room, but the alpha agent raised his hand. "Not this time, Jack. I'm going to spar with Phina."

Shaw glanced at Phina curiously. She hadn't left the middle of the floor, and she had adjusted to a loose stance to keep her muscles from tightening. He wondered if she had known Greyson Wells was going to do this. She didn't seem surprised by his announcement.

Jack wasn't happy, but he withdrew from the middle of the floor as Greyson moved forward to meet Phina.

"Weapons?" Shaw called.

The mentor and student locked gazes briefly before Greyson shook his head. "No weapons. Just hand-to-hand."

Phina removed the harness holding her two swords and placed them with the other weapons at the side of the mat.

She removed her other weapons as well, leaving herself with only her hands.

Shaw found that curious since she had fought every other bout while having weapons strapped to her. What made this one different?

They circled the middle of the room, seeming to communicate without words. The two fighters had made it almost back to their original positions when Greyson finally spoke.

"Don't hold back."

Phina had no time to acknowledge the statement before the alpha agent surged forward at a speed that belied his age. At the same time, Phina ran three steps and jumped to wrap her legs around the man and swing to pull him down on the ground.

Wells made a move on the way down that Shaw couldn't see. As soon as they hit the ground, they rolled away from each other. They were on their feet and had moved to reengage within a second, their movements fluid.

With a combination of rapid flowing movements, deflections, and using the force of the other person against them, the two fighters flowed around each other like water.

Shaw's mouth dropped open and he didn't notice. The alpha agent fought better than the last few times he had seen him. His face showed intensity but also amusement, a far change from the dour, stoic face he had shown for much of the last ten years.

More than that was the change in Phina. She held her own easily, confidently, and with a hint of amusement as well. He began to wonder if she had been holding back this whole time, but that would be a ridiculous thing to think. Right? There was no reason for it.

As several strange and startling reasons listed themselves in his mind, Shaw began to wish Masha would start making outlandish comments again.

It was certainly less dangerous than the thoughts that flashed through his head.

CHAPTER TWENTY-TWO

Gaitune-67, Spy Corps Headquarters and Base, Large Training Room

Phina slid to the side to avoid getting taken to the mat, then twisted into a roundhouse aimed at his face. The slippery man deflected it and brought down a knife-hand strike to hit her in the shoulder.

She dodged out of the way, escaping with just a light tap.

Come on, Phina. Give them a show.

Hearing the mental nudge from Link and sensing an amused cat grin from Sundancer, Phina decided to bring out some of her showier moves, although they were more difficult to do without being able to move at full speed.

Adding a side ariel here, a twirl or spinning back-roundhouse there, Phina lengthened her combinations and added more movements. Link dodged or deflected most of her strikes and kicks, but the point of the bout wasn't to score.

It was to show how many ways she could kick a man's ass.

After another minute of showboating, including a move where she lunged into a handstand and caught Link around the neck with her feet and pulled him to the mat, Phina decided that it was time to get serious.

Phina dropped the gymnastics and moved on to the quick and dirty techniques that Todd had taught her, as opposed to the strike and takedown method she'd learned from Maxim or the fluid and graceful deflect and strike method she'd learned from Link. Whatever action Link used, she did the opposite. If Link used a lengthened strike, she used a short block. If he used a graceful deflection, she used a brutal kick. The result brought tension to their bout that hadn't been there before.

Just as they approached a full minute of this tension where the audience had been gasping and staring with bated breath, Jack called the time.

Phina threw herself into a backflip, landing several feet away. Link had jumped back as well, so they were a couple of yards apart. They bowed to each other as almost everyone in the room erupted in cheers and whistles.

As she straightened, Phina glanced at the agent who had prompted the demonstration and found him gaping at her with disbelief. She grinned. Her message had been received loud and clear.

Jack joined them on the floor and raised his hands for silence. After a few seconds, the cheers and clapping reluctantly died down so everyone could listen.

"After that demonstration, it may be anticlimactic to

announce Seraphina Waters as the winner of the bouts today," Jack announced dryly.

The cheers grew even louder. Jack had to wave his hands again several times to quiet them. Phina knew that many of the agents hardly knew her and were only reacting to the show she and Link had put on. Still, she couldn't control the smile and flush that warmed her face as she bowed her head in acknowledgment.

"Thank you."

Her bashfulness only served to heighten the volume of the cheers. Jack's subsequent announcement giving Felan and Savas second and third place respectively was anticlimactic in comparison.

Gaitune-67, Spy Corps Headquarters and Base

The devoted man entered the presence of his Empress and bowed before her.

"I'm waiting."

Dread filled him at the flat tone in her voice. "My Empress?"

"Have I or have I not informed you of the danger Seraphina Waters poses?"

He swallowed roughly. "You have, my Empress."

"Have I or have I not given you the command to kill this traitor before she destroys the Empire?"

"You...you have, my Empress." He had to force himself to speak above a whisper.

"Have you killed this traitor?"

Her soft but stringent tone caused frozen ripples of dread to run down his spine.

"No, my Empress," he responded softly.

The silence stretched into eternity.

"Have you decided to turn against me, my chosen warrior?"

Shock broke the hold on his body, and his head jerked up as he protested, "No, my Empress!"

He looked down immediately, but he hadn't seen her face through the shadows.

Only her glowing red eyes.

Silence fell as the devoted man suppressed his nervousness. Red eyes meant anger and temper and death. Finally, the Empress began to withdraw, her voice echoing in warning.

"You have three more days."

The devoted man waited quietly, anguish in his heart. Either he betrayed his beloved Empress...

Or he killed a woman he had come to respect and admire.

Phina started awake, her heart racing. Sundancer yowled as her movements dislodged him from his position at her back.

"Quiet, Sundancer. Listen. Don't you feel that?"

The Previdian tilted his pink head, ears perked.

Phina held still as well, perched on the edge of her bed with her eyes closed to better feel the fluctuations of the Etheric. She whispered, "There's been a disturbance."

Yes. He turned his head toward her, showing the

glowing eyes of a predator, but Phina felt only comfort in his presence. *It feels familiar.*

Her eyes flew open. "It does, doesn't it?" She opened her senses fully. "Doesn't it feel..."

A spike of Etheric energy rippled toward her, flooding her senses and overwhelming her. She raised her shields, leaving only the connections to Sundancer and Todd open since they were permanent.

Sundancer nudged her with his head, rubbing his face against her for comfort. *You know what it is now.*

"Yeah," she whispered as she took deep breaths to control the involuntary trembling of her body after the sensory overload. "Another piece of the puzzle."

It's a big piece.

"But it doesn't tell us who the traitor is, just that they are connected to the Qendrok's 'goddess,'" Phina pointed out as she maneuvered her body to lie down.

Not that I doubt you...

"But you do."

He continued as if she hadn't spoken. *Could it have been one of the Qendrok? They were the ones who had the devices.*

"No." Phina shook her head. "They are straightforward in their way. They wouldn't have pretended they were done with the devices and keep some for themselves. Besides, we have the power source."

Sundancer sniffed. *Well, we still have to figure out who this traitor is, and now how he's connected to this goddess person. I haven't heard anything. No one is talking out of turn, not one blackmail or threat, no one sneaking around more than normal or hiding things unless it's for mating. Only humans are silly enough to think that hiding matings is important. You don't see Nodin and Savas hiding anything, do you?*

Phina blinked in surprise. "Well, they aren't talking about it, either. I only know because I read their minds."

That's because mating is a private ritual, but relationships are accepted before all. Humans get it backward with public affection displays and hiding matings like it's shameful. Sundancer turned in a circle before finding a cozy spot to lie down.

Used to Sundancer's scathing critiques of humans, Phina pulled the covers over her and rolled over. "The point is, we've still got nothing on the traitor."

Haven't you scanned them all by now?

"There's a few I haven't done yet," Phina told him reluctantly. "One in particular."

His ear turned toward her. *Who?*

"Shaw."

Then he should be first tomorrow night. Agreed?

Phina recognized that she had put off scanning Shaw because she liked what she knew of him. He treated her like an equal, even though he was her trainer. She didn't want him to be the traitor. Even though he had remained on the shortlist after everyone else had been eliminated, she didn't want to believe it was him.

Still, it had to be done.

She sighed and nodded. "Agreed."

As they settled down to sleep again, Phina continued to feel uneasy. She felt like something was ticking down.

As if time were running out.

Phina yawned as she stretched to wake herself up. The movement disturbed Sundancer, who was sleeping curled up next to her. He hissed in displeasure and repositioned himself with his nose buried under his belly.

As had become her morning ritual since she had been on the base, Phina strengthened her connection to Todd, sending him warmth and love. She wasn't able to mentally speak to him from this distance, but she could feel him. From past conversations, she knew he could feel the emotions she sent his way, although the strength waned and waxed.

Once finished, she thought about the incident the night before and concluded there wasn't anything she could do until tonight. Her thoughts turned to the instructions they had received to report to a small training room for the briefing on today's task.

The trainers have been quiet on the subject, so she'd figured they didn't want to give the trainees time to prepare.

Which begged the question as to what it could be. Phina wasn't a betting person, but if she had been, she would be tempted to put her credits on the task being spy skill-related as opposed to fighting. The whole competition was a means for evaluating all their skills, and their spy skills hadn't been tested yet.

After showering and dressing in comfortable, stretchy, and protective clothing, Phina joined the other trainees for breakfast. As she listened to the speculation, along with some needling about their fighting skill placements, she determined that they had no idea what today's task would be either.

"Hey, Phina, where are you off to?" Nodin asked curiously as she rose from her seat with her tray.

She flashed him a smile. "Since we don't know what today's task will be, I'm going to get a warm-up. I want to make sure I'm loose and awake."

"This is why you've gotten so far ahead of the rest of us," Ian teased. "You focus on the goal and not the journey."

"Hey, speak for yourself, suck-up! I still think this has all been rigged," Cade sneered. "She's the alpha agent's slut, so of course she's going to win."

Angry rumbles and protests erupted from several of the other trainees, but they all ran together in a blur as Phina's anger flashed hot. She moved fast but had just enough presence of mind to keep it to human speed as she dropped her tray back on the table and grabbed Cade's throat as he cried out in pain from her mental jab.

The trainees quieted to hear as Phina leaned down next to his ear while she pushed his head forward and to the side just enough to make her point.

"Let me make this very clear, Cade." Her voice roughened as she spoke. He reached up to knock her away, and she pulled his hands into an immobilizing hold with her free hand. "Say whatever you want about me. Call me a slut if you want. Tell me you think I'm a cheater, whether it's true or not. Feel free to despise me in whatever way you wish. But don't you *ever* say anything about the Alpha like that again. He has never behaved inappropriately with me or anyone else, and it is both in very poor taste and extremely hazardous to your health to insinuate otherwise."

She let go of his hands and pushed him forward with

the hand holding his neck before stepping over to pick up her tray just as another agent stopped at their table.

"What's going on here?"

Phina glanced at him as she passed, recognizing Team Leader Nicholson. She nodded and responded, "Teaching."

She listened in using her enhanced hearing as she walked away.

"Is that true?" Agent Nicholson asked Cade.

"That bitch just put her hands on me!" Cade seethed.

Phina wished she could see Agent Nicholson's face as he responded, "Son, if that's how you talked to her, I can see why. I'd advise you to keep your mouth shut and open your ears, or you won't make it very far here."

She glanced at the table as she placed her tray into the washing receptacle and saw the agent walking away.

Felan shook his head as he picked up his tray. "Some of you can't see past your noses. Phina just showed you why she's winning. She's smart, loyal, determined, and fierce when she needs to be. I'm getting the sense that she's being groomed to be Agent Wells' successor, or didn't you notice all the underlying tensions and glances between the senior agents yesterday?"

Huh. Phina hadn't put that together before since she had been so focused on finding the traitor, but now that Felan mentioned it, that probably was what the senior agents were speculating about.

"Yeah, Cade, that's why you aren't winning. You aren't loyal or smart," Ian snarked.

"Shut up, McCallister!"

Phina shook her head as she walked out of the dining

room. Time to warm up and find out what entertaining torture they were in for today.

Gaitune-67, Spy Corps Headquarters and Base, Small Training Room

Shaw waited patiently for the trainees to arrive. Phina had been in the room when he arrived. As they waited for the last few to slip into the room, Shaw couldn't help the involuntary pull on his gaze toward the younger woman.

Every time he tugged his gaze away, it found its way back. Part of it was the growing attachment he felt toward her—an unfortunate and ill-advised attachment. The other part just seemed to be her natural magnetism. It felt like she drew every gaze to her.

A good portion of the agents he interacted with seemed infatuated with her, and they hadn't even spoken half a dozen words to her. He didn't delude himself into thinking he was any better than they were, even though he had spent a lot more time with her.

Then again, he was more than half in love with her. Much more.

Hell, he might as well torture himself. He was all the way in love with her, and it didn't matter one bit. He still had his duty, and he didn't see that changing. Not to mention that she was in love with a man who he admired and respected.

Shaw put his thoughts aside when the last two trainees slipped in as the clock ticked over on the hour.

"Attention!" he called.

The trainees straightened. They stood in small groups

in front of him. He observed them gravely, thinking about the task ahead.

"This will be the last day of the competition. This task is, as they say, the one to win." He saw a competitive light spark to life in many of the trainees as he continued, "We are putting a new spin on two classic children's games—hide and seek and capture the flag. Items marked with this symbol scattered throughout the facility."

He held up his tablet, which showed the black silhouette of a female vampire with teeth and long hair—the symbol of the Queen Bitch, Bethany Anne. "The objective is to be the last person caught by the end of the day and to have the most items captured. Now, you are allowed one question each. Balehn, we will start with you."

The Yollin shifted on his clawed feet as he searched for a question. "You said the objective is to be the last person caught. Who's doing the catching?"

"Very good question, Balehn." Shaw nodded in approval. "If either the beta agents or I put our hands on you, you can surrender or fight. If you can get away, you have another chance. If you are defeated or incapacitated, you are automatically out. Until then, you are free to evade us however you wish. Cade."

The belligerent young man crossed his arms as he spoke. "Can we take those special items from other people who have already gotten them?"

Shaw's eyebrows rose. "Well, I can see where your mind is. Yes, you can steal items from others if you can manage it, or fight for them. If you are defeated, you must relinquish one item you possess. However, unnecessary violence, such as if someone is already defeated and is struck by the winning person, will result in that winner being disqualified from the competition. Felan."

The large man stood with his hands clasped together behind him as he spoke thoughtfully. "Will we be monitored?"

Shaw nodded decisively. "You will be monitored *and* evaluated. Do not think you can be so sneaky that you will get away with not being seen. It won't happen. Gina."

"Are there any areas out of bounds?"

"Another good question." He pulled his lips back, not quite smiling. "Yes. The door up the stairs in the hangar and beyond is out of bounds. Everywhere else is in bounds, but not every space is advisable. Ian."

The young man spoke earnestly. "Can we use anything to help us hide or fight?"

"Yes, you will have thirty minutes to prepare yourselves, including grabbing practice weapons or other equipment. However, if you use live weapons, you will be disqualified. Jahlek."

"Will there be any other obstacles we will have to deal with?"

Shaw grinned. "Yes. It will be up to you to identify them and either avoid the obstacles or escape them before you are caught. Jasper."

The young man tilted his chin arrogantly. "What happens if one person holds out the longest, but another person holds the most items?"

"A tie," Shaw answered simply. "Kabaka."

"Aside from unnecessary violence or live weapons, are there any other actions with penalties?" He stood quietly to the side with Jahlek and Phina.

Shaw tilted his head in thought. "You all have read the mission, purpose, and code of conduct for Spy Corps, correct?"

After a chorus of yeses rang out, he continued. "As long as you follow those guidelines, you will not incur a penalty. Nodin."

The Estarian's features bunched together as he thought. After several seconds went by, he lifted his head. "Will there be any participants other than the people you've mentioned?"

"Yes." Shaw smirked in satisfaction at the quieter being's intelligence. "It's up to you to determine in what way they are participating. Phina."

She spoke quietly. "Are all skills, talents, and abilities we possess allowed, or only ones that others might have as well?"

Shaw tilted his head as he thought her question over. He thought it intriguing that the very same question had come up in the planning conversation. It was Alpha Agent Wells himself who had brought up that same point. If he didn't know the two of them had integrity and wouldn't find it fair to cheat, he would deem it suspicious. However, Alpha Agent Wells had brought up a good point—that they were testing the full breadth of the potential agents, and they couldn't do that if they were all limited to the same scope of abilities.

"Yes," he answered. "Use everything in your personal arsenal to complete the objective. The prior stipulations I mentioned still apply. Savas."

As he turned to the last trainee, Shaw caught the

corners of Phina's mouth tilting up. Fascinating. He made himself tear his gaze away to focus on the Shrillexian.

"When does the challenge end if people still aren't caught?"

Shaw nodded in approval. "One way or the other, the challenge will end at midnight tonight."

He straightened his shoulders and addressed the whole group. "That gives you fifteen hours. Survive to the end or be caught. Your thirty minutes of preparation begins… now!"

CHAPTER TWENTY-THREE

Gaitune-67, Spy Corps Headquarters and Base

Phina grabbed her practice weapons from her storage locker and dashed to her room, maintaining an easy speed as she weaved between other trainees and agents darting around to make their preparations.

She was changing in her room when she heard Shade speak over the intercom.

"Twenty minutes remain until the exercise begins."

Hearing the EI's voice gave Phina an idea.

"Hey, Shade?"

"Yes, Phina?"

She strapped on her weapons. "Shaw told us we are allowed to use all our skills and abilities. My skills include hacking. Would you be willing to step aside so I can use those skills? I wouldn't need you to help, just not stop me."

Phina tightened the last of her straps as she finished speaking, then packed her go-bag with several items she thought she would use while she waited for the EI to reply.

Shade responded. "I have checked with ADAM and Alpha Agent Wells. That is a request I can grant."

"Thank you, Shade!"

The EI spoke again. "Ten minutes remain until the exercise begins."

Phina understood that it had been a facility-wide announcement. She slung the pack on her back, taking care to avoid tangling it in the straps of her back sheaths, and headed swiftly to the kitchen.

Phina swung inside the door just as she heard, "Five minutes remain until the exercise begins."

Lourise Brown and Reese Claire, the two chefs on the base, glanced up at her entrance. Lourise pursed her lips in disdain and turned back to the mass of bistok meat she was butchering with a sharp knife.

Reese gave Phina a grin and waved her in. "Come on in. They told us to get you whatever you wanted if any of you came in here."

Smiling appreciatively, Phina carefully moved forward, keeping Lourise's knife visible at all times. "Thank you. I need nutribars or something that won't take up much space, is filling, and doesn't need to stay cold."

The good-natured older chef snapped his fingers and pointed at her. "I've got just the thing. Give me a minute."

"I think that's about all I have." Phina smiled ruefully.

"Right, right." Reese kept up a one-sided conversation about what they were cooking that day as he entered a pantry and rummaged around out of sight. He didn't seem to expect a response from her. Then again, with a silent and seemingly unpleasant woman like Lourise for company, perhaps he had just gotten used to it. He came out of the room with a smile and a flourish as he handed over five AIOs, All In One bars.

"Here you are. We get the good ones so there's two fruit-flavored, two peanut butter, and one double chocolate." He gave her a wink while Lourise scowled.

Phina accepted them gratefully. "Thank you very much!"

He grinned and shooed her toward the door. "Just do your best to win. I saw the fights yesterday. I've got my money on you."

She laughed as she slid the bars into her pack and moved back toward the door, keeping a wide berth around the disgruntled woman. "I'll do my best. Thank you both for giving us all such delicious food every day!"

She waved goodbye to Reese and finally saw the woman's body posture softening as she stepped through the door. The door gently closed just as Shade's voice spoke over the hallway speakers.

"Today's exercise begins...now."

Phina smiled as she moved toward a quiet spot to begin using her tablet unnoticed. It was time to flex her skills.

"Today's exercise begins...now."

Balehn panicked. He wasn't ready for the exercise. He was a Yollin, for *tak* sake! Everyone knew Yollins weren't small and sneaky. What had made him lose his mind enough to think he could be a spy?

He was a decent fighter. He could haul ass when he needed to with his long legs and sharp talons that could grip the ground beneath him. If only the universe had also given him natural camouflage.

After calming himself down, he decided to use logic to figure out where to find the items they were supposed to search for. Of course, Sergeant Hardass hadn't told them how big these objects were or how hard they would be to find. No, that would have been too easy!

Balehn decided the best place to start would be the training rooms. It was where they all spent most of their time, so it made sense to try there first.

He rushed past a few agents who tried to speak to him, but he didn't notice them in his hurry to find something. Balehn reached the small training room where the advanced classes took place. It made sense that something would be hidden in the room they all desired to reach.

He began on the right side of the room and searched counter-clockwise. He heard the door open, but when he turned, no one was there. He shrugged and continued his search.

Balehn almost cheered aloud when he found a dagger with the symbol they were supposed to search for mixed in with the weapons hanging on the wall.

He lifted the dagger triumphantly. He had done it! He had found one of the items using logic and his vision to search it out. Perhaps he could do this after all!

He eagerly slipped the knife into the bag slung over his shoulder and finished his search of the room. Finding no other items, he straightened and turned toward the door. He reached into his bag to reassure himself of his find as he lifted his other hand to open the door.

Alarm flooded him as he groped his clawed hand

around inside the sturdy bag. Balehn glanced down to see inside the bag he pulled open just as the door slid to the side.

The item was gone!

"Ah, Balehn." The familiar voice came from in front of him.

Jack Kaiser stood just outside the door with an expectant expression on his face as he reached out to clasp his arm, indicating he was caught.

Son of a bistok! What the hell had just happened?

Gaitune-67, Spy Corps Headquarters and Base, Lower Armory

Cade peered around the corner, prepared to dart back. Only one person was visible in the hallway. They were facing away from him and walking to a room near the end.

Pulling his head back, Cade glanced behind him and around in the hangar. No one looked his way, and there was only one pitiful weakling of a man working on a land vehicle. He triumphantly slipped around the corner and through the door on the right. He saw a blur out of the corner of his eye as he turned to close the door and thought he might have been seeing things, but it went away, so he dismissed it.

Turning back to the open room, Cade practically salivated at seeing all the guns, knives, and swords. So many weapons, so little time. He got down to business and began searching. He found nothing on any of the weapons and was about to leave when he noticed a large cabinet at the front of the room that might hold something.

He opened the doors and pulled things out one by one. He turned his wrist to toss another reject when he saw the edge of a patch on the sleeve of a protective shirt hanging to the side. He dropped the gloves in his hand when he heard something clatter on the floor behind him.

Cade whirled as he pulled his knife out of his thigh sheath. "Who's there? Show yourself!"

Silence reigned, though his eyes blurred as that funky thing happened with his vision again. Cade shook his head and scanned the room warily.

He had just been hearing things, right?

His Grams, a batty old woman who'd made it her mission in life to drive him insane, had always told him that ghosts were real and that he should listen when they spoke.

Cade had always scoffed and dismissed the woman, but he would admit—only to himself—that he felt very uneasy now. As if someone else were in the room with him. But ghosts weren't real.

He wished he had a gun to use but made do with his practice knife as he searched the room for any sign that someone was in there with him.

He found nothing except a lone knife that had fallen on the floor.

Cade's mind whirled. The knife had been resting inside a foam cutout. There was no way for it to fall on its own.

Flustered and a little scared, Cade returned to the cabinet to take the shirt with the patch and get the hell out. He was determined to gather more items than anyone. He had already found one in the large training room they had been in earlier for Agent Shaw's announcement of today's activity.

They thought they were so smart hiding it in plain sight, but he had outsmarted them. He would find all the items and outsmart everyone. He would win, and those suck-ups would see that their precious Phina wasn't so special!

Cade stood in front of the cabinet, but he didn't see the shirt with the patch. Frowning, he searched through the entire row of clothing, but they were all normal items, no special symbol at all.

Cade froze. His eyes must have been playing tricks on him, but no, he remembered seeing it! It had to have been there.

But that would mean...

He began to hyperventilate as he threw everything back in the cabinet with no regard for order and slammed the doors shut.

He rushed to the armory door and ran through it when it opened, making a beeline for the hangar, where there were more people. Real people he could see.

Cade shoved the doors open to the hangar and rounded the corner. He almost bounced right off of another man just a little taller than himself. In his panic, he didn't recognize who it was at first.

"Whoa, slow down there, Cade. No need to rush. But yeah, you're caught."

Cade realized that he had run into none other than Agent Shaw. Hissing, he tried to pull away but couldn't free himself from the beta agent's grip.

Damn it! He was caught. He gritted his teeth and patted his bag, reassured that he had at least gotten one item.

The bag was empty.

Cade seethed in anger. Phina had to have been part of this. He just knew it!

Gaitune-67, Spy Corps Headquarters and Base

Nodin had been tiptoeing around the facility for over an hour. The first item he had found by accident in a lounge that he had hidden in when he saw Beta Agent Masha approaching. The book had been lying there on the side table in plain sight.

Since then, he had found three items, and he hadn't had to search for any of them. He began to wonder if their trainers were using reverse psychology. Making them believe the items were in hard spots to find to see who was paying attention.

If there was one thing Nodin was good at, it was being observant.

He wasn't smart, strong, or especially skilled, but he noticed things, and he had a great memory.

Nodin crept down the corridor, approaching the trainee lounge. He had found items in all the other lounges, so he was hopeful he would find something in the room.

He held his hand up to open the door when he felt someone behind him. He turned his head quickly, but not quickly enough to avoid the hand that now clamped on his shoulder.

"Come on, Nodin," Beta Agent Masha said kindly. "You've been caught, so it's time to go."

"Go?" Nodin was startled. Was he being thrown out of Spy Corps? His parents had disowned him when he didn't want to be a part of their business. He didn't have anywhere else to go.

"You'll see. So how many did you get?"

"Umm...three."

She turned to him curiously as she gently tugged his arm for him to follow her. "You still have all three?"

He blinked in confusion. He felt like he was hearing only half of the conversation. Why wouldn't he still have the items? Nodin grew anxious, so he checked his bag.

Nodin nodded and patted his bag closed. "Yes, all three are there."

"Huh." Masha fell silent as they continued walking, causing Nodin to scratch his head in confusion.

She had expected them to be gone. There must have been other items that had disappeared. Were they supposed to have disappeared on their own?

Or had they been taken?

Gaitune-67, Spy Corps Headquarters and Base, Library

Gina frowned as she scanned the library she had spent the last forty-five minutes searching one last time. She had found two items, but she couldn't help thinking she was missing something.

She sighed and shook her head. Phina probably would have found all of them in half the time. That woman was seriously amazing, and Gina had no idea how she did it. She could call emulating Phina's awesomeness her life goals, but the girl was at least a year younger than her.

Phina wasn't even stuck up or boastful about her skills. She just...did the thing, and she did it better than most of the rest of them combined. Phina even helped out when she saw someone struggling or shared what she had learned in an unassuming way. If she wasn't so likable, Gina would probably hate her.

Then again, Cade seemed to manage it. Maybe that was his problem; he saw what she did, felt inadequate, and hated it. Stars only knew Gina felt inadequate herself, but she couldn't bring herself to hate Phina. She was self-aware enough to know it was a problem with herself.

She could hear her mother's phantom voice in her head, *Work with what you've got, Gina! So what if someone else has something you like better? Stop the pity party and get moving on making your life better for yourself!*

Thank the Empress, her mom supported her even though her dad thought she should be doing something more domestic.

Gina saw a small picture on the wall from the corner of her eye. She hadn't noticed it before, but as she drew closer, she saw the symbol in the corner.

She had her arms outstretched to grab the painting when she heard the door open behind her. She quickly pulled it off the wall and turned to see who had come in.

Jasper grinned at her with a glint in his eye she could only call evil.

He strode toward her and held out his hand. "I'll take that from you, little mouse girl."

She stared at him incredulously. "Are you kidding me? This is mine! And 'mouse girl?' Seriously? That's the worst nickname ever!"

The grin morphed into a snarl as Jasper reached her. "You can't take me down, so I don't care what your name is. I'm taking that."

Gina internally winced. He was right. She hadn't managed to win a fight against him yet. She failed to dodge before he grabbed the small painting and pulled. She felt the material give a little and let go so it wouldn't break. Jasper seemed to count on that as he turned his momentum into a dash for the door.

"Hey!" Gina raced after him but was a couple of steps behind him as he reached the door and opened it.

She heard a startled sound outside just before she ran through and found Jasper facing the stoic Sergeant Hardass, aka Agent Shaw. Gina groaned in frustration.

"We can take him if we fight him together!" Jasper shouted as he went into a defensive stance, his focus on Shaw.

"Oh, hell no!" Gina scoffed and slid her foot to pull Jasper's back leg out.

She felt a shiver of delight run down her spine when the jerkoff fell to the floor. She placed her boot lightly on his neck.

Gina leaned down and plucked the painting out of his hand. The pressure on his windpipe made Jasper reflexively let go of it in favor of reaching up to grab her foot.

"I'll take this back, thank you very much."

"Very nice job, Gina." Agent Shaw spoke approvingly.

She flashed a grin. Maybe she had some awesomeness of her own.

Jasper groaned and pushed against the foot on his neck. Bitch! Who did she think she was?

He stopped when he heard Agent Shaw's next words.

"That was such a great takedown that I think you deserve one of the items Jasper has too."

Gina gasped. "Really?"

Jasper frowned. The man couldn't do that! It had to be against the rules. He tried to yell, but the pressure of the boot on his neck rendered his words unintelligible.

"You can let him up now, Gina."

She removed her foot, and he took deep breaths. His throat felt bruised. He patted his neck as soreness flooded his system, then glared up at the agent.

"That's mine," he rasped.

"Not anymore." Shaw smiled pleasantly.

The trainer leaned down to pull Jasper's bag off his shoulder. Jasper clenched his hands and wanted to pummel the man for taking what was his, but he knew he would be kicked out. The tradeoff wasn't worth it.

But it was tempting.

Jasper got to his feet as the man held open the bag for Gina to pick an item. He seethed at the show of delight the bitch made as she put her mousy little hands all over his items. *His items!*

Not that they were worth anything. His family had enough money to buy everything several times over. It was the hunt and the chase he relished and the satisfaction of knowing he had won.

When they were finished, Jasper held out his hand for his bag. Shaw stared at him while he slowly put the straps into Jasper's hand.

"Are you both going to come along quietly and accept that you are caught?" the agent asked.

Neither of them spoke for several moments, then Gina sighed. "Yes."

When a few more seconds had passed without Jasper speaking, Shaw raised an eyebrow at him.

"Unless you want to fight it out?"

Jasper scowled. "Fine. Yes."

"Good."

They fell in next to him as they passed agents who had been giving them a wide berth in the hallway until now.

Jasper blinked a few times when his vision went blurry for several seconds, but it passed.

"Where are we going?" Gina asked.

Trust the mousy suck-up to make conversation with their captor. Jasper had wondered the same thing, and it was better if she asked.

"You will see when you get there." Shaw was amused at their expense, judging from his tone.

Great. Just great. Cryptic comments from the almighty Hardass. He didn't think he could take much more of this.

But wherever they were going should be with the other trainees. Jasper couldn't wait to see Phina's face when she found out he had won with the most items.

Priceless.

There were some things even money couldn't buy, and not for lack of trying.

Gaitune-67, Spy Corps Headquarters and Base, Movie Theater

Ian casually slunk around the corner as he headed for the movie theater. It was the only room in the central wing he hadn't searched yet.

He had completely changed his appearance, spiking hair instead of his usual shaggy style. He had also put in colored contacts and borrowed clothes from Kabaka. Ian had found some strange objects early on in his explorations on the base and had later been pleased to learn that they were to place in the back and sides of his mouth to elongate his jaw. This one change served to not just elongate the length of his face but how he spoke, so his speech pattern sounded different.

His disguise had worked. He had been wandering around with the agents none the wiser for hours.

Grinning, Ian danced a few steps once he entered the room and found it empty. Hah! Screw you, Jasper and Cade! He was tired of the constant flak from those assholes. Ian bet they hadn't made it nearly as long since they were both cocky bastards.

He shimmied and whirled in self-congratulation, then froze. An agent in a form-fitting atmosuit leaned against the wall with a grin on her face.

A very attractive and sexy agent.

His mouth dropped open, and words fled his brain.

"Hey, what's so exciting?"

"I...uh..." Ian flapped his mouth ineffectively, struggling to put his thoughts together. Damn it. This always happened.

"Is it the competition the newbs are having?" She straightened and walked over with a friendly smile.

Ian blinked. This beautiful woman thought he was another agent. He finally got his mouth working.

"No...I...uh... No." He shook his head.

Well, sort of got his mouth working. Seriously, why couldn't he have gotten the gregarious gene from his mom to come out around attractive women? Instead, he got his awkwardness from his dad.

"So..." She stopped in front of him and peered up with dark lashes framing amber eyes. "What are you so excited about?"

You, he thought and flushed, happy for once that his brain-mouth filter didn't always work right. The extra blood flow finally helped his brain to begin processing again.

"Just, you know, life in general, and working on being the best agent." He stopped as his mouth dried up.

"You know what they say about being the best agent?" The woman flashed him a grin as she leaned in and put her hands on his chest.

"Wh-what?" he whispered faintly.

She turned her head to whisper in his ear. "You always have to be alert to your surroundings."

To his disappointment, she eased back and flashed him another easy grin before calling over her shoulder. "You got it from here?"

"Yup," a voice next to him answered, startling him.

Ian blinked at Beta Agent Masha and at the woman leaving the room. When the door closed behind her, he was able to breathe normally again. "Who was that?"

Masha glanced at the door. "That was Gen, short for Genevieve."

"Genevieve," Ian repeated as he stared at the closed door. "I'm going to marry her."

The beta agent sighed. "Come on. Let's get you to the room."

"You don't believe me." Ian tried to grit his teeth but remembered the mouthguard that kept his back teeth from meeting.

Shaking her head, Masha gently tugged Ian by the shoulder to lead him out of the room. "That woman hasn't dated anyone since she joined the agency, and she's determined to keep it that way. I doubt anyone is going to change her mind."

"Well, it's going to be me," Ian declared.

"You stalk her, and I'll break your knees." Masha spoke matter-of-factly.

Ian turned another shade whiter but shook his head. It didn't matter.

He was already more than half in love with the woman.

Gaitune-67, Spy Corps Headquarters and Base

Kabaka skeptically appraised the group of agents chatting casually in the lobby.

Too casually.

He had been waiting around the corner when Ian and Beta Agent Masha had come out of the movie theater, talking about a woman. The way they spoke made him think that the woman had waylaid Ian so he got caught.

Since then, he had grown very suspicious about any seemingly innocent agents. Agent Shaw *had* spoken of "obstacles" and other agents participating.

He knew some of the other trainees had been caught already, including Jasper and Cade. He felt no sympathy for those men. They were honorless, self-focused, and lacking any concern for Justice and integrity.

Kabaka was the youngest child of Bandile and Dova Annane and had been taught by both to value all people and act with care so he could be proud of his actions and be able to look at himself in the mirror every morning. It had been a struggle to convince them he could keep that integrity and join Spy Corps, but they had accepted that he knew his own mind. He wasn't easily swayed by others.

To Kabaka, those two trainees were reprehensible, and he had difficulty trusting that the agents in charge understood what sort of men they had allowed into the program.

Still, it had given him great satisfaction to see them caught.

Seeing the agents turn their heads as if searching while they talked also gave him great satisfaction in knowing he was right. They had to be involved somehow.

Kabaka's vision blurred suddenly. He closed his eyes against the sudden dizziness. The blur had tracked from right to left in his vision, almost as if...

He opened his eyes and searched the room, noting that the blurriness was gone.

Strange. It couldn't have been an eye problem. He knew he had excellent vision. That would make it a problem imposed upon him by outside forces.

Which led him to the fantastical conclusion he came to.

The blur had been an unseen person moving from one side of the corridor to the other.

But who—or *what*—could manage that?

Felan leaned against the wall on the other side of the room, staring at Kabaka, who was staring at the agents. It amused him to see how wary the brilliant young man was.

Of course, Kabaka's wariness was justified. Having every agent participating in the task with a goal of distracting or waylaying the trainees was a tactic the sly agents who oversaw their training would use.

Catching something out of the corner of his eye, Felan turned and saw a female-shaped blur that could have been Phina move along the corridor and stop behind Kabaka before moving on.

He grinned. On the inside, of course.

Phina's movements and interactions since she had arrived on the base had been a source of interest and amusement to Felan. The young woman had spunk and a core of strength that drove her to find the answers she was clearly here searching for. What those answers were, Felan didn't know, although he suspected it was serious and a matter of great secrecy since it was clear that not even the beta agents knew.

Although... Both beta agents had altered their manner toward Phina recently, so perhaps one or both knew about her objective. Not that he would ask either of them.

Felan was fine keeping his thoughts to himself, something his ex-wife had often mentioned to him with exasperation. Telling her he didn't feel like sharing his thoughts with her so she could pass them off as gossip to her friends had probably been the final nail in the coffin for their marriage.

That was all right with Felan. The woman had talked far too much for his liking. He couldn't remember what about her had appealed to him, but perhaps the adage was true that opposites attract. More likely that they drove each other crazy in the long run, but that was his personal opinion.

Sensing someone approach, Felan took his gaze off the wary dance Kabaka had entered into with the agents and turned to see Shaw.

The trainer nodded in greeting and raised an amused eyebrow at the agents, who had been gradually spreading apart as they talked in an attempt to draw Kabaka in.

"What's going on there?"

Felan shrugged. "An awkward dance between suspicion and futility."

"Huh. Sounds somewhat intriguing. Any particular reason you are not participating?" Shaw's inquiry was curious but also friendly. They had known each other in the Guardian Marines before becoming involved in Spy Corps, and they had spent many hours over beers after training.

The Wechselbalg gave the man a faint smile, which Shaw knew for him was the equivalent of a maddened grin. "Because I know how this exercise will end, so I might as well get my amusement in the meantime."

Shaw's eyebrows rose in surprise. "You have insider knowledge I haven't given you?"

Felan leaned back on his heels. "Let's just say I've weighed the odds, and the odds are good that it will end how I think."

Shaw shook his head with a rueful smile. "And you know the odds because..."

"Know the players, know the odds." Felan offered his old mantra and glanced at Kabaka, who had turned his wary speculation in their direction.

His old friend followed his gaze. "Think he'd stay if we walked over there? I'm assuming you're accepting being caught."

"He's too curious not to." Felan nodded. "Told you, I know how this ends."

Shaw shook his head in amusement as they walked around the frustrated agents, who turned toward them and realized theirs was an exercise in futility. "This is why I recommended you, man. You have that uncanny knack of knowing what's going to happen."

Felan shrugged. "It is what it is. Weighing the odds is a lot like predicting the future. Slippery as hell, but manageable if you know the players and the layers."

"Still remarkable."

The Wechselbalg remained silent as they approached Kabaka. The younger man glanced at the two of them uncertainly, ready to dash away at the slightest provocation.

Felan gave him something else to think about.

"Want to let yourself be caught so we can end this and finally see the show?"

Kabaka was startled, then thoughtful, then he visibly relaxed. "Sure. Why the hell not?"

. . .

Gaitune-67, Spy Corps Headquarters and Base, Office Area

Jahlek gingerly opened the door and peeked out into the corridor. Not spotting anyone around, he slid out the door and down to the next one.

He frowned when he met resistance and pushed a few more buttons on the device in his hand before trying again. The door slid open. Jahlek allowed himself a quick grin since his hands were too occupied for a fist pump before cautiously entering and closing the door behind him.

He surveyed the office, which contained a large desk stacked with papers. Jahlek shook his head at the waste. He didn't see any need for the human fascination with paper. Tablets and devices could do so much more in an easy to hold and store fashion. He gave the papers a cursory glance before slipping between the end of the desk and a potted plant.

After a glance filled with envy at the beautiful katana and daggers displayed on the wall, Jahlek got down to the business of searching through the drawers. Not even a minute had passed before the quiet clearing of a throat came from the corner.

Jahlek froze.

He didn't want to look but couldn't help himself. As his gaze rose and met with the owner of the noise, Jahlek wished he had never gotten out of bed that morning.

Alpha Agent Greyson Wells leaned against the wall in the corner staring at him expectantly.

"Um..." Jahlek mumbled unintelligibly.

"What was that, kid?"

Jahlek's skin flushed rosy pink under his fur. "Um...I...ah...I said I didn't see you there."

The alpha agent flashed him a look that clearly said, "No kidding." "Is that it?"

"Uh, no?" Jahlek's thoughts reeled as he searched his brain for a reason he would be going through the alpha agent's belongings. "I didn't know this was your office? I mean, uh..."

"Well, at least you're trying." Greyson Wells sighed. "Lesson number seven: Always have a plausible reason for being where you are, kid. And lesson number eight: If you don't have one, create the reason before you get there. Want to know why?"

Jahlek blinked and scratched the back of his head. "So I don't freeze up?" he answered tentatively.

Wells pointed at him. "Exactly right. The brains are oozing back now, aren't they?"

The Noel-ni had no chance to wonder if that was an insult before the man moved on. "Have your reason set in your head so that even if you do freeze up, you already have a handy reason to fall back on."

"Right." That made sense and would have prevented him from looking like a moron.

"Want to take your hands out of my drawer, kid? You won't find what you're searching for in there anyway."

Jahlek flushed again as he snatched his hand out and slammed the drawer shut. "I'm...uh, I'm trying to find those items with the symbol."

Alpha Agent Wells shook his head sadly. "Yeah, that's not gonna cut the mustard. See, we know who comes through these doors and why." He pursed his lips in distaste. "Well, someone missed Blayk, but he had his issues tucked down inside for the most part."

Jahlek's ears perked up. That was something he hadn't heard about Blayk's unfortunate demise. Before he could wonder any more about it, the alpha agent's next words caused his blood to freeze.

"Rest assured, however, that our sources were very thorough where *you're* concerned, my lad."

Deflect and distract. The actions that had been recently drilled into him thundered through his head.

"I don't know what you mean, sir." Jahlek eased back, wishing he had a way to flee. Unfortunately, the alpha agent stood between him and the door.

The man grinned. "Oh, I think you do, but don't worry. You aren't in trouble." He paused, then spoke deliberately. "At the moment." He stared at Jahlek to get his point across before continuing in a lighthearted tone, "We'll have a little discussion later. Right now, I believe things are just about set for this evening's show. Follow me."

Jahlek frowned as he hesitantly followed the man out of the door at his gesture. "Is something happening after the end of the exercise announcement? They haven't said anything."

"Nope." Greyson Wells spoke almost cheerfully. "That *is* the show."

"I'm not sure I'm following."

The human grinned, causing Jahlek to cringe. It still gave Jahlek the willies to see teeth bared that weren't pointed and nicely sharp. Bared teeth were supposed to be a warning that the other was encroaching on your territory. These humans flashed their teeth at everything. Ugh.

"Well." Agent Wells unknowingly broke into his thoughts with another cringeworthy grin. "Phina's undoubtedly going to be the last person caught. If I know my girl, she's going to do something ballsy and clever."

Gaitune-67, Spy Corps Headquarters and Base, Assembly Room

Savas fingered the hilts of his practice knives, wondering if he should fight Jack Kaiser and get away.

"I wouldn't do it." The beta agent spoke calmly as he opened the double doors Savas hadn't entered at the end of the dining room corridor.

The large room beyond held the majority of the Spy Corps population currently on base. Murmurs and whispers combined buzzed around the room as Savas followed Jack up toward the dais at the front of the room.

The trainees had been lined up in the middle of the platform to face the growing audience. They all had backpacks or bags on and had dressed in a variety of clothing between casual and what could be termed spy wear. As Savas scanned the line, he began to hope that he had been last.

His hopes were dashed when he reached the end and realized that Phina was not among their number.

Ah, well. He hadn't really thought he would win, but it would have been nice. He stepped onto the dais at the beta agent's gesture and took his spot at the end of the line.

Jack turned toward them and spoke so only trainees could hear. "Shaw and Masha are searching for Phina. Once they find her, we will continue."

Savas glanced at the door and was alarmed when his vision blurred for a few seconds. That had never happened before. Why was he having eye problems all of a sudden?

He felt a slight tug on the bag on his back. Gripping his bag with firmer hands, Savas turned his head to see if Jahlek was messing with it. The Noel-ni glanced at him with a puzzled expression but didn't appear to be interested in his bag, so Savas remained silent.

After another minute or two, his right eye went blurry. He closed it, hoping no one would notice. Gingerly, Savas opened his eye again, but his vision seemed normal. Just in case, he decided to get checked out by Medical the next day.

It hadn't been long until Beta Agents Masha and Shaw came in the room, subtly shaking their heads when Jack sent a silent inquiry.

The beta agent frowned and turned to Alpha Agent Greyson Wells, who sat in the front row, grinning like a fool.

Not that he thought the man was a fool. No, no. Far from it.

The three trainers glanced at the alpha agent occasionally as they talked, their voices low. Savas made out one phrase, a phrase he wondered if he had heard correctly.

The EI can't find her.

Savas didn't know everything EIs could do, but the thought that Shade couldn't find one woman on the base was troubling.

Jack Kaiser moved to the front of the platform and clapped his hands twice. The whispered conversations died as the agents turned to listen.

"Seraphina Waters, if you are present, please show yourself. You have won the challenge for the last trainee caught."

Silence filled with anticipation fell in the room as everyone searched the room to see if she was there.

After ten long seconds, a woman popped up in the back and stepped forward. Whispers began to grow again as the woman walked past the rows until she reached the front.

It wasn't until she stopped halfway between the audience and the dais that she spoke. "Present and accounted for, Beta Agent Kaiser."

Savas straightened his spine and craned his neck. It was Phina's voice, but he hardly recognized her.

He stared at the changes Phina had made to her appearance. She'd lightened the skin on her face and neck by several shades, and the contours of her face had been altered with makeup, making her face look entirely different. Her nose looked thinner, and her cheeks showed more sharply. Even the shape and color of her eyes was different. Her hair was pulled up in what Gina called a ponytail, a style he'd never seen Phina wear since she liked it either down or in a braid.

Lastly, she wore the uniform of a full agent.

Phina looked nothing like herself except for her height and hair color.

Savas shook his head in wonder.

She had already earned his respect since she had beat him in a fight several times. But now...

Well, he didn't feel quite so bad about coming in second place.

Phina stood waiting in front of Beta Agent Jack. She could hear the whispers behind her, as well as the astonished gasps of surprise of the trainees in front of her.

She heard the questions passing through everyone's mind and put up a stronger mental shield that only let select thoughts through.

Nice job, my dear. Shock and amazement are always the way to go.

I don't think your old pal Jack agrees with you, Link. Phina saw several fleeting emotions that confused her cross Jack's face.

He'll get over it.

The beta agent in question nodded and gestured for her to join the line onstage. "Beta Agent Masha will count your items."

Phina handed over her backpack. Masha set each item to the side as she counted, finally announcing the number. "Five."

Jack glanced at Phina and spoke softly, though she could still hear him easily. "Strange. I would have expected more."

She gave the agent an enigmatic smile and moved to stand at the spot next to Savas, who handed over his bag when Shaw held out his hand.

"Five," Masha called after counting and lining up the items on the table.

Next was Jahlek.

"Five."

The Noel-ni was confused.

The murmuring from the audience grew louder as the next few trainees handed over their items to be counted with the same result of five. The other trainees gradually became more intrigued and more surprised.

Masha reached Jasper. "Two."

The room buzzed louder as Jasper protested, "Hey! I had more than two. I had at least six of those things before Gina took two for herself!"

Gina and Nodin were pleased but confused with five apiece.

Cade had only two, and his face showed both anger and confusion.

Finally, Balehn had a total of five.

Masha looked at Jack in confusion. "I don't know how this could have happened, but they all are tied with five, save for Jasper and Cade who are tied at the bottom with two."

The whispers rose in volume, causing a buzzing within the room. Jack held up a hand and turned toward Phina, and the volume dropped again.

Masha and Shaw watched from the side with curiosity and confusion.

"How did you do it?" The beta agent's voice was strident and demanding.

Phina's expression gave nothing away. "Pardon?"

"The items," he responded impatiently, ignoring the agents' astonished reaction to his harsh manner. "How did you redistribute them without anyone noticing?"

She remained silent.

He visibly took a deep breath and glanced along the

row at the other trainees before turning back to Phina with a frown. "I know it was you."

Absolute silence fell in the room.

Phina feigned sheepishness as she shrugged while turning her hands palms up.

"Magic?"

CHAPTER TWENTY-FOUR

Gaitune-67, Spy Corps Headquarters and Base

Shaw slipped in between agents as they all talked together in groups. He felt the pulse of the music playing in the lounge spilling over into the library, a rare occurrence on the base.

A hand grabbed his arm, and he swung around at the interruption. Jack stood to his right, tense with impatience and anger. "What the hell was that about, Shaw?"

He dislodged his arm and stared at the man with a frown. "What the hell was what about?"

"That whole display with almost everyone being tied," Jack ranted. "Is she making a mockery of our training? Does she have it in for someone? She doesn't like Cade and Jasper for some reason. And how the hell did she pull it all off?"

Shaw held on to his patience. "If you mean Phina, how should I know? I'm not in her confidence."

Jack's eyebrows rose. "You certainly keep your eye on her enough."

Shuttering his expression, Shaw barely kept his hands from clenching. "Are you accusing me of something?"

"Of course not." The beta agent appeared to calm, although the light in his eyes made Shaw nervous.

"Well, then." Shaw glanced around and caught sight of Cade and Jasper speaking intensely. He continued to watch them as he threw over his shoulder, "If you'll excuse me, there's something I need to do."

The devoted man guided his chosen tool down the corridor and into an unused training room.

"What is this all about?" Cade demanded.

The man stared at the trainee in disgust. Cade's arrogance compared to his usable skills was laughable at best. Still, there was a reason the devoted man hadn't done anything about him yet.

"I have a proposal for you. Tomorrow it will be announced that Phina is the winner and you will be dismissed from the program."

Cade scowled, his face turning red. "That's total shit. She doesn't deserve to win, and I don't deserve to leave!"

"Well," the devoted man drawled, "these decisions are based on results. However," he added before Cade interrupted, "the proposal I have would neatly solve this problem for you."

The sullen trainee scowled and asked, "What's your proposal?"

"Kill Phina." The devoted man felt a pang in his heart, but he firmed up his resolve to follow the direction of his

Empress. "Make it look like an accident if you can. If you succeed, then I'll fix it so you will be a Spy Corps agent."

Cade smiled triumphantly.

Gaitune-67, Spy Corps Headquarters and Base

Phina took a relieved breath as she pulled away from the celebratory crowd. It felt like everyone wanted to talk to her about her skills, the exercise, her disguise, her relationship with Link, and a thousand other things she didn't wish to expand upon.

Not only did the questions make her feel uncomfortable, but so did the constant sharp and probing gazes of the other agents.

She was worn out from using Etheric energy throughout the exercise. Phina had only used her speed and a clever mind trick Sundancer had taught her that hadn't worked on everyone. Still, she needed some rest before she went out later to scan the last few minds, including Shaw's.

It had been extremely satisfying to use her hacking skills to set up a tracking program so she could monitor the locations of the three trainers as well as the trainees. She could finally admit that Alina's attempts to get her interested in makeup had also had their use.

Shade had told her that putting a block on her tracking capabilities just for Phina was not permissible. Completely changing her appearance with a few products her best friend insisted she always carry had been a stroke of brilliance. Sneaking around the base unseen had given her a thrill that she usually only got when she was flying on the bars or spending time with Todd.

All of this had further solidified her decisions about the future and what she wanted it to look like. Once all this was over, she would need to have a long talk with Link that he may not be happy about. That was all right with Phina. The man needed a reason to stay on his toes.

She turned the corner of the corridor leading to her room and almost ran nose-first into somebody. Phina took a step back just in time to avoid a collision, but she couldn't miss the rank smell of stale sweat. Lifting her chin, she saw Cade blocking her way and scowled.

"Something you want to say?"

The trainee shook his head as a slow vengeful grin spread across his face. "Eat this and die, bitch."

Several things happened so quickly that an observer might have seen them occurring simultaneously. Phina registered a knife—real, not a practice one—heading for her face and moved. In her tired and shocked state, she felt a bolt of panic that Cade was actually trying to kill her and pulled hard on her connection to the Etheric. Energy flooded her brain and body, urging her to preternatural speed as she dodged the knife. She heard someone call out behind her, and while the words didn't register, the alarm in the man's voice did.

Not wanting to have someone at her back while she fought, Phina grabbed Cade's hand and wrist to take control of the knife. She kicked him in the groin, causing him to crumple. As he went down, she dislocated his knife arm and side-kicked him in the head, sending him crashing into the wall across the hall.

Phina heard footsteps approaching and turned, half-crouched with the knife she had removed from Cade's slack hand raised defensively.

"Wait!" Shaw stopped a few paces away with his hands up, surprise and wariness on his face. "What's going on here, Phina?"

"You tell me," she demanded evenly.

When he frowned, Phina opened her mind to scan his surface thoughts. Unfortunately, they were racing along with his heart rate and were difficult to follow.

What's she asking... Put him down so fast... Had a knife? Must have been a good reason... Never seen... Trust... Do something...

Struggling to keep her expression even given the rush of energy still flowing through her and the confusion in his mind, Phina interrupted what he would have said with a wave of the knife.

"You just had a thought that there must have been a good reason. Who were you thinking about?"

Surprise flashed over his face. "You, Phina. You aren't the type to attack people without provocation. Want to put that knife down and tell me what happened?"

"Not yet." She surprised herself with how calm she felt.

Shaw's expression flashed with annoyance, but he nodded. "All right. So, what's going on here?"

"Cade decided to kill me."

Phina was startled to see the cold glare Shaw tossed at Cade before his gaze softened again. "Are you all right?"

She waved her free hand at herself. "As you see."

He nodded and glanced at the knife. "Can I put my hands down now?"

Phina pressed her lips together as she considered the agent. "What would you say if I said someone else had sent him after me?"

A flash of rage contorted his face before he regained control. He slowly lowered his hands as he replied. "I would say that's interesting and I'm listening."

The noise from the crowd Phina had tuned out echoed down the hall, causing her to remember they were in the open.

She stood and backed away, then gestured at the unconscious Cade. "Bring him. We should have this conversation privately."

Shaw nodded and reached for Cade's arm, then followed her as he dragged the limp body behind him. Phina smirked when she noticed he didn't show much care in protecting Cade from bruises as he hauled the man through the doorway of her room.

Phina kept Shaw in sight as she pulled out a length of thin rope and tossed it to him. "Tie him up, please."

Shaw caught it and glanced at the rope in his hand before raising his gaze to her. "Is there a reason we need to tie him up instead of taking him to Holding?"

"Yup."

He stared at her, waiting.

"I'll tell you after you tie him up."

Shaw considered and nodded. "Fair enough."

Once Cade had his arms and legs trussed behind him, Shaw leaned against the wall by the door and gestured. "Please explain, now. I'm attempting to convince myself that I have a good reason for not following procedure here."

Phina took a deep breath. "I'm not just here as a trainee for Spy Corps."

He nodded, studying her speculatively. "I had been wondering about that. So, what did bring you here?"

She spoke flatly. "I'm on a mission."

Before Shaw could question her, she spoke up. "Shade, please confirm this for Agent Shaw."

"Hello, Agent Shaw. Seraphina Waters is here with permission and approval for the objective of the mission."

"All right." He relaxed when he recognized the voice. "Shade must be the base's EI, but surely if you are on a sanctioned mission..."

Phina interrupted him while holding his gaze. "Shade, please tell Shaw the mission code."

"The mission code is top-secret, Empress' Eyes Only-slash-Alpha-One-Priority-Black."

His face paled. "You are on a mission that only the Empress and the alpha agent know about?"

She gave him a short nod. "Yes."

"How can there be something *that* big going on in Spy Corps and we don't know about it?" He shook his head in confusion and anger.

"There's a traitor here," Phina told him, maintaining eye contact and keeping a read on his mind. "Someone has sold the Empire out, and if I'm right, has both directly and indirectly caused the deaths of many citizens."

Shock filled his face as Phina leaned forward. "And before we go any further, I need to make sure that traitor isn't you."

.   .   .

Gaitune-67, Spy Corps Headquarters and Base, Dining Room

Link had been amused throughout the night. He always got a kick out of how everyone interacted: the more senior agents were either loners or highly social animals, and the newer agents vacillated between amusing attempts to be smooth like James Bond and wide-eyed awe at the stories the older agents told. All fodder for the laughter mill.

However, he also felt an odd sense of nostalgia, as if everything would change after tonight.

Strange.

He enjoyed the blend of delicious scents wafting from the kitchen until a bright flash of a smile caught his attention and caused him to begin to brood.

Ah. Masha.

Her dress uniform fit her body in ways he wished stuck only to his nightly dreams. Only young men had the luxury of daydreams, and he hadn't been young in quite some time.

Riling the woman had become one of his favorite pastimes. The brunette was spectacular when she had a mad on, her eyes bright and fiery, her strong but curvy body...

Ah, well.

He purposely turned his head away. Not for the likes of you, old man.

Link searched the crowd for Phina, wanting to give her one last congratulation before he headed up to his chambers to sleep. Or perhaps to the office to catch up on current and future missions, he hadn't decided.

When he couldn't find her, he frowned and searched

more thoroughly. Then he pinged Shade through his implant.

Shade, I can't find Phina. Do you have her under surveillance?

She is currently in her quarters with Agent Shaw and Trainee Cade, the EI responded.

His face contorted in surprise before shuttering his emotions. Masha frowned at him in concern and walked over. Before either of them could say anything, a drop in the volume of conversation caused them both to stop and glance around.

A familiar figure had stepped onto one of the tables and stood with an air of enlightened authority.

Link put two, three, and five together to make ten. A dismaying, disillusioning ten that scored his heart in the middle.

He shook his head and murmured, "Bloody hell, Phina. This couldn't possibly be any worse."

Gaitune-67, Spy Corps Headquarters and Base, Phina's Room

Phina thought she knew which way the wind blew when she saw devastated fury cross Shaw's face.

"You are telling me that we've had a traitor here at Spy Corps, giving our information to our enemies?" he snapped angrily.

"That's about the size of it."

"How long?"

"It's only speculation at this point, but if I'm right, it's been years."

Shaw blinked and took a breath as he glanced at Cade on the floor. "So, not one of the trainees."

"It's not very likely," she agreed.

"Which is why you said earlier you thought he had been sent."

"Yes."

He fell silent for a few moments as he thought before turning his gaze back to her. "You obviously don't know who it is since you said you had to make sure it's not me."

Phina spread her hands. "I've checked out everyone except a handful of people, but as far as suspects who had access and means, it's a short list."

His gaze turned intent. "How short?"

She gave him a thin smile. "Pretty damn short."

"All right." He lifted his chin. "What do I need to do to prove I'm not the traitor?"

Stepping forward, she stood in front of him as his gaze remained trained on her. "Do you trust me?"

With his life. "Yes."

"Will you let me do what I need to do to prove it one way or another? Even if it feels like a violation or makes your skin crawl?"

Confusion and puzzlement crossed his face before clearing into determination. "Do whatever you need to do so we can find this bastard."

She nodded at the bed. "Sit, then."

Confusion crossed his face again though he did as directed. "What does it make a difference if I'm sitting?"

"Because if you are aware, this can be disconcerting," she told him.

He did as she asked. "What now?"

"Hold still." Phina didn't have to, but she put her hands on either side of his head and held his gaze as she opened her mind to his to do a deep scan. She still felt a bit jittery from the pull earlier, so energy wasn't a problem.

Shaw was startled when he realized what was happening. "Oh, shit!"

Phina didn't answer, her mind focused on his thoughts and memories. His present, and what had happened today. His childhood growing up with his mother after his father had died during a skirmish with rebel Yollins when the Empire was still young. His time as a Marine and his relationships with Todd and Felan. His first kiss, his last girlfriend. His memories of his father and the memories of training with Link, Jack, and Masha. Training his own students, training her.

Flowing through it all was the dedication to his duty and love for the Etheric Empire his father had died for, his determination to take care of and protect his fellow soldiers and agents—especially those he cared about, his sense of honor, and his respect for the position he held, thinly-veiled impatience and disregard for those who disrespected others, the responsibility he felt for training agents to be prepared so they wouldn't die carelessly and needlessly, his love and respect for his mother, anger, sadness, and disappointment that someone would betray them all by turning traitor, a flare of rage for whoever sent Cade after her, and—

Her face showed shock and surprise as she withdrew gently and dropped her hands. She took a few unsteady steps away from him.

"Are you all right?" Shaw asked.

Phina nodded jerkily. "Shaky, jittery. It takes me a minute to..." she waved a hand and grimaced, "feel completely myself and compartmentalize. I was already zinging from the encounter with Cade."

He nodded but remained silent and watchful.

"Shaw..."

Pressing his lips together grimly, he shook his head. "Later. Do you have what you need to be sure the traitor isn't me?"

She gathered her thoughts, running through her sense of him again. Then she carefully packaged it together as Sundancer had shown her and sent it to the back of her mind. "It's not you."

He stood, visibly steeling himself before meeting her gaze again. "What is your next step to finding this traitor?"

Phina assessed him, although she purposely kept from reading his thoughts again. "Can I talk you into letting me handle this?"

"If you did what I just think you did, you should know the answer to that, I imagine."

She nodded, turned to Cade, and knelt. She didn't need to put her hands on his head as she'd done with Shaw, but she did so anyway. The action helped her focus on what she was doing, and she needed that focus after everything that had happened.

Her lip curled in disgust as she read his mind. She did a deep scan but focused on his recent memories.

Shaw's voice broke her concentration. "What is it?"

"Shh." Phina shook her head. "Need to focus."

He fell silent, and she continued to examine Cade's consciousness as it flowed past her. She withdrew and shook herself as if she could throw off the memories she had seen and the feel of his mind.

Phina stood and closed her eyes, bringing his most recent memories to the forefront of her mind to be cataloged. Again, she packaged them and placed them in the back part of her mind, where she didn't need to touch them anymore.

Phina opened her eyes to see Shaw focused on her in concern.

"What is it?"

Before she could answer, she heard Sundancer's agitated voice. *Phina, come quickly to the dining room and lounge. It's bad and getting worse. Bring everything.*

She straightened in alarm and dashed around the room at full speed, gathering her hidden weapons and strapping them on. She grabbed her tablet and everything else she had stowed away for this moment.

She was moving toward the door when Shaw's urgent words penetrated her alarm.

"Phina! Damn, she's fast. Phina! What's wrong?"

Turning to face him, she let her alarm, fear, and anger show. "I know who the traitor is, and we're all in trouble."

Shaw's eyes hardened even as he cursed and shook his head.

She gestured impatiently at Cade. "Follow me to the dining room quickly, and bring him."

Without waiting to hear his response, Phina turned and ran as fast as her enhanced body would carry her.

CHAPTER TWENTY-FIVE

Gaitune-67, Spy Corps Headquarters and Base, Dining Room

Link's heart sank as he heard the words coming out of the mouth of one of his oldest friends.

"I have an important announcement to make." Jack Kaiser had a fervent light in his eye as he spoke solemnly. "There has been a cancer among us, eating our organization from within."

Shocked whispers spread through the crowd, and a few people yelled to demand to know what he was talking about.

"It is to my great regret that I inform you one of our own has turned traitor."

Link shook his head in disbelief. He felt a tug on his arm, and Masha whispered, "Did you tell him?"

"No," he responded softly.

"Phina?"

"No." She wouldn't have.

Masha glanced between Link and Jack in confusion as

Jack continued. Link couldn't bring himself to spell it out for her.

"It deeply saddens me that one of our brightest students chose to betray our beloved Empress and Empire, but it remains the truth, unfortunately."

"Who is it?" someone in the crowd called angrily from behind Link. Murmurs and similar calls rang out until Jack raised his hands for quiet. The noise of the crowd of agents used to following Jack's orders dropped into silence.

Jack glanced at Link, his expression regretful, though who knew if it was genuine or not, before turning back to the crowd.

"Seraphina Waters!"

As the crowd reacted with surprised outrage, Link reflected that he hadn't realized he had been holding onto a smidgeon of hope until it had died. There was no chance that Phina, his adopted niece and the child of his heart, had turned.

The traitor had to be Jack.

Hadn't he made unexpected trips to the *Meredith Reynolds*? Hadn't he been there at the same time as the trouble with the Qendrok? Link had accepted the reasoning Jack had given, but there couldn't be any hiding Jack's actions now. Further, Jack's words and actions were out of character. Clearly, something was wrong.

Link raised his voice and spoke firmly. "That is a lie, Jack. Phina would never betray the Etheric Empire. The only traitor here is you for turning against her."

The crowd was hushed. He could still hear some angry murmurings and knew this situation was a powder keg waiting to explode.

Masha gasped and clutched Link's arm, her voice devastated as she whispered, "No, *no*."

Link sympathized with her since he felt the same way. It was unthinkable that Jack would turn traitor. Yet, the evidence was being played out before his eyes.

Jack stood strong and stared pityingly across the distance that separated them. "It is unfortunate that the traitor has convinced you with her lies, Greyson."

"Dammit, Jack, she hasn't lied! I don't know what screw got loose in your head, but I know exactly where her loyalties lie, and she isn't a damned traitor!"

The beta agent continued to shake his head sadly while the crowd kept swiveling their heads between them. "I didn't want to have to fight you too, Wells."

Link straightened to his full height meeting his friend's...his *former* friend's gaze. "If you go against Phina, you go against me, Jack. You know who her parents were. There's no chance she would turn traitor."

Jack scoffed. "Her parents? She turned traitor *because* of her parents. The Empire took her family away, and she wants revenge."

Masha spoke firmly, all traces of the devastation removed. "You're being very brave here, Jack, accusing her without her being present in the room. You aren't giving her a chance to defend herself, just slandering her with your opinions."

Pressing his lips together, the traitor nodded. "True, true, but unfortunately, she has been waylaid and won't be able to be here."

Link narrowed his gaze in suspicion. "And why is that?"

"Why, because she's dead, of course."

"That report is grossly exaggerated, I assure you," Phina called in a voice that carried from the back of the room. "You chose the wrong tool, Jack."

Link had never been so happy to see someone in his life. He sagged in relief when he saw her decked out in her full kit and weapons.

"Phina." Jack spoke tightly.

"Jack," Phina replied brightly as she advanced, the crowd inching away to let her pass, though she felt their gazes on her. "So kind of you to show yourself so we could see you as the traitor for ourselves."

He scowled. "Stop calling me a traitor, young lady! *You* are the traitor!"

"Huh." Phina paused her momentum as she tilted her head. "You believe that. Interesting. What makes you think I'm the traitor? What proof do you have?"

Jack drew himself up, his chest puffing out. "I have it on the highest authority."

"Oh?" She paused, confusion passing over her face. "Why am I hearing a clock ticking in your head?"

Phina shook her head as if it didn't matter before calling, "I find that hard to believe."

"It's the truth!" Jack exclaimed. "Not that anyone could believe anything that comes from the mouth of a traitor."

"Exactly." Phina nodded as she continued toward him with all the casualness of a leisurely stroll. "Just who could this highest authority be? It can't be Greyson Wells because we've been working together to uncover the real traitor's identity."

"What?" Jack stared at Link with horror, betrayal, and devastation. "How could you?"

"What the hell, Jack? You aren't listening or making any sense!" Link got a bad feeling and tugged Masha behind him.

"You want my authority?" Jack bellowed as his grief switched to anger. "It's from the Empress!"

The crowd startled into the noise of awe and confusion.

Phina stopped and stared at Jack. "That can't be, Jack. That's just not true."

"Again you call me a liar!" He scowled, his face twisting.

"Because we have a problem. See, Greyson and I spoke with the Empress just before we came here, Jack." She spoke calmly and firmly, with a note of kindness. "She gave us the mission to come to Spy Corps and find a traitor we had gotten wind of. Someone who had caused problems with previous assignments. Our mission is classified as Top-Secret: Empress Eyes Only-slash-Alpha-One Priority Black. The base's EI Shade can confirm she received orders to assist us from ADAM."

Jack Kaiser stared at her in bewildered confusion.

"You see, Jack," Phina continued gently, "we can't *both* have been sent by the Empress. That makes no sense since Bethany Anne is a straightforward person. She always has a reason for the actions she takes and the orders she gives. She would not have given us conflicting orders."

"No, no, no!" He shook his head as his confusion and disbelief turned to outrage. "You're trying to trick me!"

"There's no point in that, Jack," Phina answered absently. Her brow furrowed. "Seriously, how can you stand having that ticking sound in your—"

Phina broke off and stopped ten feet away from Link.

"Not ticking, but counting down." She turned to Link in alarm as she repeated, *"Counting down."*

His stomach dropped, and he swung back toward Jack in time to catch him aiming his pistol.

At Phina.

Link didn't stop to think. He didn't even remember that Phina could heal from most wounds. He just reacted to the threat against his only remaining family by throwing himself in front of her just as the gun went off.

Masha tried to catch him, but his momentum helped him slip out of her fingers.

Fire, then numbness and pain sprouted between his heart and his shoulder. His legs seemed to have lost their bones.

Link collapsed to the floor as shouts erupted around him.

Phina felt the blood rush out of her head as she realized that Link had been shot instead of her. She pushed herself out of her momentary paralysis and rushed to his side.

Masha held onto Link, her voice shaky as she pleaded with him.

Phina saw Jack lifting the gun again. Fear for Link and anger that he had been shot caused her emotions to erupt as she raised her hands and yelled with both her mouth and her mind, "Stop!"

Everyone froze in surprise, including Phina. Jack's hand involuntarily opened and dropped the gun.

Phina recovered quickly and rushed to Link. The

wound was close to his heart, but he was not in immediate danger. He still had to get to a Pod-doc urgently.

She searched her mind for something she could do, then grabbed one of her knives and sliced open her hand, focusing her mind and will on her blood dripping onto the wound.

Heal, heal, heal...

She ignored Masha's startled protests and focused on Link and Jack. When Jack began moving again, she sent energy to her hand to jumpstart the healing process while she dug into a pocket and slapped a bandage into Masha's trembling hands.

"Put that on him."

Phina didn't wait to see if she responded. She threw her knife at Jack and charged him, dodging the agents who sided with him.

She reached the table as her knife hit Jack's wrist, smacking the other pistol out of his hand.

"What?" Jack cried in confusion as the gun tumbled to the floor. "You can't move like that!"

"Sure I can."

"Only the Empress can move like that!" he protested angrily as he pulled out his double blades.

"Jack, Jack, Jack," Phina chided as she slid her short swords out from her back sheathes. "For a spy, you have been limiting yourself. If you've missed the information that there are more than the Empress with these abilities, I wonder what else you've missed."

He shook his head as if it pained him, his mouth twisted in a grimace. "It doesn't matter. You still have to die."

Phina met his double blades with easy strokes. She no

longer had to hide her enhanced speed and reflexes. She saw a few agents moving toward them with intentions to subdue her.

"By the authority granted to me by the Empress, I order you all to stand down."

She pointed one sword at them for emphasis as she continued to block Jack with the other. The agents halted, shuffling uncertainly.

"Don't just stand there!" Jack yelled as he jumped off the table to gain more space. "Come get her!"

The agents gathered themselves to obey him but were stopped by Felan and a few other agents.

"We've got this, Phina," Felan called. "Do your thing."

She flashed her fellow trainee a smile and flipped to the floor, her swords outstretched in front of her.

"Damn and blast!" Jack grimaced as he lunged at Phina. "I'll just have to do it myself."

They exchanged strikes for a minute, the beta agent's face growing red as he threw all his effort into defeating her.

It still wasn't enough.

Phina decided enough was enough and hooked one of Jack's swords, pulling it out of his hand. He growled and grabbed a dagger strapped to his thigh, refusing to give up.

"Come on, Jack. You can't keep going like this." Phina spoke softly as she continued to disarm him one weapon at a time.

"No!" His voice grew more desperate as he pulled out his last knife. "You can't beat me! I was teaching you just last week! How can you beat me this easily?"

"I was always a good student." Phina swatted Jack's

hand with the flat of her blade, forcing him to drop the knife. "And I've had several good teachers."

Now that he was disarmed, she dropped her weapons and glanced around the room. Link still lay on the floor with Masha right beside him. Shaw had finally joined them and was working to regain control of the room, along with Felan and the team leaders.

Phina reacted in time to grab the fist that had almost hit her. She turned her attention back to Jack and shook her head. "Wrong move."

She held onto his arms and pushed the beta agent back until he landed in a seat at the table behind him. She ignored his grunts of protest and the startled glances as she hauled around a man almost twice her size.

"What are you going to do to me?" Jack asked, showing a hint of panic as he tried to fight her off. Phina took out a restraint and wrapped it around his wrists, pulling it tight. She placed her hands on either side of his head as he shook it, his eyes wheeling. "No! The Empress told me to stop you!"

"I'm finding out who screwed up your life, Beta Agent Kaiser, and for the last time, it *wasn't* the Empress." Phina stared into Jack's eyes until he stopped thrashing and she knew for sure he wouldn't fight her.

Shaw, watch my back?

Phina didn't realize she had spoken mentally until she felt his surprise, then he answered.

Of course.

She shut her eyes and scrolled through Jack's memories until she found the most recent blank spot. Phina proceeded to do what she should have done weeks ago. She poked at the grayed-out memories that had been hidden and realized it had a command similar to the mental trick she had just used for the exercise attached to them. The command told anyone that messed with the memories to forget the importance of them. No wonder Phina had floundered.

Grumbling to herself, Phina increased the amount of energy she was using, which allowed her to ignore the command and focus on the memory. She didn't think it was possible to erase memories. Not completely. Something else must have been done to Jack's mind to make them appear absent.

Phina gently probed, but that didn't do much more than it had the last time. After some thought, she tried sliding around the absent memory until she found a nearly invisible crease. She did the mental equivalent of slipping her fingers underneath to separate the layers and realized that the very top layer was a compulsion for Jack to forget what had happened aside from the orders he had been given.

Hmm...

She withdrew enough to speak. "Jack, I can see the compulsion, and I think I can remove it, but I don't know how you will feel when I do or what you may remember."

She didn't get an answer, so she opened her eyes to see the large man had become subdued. Shaw stood nearby, keeping his word to watch her back.

"You really think someone messed with my brain and made me believe things that aren't true? Pretended to be the Empress?" Jack's expression had turned bilious.

Phina responded simply. "Jack, I know someone did. I

want to find who did it and make them pay for it, among many other things."

He sighed but nodded. "Do it. Get the proof you need."

She smiled in encouragement before she closed her eyes and dived back into the anomalies in his brain. She slipped her fingers back underneath the top layer. Once she had a firm grasp, she tried tugging gently, but it didn't go anywhere. After a brief contemplation about how she had compelled Jack to drop the gun, she sent a quiet but firm command right to the memory.

Remember.

Remember.

She slowly peeled the memory up. The compulsion clung to his mind as if stuck with sticky taffy. Both she and Jack winced at the pain.

She spoke quietly, her eyes still closed. "Jack, I want you to focus on remembering what happened. There are blank spots in your memory. Don't hide from them, even if it's painful. Decide you want the memory no matter the cost."

He responded with a hint of the steel that had allowed him to survive decades of war and spy missions in his tired voice. "I'll do my best."

Phina nodded in satisfaction and went back to her task, pulling energy and pushing it into the command she sent through her mental fingers. She realized the originator was female and she had talent with mental manipulation.

She pushed the realization to the back of her mind until later and focused on releasing Jack from its hold. After a few agonizing minutes, she decided to reassess.

"Phina?"

"Shaw. Just give me a minute. She's got her hooks in him tight."

A short pause. "So, he was brainwashed?"

"Definitely. Hmmm... Brainwashed. That's a good term for it." She opened her eyes to see Jack with his eyes closed in pain. Former soldier. Spy. Trainer.

Phina tilted her head as she considered what made up the man and the female who had deceived him and decided on a more subtle approach. She closed her eyes and changed the thought she was sending to the memory.

Mission accomplished. Your task is now complete.

As she did so, she lifted the command in a spiral, as if she were untwisting a cap on a bottle. It began to move. Once the compulsion had fully let go, she disintegrated it.

"Yes!" Phina couldn't help but cheer.

Jack gasped in shock and dismay. "No! Oh, no, no. I remember. I remember her telling me to kill you."

"Good." Phina gave him a fierce smile of satisfaction. "Now, let's get the rest of your memories back before something else happens."

"Yes." Jack appeared shaken but resolved to continue.

Link coughed and winced as he opened his eyes. He ignored the sounds of everything happening around him and focused on the wide, gray eyes staring at him with fear and concern.

"I'd say I'm in heaven since you're here, but I'm in too much pain to believe it." His voice rasped as he spoke, causing him to whisper the last words.

Masha wiped away her tears, then she grabbed a bottle of water and opened it for him to drink. "Hush now. You were shot. You need to rest and not say ridiculous things."

After half choking down some water, Link tried to look down at the wound. He stared in shock. "Hellfire and damnation! How am I not dead?"

"Phina." Masha gave him a watery smile, which pulled his gaze away from the bloodstains all over his shirt.

"Are you all right?" He frowned in concern.

Her face scrunched as if she wasn't certain how to respond. Then she scowled and put her hands on her hips. "Am I all right? *Am I all right?* Don't be an idiot! Of course I'm not all right! First, Jack is a traitor, and he tried to kill Phina. Then you were shot." Her voice wobbled, but she continued, "All the agents have been fighting each other, and everything is a shambles. Of *course* I'm not all right, you ridiculous man!"

"Bloody hell, woman," he muttered. "It was just a question."

"Do you know what's the worst thing about that question?" Masha continued as if she hadn't heard him. "It's that asking me is the nicest thing you've said to me in years. *Years*! And it took a bullet to do it!"

"Hey, I've said plenty of nice things to you!" Link protested but winced as he felt a streak of pain.

"Oh?" Masha retorted ungraciously. "Name one."

"Well..." Link hesitated before he found something to grab onto. Like just a minute ago when he'd compared seeing her to heaven, although he shouldn't have said that. "I told you last week that your sword work has improved."

Masha pressed her lips together and glowered at him

with disapproval. The tear tracks on her face had already begun to dry, thankfully. It had taken five years off his life to see her so scared. Mad was much better, even if it was directed at him. Mad he knew what to do with. Mad didn't scare him to death.

"Ooh, you make me so mad sometimes," Masha seethed. Link wondered if he had gone too far this time in pushing her buttons.

"Yes, I'm getting that distinct impression," he mumbled as he turned his head, wincing at the sharp pain running through him. Phina had her hands on Jack's head while Shaw stood guarding her back. Good on them.

After another stab of pain, Link began to wonder why they hadn't made a run to a Pod-doc yet. He weakly called, "Medic."

Masha remained oblivious as she continued on a tirade of his characteristics. "Oblivious, arrogant, rude... Obnoxious! Abrasive! Childish!"

Link blinked in disbelief and mentally sounded a retreat. "Can we get back to part with the tears and concern for my welfare? That was nice..."

Masha froze before exploding. "Ugh! If you weren't wounded already, I would slap you *so* hard!"

"What?" Link frowned. "What did I say?"

She fumed as she rose on her knees. Link thought she had never been more beautiful. "I'm explaining that I've been waiting for years for you to finally wake up and see me for *me* and not just as your beta agent! I can't wait any longer for you to realize I love you and maybe decide you love me, too."

Link had felt like a steam roller had flattened him

already from the bullet, but now it seemed to have another go at it. He almost missed Masha's next words.

She glared at him, broken-hearted but resolved. "So, I'm leaving! I won't leave you in the lurch and I will help clean all this mess up, but I can't stay any longer than that. It's all clear now."

"No!" he protested, reaching for her and grunting when he used the wrong side. "You can't go."

"I have to." She shook her head sadly. "I can't go on like this."

Masha pushed herself to her feet and was about to call another agent to help him when he couldn't take it anymore. The words burst out of him in a pained gasp.

"Bloody hell, woman! Can't you see I'm trying to tell you I love you too?"

Masha froze a second time, then turned her expression-less face toward him. "What did you say?"

All the agents in hearing distance stopped fighting and stared at them. He sighed and mentally assigned his dignity to the recycle bin. He'd come this far.

Link cleared his throat. "I said I love you too, Masha. I have loved you for years."

She stared at him for long enough that he began to wonder if he'd made a terrible hash of the business. He'd never told a woman he loved her before, so how the hell would he have gotten any experience in doing so?

Masha sank back down on her knees and whispered, "You aren't just saying that because I want to hear it so you can keep me here at Spy Corps?"

He huffed, attempting to save a scrap of pride. "Does that sound like something I would do?"

"Yes."

"Hmm." Link reflected on the idea of karma. When Masha made to move away again, he reached out and grabbed her hand. He spoke with all sincerity in his heart. "Masha. I meant it. I've loved you for years. It's always been you."

"Then why didn't you say anything before now?" Masha vacillated between elation and irritation.

Link thought she was beautifully perfect that way and resolved to keep her in that state as much as possible. He splayed his free hand out regretfully. "I'm the boss, love. You had to make the first move, or it could be considered sexual harassment or coercion."

"Of all the things!" Masha gaped in astonishment. "Really? You were just waiting for me to say something?"

He nodded. "Every day."

Masha choked up again with tears. "I love you, Greyson."

"I love you, Masha."

Cheers sounded from the agents surrounding them.

"Kiss her!" an agent called.

A chant began. "Kiss! Kiss! Kiss! Kiss!"

They glanced around in surprise before their gazes caught. They smiled, finally allowing themselves to see the love in each other's eyes. Masha leaned over and obliged them amidst more cheers, though Link was able to hold on with a surprising grip considering he'd been shot.

Masha leaned back and shook her head in bemusement. "Phina completely called that. She told me to tell you how I felt."

He grinned. "She's good that way. Helping without revealing other people's secrets."

"You love her, don't you?" Masha asked.

Link didn't see any reason to deny it. "She's family. Like a niece or an adopted daughter, but yes. I do love her."

Masha gave him a wide smile and leaned down to give him another kiss that was far too short. She turned toward Phina as she leaned back but quickly stopped.

Her expression of alarm caused him to whip his head around much faster than his wound allowed.

The pain alone caused him to feel faint, but the sight in front of him almost stopped his heart.

CHAPTER TWENTY-SIX

Gaitune-67, Spy Corps Headquarters and Base, Dining Room

Phina opened her eyes after she'd finished releasing all of Jack's suppressed memories when she registered gasps of shock. Jack opened his eyes a beat later, intense relief on his face.

Shaw's voice rose in a warning. "Phina."

They both turned to the left and saw a tall female alien with purplish skin and flat black eyes standing beside them. Her humanoid body resembled an insect in appearance. She wore a simple robe as clothing.

The alien viewed them with all the emotionless curiosity of a scientist examining an interesting experiment. Her head tilted to meet Phina's gaze.

Jack reached out and grasped Phina's hand in a strong grip. "Phina," he said urgently. "That's *her.*"

Phina gently broke his hold and patted him reassuringly. "I know, Jack."

The alien smoothly pulled Phina's last knife out of her sheath and thrust it into Jack's chest before anyone could react.

Phina had seen it coming, but the alien's speed caused her to be just a hair too late.

"No!" Phina cried, staring at the wound in the middle of Jack's chest as he jerked in response, pulling in air with choking gasps.

She felt a dry hand with segmented fingers grasp her arm. Before Phina could respond, the view of her surroundings changed from the base's dining room to a gray-white space with lightning storms spreading in the distance.

For the third time in her life, Phina found herself in the Etheric involuntarily.

Shaw was angry when he couldn't move in time to save Jack from the alien. When Phina disappeared right in front of him, that feeling changed to helplessness.

Jack's choking gasps brought him out of his frozen stupor in time to hear Greyson Wells calling in a struggling voice, "Don't just stand there, Shaw! It's the Pod-doc for both of us. I can use the one on my ship. Take Jack to Medical. Now! There's a chance we can save him, and Phina's not here to do whatever she did to save me."

Shaw shook off the emotions freezing him up and did his job. The top three agents in Spy Corps were essentially out of commission, considering Masha wasn't going to take even a step away from Greyson Wells. He had to pick up the slack, no matter how he felt.

He pointed at Felan, Savas, Ian, and Kabaka, assigning two each to quickly carry Jack and Greyson to the appropriate locations and get them into the Pod-docs. He told two of the team leaders to show them where to go and use their authorization.

"As for the rest of you," he spoke firmly as he scanned the room, "we need to have a little talk."

The Etheric

Phina rose from her knees and stepped away from the alien, keeping her in her sight as a memory crashed into her.

"Phina, there will come a day when you will be up against someone without being able to do all your background checks on them." Link waved his beer in the air as they lounged at the bar. *"It's just the nature of the work. So, when you meet them, they will be a blank slate to you. Remember the rules I taught you. Notice everything, keep your mask on, and be prepared for anything. Draw information out of them. The more you know, the more choice you have as to how to handle them. While you do all that, remember to lie through your teeth if you sense that truth will be a danger to you. Don't let them catch you off guard."*

She kept his words in mind and held herself back, waiting for this isopod-like alien to let her know what the agenda was. However, she began to rethink that strategy.

If this was who Phina believed her to be, this alien was dangerous without speaking a word.

"Why did you come yourself?" she finally asked.

The alien continued her slow movements from one foot to the next. Phina had the sense that she had been surprised.

"An intelligent question." The alien's voice was as dry as bark. "Depending, of course, on the reasoning by which you came to it."

"An intelligent question usually seeks to achieve an answer." Phina spoke mildly. "However, I can see you do not have much respect at all for the asker, and you have no intention of answering."

"A reasonable assumption based on my given response." The female tilted her wide head to the side as she continued pacing around Phina. "In this case, it is the correct one. What respect does one give to chattel? For that is what all lesser species are to us."

"Ah." Phina spoke with satisfaction. "You are Kurtherian. I had thought as much."

The alien stopped, her flat black eyes blinking so quickly Phina almost missed it. "You expected a Kurtherian?"

"It was the only logical answer." Phina spoke modestly but with a slight tone of surprise that she hoped would draw the female to elaborate. She suppressed her grin of triumph when the female asked the question Phina hoped she would.

"The answer to what question? There was no reason to expect me. I left no tracks anywhere." She spoke with impatience.

Phina shook her head. "I'm afraid it was obvious."

"Ah. You recognized something in the methods by which I utilized my failed acolyte just now."

"No, it wasn't Jack."

"Nonsense," the Kurtherian said crisply. "You could not possibly have connected me to the Baldere experiment. Only their leader and the leader of the Gleek faction were influenced to cause subversion." She paused, then continued impatiently, "I suppose the so-called ambassador of the Empire counted, though he was barely touched."

Phina barely remembered to keep her face impassive. That *experiment* had killed dozens of people and could have killed thousands if it had reached its conclusion without interference. "That situation was of note, but no, I was not referring to that incident."

The female frowned. "Then that overeager Aurian remembered who gave him the device. I noticed the remnants had let him live even though he had used it as designed. They must have accepted his testimony about its origins."

"It was a very clever design. Your plan had been working flawlessly." Phina had to draw on every ounce of control not to yell at the female for her callousness. Tens of thousands of Aurians had died. Speaking of which... "What were you going to use the energy for?"

She kept her tone level with a note of admiration. Even though those emotions were not what Phina felt. Not even close.

"As a weapon, naturally," the Kurtherian answered as if it was of no consequence. "The Aurians were a failed project, so scrapping them was necessary. Utilizing the device would have collected enough energy to be used as a weapon useful as a countermeasure."

Phina gritted her teeth at the dismissive tone as she put the pieces of the puzzle together to find the Kurtherian's agenda. A countermeasure weapon. An energy weapon. She froze with incredulity. Holy fudging crumbs.

"You wanted it to counter the ESD Beam on the *Meredith Reynolds*."

The Kurtherian was crazy. Had to be. At the end of the war with the Yollins a quarter-century ago, the rebel Yollin faction had sent superdreadnoughts against the budding Etheric Empire. Bethany Anne and General Reynolds had sent out their fleets to take down the first two massive ships. There was a third, however, that had tried to sneak up on the *Meredith Reynolds*. There were no ships large enough left to defend the space station and its hundreds of thousands of civilians, many of them women and children.

Thanks to clever foresight and engineering by the R&D dream team BMW, the station hadn't been defenseless. The Arti-sun, the energy core that powered everything on the station, had been utilized as a weapon of last resort.

The ESD beam had destroyed the superdreadnought and reduced the accompanying armada to debris.

The Kurtherian clasped her violet hands behind her back and examined Phina. "That is correct. It is too much power in the hands of Death."

Phina desperately clung to her need to conceal her horror and strove to match the unemotional tone. "You realize that the two cores of energy emitted together would most likely cause a massive explosion that would decimate not just the station but also the entire Yoll system?"

"Of course. The Yollins were useful at one time, but they are now contaminated by their prolonged exposure to humanity. Their species needs to be eliminated. The system would be a loss, but not an insurmountable one."

"Contaminated by humanity?" Phina repeated slowly.

Those flat black eyes remained expressionless. "Yes. Humans are dangerous, commonly lacking intelligence and perspicacity. Your planet should have been recycled long ago."

"Sorry to disappoint." Not sorry at all, you batshit-crazy Kurtherian.

The Kurtherian began pacing again. "There is no disappointment. Disappointment implies expectation. We have none for you humans."

"Except to die."

The Kurtherian inclined her head. "Precisely."

Gaitune-67, Spy Corps Headquarters and Base, QBS *Stark*

Masha walked with Greyson as he was transported on a hovergurney up the ramp into the cargo bay. The trainees had been dismissed as soon as the gurney had been found in the mission's ready room.

"You'll stay with me?" He spoke softly, his intense brown eyes on hers.

She thought of the shambles they had left in the cafeteria, the myriad tasks now on their slate with the upheaval, betrayal, and uncertainty. Masha set it aside and nodded with a warm smile. "Of course."

He tightened his hand on hers, the only outward indication he gave that he was pleased and wanted her there. Masha suspected she would need to make studying his body language a priority since it was unlikely he would suddenly become effusive about his emotions.

They arrived in the medbay on the ship as a medical technician ran into the room, puffing.

"Sorry, Alpha. Beta. Just got Jack into the base's Poddoc. Here, let me help."

He rushed forward and began rapidly pressing buttons on the panel on the side of the machine. The wide door opened with a tiny hiss.

The two of them helped Greyson into the Pod-doc and the technician returned to his preoccupation with the buttons. Greyson laid back and stared at her intently, something clearly weighing on his mind.

"I apologize for the interruption."

They both looked up as ADAM's voice came from the speaker overhead. The medical technician stepped back when the Pod-doc began to configure itself.

"Hey!" The technician scowled in irritation.

ADAM spoke calmly. "Please step outside, Hugo Haines. I will take it from here."

The man exited the room, muttering, "Couldn't have told me this before I ran a mile from one side of the base to the other, of course."

"ADAM, what's going on?" Masha asked when the door had closed behind the man.

"Stark and Shade notified me as soon as the confrontation with Jack began. I have been reviewing the footage and have an urgent question."

"What is it, ADAM?" Greyson asked impatiently.

"It appeared that Phina gave you her blood. Is that what happened?"

"Yes." Masha smiled. "It kept Greyson alive by at least partially healing the wound. It gave us time to get him here."

"I was concerned that would be the case."

"What's wrong with Phina's blood, ADAM?" Greyson asked wearily. "I thought you fixed that."

Masha nervously scanned the bandage-covered wound through the hole of his blood-stained shirt. His body must be exhausted with all his energy focused on healing him.

"Phina's nanocytes are not like Bethany Anne's nanocytes. Bethany Anne's nanocytes could remain in your body without issue while they healed you, as you know from Anna Elizabeth. Phina's nanocytes will need to be cleansed from your system."

Masha stiffened but asked anxiously, "But he will be all right?"

"Yes," ADAM assured her. "They have not had time to bond to his DNA yet. It will take some time in the Pod-doc to cleanse his system of the nanocytes and finish healing him. My best estimate is twenty-six hours."

She sagged in relief and turned to Greyson. "You'll be all right."

"Thank you, ADAM." Greyson spoke without taking his gaze off her.

"You're welcome, DS."

Masha squeezed his hand, gave him a warm smile, and

pulled back to move away. He tightened his hold on her hand and didn't let go. She looked at him in concern.

"Greyson?"

He spoke quietly. "Would you still love me if my name wasn't Greyson Wells and my life was a great deal more complicated than it appears?"

Masha frowned. "Don't be an idiot. Of course I would. And your life more complicated than it may appear? My love, I think your picture must be etched next to the word complicated in whatever passes for a dictionary these days."

He gave her a faint smile but his gaze warmed by an infinite degree. Yes, she needed to make studying his body language a master class. The man kept secrets better than anyone she had ever known. Speaking of which...

"Am I allowed to know what your name is?" Masha smiled at him in return.

He tugged at her hand to bring her forward and she obliged, leaning close enough to hear a whisper. "Lincoln Sherwood Grimes."

She straightened in surprise. "Wow! A Grimes? As in, related to..."

"Yes, John is a cousin."

Masha gazed at him in amazement. "I had no idea."

"That was the idea." He smiled in amusement.

She thought about it for a minute. "Does anyone else know about this? And what should I call you?"

"Link is what I told Phina. It was a nickname long ago. She is the only one I told before you. It felt right since even from the beginning, she's been family. The Empress and Barnabas probably know since they are telepaths. I don't think many other people know, and I'd like to keep it that way."

"Of course," she assured him. "But why keep it secret if there isn't anyone else who knows your name?"

"Two reasons. John doesn't know, so another Grimes would kind of rub it in his face with its obviousness."

"True."

He brought his other hand over to hold her. "The other reason is that there might be a day when I want to disappear from the life of a spy, perhaps to retire and have a family. I would rather retire as myself than live with a name that's a lie."

She gave him a warm smile. "Excellent reasons."

Link gave her a satisfied smile. "I thought so."

She straightened to her full height and took a step back, her smile turning playful. "Now get yourself fixed, mister. I've got plans for you that necessitate your body being intact and healthy."

"I like the sound of that." He gave her a grin though she could see the weariness in him.

"Yes, sparring is always excellent exercise."

She pushed the button to close the door of the Pod-doc on his groan. She gave him a quick grin while his expression turned injurious. The door slowly but smoothly began to close.

"You are a cruel woman," he called.

She blew him a kiss. "I love you."

"I love you too."

The door slid shut with a click.

．　．　．

The Etheric

The casual arrogance of the Kurtherian grated on Phina. She refocused and pushed her emotions to the side. "To get back to your original question, no, the Aurians were not what gave the presence of a Kurtherian away."

"It was not?" The Kurtherian frowned as if puzzled. "You humans are against order and rationality. Perhaps a pattern resulted. Your father's littermate, perhaps?"

Phina's heart fell into her stomach. Had ADAM and Todd been right? Had this Kurtherian female done something to her aunt to change her so drastically? She could honestly say she had wondered once they knew Jack had been mentally manipulated.

"What about my aunt?" She feigned indifference.

"Come now." The female sneered. "Are you that oblivious?"

"Apparently." Phina scratched her chin as she assessed the Kurtherian. "What brought my aunt to your attention?"

The Kurtherian opened her mouth but shut it before shooting Phina a glance. After a moment, she responded stiffly, "It came to my attention that the female worked with nanocytes. An inferior version compared to the original, of course."

"Ah," Phina responded as if it had all become clear, even though it brought up several questions. Primarily, how had it been brought to her attention?

"Yes." The Kurtherian's expression soured. "It was unthinkable that humans had found the path to Ascension. I had to take steps once I discovered this travesty."

"Of course you had to take steps. How long did it take to accomplish them?"

"It is ongoing," she responded with a tone of...not quite bewilderment, but something akin to it. "There have been many setbacks. I had to return to reaffirm the tasks I had set for the female once a year since she usually managed to partially lift the compulsion by then. Still, if she had accomplished her task to recreate the formula that had been used on Death as ordered, my endeavors would be much farther along."

The Kurtherian shook her head in disapproval. "She was a poor subject. I assume she is still in your medical ward due to mental deterioration? A pity they detained her before she had achieved something useful."

The cold dismissal of her aunt shook Phina, but she kept it together. "What other commands had she been able to lift?"

Focused on an internal question, the Kurtherian answered absently, "To drive you away, of course. You had knocked on the door and almost entered when I gave her the commands that first time. I couldn't have you interfering, so she was told to do what humans do to push their children away. It worked for a while, but she had almost lifted it by the time I came back each year." She shook her head with a frown. "A failed subject."

Phina wanted to cry and scream and rage. The unfeeling arrogance of this Kurtherian staggered her. She had thought Greyson arrogant at times, but this was a whole different level of superiority. Sorrow crept into the anger. Her poor aunt never had a chance! She had killed Phina's relationship with her only remaining relative by being so cold and unfeelingly focused on her objective.

Rein it in just a little longer, Phina.

Sundancer.

He was right. She had to elicit all the information she could from this unfeeling, arrogant...

She focused on her breathing to calm herself. *Breathe in. Keep everything hidden from prying eyes. Breathe out. Show only what I choose to reveal.*

Curious, detached, calm, poised, confident.

Phina refocused on the Kurtherian, who was studying her with speculation.

"For a human, you are a strange one."

"I am myself." Phina spoke mildly, her emotions under control.

"Indeed."

"Is there a name by which I can call you?"

The Kurtherian inclined her head in thought, her dark eyes nonreflective. It made her look soulless.

"You may address me as Glorious Penitent in Transcendence to Ascension."

Phina blinked as she ran that through her head. "Sounds pretentious, but all right. Sorry, but it wasn't what happened with my aunt that gave you away."

Glorious Penitent... The Kurtherian snapped her attention to Phina. Her mouth closed with an audible click as she pulled back, affronted. "It is a name of dignity and honor. It is not *pretentious*."

"As you say," Phina responded with amusement and satisfaction at the response. She knew what buttons to push now.

The Kurtherian squinted at her suspiciously while Phina maintained her slightly interested, somewhat bored expression. The Kurtherian finally turned away with a few body twitches that made Phina think she was still on edge.

"If you did not discover my involvement through any of these instances, I can think of only one other incident in which you were involved." She spoke stiffly.

"Oh?"

Glorious...the Kurtherian stared at her witheringly. "You are not lacking intelligence despite your pretense. You know exactly of what I speak."

"Yes, I first suspected there was a Kurtherian in the mix when the Qendrok arrived, speaking of a mysterious goddess who came out of nowhere and gave them amazing gifts."

"They were useful tools for a time," the Kurtherian said dismissively. A thought occurred to her. "Portraying myself a goddess has its uses. I will remember that for later experiments."

"How did you find out about Aunt Faith?" Phina pressed.

The Kurtherian stilled, then turned until Phina was in view. "It is of no importance."

"Well, now you have me all curious."

"It is not relevant to the discussion." The Kurtherian's eyes blinked a little too quickly.

Glory was a liar.

"Tell me, Glory." Phina's voice hardened.

She stiffened, affronted. "That is not my name, human."

Phina...

Her control over her emotions snapped. Phina yelled mentally and physically, *"You tell me right now!"*

She dropped the layers of shielding that kept her from

slipping into other people's minds and dived for the Kurtherian's mind.

Phina didn't have any thought in her head except for confirming the awful suspicion that had been growing ever since she'd realized a Kurtherian had messed with Aunt Faith's mind and when it had started. She didn't care that it wasn't smart. She didn't even care that she could be compromising potential intelligence she could have drawn from the Kurtherian by engaging in further conversation.

She was all feeling, and those feelings stemmed from a single thought.

One terrible thought.

She pushed into the Kurtherian's mind. It was hard. A human mind was easy to slip into. Wechselbalgs' were harder. The Nacht were harder still, although she admittedly hadn't tried all that hard with Bethany Anne and Anne. She could tell they weren't easily read.

They all were nothing compared to this Kurtherian.

Phina had a glimpse of Glory's mind before she was flung out of it.

She staggered with the force of the expulsion and coping with the images she had seen.

"I had thought perhaps to utilize you in my pursuits against the Phraim-'eh clan as well as with my calling to end Death." The Kurtherian spoke with a ragged edge to her voice. "But now I see that you are just as bad as *she* is."

Phina's thoughts raced as she righted herself. "You've got that right. Thanks for the compliment."

"It was not meant as such. You two stole the Etheric meant for us!" Glory clicked her mouth shut in agitation but collected herself. "You were given the same nanocytes as Death?"

"Nope."

"The serum. The female gave it to you when she was supposed to perfect it for me." The Kurtherian's head swiveled as she worked through her thoughts. "But the aunt gave me a sample, and testing showed the formula was not complete. The programming was not enough to trigger the full transformation."

Phina's heart pounded. If she asked...

"You." Glory lifted her face to view Phina head-on. Her eyes bored into her. "You had birth issues. They had to treat you. You had faulty genetic code that they fixed."

She had to force herself to breathe. "Yes."

The Kurtherian leaned forward, intensity pulsing from her. "What genetic material did they use to fix it?"

Drawing herself up to her full height, Phina stared at the being responsible for taking her parents away from her.

"Kurtherian."

Glory drew back, her gaze unblinking. She was motionless for several moments. "They did not."

"They did."

The Kurtherian seethed. *"Abomination."*

"Right back at you, lady," Phina growled. "You took my parents away from me."

Only her parents could have told Glory about the genetic birth issues. It had become clear once Phina had put the pieces together. She shuddered that she had anything in common with this soulless sociopathic alien.

"They were tools used to achieve my goals." Glory

curled her lip in distaste. "You were nothing, and you are worse than nothing. Abominations don't deserve life."

"Neither do murderers!" Phina cried.

"Murder is only invoked with worthy species." The Kurtherian was cold. "Humans, especially those with stolen Kurtherian technology, are vermin to be exterminated."

Phina's mind was flooded with a digging, burrowing weight. Her shields broke and she froze, unable to shore up her mental defenses. They eroded as soon as she threw them up.

Overwhelmed, she threw out the only thought she could manage.

Sundancer!

The Previdian's familiar presence came crashing through their private door in her mind, but instead of his normal mental touch, his presence was huge in her mind, like a big cat puffing himself up to attack.

Sundancer sniffed. *I'm saving your life, and you still insult me.*

He mentally leapt at the invader, snarling at the foreign weight of the Kurtherian's mental presence.

The assault ceased so suddenly that Phina staggered.

She opened her eyes to see the Kurtherian land on her back, a gratifying expression of shock and surprise on her alien face. She reached for her wristband, which used a version of the technology she had given the Qendrok.

"No!"

Phina rushed forward, but the Kurtherian was gone. She froze in shock, waiting to make sure the Kurtherian wasn't coming back. Her chest heaved with emotion, and she gasped for the air she needed in her lungs.

Her trembling fingers pressed her wristband, and she stepped out of the Etheric. Her surroundings shimmered into the familiar confines of Stark's ship, and she collapsed to her knees, tears streaming down her face.

When Sundancer nudged her leg to comfort her, Phina curled around him and sobbed for her aunt, the parents she had lost, and her younger self, who'd had to live without them.

CHAPTER TWENTY-SEVEN

Gaitune-67, Spy Corps Headquarters and Base, Conference Room

Shaw entered the room and saw Phina sitting at one end of the table. She still retained the haunted expression that she had worn since reappearing on the *Stark* in the hangar a few days before. He wanted to comfort her and ask her to share her burdens with him.

However, that wasn't his place in her life, so he pushed those feelings to the side and turned to stare at the man sitting next to her.

Barnabas had arrived the day after everything had come to a head, announcing that the Empress had sent him to help. He suspected the real reason she had sent him had to do with why Shaw had been called to the room.

He stopped at the chair next to Phina's, across from Barnabas, and sat down. His gaze never left her face.

Phina appeared nervous as she spoke. "You know why you are here?"

He reined in his emotions and focused. "It wasn't

explained to me in detail, just that everyone on base needed to come in today. I have noticed that those exiting the room are being kept separate from those who haven't entered yet."

Phina nodded and glanced at Barnabas, who inclined his head, indicating that she should continue. She turned back to Shaw and took a deep breath before explaining.

"The Empress has expressed concern about recent events. Barnabas is here to make sure that certain memories are suppressed or removed. Memories that could be dangerous to the agents or me."

She shifted uneasily as he processed her words.

"I see. May I ask what the danger is?" He glanced between them. Barnabas' face gave nothing away. The man should have been a spy with that level of control.

Phina cleared her throat, but before she responded, Barnabas spoke up.

"The Empress is concerned that if the spies here retain the memories of seeing a Kurtherian on the base as well as Phina's unique skills, they will place themselves in danger by seeking information they are not equipped to deal with or inadvertently expose Phina, thereby placing her in danger. You have to admit that they may not see the far-reaching repercussions to their inquiries, just the puzzle in front of them."

Shaw nodded. "I can see the logic in that. We are all naturally curious and independent. I could see some of the agents seeking information and poking their noses into places they don't belong. However, I do think we, those loyal to the Etheric Empire, need to find out more about this Kurtherian."

Barnabas nodded. "There is a plan in place to do so, yes."

"May I ask what that plan entails, or is that over my clearance level?"

The other man briefly smiled in amusement. "You may ask. However, since the Empress has not shared those details with either of us, there is nothing we can tell you."

Shaw nodded. Understandable but disappointing.

"So, I assume the reason I am here has to do with one of you rearranging my memories to take this information from my head?"

"Yes, I have been teaching Phina how to do so after we speak to each person and gain their permission."

Shaw gave Phina a long glance, then straightened and stared Barnabas in the eye. "I request to retain my memories intact."

Phina's quick intake of breath pulled his gaze to her. She leaned forward, her eyes showing conflicting emotions. "Even though... Well, it might make certain things easier if you forget."

Shaw's mouth tugged into a smile. "You are not responsible for my feelings, Phina." He wasn't ashamed of them, either. "They are my own, and I would like to remember why I have them."

She leaned back, and although she still seemed concerned, he could see she understood. He turned to Barnabas.

"Alpha Agent Wells and Beta Agent Masha are currently restructuring the organization so they share the Alpha role." He grinned. "The change was a stipulation Masha made before accepting his marriage proposal. Since Jack has requested to step into a different role after his vacation to recover from the trauma of what happened to him, they have asked me to become the sole beta agent. The three of us are planning to revamp everything so we are all aligned in our goals and we can better train our agents. I believe that with my new role and responsibilities, I can better help both them and Phina by retaining my memories."

Barnabas tilted his head in curiosity. "You three believe you know what the Empress has planned for Phina?"

Shaw nodded. "We've discussed it. We believe the course ahead is what makes the most sense. We think she will need all the help we can give her, even if it's from the background or the sidelines."

He glanced at Phina and found her staring at him. He smiled reassuringly. It didn't matter if she returned his feelings. It didn't matter if he remained in the background while she pursued the truth. It didn't even matter if he would ever see her again.

She was a dark angel.

Shaw believed she was as worthy of following and supporting as the Empress. Phina was a protector of others and a seeker of the truth. She would find that Kurtherian eventually. He knew she wouldn't stop until she did.

"Very well," Barnabas responded, pulling Shaw's attention back to him. "The Empress agrees. But if you ever leave Spy Corps, we will revisit this conversation."

Shaw nodded in satisfaction as he stood. "Thank you."

"You're welcome." Barnabas assessed Shaw critically and nodded. "I don't believe you will let us down."

High praise from someone in the Empress' circle of trust. He gave them both a nod, then turned to exit the room with a lingering glance at Phina, feeling a remarkable sense of clarity.

He no longer felt conflicted. His feelings for Phina and his duty to the Empire were perfectly aligned.

Etheric Empire, QBBS *Meredith Reynolds*, Phina's Apartment (One Week Later)

When Phina had finished explaining the events of everything that had happened, Todd remained quiet as they sat cuddled on the couch for several moments in contemplation.

He ran his fingers up and down Phina's arm soothingly while he thought. After a time, Phina lifted her head off of his chest and turned in the circle of his arm.

"Tell me what you are thinking?" she asked softly.

He shot her an amused glance. "You could just read my thoughts."

"I could." She rested her chin on his chest, her eyes focused on him. "We are still mentally connected, so it would be easy. I've recently come to understand that I shouldn't take this ability for granted or use it lightly. I also don't want there to be misunderstandings between us. If you want me to read your mind I will, but right now, I would rather have the conversation."

"All right. I'm still mulling everything over, but the first question that comes to mind is, are you certain this Kurtherian killed your parents?"

Phina frowned. "I was certain at the time. The glimpses I caught were difficult to understand. She had seen them at some point. They were in her mind."

She paused and rose from the couch to pace as she put her thoughts together. "When I said she took my parents from me, she didn't deny it. When I said she was a murderer, she told me they were tools to be discarded."

"But you aren't sure she killed them?" he pressed.

Phina shot him a pained grimace and threw her hands up. "She was involved at the very least. If nothing else, she may have answers as to what happened to them."

"That's fair to say."

She shifted uncertainly. "Why is it so important to you to make sure of the answer?"

Todd held out his hand, and Phina sat down next to him again. "There are a couple of reasons. The first is that I wanted you to be sure of what you saw. If she did kill them, you needed to know it and not be plagued with uncertainty. However, since you aren't sure, you will need to find out the answer."

"True. All right. And the other?"

He squeezed her hand gently. "I wanted to be certain that you aren't going to drive yourself to madness with an obsession about catching her. Find the answers, yes, but obsessions are dangerous for the person who has them."

Phina nodded thoughtfully. "Fair enough. I'll keep those thoughts in mind."

"Thank you. Now my next question has to do with Shaw."

She turned to him warily. "What about him?"

"You talked around it, but I got the sense that something more personal happened between you." He regarded her steadily.

Phina scowled. "I didn't cheat on you. That's not the kind of person I am."

Todd smiled in amusement. "I am relieved to hear it, although that wasn't what I was implying."

Phina poked his chest, a silent acknowledgment that he had succeeded in poking one of her buttons. She sighed.

"It was difficult and awkward. I had to read his mind thoroughly to make certain that he was not the traitor. While I had caught signs indicating that he had a fondness for me, it was inescapably clear that the feelings were deeper once I had read his mind. He knew that I saw it in his thoughts but brushed it aside at the time since things were happening so quickly. I went along with that since I didn't know what to say."

"I can see that." He worked to control his heart rate. "And later?"

Phina grimaced and flapped a hand. "There was no time to talk about anything but resolving the chaos and making sure everyone was healed. The agents all had understandable confusion as to what had happened and didn't know how to treat me before we adjusted their memories. Shaw was busy becoming the only beta agent and keeping things organized. The first time we had a chance to talk was several days later when he came in for the memory suppression."

Todd frowned in speculation. "So, he's forgotten everything?"

"No." Phina peered at him and shook her head, her eyes sad. Todd gently squeezed her hand in comfort. "Shaw said I wasn't responsible for his feelings, but they were his, and he wanted to keep them. He told Barnabas he could do more to help and support me and his alpha agents by remembering what happened."

"He was always a man of convictions and had a strong sense of duty and responsibility," Todd reasoned.

Phina nodded.

"Do you have feelings for him?"

Her head shot up. She opened and shut her mouth, her face morphing from bewilderment to certainty.

Todd decided he must be completely infatuated because he found it adorable, which was not something he would ever admit to anyone but Phina.

Phina shrugged. "I think I could have in another lifetime, and I can't deny there was a tug there. My heart is too filled with you to give it any weight, though, so it was easy to ignore."

The tension in Todd's body dissipated, and he gently squeezed her hand again. "I am, of course, relieved to hear that."

She raised an eyebrow quizzically. "Did you have any doubt?"

"No, but I could tell something had happened based on how you talked about him, so I wanted to clear the air instead of allowing the subject to become a cause for insecurity."

Comprehension dawned on her face, and she winced. "I'm sorry, I didn't mean to bring up painful memories for you."

Todd grinned. "Trust me, Phina, you are not at all like my ex. In hindsight, she was too focused on the superficial. You are the complete opposite."

Phina smiled with appreciation. "Thank you. I've never

really cared about my appearance, but I always wanted to be someone who does things that matter."

He tightened his arms around her. "You are that person."

Her smile grew into a huge grin. "You are overflowing with compliments tonight. Thank you." She slipped her arms around his waist and leaned her head against his chest.

Todd reflected on the direction his thoughts had taken while Phina had been away and again as soon as she had returned. It had been as if she hadn't even left, aside from having new stories to tell him. Being with her was right in a way it had never been with his ex-wife.

He leaned back and gazed into her eyes. He saw that same certainty in her.

"Phina, I wasn't going to do this just yet, but now seems like the perfect time."

"Time for what?" She frowned but waited as patiently as she ever did when she wasn't focused on maintaining her mask.

Todd let go of her, pulled a small box out of his pocket, and opened it for her. "Will you marry me?"

Her eyes rounded with shock and surprise, but she threw her arms around him. "Yes! Of course."

He pulled her close and glanced ruefully at the ring, which Phina hadn't even looked at. The black tungsten band was inset with four black diamonds and a deep-green square-cut diamond the color of Phina's eyes graced the middle, twice the size of the rest.

Todd had gotten the gems in the first shipment from Lyriasha and had worked with the jeweler for weeks to make sure the ring was beautiful, felt right, and wouldn't get in her way during her spy work. He shook his head with an inward chuckle and held her closer.

No. His Phina was not a superficial woman.

Etheric Empire, QBBS *Meredith Reynolds*, Bethany Anne's Office

"So, we have resolved our questions about your aunt and all those intersections you noticed during the events of the past few years. Now it's time to consider the future." The Empress had a gleam in her eye as she munched on a brownie and sipped a Coke.

"Yes." Phina sat straight in her seat, feeling unsettled. She smelled the chocolate from the brownies and wished she could eat one, but her nerves wouldn't let her.

Bethany Anne gestured at the ring on Phina's hand. "Speaking of the future, best wishes!"

"Thank you." Phina glanced at her beautiful ring and smiled, remembering how Todd had beamed with happiness after he'd proposed. Since her birthday had passed during the mission, her friends had celebrated their engagement and her twenty-first birthday the day before.

"Did you decide when to have the wedding?" Bethany Anne asked.

"Soon. Neither of us has any living relatives, only our chosen family and friends." Phina grinned. "Since the only request I had aside from who we invited was to not wear high heels, it isn't going to be a very formal wedding."

Bethany Anne laughed as she waved her last bite in the

air. "Well, I was going to give you a pair of Louboutins as a gift, but I'll save them for someone more appreciative."

Phina chuckled in surprise. "Well, thank you for the thought. You're right; someone else would appreciate them more."

The Empress popped the last bite of brownie in her mouth and dusted the crumbs off onto her plate.

Bethany Anne fixed Phina with a contemplative look. "So, the future. Specifically, *your* future."

Phina couldn't help noticing parallels between now and when she had been called in front of Anna Elizabeth years before to discuss what would happen to her. Phina still felt nervous anticipation as to what the future might hold, but so much else had changed.

"I am forming a unique team, and I would like you to lead it."

Phina blinked. Talk about déjà vu, though this was a twist.

"I wouldn't have thought I would be experienced enough yet to lead a team." Phina frowned. "Anna Elizabeth told me I would be a part of a diplomatic team that would also be a part of spy missions, but this doesn't sound like the same thing."

"I know. I decided to commandeer that team and change the objective." Bethany Anne glanced at the empty brownie plate as if hoping another one would magically appear.

"All right." Phina spoke cautiously. "What would be its purpose?"

Bethany Anne straightened in her chair and resumed

her persona as the Empress, not just the friend she was becoming. "To track that scheming Kurtherian down."

"Ah, I see." Phina did. Kurtherians were historically very difficult to find, and this one liked to use proxies, which made tracking her even harder.

"Yes!" Bethany Anne got to her feet and began pacing, her eyes glowing red. "I want Justice for your parents, your aunt, Jack Kaiser, the Balderians, the Aurians, the Qendrok, Spy Corps, and everyone else that malignant fucking crotch-goblin has screwed over."

"I do too," Phina agreed. "However, I don't think this will be a quick and easy mission."

The Empress nodded as she turned to look out of the large window that gave an unobstructed view of the stars. "You are right. This will probably take years, perhaps decades. She hides too easily, she has had who knows how long to hide and gather resources, and we only have what breadcrumbs she gave you." She turned to look at Phina. "However, we have a place to start."

"Yes." Phina spoke firmly as she stood. "We do have to do something about her, but don't you have someone more qualified to lead this team for you?"

Not that she didn't desperately want to be on that team.

Bethany Anne shook her head gravely. "No, I don't. Everyone else who has the experience to lead this team already has their tasks in our fight against the Kurtherian clan supporting the Leath. They have been at those tasks for years, some for decades, and most of those I trust have been at their jobs ever since we arrived here in this part of space." She paused before continuing, "When we left Earth, I asked everyone if they would come and fight to end the

Kurtherians, *Ad Aeternitatem*. You remember what that phrase means?"

"To eternity."

The Empress nodded, her gaze filled with determination and strength. "That's right. And it *will* be our fight until the end, however far in the future that end may be. I don't have anyone else available who also has the knowledge, skills, abilities, connections, and compassion that you do."

Phina glanced at her, startled.

The Empress smiled at her. "You could have killed Jack when you fought him. It was within your orders to do so since he was the traitor. Why didn't you?"

"Because he thought she was you. She manipulated him. He showed a lack of judgment, but not a lack of loyalty."

"Yes, and he will work even harder now to redeem himself once he has worked through his guilt." Bethany Anne studied her expectantly. "That's why I know you are the right person for the job. I know I can trust you without having to look over your shoulder."

Phina felt a warmth inside that gave her an urge to rub her chest above her heart. She managed a smile, but she knew the Empress could read her mind if she chose to. "Thank you."

"You're welcome." Bethany Anne returned her smile and turned back to the window. "I once told you that I needed to know if you would jump off a cliff if I asked you to jump." She clasped her hands behind her back as she spoke. "This is that cliff, Phina. I need you to lead this team and find her for me. Will you jump?"

Phina took a deep breath and walked over to gaze out

the window into the dark of space. She recalled a conversation to mind that had a similar view. She'd half-recalled a phrase she and Link had heard on an old television show, and Link had repeated it.

"*'I serve at the pleasure of the President.'*"

"*That's the one. They say it proudly, they say it with love, and they say it with determination. But you know what they don't say enough?*"

"*What?*"

"*How freaking hard it is.*"

"*Do you regret it? Do you wish she hadn't told you to take care of it?*"

"*That's the thing, Link. Swap a word, and it's the Empress that phrase could be speaking about. It's not a light matter to be tasked with an objective by the Empress, especially someone's death, or enacting her Justice for those who have been wronged. It's a heavy weight. It's not just someone's death then; it's giving that death the meaning it deserves, the Justice that's demanded.*"

She'd paused.

"*If given another task by the Empress, would I proudly serve with love and determination? Would I carry that heavy weight again?*"

After considering, she'd answered her own question.

"*I would, Link. I would do it again without a drop of regret.*"

And I will, Phina thought fiercely. *I will choose it every time.* Her resolve crystallized as she gave her Empress and friend a sharp nod.

"*Ad Aeternitatum.*"

The End

AUTHOR NOTES - S.E. WEIR

AUGUST 16, 2021

Hello again! :) Thank you so much for reading not only this book and these author notes, but these four books of The Empress' Spy. I can't tell you how much I appreciate all your support because it would take far more space than I think I'm allowed. 😄 I highly value all your encouragement and have read every word you have posted in reviews and on FB. I am extremely grateful to each and every one of you. :)

SpyCorps

What did you think? This was really just a taste of what happens in SpyCorps since it was only from the recruit perspective. There's a whole lot more that happens with missions and agent training!

One of the fun but harder parts was how many new characters had to be added to the mix since it was an entirely new location and situation. :) It was on purpose since it was the natural choice, but that did take a little

AUTHOR NOTES - S.E. WEIR

more time to set everything up. :) Hopefully you will find SpyCorps at least half as interesting as I do!

If you have read other series in the KGU you may find the base location to be familiar. In the Ascension Myth series, set roughly 120 years in the future from Phina's time, they find a base on an asteroid that had been empty for a while. The hangar and everything located up the stairs where the staff and leader room are in this book are what is mentioned in the AM series. They do describe a few doors in the hangar that they don't explore. I always wondered why they didn't and what could be back there.

When I was thinking up a location for the SpyCorps headquarters, this base popped into my head as a possibility. After some research and discussion it looked like it could really neatly fit both present and future. :) I love it when connections come together!

Apology and Thanks

I didn't add an acknowledgment in book one as I had intended to add it at the end of book two, but it didn't actually get in there since it was the only one. Here it is, belated but not forgotten as it's been on my mind.

Thank you, Peter Manis for your kindness in helping me with medical questions about what a Doctor would bring on a rescue mission! :) I wish I would have used more of your insightful suggestions. I'm sorry it took this long to get these words here so you know how much I appreciate your help.

Link, Masha and HEA's

As soon as I knew things were shifting with Phina and

Todd, I decided that Link needed someone in his life. He was too separate, lonely and cranky! 😄

All right, you got me! I'm a Happily Ever After (HEA) kind of person, which means I'm that kind of writer too.

I won't ever be the kind of writer that kills the main character, and it would have to be a super good and unavoidable reason to kill off secondary characters too. It really just destroys me for days after reading a book where the MC dies at the end (especially after a whole series), so I never want to put a reader in that situation- if I ever could actually write it myself.

I finally realized just a few weeks ago why I like HEA's- because it's all good feelings and I'm so, sooo tired of the bad ones. I have enough of that in real life, I want some good feels in my reading! 😄 And now my writing too!

I tried to keep those parts to a minimum since it's not everyone's cup of tea, but I couldn't keep them out because that's just how I work.

So, Phina and Todd, and Link and Masha were my good feels for this book. I think it worked out well for all of them and they got just the right person for each of them. :) Hopefully you think so too!

What's Next?

I know your burning question is will there be more Phina? I realize it's a disappointment, but I just can't answer that yet. Only time will tell.

My next project is an alt world fantasy with a dash of fairy tale. It began with a hypothetical situation: What if Maria Nikolaevna Romanov didn't actually die, but was taken into another dimension? What if by the time she returned to our world she had lived only a year and a day, but 100 years had passed by on Earth?

I had intended to write an urban fantasy series starting after she had come back to our world. However, I quickly realized that year she was gone would be pretty important to her personal development. So, I decided to do a prequel novel and had actually started writing it for NaNoWriMo before I got into Phina.

Well, that novel is now going to be a trilogy because there was too much happening to fit it all in one book, and that's what I am working on now. Some things will need to be rewritten, both because of the split and reworking some things with the plot, and a great many more scenes need to be added.

I don't have a title for either trilogy or series yet, but it will take some time to get it all written since I've been setting up a whole new universe with new rules, new history, new everything. I can't deny that I love world-building and creating characters and discovering their stories, but it does take time. :) I will say I'm really excited about it because there's just so much going on with Maria and this new universe, and I have big plans for both of them!

AUTHOR NOTES - MICHAEL ANDERLE

AUGUST 17, 2021

Thank you for not only reading this book but this entire series and these author notes as well.

So, I am writing these author notes from a new Mexican restaurant about ten minutes from my house named Tres Amigos. Apparently, there is an existing Tres Amigos which is more a hole in the wall, and this restaurant is a very well-appointed sit-down version, complete with beautiful wall paintings and amazing fabric on the chairs.

They say a picture is worth a thousand words, so there you go!

I've been the only customer for the last hour or so, and I feel special. The Coke is delicious, the eggs are wonderful, and the rice and beans are on point.

In short, I will be back for lunch (I had the breakfast.)

I hope this restaurant makes it since they obviously put in a lot of money and effort to set it up. Plus, I'll have another breakfast/lunch location for Monday mornings when my normal location is closed.

Support local businesses.

There is alcohol, and then there is NAVY Rum.

So, Judith (my wife) surprised me with tickets for the two of us to go on a date to support a local distillery opening at Area 15 (not 51) here in Las Vegas. The picture showed a nice room with dark wood walls and leather chairs.

Very high-end.

The reality was very different. It was cool, just different.

So, the location is Lost Spirits (https://www.lostspirits.net), and the experience is more of a cross between a haunted house and drinking rooms. The only problem?

Neither Judith nor I drink whiskey or rum.

So naturally, the first sample of the night is something called Navy Style Rum, which we are told by the pourer was 68% alcohol. That's 136 proof, or essentially turpentine.

It wasn't, exactly, but for someone who considers an 80-proof Drambuie to be WOW, this tastes like something that takes paint off the walls.

By the time we had our third tasting, there were two things I was grateful for.

One, I'm happy to have had the chance. The tasting experience was really cool. The architecture, little battery buggies, the submarine room, and the hosts were all amazing.

Two, I have now tasted different high-quality whiskies, and while I've now tasted rum, a Framboise, and a Cuban Inspired Anejo Blanco, I am not going to leave my (admittedly minor) passion for Drambuie any decade soon.

It's probably like trying a police procedural thriller instead of an action-adventure and deciding it's just not for you.

The most amazing aspect for me was the discussions I had related to how they can now create chemically equivalent twenty-year-aged whiskey in just a few weeks. It has to do with light, and for those who do enjoy the idea of doing your own distilling, that portion of the show-and-tell was worth it. Just make sure you ask the questions about the real detail since our host just skipped the details until I asked.

Thank you so much for supporting Sarah's series and her stories. For a new author, your reviews help them realize they aren't just hobbyists but rather professional authors who are appreciated by their readers.

And Sarah has earned her title.

Anyway, stay safe and sane out there, and I look forward to talking to you in the next book!

Ad Aeternitatem,
Michael Anderle

CONNECT WITH THE AUTHORS

Connect with S.E. Weir

Website: http://seweir.com/

Facebook: https://www.facebook.com/sarahweirwrites/

Connect with Michael Anderle

Website: http://lmbpn.com

Email List: http://lmbpn.com/email/

https://www.facebook.com/LMBPNPublishing

https://twitter.com/MichaelAnderle

https://www.instagram.com/lmbpn_publishing/

https://www.bookbub.com/authors/michael-anderle

BOOKS BY S.E. WEIR

The Empress' Spy
Diplomatic Recruit (Book 1)
Diplomatic Crisis (Book 2)
Diplomatic Resurgence (Book 3)
Diplomatic Agent (Book 4)

Printed in Great Britain
by Amazon

82517868R00236